I0576704

Rebecca Donaldson Beach, Rebecca Donaldson Gibbons

The Reverend John Beach and His Descendants

Together With Historical and Biographical Sketches and the Ancestry....

Rebecca Donaldson Beach, Rebecca Donaldson Gibbons

The Reverend John Beach and His Descendants
Together With Historical and Biographical Sketches and the Ancestry....

ISBN/EAN: 9783337031152

Printed in Europe, USA, Canada, Australia, Japan

Cover: Foto ©Raphael Reischuk / pixelio.de

More available books at **www.hansebooks.com**

The Reverend John Beach

AND HIS

Descendants

TOGETHER WITH

Historical and Biographical Sketches

AND THE

Ancestry and Descendants of John Sanford

OF

Redding, Connecticut

BY

REBECCA DONALDSON BEACH

AND

REBECCA DONALDSON GIBBONS

—●●●—

NEW HAVEN:

THE TUTTLE, MOREHOUSE & TAYLOR PRESS

1898

PREFACE

Under the present critical genealogical eye it would be impossible to produce entirely satisfactory results in any such field of labor. This should not and does not prevent the imperfect effort. In this case no apology is intended for that portion of this work which, without undue arrogance, can certainly be pronounced unusually complete. For the rest, however, the compiler expects differing opinion. History is not made of mental arithmetic statistics alone—tradition, the twisted tale of the once swift wheel in the quiet corner, the touch of local color and how that "*Once*" springs into life! Without this there would be no environment—even no panorama. Redding has been honored, and by one of her sons, Charles Burr Todd, whose history of the town and country is full of interesting material ; but Newtown, aside from historical sermons and addresses, and a sort of high-class advertisement called "A History of Fairfield County," has been too long without due distinction.

This effort, therefore, has been made and is offered in all its crudity and by an inexperienced pen, in order that some future hand may be led to correct and perfect her record. Discarding some of the usual adjuncts to such pages—such as the irritating foot-note, or the interfering explanation, and giving references at once and in the lump, has seemed to add continuity to an otherwise frequently broken narrative, and unless important to the context will not be again introduced. But one entire contribution from outside is included, and that is the sketch of the present Episcopal Church in Newtown, by the Rev. Mr. Linsley, and to him I am also indebted for much kindliness by the way. Family MSS., letters and papers hitherto unpublished have been copied, some entire, others in part, and in this connection valuable additional data have been secured. The readiness with which such material was forthcoming and the wide interest taken in its search, leads me to a different point of view to that taken by some of my predecessors in these fields. The three divisions into which these records have naturally fallen, historical, bio-graphical, and genealogical, will at least give opportunity to avoid that portion which may seem superfluous. No numerical system is adopted in the genealogy, but with continuing each family through its generations before returning to the next, and a complete index, it is hoped the arrangement may prove easily followed and consulted. Aside from the lengthy list of publications, references and records, special mention should be made of a few earnest helpers by whose assistance we have such full records to present. Among these are Mrs. Philo Nichols of Newtown, Mrs. George H. Chase of Sharon, Mrs. William E. Duncomb of Redding, and Mr. Charles H. Peck of Newtown. In the Sanford connection: Mr. Edward Jackson Sanford of Knoxville, Tenn.; Mrs. James P. Brayton of Chicago, Ill.; and Mrs. Charles W. Kelley of Redding. To these and to many other equally helpful hands this recognition is added to previous acknowledgment.

REBECCA DONALDSON BEACH.

New Haven, Conn., June, 1898.

LIST OF REFERENCES

New Haven Colony Records.

Connecticut State Records.

Town, Land, Probate and Church Records of New Haven, New-town, Redding, Stratford, Fairfield, Danbury, Bridgeport, Shelton (Huntington) Milford, and Hartford in Connecticut; Rochester, Albany, Troy and Brooklyn, New York State; Elizabethtown, New Jersey; Chicago, Ill.; Milwaukee, Wisconsin; Wilmington, Delaware. Other town records examined and sent in by descendants in the West, South, California and Canada.

Trumbull and Hollister's State Histories, Bacon's Historical Discourses, Barber's Historical Collections, Orcutt's Bridgeport and Stratford, Torrington and local histories, Davis' Wallingford, Schenk's Fairfield, Lewis' Fairfield County, Cothren's Woodbury, Stiles' Old Windsor, History of Hartford County, Todd's Redding, Baird's History of Rye, Boyd's Winchester and the histories of Durham, Goshen, Danbury, etc., etc.

Beardsley's History of the Church in Connecticut; Perry's American Episcopal Church; Life and Letters of Dr. Samuel Johnson; Life and Letters of Bishop Seabury; Sprague's American Pulpit; Sabine's Loyalists; Documentary History of the Church in Connecticut—Drs. Hawks and Perry; Yale Biographies—Professor Dexter; De-Forest's History of the Indians in Connecticut; Connecticut Men in the Revolutionary War, and War of 1812; The New England Historical and Genealogical Magazine; Dodd's East Haven Register; the Family Records of Booth, Burr, Hawley, Platt, Tuttle, Morse, etc., etc. The English authorities are given in their place, though I should mention, perhaps, that the Minster records at Warminster were consulted by permission of the then vicar, Sir James Erasmus Phillips, bart.

CONTENTS

_____

LIST OF ILLUSTRATIONS

A Historical Sketch of Newtown, Connecticut.

1686-1800

AS no history of any part of Connecticut could be properly entered upon without an Indian prologue, so no history of Newtown could be begun without first mention of Stratford also. This seventh child of the Colony proved its birthright in the older parent country by a good fighting disposition and ready ability to acquire fresh pastures in the new. Fast and strong it grew and in turn sent out its sons to conquer. Among the first of the Indian deeds to individuals was one to "my loving friend, Joseph Judson" of Stratford, in 1661, consisting of a tract of land in the "Mohican Hills"; another in the same year from Towtonamy and his mother (the wife of Ansantawae) to Samuel Sherman, John Hurd and Caleb Nichols; and in 1671, Pocono the Sachem of Weantinock (New Milford) gave a deed for more than 25,000 acres to Henry Tomlinson—this was confirmed in 1702 with two additional names, Richard Blackleach and Daniel Shelton ; the land ran as far as Newtown and included property to which John Read, Junr, afterwards fell heir, and it is said, he sued the New Milford purchasers for trespass, winning his case fifteen times, but losing it the sixteenth ! Pootatuck was the original name of Shelton, and it was not until later that it was brought to Newtown.

The following description, taken largely from Orcutt's "Bridgeport and Stratford," will make this more clear: "About 1680 the Indians on the lower part of the Housatonic made a considerable migration with their wigwams up the river, those on the South Side to Potatuck in Newtown, and those on the East Side to the mouth of the Shepaug on the North. In 1681 the Pequonnock Indians sold their old planting field in Fairfield, and in 1685-6-7 they completed the sale of all their claims in that town. . . . . ."

Newtown and New Milford became the points of rendezvous, from 1680 to about 1705, when they sold again and

moved on west. Of course these localities were not yet so
named or called, but it would be difficult to recognize the
many stages of this movement in the Indian prototypes.

Newtown must have been from 1680 until 1705 the home of
several hundred natives : in the latter year they sold the terri-
tory for that township, making some reservations, and in
1723 they—by their chief Quiomph (or Quiump)—sold all
their claim in that town "except a corner of intervale lying
by ye river where Cocksures fence is." The Newtown deed
of 1705 contains the names of several Indians who signed
deeds in Fairfield and Stratford, thus showing that they had
retired from their old wigwams along the coast to Pootatuck
in Newtown.

"New Milford and Newtown were purchased at nearly the
same time. At New Milford they sold their last land, which
was the planting field, in 1705, and with those from Newtown
and Shepaug in Woodbury began to center in considerable
numbers at Kent. . . . . ." Mr. Orcutt goes on to say that
to him "there is a sense of sadness connected with these
forced migrations and giving up of their old council places
and wigwams," and he describes very beautifully the charming bluff and valley which is pictured in an illustration from
a recent photograph.

The following list is taken from Vol. I, page 263. It is not
the whole list of early Stratfordians, but only *forty-seven*,
whose names appear in the genealogy and as property-hold-
ers in Newtown.

Eben' Booth, 18½ acres.
John Booth, 18½ acres.
Samuel Judson, 24½ acres.
Samuel Galpin, 12 acres.
Josiah Nichols sen, 17 acres.
Mr. Samuel Hawley, 39 acres.
Timothy Titharton, 18½ acres.
Daniel Titharton, 14 acres.
Joseph Booth, 6 acres.
Mr. D. Mitchell, dec'd, 47 acres.
John Hurd sen, heirs, 36 acres.
Edward Sherman's heirs, 12 acres.
Zechariah Fairchild, 20 acres.
Cap' James Judson, 32½ acres.

Nath' Porter, 6 acres.
John Peacock's hrs., 14 acres.
Moses Wheeler, 31½ acres.
Mr. Sam' Sherman, 17½ acres.
Matthew Sherman's hrs., 12 acres.
Lieut. John Hubbel's hrs., 18 acres.
John Thompson and }
Ambrose Thompson, } 44 acres.
Mr. Dan' Shelton, 28 acres.
Mr. Joseph Curtis, 34 acres.
Mr. Ephraim Stiles, 30 acres.
Mr. Sam' Sherman Jun', 20 acres.
Capt. Stephen Burritt, 20 acres.
Mr. John Wells, 30 acres.

John Curtis, ", 12½ acres.
Benj⁰ Curtis, 9½ acres.
Isaac Stiles, 6 acres.
Isaac Bennit, 6 acres.
Joshua Curtis, 14 acres.
John Porter, 15 acres.
John Sherwood, 28 acres.
John Beach, 12, and 8 acres with⁰ 5 miles.
Nath¹ Beach, 6½ acres.
Benj⁰ Beach, 14 acres.

Deac. Timothy Wilcoxson, 29½ acres.
Captn. Wm. Curtis, 26 acres.
Josiah Curtis, 6 acres.
Sam¹ Uffoot, 35 acres.
John Birdsey, ", 21 acres.
John Birdsey, ʲʳ, 12 acres.
John Burritt, 19 acres.
Sam¹ Beers—in right of his father —John Beers, decᵈ, 6 acres.

Many other names appear elsewhere similarly connected.

From all that has been gathered into history concerning the Connecticut Indians we are enabled to place the Pootatuck family as a branch of the great Mohican tribe—from the Hudson River. These coming down the Housatonic valley and finding many falls in that stream, named it "Potatuck," which is Indian for "falls river." Their chief was Okennuk, son of Ansantawae. The Newtown deed of 1705 was for "a tract of land bounded South on a Pine swamp and land of Mr. Sherman's and Mr. Rosseter (later belonging by will and lease to Richard Nichols, Mr. Sherman's son-in-law), Southwest upon Fayerfield bounds, Northwest upon the bounds of Danbury, Northeast on land purchased by Milford men at or near Caentenoak, and Southeast on land of Nunawauk, an Indian, the line running two miles from the river right against Potatuck, the said tract of land containing in length eight miles, and in breadth six miles . . . . in consideration of four guns, four Broadcloth Coats, four Kettles, ten shirts, ten pair of stockings, fortie pound of Lead, ten Hatchetts, ten pound of powder, and fortie Knives . . . . ." Signed by thirty-four "marks" representing so many dusky figures, male and female, who, tricked out in their "Broadcloth Coats, Stockings, etc."—according to the taste of the wearer—caroused for several days on the *proceeds.*

Mr. Orcutt does not further qualify the *brand*, but says the new "proprietors" were obliged to remain quietly at home during the orgy. The later deed, called the second purchase, was not made until the August of 1723, and is called "The Quiomph deed." On the Newtown records Quiomph makes over all his land in the boundaries of Newtown "not purchased by ye English before ye date of this purchase (Aug. 7, 1723) to John Glover and Abraham Kimberly for ye proprietors of Newtown.

Signed Quiomph his mark

Signed in the presence of
ROBERT SEELYE.
EUNISS BENNET.

Recorded Jan. 21, 1725\6."

This is the Eunice Bennet, daughter of Capt⁰ Thomas and afterward wife of Daniel Booth.

In Mr. John W. DeForest's History of the Indians in Connecticut this family (the Potatucks) is put off with a short shrift. He says: "Northwest of the Paugussets within the limits of Newtown, Southbury, Woodbury and some other townships resided a clan known as the Potatucks, their insignificance is sufficiently proved by the silence of authors concerning them." Again: "The Potatucks of Newtown and Woodbury appear to have been a small community. They never gave any trouble to the English settlers. . . . (!) . . . One of the first, if not the very first *acts*" (correctly quoted except for the italics) "recorded of them is the sale (*1728*) of forty-eight square miles of the river right against Potatuck, the said tract of land containing in length eight miles and in breadth six miles . . . . . in consideration of four guns, four coats, four blankets, etc., etc." Perhaps, in view of the questionable grammar, the unquestionably false statement in regard to the entire agreement of sentiment between these gentle aborigines and the English settler, and the remarkable confusion of deeds and dates, a further "silence of authors" would have been advisable. The only Indian deed on the land records of Newtown, after 1723, is one to the Hubbels, which will be mentioned in its place. That the Indians gave a great deal of trouble to the first settlers and indeed later comers, can scarcely be denied. Even as late as the middle of the century, there is a tale which may be told here in this connection. It was well known that at the time the Rev. John Beach returned from England in 1732, some of those who were the most bitterly opposed to the Church of England and resented his return to Newtown in the capacity of missionary,

incited the Indians to annoy him, and at a later period a band
of them entered his house in his absence and tried to frighten
the children into telling where the money and valuables were.
One of the daughters, Sarah, had been left in charge and told
to be sure and hide a certain silver tankard in case of danger.
This brave little girl gathered the children round her, slipped
the tankard out of the closet and under her skirts, and they
all huddled in a corner and refused to move or answer any
questions. The Indians, after frightening them, made off
with what they could themselves find. The members of
Trinity Parish have now the privilege of communing on silver made over from the tankard and other pieces of historic
value, collected, melted over and presented by a recent parishioner, through whose mistaken zeal more than one old
Newtown family is to-day mourning its lost heirlooms.

We can not consider that after our own treatment of the
Indians—in the Pequot and King Philip's wars—it should be
surprising they felt distrustful of our ideas of justice. Historians have hushed up this early national disgrace, as they
will the repetition of it, in the same connection which is at
present rendering another "silence of authors" necessary.
How many tales of wanton cruelty and double-dealing must
have been handed down from father to son, and it was always
easy to excite their animosity—*after* the *pale face* had cheated
them of proffered friendship. On the other hand, we have on
our side much to remember of misplaced confidence to the
innate barbarian.

The phrase Indian summer, which is so suggestive of soft-
ness and beauty and the last warmth of a fading sun, bore in
those early days quite a different inner meaning. It meant
that time after the housing of the grain and preparation for
the long winter, when by incessant labor and forethought the
tired farmer had battled with nature to secure the absolute
needs of his little family in their solitary makeshift called
home, and the first chill had touched with its ripening hand
the fruits of the earth ; it meant that *then* came the "Indian's
summer," when the shiftless and lazy dweller in the woods
who had watched some one else growing and gleaning for
him, broke cover and stole out as fully armed and a thousand
times more sure of aim, and raided the farm, gathering up the
very food of the day—and fortunate was the little settlement

that escaped without fire and desecration. Connecticut suffered in this way less than New York State, but this was the
true sentiment of the phrase " Indian summer."

Chicken Warrups, the Sachem of Reading, was long a
dweller on his reservation, and his children's children claimed
inheritance, but of him we shall read in the description of that
locality. With this brief introduction we pass at once to the
actual center of interest.

NEWTOWN.

When Mauquash, Nunawauk and Massumpas sold their
own and their children's birthright in this happy hilltop
valley for such literal coin of the realm as "four coats, four
guns, four blankets, ten pounds of powder," and some small
gear, they had but begun experience with the already thrifty
New England farmer.

The first purchasers were three also, Hawley, Junos and
Bush, the latter always spoken of as "of New York," and
indeed never appearing in person. This small syndicate was,
however, well backed by many Stratfordians who sought to
emulate their sires in founding still another settlement. In
the Colonial Records of Connecticut, the first mention of
Newtown is at the May session of the Assembly, 1703, when
in regard to "a pattent to Newtown or Preston dated 4th,
Feb. 1686, this Assembly grants to the Petitioners herein-
after named, all that tract of land lying on the west side of
Stratford and part of Fairfield, westerly upon Danbury and a
line running from the southeast corner of Danbury, paralell
to the east line of s^d town to Fairfield bounds, northerly upon
New-Fairfield purchase and Potatuck River, should be one
intire town called by the name of Newtown, & do appoint
& impower Jos Curtice of Stratford Esq, Captain Joseph
Wakeman of Fairfield, Mr. John Sherman of Woodbury, and
Mr. Thomas Taylor of Danbury, a Comt^{ee} to survey the said
track of land, and consider what number of inhabitants the
said track of land will conveniently accomodate, and accordingly determine where the town plot shall be, and lay out a
suitable number of home lotts, and order all the prudentials
of said town until such time as the General Court shall order
otherwise. Signed, Jos Curtice, James Judson, Samuel
Hawley, John Read, Jno Burr, Theophilus Hull, John

Minor, Benjamin Sherman, Josiah Curtis, Dan[l] Burr Jr.,
Daniel Curtis, Rich[d] Hubbell, Jun[r], John Judson, Jno
Seelye, Jun[r], Daniel Beardslee, Jos Fairchild, Benj[n] Hurd,
Benj[n] Nichols, Peleg Burritt, John Griffin, Tho[s] Sharp, ——
Dunning of Stratford, Dan[l] Beardsley, sen[r], Zechariah Ferriss,
Will Mallorie, Sam[l] Hubbell, J[r], Jonathan Booth, Jno Haw-
ley, David Whitlock, J[r], Jno Glover, Dan[l] Foot, J[r], Ab[m]
Kimberly, Benj. Peck, Daniel Burr, S[r]., Mr. Richard Brian's
heirs, Sam[l] Eels —— ——."

Accordingly, we find, on a leaf torn from the first Newtown Record book, and now preserved in the present copy,
the following. On the outside is written, " The Draught of
ye twenty acre Lotts Divi[d], by ye Comm[ttee] pr order of the
Generall Court Recorded folio 84 first Book, pr Joseph
Peck, Town Clerk." (Inside.) An acco[tt] of a division of
Land laid out March 24th 1709/10, of the Committee for Newtown, each lot containing 20 acres, namely, on the Hill on
the west side of the town 14 lots already laid out to ye following persons named, to wit: Josiah Burit the North lott &
Abraham K(imberly) the South lott, only, Kimberly's Lots
containing but 7 acres is to have eleven acres more adjoyning to the west side of M[r]. Sherman's farm to front w[st] on ye
line of s[d] farm, forty acres laid out to M[r]. Glover in and . . .
. . being for the 2 allotting's due to him, lying northward of
the said town on the north side of a br(ook) Note, that John
Griffin in lieu of ye home lot laid out to him, accepts of land
layd by his dwelling house, & hath two acres layd at the
ea[st] end of his 20 acre lott, & . . . . . twenty acre lotts to
be laid out west of Josiah Burit's lot and that rang(e) of 20
acre lotts, in three parcels, the first rang(e) on the west of
aforesaid continuous rights, lotts of 20 acres each, from the
south to the north upon the first hill, & three lots on a hill
of 20 acres lying west of the northerly end of the next above
hill, five lots to be layd out on the southerly end of Mr.
Sherman's farm & Kimberly's Land above mentioned, each
containing 20 acres, three lots of 20 acres each to be layd out
on the West side of the new country road southerly of the
Brook called by the name of deep-Brook, five lots to be layd
out of 20 acres each, lying on the hill eastward of the long
medow adjoyning to the deep Brook on the North end.

1 Ensign Hubbell, Rec[l]	0.13	1 Joseph Curtis	3
2 Daniel Beers, sen[r]	7	2 Joseph Osborne	12
3 Theophilus Hul	5	3 Joseph beach	14
4 Daniel Beer, Jr	12	4 James Lewis	15
5 ——— yet burr	8	5 Josiah Curtis	10
6 ——— ———	2	5 ——— Fayerweather	2
7 Mr. John Reed	10	7 Capt[n] Judson	7
8 ——— Chancey	3	8 Jon[n] Morris	8
9 Jon[n] Booth	9	9 Wm. Junos	11
10 Jon[n] Minor		10 Joseph Beardslee	9
		11 Eben[er] Prindle	5
11 Capt[n] Hawley		12 Jere Turner	4
12 Tho[s] Lake	6	13 Edmund Lewis	12
13 Mr Sam[l] Hawley	3	14 Daniel Judson	1
		15 Benj Sherman	6
		16 tho Curtis	16

Three lots on ye west of ye country road south of ye deep brook.

South of Mr Sherman's   Lieut Sam[l] Hubbel's 1 lot N[th]
     farm, five lots   Mr Chancey's 3 lots
                    Mr Sam[l] Hawley's 2 lot

     Eben Booth 3 lot
     Mr Reed 5 lot
     Capt Jos Hawley 2 lot
     Daniel Burr Jr 1 lot
     Ensign R Hubbel 4 lot

Town   ——— Minor 1 lot at North end
     Capt[n] Hill 2 lot
     Tho Lake 5 lot
     Daniel Beers [sr] 3 lot
     Capt[n] Burr 4 lot

To the north end of ye town 16 lots the first hil 8 lots.

Daniel Jackson   J B
——— Fayerwether   Josiah Curtis } On the hill of
Joseph Curtis   Wm Junos }   3 lots
Jon Turner   Joseph Osborne 5 lots
Eben Prindle   Edmund Lewis 1 lot
Benj Sherman   Joseph beach 4 lots
Capt[n] Judson   James Lewis 3 lots
John Morris   Tho[s] Benit 2 lots
     Five lots on the Hill Southwest
     begins at Southward

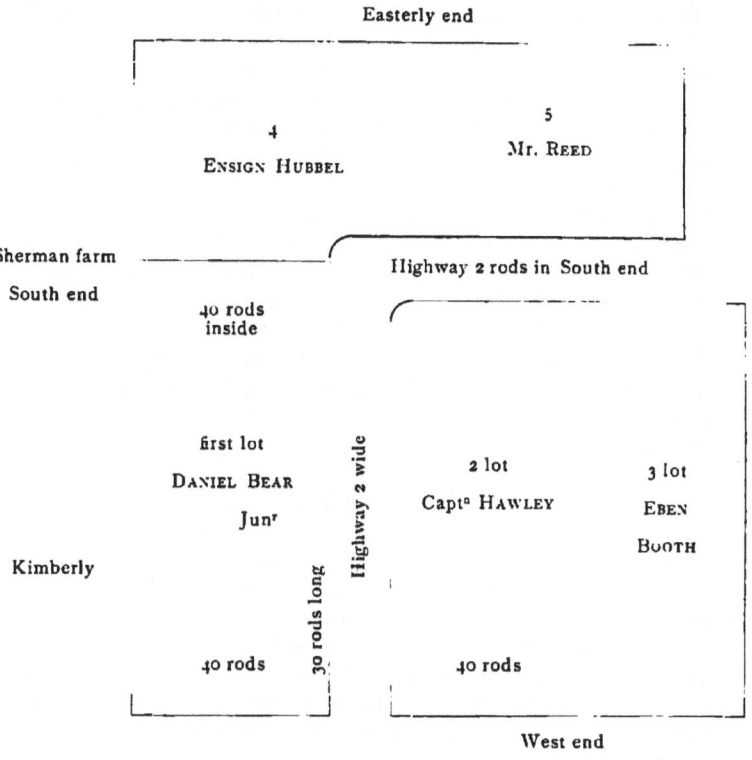

Easterly end

4
ENSIGN HUBBEL

5
Mr. REED

Sherman farm

South end

Highway 2 rods in South end

40 rods
inside

first lot

DANIEL BEAR

Junr

Highway 2 wide

2 lot

Captn HAWLEY

3 lot

EBEN

BOOTH

Kimberly

30 rods long

40 rods

40 rods

West end

JOSEPH CURTIS   } Com
THOMAS SEELYE JR   } tee

North end
The Hill containing 8 lots
1 2 3 4 5 6 7 8
Five lots south of Sherman's farm
9, 10, 11, 12, 13

North end of ye town on the hil
contain^g 3 lots, 9, 10, 11.
North end on the Hill contain^g five
lots 12 13 14 15 16.
Five lots Eastward, 4-5
(torn ——)

On this list and map are thirty-two names, seventeen of which will be found many times recurring in this genealogy.

The first town meeting of which we have any record is dated 1711, for the election of officers, and being "Leagally met at ye house of Peter Hubbell yt was then voted that Peter

Hubbell shall be town clerk for the yeare ensuing. Voted
that Abraham Kimberly shall be Constable for the yeare ensuing. Voted that Ebenezer Prindle and Thomas Sharp shall
be Surveyors of Highways for ye yeare ensuing." At the
same meeting "Daniel foot and Joseph Gray" are appointed
fence viewers, and Thomas Lake is ordered "to slip his 20
acre divition and take it up on the west side of the rhoad, to
be laid out by the Committee upon the s^d Lake's charge."

At the May session of the Assembly in that year (1711), a
committee consisting of "Captn John Hawley & Mr. Benjamin Sherman of Stratford & Mr. Platt of s^d Newtowne" is
"to lay out such divisions of land within the s^d town of Newtowne, with the advice of Mr James Beebe and Mr Thos Taylor of Danbury as shall be agreed upon by ye proprietors
there-of." And in October this committee reports and petitions for full town privileges and the number 7 for its brand
mark, but in the May of 1712 the Assembly "being informed
that sundry of the grantees of the land at Newtowne have not
amended the conditions of the said grant so that the good settlement of the said towne is (in) danger of being greatly
defeated, & where as this Court did in the same grant of the
said towne, reserve a power to add such others for settlement
in the said towne as they should think meet, do therefor
desire and appoint the hon^ble Nathan Gold Esq. Joseph Curtice and Peter Burr Esq. and Captn Joseph Wakeman them or
any three of them to be a committee to view and inspect the
whole affair relating to the settlement of the said towne in
the next Sessions," . . . . ending with the proviso that "no
charge shall arise hereby to the colony."

While these committees were going and coming between
State and town, seeing to it that proper legislation and recognition was assured them, the proprietors busied themselves
about matters of equal importance, for in the earliest volume
of the Town Journal we read: "May 3d, 1712 . . . Voted, to
swap one rod of land with Mr. John Glover, & one rod with
Jonathan Booth off from thire hom lots at the north end of
the towne. . . . . . Voted, by ye maj^r part for Mr Phineas
fisk to be the minister for Newtowne,—voted, to give the
minister that comes and settles amongst us as a minister of
the Gospel to preach the Gospel amongst us, that he shall
have a petition Right in full . . . ." In another place—it is

chronicled that at a town meeting (probably the same or next one) it is voted—"that Mr. Phinehas Fisk is invited to come to this place to preach a sermon amongst us & that we may discourse him about setling among us a minister of the Gospel for half a year or some other space of time as may be agreed for a Tryal, and that Mr. Adams be the person to invite him on that Design." In face of such a " Tryal " we can imagine the trepidation with which Mr. Fisk first addressed and then discoursed his critics. Nor are we surprised to learn that the reverend gentleman declined so hazardous a call.

In October—that year—" John Glover is appointed to confer with Rev^d Mr. Charles Chancey and Rev^d Mr. Joseph Webb & some other minister of ye county if they think needful that one or two or as they see meet, come & assist & carry on and advise us at Newtown & keep a Day of humiliation with us, that God in mercy would Direct us & prosper us with a man to Preach the Gospel with us," and John Glover is also appointed Town clerk, "for the year ensueing." Peter Hubbell petitions for & is allowed to keep " a house of Entertainment " (Inn), & a three shilling fine for non-attendance on Town meetings, is voted. " The inhabitants afores^d made choyce of John Glover James Hurd, Jas Turner & John Platts a committee to measure ye land & settle ye bounds with ye Indians of that purchase which William Junos purchased of ye Indians with his asotiates in ye boundarys of Newtowne & to Requeste Col^l Johnson & Captn Wines of Woodbury to declare to ye indians what land the indians hold & ye Deed ; Also to procure four gallons of Rum to treat ye Indians and to Refresh y^urselves." So long ago was it thought necessary to "treat " the Indians when the subject of land was to be discussed. This large order for rum seems to have occasioned no debate. This Deed was the one drawn in 1705—spoken of above. The wheel of industry began early to revolve, for even in the heart of that winter "at ye house of Daniel foot it is voted, that Mr. Benjn Sherman Eben^r Prindle & Mr Samuel Sanford [from Milford] " shall agree with said Turner & draw up an agreement concerning a Grist Mill on s^d brooke." This Jonathan Turner had already been voted a " 40 acre lot adjoining ' *after* ' he hath built the Mill," and in March Benj Sherman Captn John Holly and John Seely "have libertie to gat a

saw mill on ye Deep brooke South of ye town," and Joseph
Dudley is allowed the first fulling mill "provided he do not
damnifie the saw mill." "Pitching" for land was the recognized manner of lawful division, and lest the reader should
share the previous ignorance of the writer, the process is
quoted, "They shall go out 8 in a companie & draw by
figures 1. 2. 3. 4. 5. 6. 7. 8, till the whole number of 40 lotts
be layd out." This seems fair enough and without favoritism, though large proprietorship and coin of the realm
obtained then as now. "Mr John Glover shall have his pitch
at the rere of his house lott and the highways west & north,
so fur as it will hold out, & s⁴ Glover will paye to the town
treasurer 12 shilgˢ for his pitch." "Abᵐ Kimberly shall take
his pitch at the rere of his home lott so fur as it will hold
out," and "voted, that Abᵐ Kimberley shal draw for all the
Proprietors of ye town" and the 7ᵗʰ day of April "shal be
the Day for the companye to pitch, and successively till they
have done, exceptin fowl weather hinder." And while they
so carefully protected the living, it is pathetic to read in the
small, clear, little cramped handwriting that one of their
number, Stephen Pamerly "has the use of an acre & a half
which is the burying place, provided he clear the bushes and
sow English grass seed."

To return to the Colonial Records, in October 1713 a
list of "rateable" estates is ordered, "& for the promoting
of the New Plantation called Newtown for the defraying
of the charge of building a meeting-house there, & the maintenance of a minister each owner of a petition right shall
for the next four years annually pay 30 shillings money
& all the rest of the said charge shall be raised upon the
heads & stocks of other estates of the s⁴ Town except so
much as this Court shall next May order to be payd annually during the four years aforesaid by the Farmers." A very
important point in the early history of this interesting town
was reached when, at the October Sessions of 1714, "a tax of
one penny pr acre is levied on the farmers, and those who
have not already settled for their petition rights are allowed
3 years to do so, & five lb an acre for delay in so doing,
payable to the Selectmen, and the s⁴ Newtown is annexed
to the County of Fairfield." And the next year they are
"granted liberty to embody in Church estate as soon as God

in his providence shall make way therfor." Newtown figures largely in State and Town records as of the Church militant : this was, however, not an unusual state of affairs in New England at that time, and in the language of one of the divines concerned, not a hundred miles distant, 'twas "no great marvel my Brethren, for surely there be a superabundance of heavenly ministrants amongst us."

Cut off as they were from intercourse with the great march of mind, obliged to become toilers in, and of, a land yet unredeemed, religion itself was to them the only center of literature and argument ; the prayer-meeting was the vent for pent up enthusiasm, the psalm their music, and in the "preachings of the Gospel" so ardently longed for they wished to find an uplifting power—something to help them shoulder their burdens. We too often forget that our hard-working forbears in this new country were, many of them, untrained to such exertion, or their wives to the manual toil of primitive homes in half-felled forests. We are shocked when we come across a remarriage on the same page with the death of the first wife, but what was to be done? No respectable woman would care for his children, and the day of other female servitude had not dawned for them. By this time they had secured the Rev Mr Thomas Toucey and the year before had voted to "soo all ye ministers home lot with wheat that . . . . Mr. Towse have ye crops Provided ye s⁴ Mr. Thomas Towsee preach ye Gospel amongst us a yeare" and "Abᵐ Kimberley John Glover Ebenʳ Smith Ebenʳ Prindle & John Griffin are a comᵗᵉ to discourse Mr. Towse in order to settlemint to know whether he is willing to cary on ye work of ye ministry in this Place as long as God shall grant him life & health & the salary that ye town and hee shall yearly agree for" ; by another vote at the same meeting "voted to give Josiah Burrit 20 shillings in Pay or two thirds money for meeting *in his House* on ye Lord's Day from yᵉ Daye until next May ensueing," but preparations are also immediately made for the building of a suitable edifice. "John Glover James Hard & Ebenʳ Smith are a "comᵗᵗᵉ to hier workmen on ye Towne A-compt to builde a meeting house to serve God in 40 foot Longe & 30 foot wide & 20 foot between ye joysts." Joseph Peck becomes town clerk.

The Rev. J. P. Hoyt, quoted in Lewis' history of Fairfield County, says that there was a rude church edifice of some sort in 1710, but this minute would seem to indicate that as late as 1713 they were holding their services in a private house and expected to do so until "the next May ensuing," and his measurements of "50 + 36 feet," do not follow the original plan; however, he says, "this was not built until 1717, and was situated at "the intersection of Main st. & a lane running east & west," where the liberty pole now stands.

Growth progressed in natural sequence, first the tilling of the land, then the building of the church, and then the schooling of the "weans." In each of these movements we trace the greatest care that everything should be firmly based on exact measurements, no favoritism or unequal division of labor, no underhand advantage or release from duty assigned; they would not spare the rod to its just dividing line nor spoil the child for want of it. To every man his 40 × 16 home lott, and if by some chance influence in high quarters an advantage seemed secured, justice overtook the clever one and his little day quickly waned; for instance: "Jonathan Hubbel hath pitched for his ten acre lott in ye swamp at ye north corner of Mr Read's lott, now in ye improvement of Stephen Parmerly & on ye southeast side of ye path which goes from Potatuck to Danbury," "entered this fourth Day of November, 1714, pr Mr Peter Hubbell." At first glance "ye swamp" might not seem to betray any special wealth of property, but "Mr Read's lott" was unquestionably the best in the settlement, and the "improvement of Stephen Parmerly" would indicate good clearing in that direction, while the "path" between Potatuck and Danbury meant a highway shortly, and a very available cart road for his present use! So, we are not much surprised to find the next entry reading, "These presints may sartify that ye above[sd] Jon[a] Hubbell had no right to pitch upon or take ye land in his oune name & that lef[t] Richard Hubbell hath taken up his ten acre pitch of land elsewhere, as ye Record will discov[r]." Poor Peter, the *Recorder*, must have found his family connections almost as difficult as they were numerous, for he is many times called upon to register their squabbles and re-arrange their "bounds."

The first school was started in 1717, and the building

answered the double purpose of class room by day, and town meeting by night, or out of school hours, for many years. Although they had, as early as 1713, voted to build their meeting house on the modest lines as above given, it was not until 1717 that they really accomplished anything. At a town meeting held Dec. 26th (the day after Christmas when they might be supposed to feel a devout sense of their needs), we read " Consulted, agreed upon, concluded and voted by ye Inhabitants above^sd at s^d meetinge to build a meeting house so that ye aforesaid Inhabitants of ye s^d Town might be under better advantage for ye enjoyment of all ye ordinances of God in his sanctuary according to Divine appointment : enter^d by Jos Peck, Town Clerk.

Along the margin is written " Joseph Peck will give 1,000 of shingles (&) find nails to lay them." This is crowded in on account of a similar offer of Peter Hubbell, who, "will give for ye Incouragement of Building ye above^sd House one Thousand of sawn board & one thousand of shingles." Fired by these promises, " John Glover will give the making of all ye window frames at ye front," but lest his noble *sounding* offer should mislead he adds, "note that ye Town is to find Timber for ye frames." The boundary lines between Stratford and New Milford and the township of Newtown become material for more than one year's petitioning, but in the next year at the May sitting, the Assembly refuses their requests in respect of a re-survey, but levies a fine or tax of a penny pr acre for four years on town proprietors and of farms, proportionably, "the same to be used for Church purposes." The laying out of highways and the difficulties attendant on due proportions in county road expenses, the trials and tribulations of religious differences and adjustment of land " Rights " and the more recent Indian purchases, make many town meetings necessary, but not so interesting for the next two or three years.

In 1723 Mr. Thomas Towsey presents a memorial to the General Assembly complaining that his salary is not forthcoming. Whereupon orders are issued that the "Inhabitants of the town of Newtown in compliance with the agreement with Mr Tousey shall paye to the said Mr Tousey 60 lbs of money beside a resonable consideration for his firewood for the year 1723 which ended the 8th of March last," and doubtless at the instigation of the "fighting preacher" as he was called, the "Governor, Council and Representatives in General Court assembled" . . . . further enact a "rate of five pence on the pound on all the polls & rateable estate within the said Town & collect & gather the same & pay it to the said Mr Tousey on or before the third Tuesday in July next," and still further, should this fail, the "Secretary of the Colony is ordered to issue a warrant of distraint to the Sheriff of Fairfield County," who is to be allowed 15 shillings fee, and is to "send forthwith a copy of this Act to Mr Thomas Bennit Justice of the peace : . . . . who is herebye required" to see it properly served. These two must have been congenial spirits, captains both, acknowledged leaders in affairs, disciplinarians in peace·and war, and if Mr. Tousey excelled in literary and educational privileges "Captⁿ Thos Benitt" ran him close in public preferment and overtopped him in the hearts of their fellow townsmen. They soon learned the value of their former rather objectionable minister, for, as a diplomat he stood between them and their overreaching neighbors more than once and became, with Mr. John Read, Jonathan Booth, and later, the brilliant Edmond, one of Newtown's most honored defenders. This year (1723) also saw the completion of the "Second purchase," as it is called in the "Quiomph Deed" (fully described in the account of Indians), but not divided until 1726.

At a town meeting "Holden may ye 4, 1724, the Bisness to be attended at said proprietores meeting is to make Choyce of a proprietor's clark to Consult about a pattent for the Township of Newtown to pitch upon a time when to begin to lay out ye 30 acre Devitions & do sumthing about ye land of Mr Reed John has laid out in the neck so called above the pound brook. Peter Hubbell by vote . . . Chosen clark & sworn by Thos Bennit Justice This meeting ajourned to ye 13ᵗʰ Day of Instant May at 5 of the clock afternoon." . . . . . This notification is set up in three different places, "One at the north end of ye town near Captⁿ Bennits one at or near Abraham Kimberly's shop and the other near Joseph Botsford's house," and the town clerk is to see that this is always done ten days before the date of the meeting, and "the Proprietors are to Asemble or to Conven to gether at the beat of ye Drum at ye time & place appointed." Accordingly, such a meeting having been "leagaly" called and named for the purpose of appointing a committee to meet with the Stratford representatives on boundary interests, "Ye Rev Mr Tousey Mr John Glover Mr Jno Leavenworth Mr Joseph Peck & Mr Ephraim Peck" are chosen to conduct the parley, and in case of necessity to agree with the other committee on a third, of three "uninterested gentlemen to determine as above[ad]" and they agree to "sett Down forever satisfied as they in their wisdom shal see fitt." This sounds well and plausible, but that vexed boundary was not so easily laid ; those three public spirited, but "*uninterested*," gentlemen were not then forthcoming, and so we shall find other committees and meetings called and much discussion before a conclusion is reached although the original committee reported the "boundaries erected by s[d] Edmond Lewis, county surveyor." Joseph Curtis, James Lewis, John Wilcoxson, Jr., Joseph Judson, Joseph Peck, Peter Hubbell and Jeremiah Northrup "are to take charge of ye highways, & to setle" with those whose lands border on or are needed for such purpose & Mr Eben[r] Prindle shall slip an acre of land from the west end of his house lott & take y[t] up ajoyning to the six acre pitch, and John Foot shall have libertie to lay six acres of land being part of a 30 acres which he the s[d] foot purchased of Joseph Bristol as appears of Record, viz ajoynin to s[d] foot's own land at the upper end of the home meadow so called, provided that s[d] land damnifie no highway. "Voted in ye A fermativ." It is very soon found advisable to do away with so much advertisement of town meetings : whether the drum proved too attractive music or was thought sacrilegious (being beaten on Sundays as a summons to that rather different style of meeting), we can only surmise, but it is "voted y[t] shall be suffishint to warn Proprietors meetings without the beet of the Drum in futer

Peter Hubbell, Town Clark."

Returning to the State records, at the October Assembly of 1725 "Upon the memorial of the Town of Newtown shewing to this Assembly that s[d] Town is at present under pressing circumstances occasioned by the removal of the former min-

ister (Mr Tousey) & the settling another (Mr Beach) being
weakened by the disunion in opinion which hath been *and* is
still among them, & remarkably cut short in the crops this
present year by the Frost, by the which they are much
straightened & incapacitated to paye a rate to the publick,
this Assembly therefor upon the special reasons aforesaid
doe see cause to free & do hereby exempt & free the Inhabitants of s^d Town from payinge any country rate for the next
yeare ensuing, Provided the town of Newtown draws no
money for the schools nor send representatives to this Assembly during the exemption." (A more particular account of
the religious life of the town in this transition period will be
found in the biographical sketch of the Rev. Mr. Beach.)   The
most important, or *next* most important, matter to be settled
was the dividing of the Quiomph purchase, already made by
Mr. John Glover and Abraham Kimberley, which "shall be
equally layd out & sized Quantity & Quallety to every person
according to their Right."   John Read is appointed "atturney"
for the town, "to conduct & defend them against ye proprietors of New Milford."

The following extracts from "Hawks and Perry's Documentary History of the Protestant Episcopal Church" will
present the state of that body in Newtown at that time.

In one of Mr. Pigot's letters to the Secretary of the Society,
written from New York, Oct. 3d, 1722, he says: "I shall
before Christmas, according to appointment, preach thrice at
Fairfield, which is eight miles distant from my abode, as often
at Newtown, which is twenty-two miles from Stratford—thrice
also at Ripton at the same distance. . . . . Nay Sir—
Newton (Newtown) and Ripton if not Fairfield do intend to
petition the Honorable Society for Church Ministers."   In a
later letter to the same, from Stratford, Nov. 6, 1722, he says:
"The Subscribers of Ripton have been of long standing
inclined to the Church . . . . . but those of Newtown, to a
man, have been induced by my means to embrace our profession."   From the same to the same, Stratford, June 3d and
7th, 1723: "This is the sixth letter I have sent you without
the satisfaction of one in return, so that I am to seek whether
Fairfield, Ripton or Newtown petitions have reached you or
not. . . . . . . I have been once to Norwalk, once to North-

Haven six times to Fairfield, Ripton and Newtown, each, at which last places I have administered both sacraments once already, & do intend it once more before my departure." Again, from Providence, January 13th, 1723-24. . . . .
. . . . "as to the out-Towns, it is my humble opinion that Newtown merits the preference in the Honorable Society's regard; both as it is more remote from Stratford and also, as its inhabitants are above half come over already, insomuch that Mr Johnson (Mr. Pigot's successor at Stratford) may expect thirty communicants there. . . . . . . Mr Johnson will find it a most difficult task to answer the expectations of the Towns around him, there being work enough for Sunday Labourers in the Lord's harvest; however, if Newtown were supplied with one, he might take care of Ripton, and Mr Johnson might of Fairfield and West-Haven."

PETITION OF NEWTOWN.

Members of the Church of England at Newtown, Connecticut, to the Secretary.

Oct. 19th, 1722.

Honorable Gentlemen:

We the subscribers, inhabitants of the Town of Newton (Newtown) in the province of Connecticut, being cordially included to embrace the articles and liturgy of the Church of England, and to approach her communion, do humbly and earnestly request your Honorable Society to send us a lawfully ordained minister. We are heads of families and with dependents shall appear the major party here; therefor we intend to set apart for our episcopal teacher, whensoever it shall please God to inspire your Venerable body to appoint us one, at least two hundred acres of glebe for the support of a church minister forever. And this we are emboldened to hope, because our town is at so great a distance from Stratford as twenty-two miles and also situated in the center of all this country, being surrounded with more than ten other towns at no vast distance.

We do likewise return our most hearty thanks for that which Mr. Pigott introduced among us, who has inclined us to declare boldly for the Church, & thereby to be exposed to the resentments of the Independents, to his and our, no small disadvantage and reproach; indeed we are placed in the midst of an insidious people, but should quietly enjoy our persuasion without the intervention of others, if an Episcopal minister were once settled among us, which we beg of Almighty God to induce the Honorable Society to nominate; and in the meantime we remain their very humble servants and well wishers.

John Glover, Ebeneezer Booth, Stephen Parmelee, Samuel Henry, Moses Knapp, Dan[l] Jackson, John Seeley of Chestnut Ridge, Jeremiah Turner, Sam[l] Mosher, Eliza Sharp, widow, Thomas Wheeler of Woodbury.

Rev. Mr. Johnson to the Bishop of London.

STRATFORD, January 18th, 1723/4.

. . . . there is not one Clergyman of the Church of England, beside myself, in this whole colony, and I am obliged, in good measure to neglect my cure at Stratford, (where yet there is business enough for one minister) to ride about to the other towns (some ten, some twenty miles off) where in each of them, there is as much need of a resident minister as there is at Stratford, especially at Newtown and Fairfield. . . . . ."

From the same to the Secretary, June 11th, 1724. . . . . . . "Newtown is distressed for a minister, their teacher . . . . . being quite beat out ; and the whole Town would I believe embrace the church if they had a good minister at Fairfield."

From the same to the same, Sept. 16, 1726 : "At Fairfield, however, the number daily increases, and they have erected a small Church, which I opened last fall . . . . but while the Church in the country continues under the present oppressions—little or nothing can be expected of Newton (Newtown) or Ripton to encourage the Society to send them a missionary."

Rev. Mr. Caner to the Secretary (his first letter after his return from ordination):

"FAIRFIELD March 15th, 1727–8.

. . . . . There is a village northward of Fairfield, about 18 miles, containing near 20 families—where there is no minister at all of any denomination whatsoever; the name of it is Chestnut Ridge, where I usually preach or lecture once in three weeks. Newtown—which is about twenty-two miles northwest of Fairfield, Mr Johnson and I supply between us, it being equally distant from us."

During this interval Mr. Toucey had gone to England, returning with his commission of Captain in the King's army, resigned his pastorate and settled down in the village as an influential man of affairs ; his name and his wife's name, Hannah (Clark), are found on many records of deeds and sales, and he at once became a bulwark to those who could not before " sit easy under him."

The calling and settling of the new minister is thus described in the town records :

"Att a lawful Town meeting of ye Inhabitants of Newtown Held Oct ye 8ᵗʰ 1724 Orderᵈ & Apointᵈ foʳ ye making Choyce of a Gospel Minister in order to Settlement The Voters wear ordered to bring in there votes for ye Man whom they Desired should be there Settled Ministʳ wiᵗʰ ye Man's name fairly written on a pece of paper wiᵗʰ thʳ owne names to itt also and Mʳ John Beach of Stratford was made Choyc off for to be ye Gospel Minister in Newtown.

JOSEPH PECK, *Clark.*

Entered for Record ye

Date above.—Recorded pr

JOSEPH PECK, *Clerk.*

A week later they vote to give him a "home Lott containᵍ 94 acres—. provided Mr Beach Setle in Newtown in ye work of ye Gospel Ministry. Likewise to build or Erect A House on said house Lott for Mr Beach forty foot Long & twenty one foot wide and in heith as Generaly Two Storey Houses are built and erect a chimney in midst of said house of three Funnils two fire places below & one in ye Chamber Mr Beach finding glass & iron." Then follows the pasture bordering on " Mr Samuel Ferriss land," and a committee consisting of " Captᵃ Thomas Bennit Samuel Beers & John Leavenworth " is appointed "to give bond for ye Land as they shall agree," and on Nov. 9 " Then unanimously agreed & voted that Mr John Beach of Stratford should be ther Settled Minister in Newtown & that he shall be Ordained As soon as may be with convaniancy." Peter Hubbell, Samuel Beers and John Leav-

enworth are "to treat with Mr Beach conserning ye above
mentioned premises—the Town Ratifying & confirming whatever ye above s^d Com^{tee} shall do in all Respects." Then we
have in the records most minute descriptions of the various
conveyances of land for his "Incoragement."

Newtown Land Records, page 6.
November ye ninth 1724, we the subscribers Doe freely give
for the in Coragement of Mr. John Beetch his Settlement for
the ministry for Newtown ; that is to Say out of the thirty
acres, Devition all Ready agreed upon to be laid out ; Capt.
Thomas Bennitt five acres.

Sam^{ll} Beers, five acres.
Ebenez^r Booth, Six acres.
Joseph Peck, five acres
Ebenez^r Pringle, Two acres & an
    half
Stephen Pamerley, five acres.
Sam^{ll} Sanford, five acres
Ephraim Peck, five acres
Mathew Sherman, five acres
John Northurp, two acres
Josiah Burrit, four acres,
Jeremiah Northurp, four acres
Joseph Botsford, two acres
Nathan Baldwin, four acres.
Benja^{en} Duning, three acres
Jonathan Hubbell, two acres
Lemunuel Camp, three acres
Hugh Stilson, five acres
Adonija Morris two acres
Peter Hubbell, five acres
Joseph Gray, five acres
Jonathan Booth, boggy lot
Joseph Briftol, two acres.
John Gillit, seven acres and an
    half.
John Plat, five acres
Andrew Wheeler, one acre.
Thomas Sharp, one acre
Benjamin Northurp, one acre
John Griffin, four acres

given out of Quisomps purchas, by
these persons herafter named viz :
Moses Stilfon four acres, Sam^{ll}
Bryan six acres Thomas Skidmore,
four acres

John Lake two acres of his twenty
acre lot.
November ye 9th 1724, voted by
the proprietory to lay out the two
acres of land of John Lake's twenty
acre lot to Mr. Jno. Beach easterly
on John Glover's farm land and
north on Nathaniel Pamerly's land,
the other sides on common land or
highways.

The land given to Mr. Beach out
of ye thirty acres, is 107 an half.

att a Lawfull Meeting of the proprietors of Newtown, held
November ye ninth 1724, voted whether Mr. John Beach shall
have the improvement of four acres farther land, lying South
on the land of Thomas Sharp's home lot, westerly on Sam[ll]
Ferriss, southerly on common land or high way, Durcing the
said Beach his Naturall Life, viz : if he shall settle in the
work of the ministry in this place of Newtown. Voted in ye
afirmative : enter[d] per me

Peter Hubbell proprietory Clark.

page 7.

att a lawful proprietors meeting legaly warned, held November ye 9, 1724 ; then Voted that those proprietors which have
or shall give by subscription to Mr. John Beach, for his
encoreiagment to setle in ye work of the ministry in Newtown, according to the Constitution of this Goverment, that
is to say that the persons soe subscribing shall have Liberty
to say what they have subscribed out of their thirty devitions
for one or two   tract, that is to say one part on bushy hill
neare the south end of the towne on the westerly side, the
other part or tract without the Seequesterment, Voted for the
afirmative

Peter Hubbell.

page 22.

Voted that Mr John Beach shall have liberty to take up 30
acres of land, that was given him, after ye thirty acres as it
apears on the records ; viz : att ye end of one mile from ye
meeting house, to be taken in two or three peaces, at his election, provided it be taken, so that it damnifie no highway,
this meeting ajoyrned to the 20th of this instant Aprill at five
of ye clock afternoon.

Peter Hubbell, Clark.

Newtown Aprill ye 6, 1726."

It is quite a little time before they finish up these transfers
and in 1729/30 we find them laying out to John Beach of
Newtown, a *part* of that land that was given him by certain
proprietors . . . . . . at ye mile from ye meeting house . . .
. . . north of Benjamin Dunning's, and another lott, next to
Ephraim Peck's land " & make a drawing of it," which looks

like the side of a barn, toppled over, and pointing eastward,
another portion abuts "north^{ery} on John Glover's home
land," and yet another touches on Thomas Skidmore's 6 acre
divition by ye end of ye pond" and the closing survey takes
in "Samuel Turners, his house." For the consideration of
"fivety pounds" Jonathan Hubbell sells "unto Mr. Beach
. . . . . . the land which was formerly David Jenkins, his
home Lott . . . . . . " " 4 acres be it more or less . . . . . .
with a certain dwelling house now upon ye same, this 16th
Day of February, Anno Dominni, 1729/30. On the same page
follows a deed from Juhn Gillet "for ye love & goodwill I
have to John Beach of Newtown, etc.," so that by purchase
and gift his acres swelled to a goodly share of earthly posses-
sions, and it is evident he had no great doubt of his ability to
hold them in any event.

But the storm was brewing and he announced to his
beloved parishioners that he had grave doubts of the validity
of his ordination and felt called to express them. As was
said of him in a sermon preached at the consecration of the
fourth church edifice of his parish, by the Rev. David Platt
Sanford,—"He was of that honest make-up that his practice
followed closely upon his belief—truth with him was for use,
not for mere speculation and discussion." And yet, judging
from the letters and papers written by him during his long
life of controversy, he was certainly fond of argumentative
and debatable subjects. This avowal brought the less surprise as he frequently made use of the Lord's prayer and
other as they called them "*set*" prayers, but nevertheless,
once again were they troubled in their souls. "Att a lawful
Town" meeting of ye Inhabitants of Newtown, held Jan. 14,
1731/2, appointed to consult what was prop^r to be done with
ye Rev^d Mr John Beach, regarding Present Difficulties of ye
town, by reason y^t, said Mr Beach hath declared himself to be
of ye Communion of ye Church of England, ye meeting is
adjourned until ye 19th of present January at 3 o'clock in ye
afternoon. Att ye afores^d ajourned meeting, voted by ye
Inhabitants aboves^d to keep a day of solemn fasting and
prayer under ye present Difficul Circumstances, also to call
in ye Ecclesiastical Council of ye County of Fairfield to
Direct & Do what they shall think Propper under ye present

Difficult Circumstances of ye said town of Newtown. Also ye first Sunday (?) of February next is ye Day appointed for ye Fast, also voted by ye Inhabitants afores[d] that Capt[n] Thomas Toucey, Mr Peter Hubbell & Mr John Leavenworth should be a Com[tee] in ye behalf of said town to write to ye Reverends Eccle[s] of ye County as afores[d] for their assistance." Immediately following is this significant entry "Whereas there being a town meeting held in Newtown on ye Instant Jan[y] ye 19th Day 1731/2, it is voted in s[d] meeting to keep a Day of fast & to send out for a Council of neighboring elders to consult what method to take in ye present Difficulty of ye town above[sd]. We whose names are hereunto subscribed Do enter our protests & dislikes against said vote," and this is signed by nine prominent men of the town, Mr James Hurd, Benj[n], John and Henry Glover, James Hurd, Jun[r], Robert and Nehemiah Seelye, Samuel Sherman and John Fabrique.

Capt. Thomas Toucey must have been less than human if he had not some private and it may be public comment to make on the failure of his successor in office to please and satisfy the critical villagers, and he must have taken a melancholy pleasure in performing his share of the duty of writing to the "Reverend Eccle[s]." Indeed, being probably the most capable penman, his was the actual hand, not to add *brain*, in the affair. The result was that the committee were, with the town clerk Joseph Peck "to pursue ye accomplishment of ye advice of ye Reverends Associates late given to ye town of Newtown with Respect to ye obtaining if it may be either Mr Samuel Sherman of New Haven or Mr Hinsdale of Deerfield to come & carry on preaching in this place in order to a Settlement in ye Gospel Ministry here. In case there shall be a Good Liveing & Agreement to that end between those calling & him called & In case that neither of those Gentlemen can be obtained that the said com[tee] shall have pow[r] with good advice to apply themselves to any other suitable person for the end afores[d]." The day before, February 7th, a little company of staunch churchmen met together and signed their names to the following agreement :

"Newtown, Feb 7, 1731/₂: We whose names are hereunto subscribed do herebye declare that we are desirous that Mr John Beach may be our minister notwithstanding his declaration for the Church of England and we are jointly willing to await until he shall get a regular ordination by which authority he may administer in faith the holy sacraments & further do hereby declare our protest against the settling or maintaining of another minister, and we will pay our rates to him the aforesd Mr John Beach Salary as he shall continue to be our minister according to the Law entituled An Act providing how the taxes levied on the professors of the Church of England for the support of the people shall be disposed of,

James Hurd	Jeremiah Turner
Wil . . . Sherman	Moses Lyon
Ebenezer Sanford	Daniel Sherman
Easter Sanford	Robert Seelye
John Glover	John Foot
Samuel Sherman	Benoni Sherman
Nehemiah Seelye	Henry Glover
Robert Seelye Junr	Benjn Glover

John Beach ordained an Episcopal Clergyman 1732 over about 15 families

ISAAC BEERS."

This is copied from a note-book of the late Isaac Beers of Sandy Hook, himself a descendant and to whose valuable papers I am, by the kindness of Mrs. Beers, indebted for many important items. In the old Congregational record the following brief synopsis is carefully entered: "Newtown first settled A D 1709—settled Chiefly from Stratford & Milford. The first minister Mr Thomas Tousey ordained & a Church Gathered (being about 30 families) A D 1714. Mr Toucey dismissed A D 1724. Mr John Beach called to the ministry. Mr Beach declared for ye Church of England & sent for orders for Newtown over about 15 families & for Reading A D 1732. Mr Elisha Kent ordained in Newtown over about 60 families Sepr 27, A D 1732. Mr Kent dismissed A D 1742. Mr David Judson ordained in Newtown Sep 21—A D 1743. All which ministers were living 1760. The present number of families in Newtown A D 1770 being about 350—and about one half of them of the Church of England. A D 1765 Sep 9—Dea^c Daniel Booth resigned of his own motion his office of Deac^n in this Church & also his relation as a Brother, because he could not as himself Declared be easy under ye Calvinistic Doctrine as therein taught." Mr. Booth declared for the Church of England and became one of its foremost men. His character and family will be found fully described among the sketches of ancestors.

At the risk of some repetition but with no other apology, the petition of Newtown and Reading churchmen—for the return of their beloved minister—is given in full.

Petition of Several Members of the Church of England in Reading and Newtown in Connecticut :

NEW ENGLAND, March 20, 1732.

May it please the honorable Society,

We, the Subscribers, members of the Church of England in Reading and Newtown, within the County of Fairfield and Colony of Connecticut in New-England, being under very great difficulty to com at the worship of God according to that excellent establishment by reason of our distance from the honorable Society's Missionaries the Rev Mr Johnson and Mr Caner which is about twenty miles, and being, in-deed some of us, at a great distance from any publick worship at all, whereby not only we ourselves, but our poor children also suffer, and are like to be trained up in very great ignorance of the knowledge of the Gospel, do beg leave to lay this, our Calamitous State before your venerable board, and become very humble petitioners for a share in that Charity which is conspicuous even in this dark corner of the earth. To this we are rather encouraged by a favorable letter to Some of our number from the honorable Society, obtained about two years after the Rev Mr Johnson's first coming among us, wherein the honorable Society, were pleased to offer us a Missionary upon certain conditions, which at that time we were not able to come upon by reason of the settlement of the bearer here of, Mr John Beach—a gentleman at that time of a different persuasion ; but now more and further encouraged by the said Gentleman's being reconciled to the established Church of England, especially in that being now bound home to receive holy orders from the Lord Bishop of London, he is willing to return to this place of his former settlement and abode, if his Lordship and the honorable Society shall think proper.

The good opinion that persons of all persuasion have of him here, where he has been known for several years past, and accounted a gentleman of remarkable sober and regular conduct, and of learning and good ability to discharge the ministerial office, gives us reason to promise ourselves a great deal of happiness and comfort from his future ministration, if the honourable Society shall think fit to return him to us. Though we are poor, the unavoidable consequence of settling an uncultivated country, and so cannot possibly with-out assistance provide a suitable support for the aforesaid gentleman, yet what we are able we are very ready to engage and have affixed to our respective names underwritten; and we do humbly hope and pray that the honourable Society out of their great charity will supply wherein we are wanting toward the said gentleman's support, as we flatter ourselves with hopes of success in this affair, from the former goodness and great charity of your venerable board, so we would humbly hope that the consideration of several towns lying about us, at a distance of about seven miles, as Danbury, Ridgefield, Woodbury and New Milford, and numbers of Indians, would be of some further inducement toward some suitable relief to our truly deplorable state; for indeed we are not so selfish as to expect Mr. Beach's service should be wholly confined to ourselves, but that he may be capable of propagating Christian Knowledge in those other towns like-wise. Thus, the Rev. Mr. Johnson and Mr. Caner, though settled at Stratford and Fairfield, have been and are still very ready to assist us, so far as is consistent with the distance between them and ourselves, for whose service, as flowing from the Society's charity, we are truly thankful, wishing withal, there may never be wanting pious men in these parts to promote the Church's interest. Fearing we have been already too tedious, we only add our hearty and fervent prayers to Almighty God for success in your truly charitable designs to the souls of men.

> " We are, etc., etc.
>
> SAMUEL MOREHOUSE and others."

At this time, or shortly after, the Rev. Mr. Kent was, as we have just seen, ordained in Newtown, and the town was greatly distressed and disturbed over the difficulties of set- tling two ministers of different denominations harmoniously. In consulting the list of Selectmen it will be seen that the Booths, Beers and Hubbells were not as often on duty ; other names appear. Whether this had any political or party signi- ficance let him who can, tell.

We may take note of a couple of strays of the period. "Then taken up By Left Samuel Griffin, a Read Brockled faced Bull with white under his Belly marked with one half peney ye under side of the neare eare & one half peney ye upper side of ye off eare Being about two yeare old past." Whatever a "read brockled faced" creature may be, it was as well he should have been taken up, by somebody.

"Then taken up in a sufering condition by Daniel Beers, a Bey Mare, with two Knics in the inside of the rite eare," and follow some charges and fees, and an indication that the finder was on this occasion the haver.

In 1741, Tanton applies for a "liberty. "Att above s^d meet- ing voted & agreed that ye west farm" called Tantoun shall have ye liberty to Build a Schoolhouse upon their oune charg, and to have their proportion of money, voted for ye School from time to time according to their list of Rateable Estate, provided they lay out the incomes for ye School within the year," and a rate of one penny upon the pound is voted for "school in ye winter season." John Glover and Abel Booth, a com^{tee} for ye North School, and John Lake & Nathl Nickols for South School. Previous to this date, it had been found necessary to have two schoolhouses and the town meetings were held sometimes in one, sometimes in the other; they had also ordered a "horse bridge erected over the pond brook as they pass in ye Country Road to benjamin hawleys and as they go to Benjn Dunnings," and that "ye grass shall be cut for Clearing Commons at ye South End of ye Town, namely in ye town street to Bearses house Lott & from thence to ye Deep Brook so called that peece of Land from ye Deep Brook where it emties out of ye Hom medow to Jos Prindle's house, and also between Captn Towsey^s Esq. home Lott & henery glover's home Lot, and also ye North ende of ye Toune ye valley that Runs northward from ye northwest corner of Mr Heth Peck home Lot to ye house of Thomas Pearce and also apece of land lying East of Sam¹ Turner's Twenty acre Lot." Thus early was there a village improvement society. "Att aboveᵈ meeting voted & agreed that Jeremiah Northrup should Have Liberty to set a small Saboth Day House In ye Land by or against . . . . . Captⁿ Nathan Baldwin's orchard."

Rev. Mr. Beach to the Secretary (first letter in this collection, but evidently *not* the first since his settlement) :

AUGUST 7, 1735,
NEWTOWN IN CONNECTICUT.

Reverend Sir,

      I think it my duty to acquaint the venerable Society with the present State of my parish, although the alteration since my last has not been very considerable. I have baptised twenty-nine children, and admitted twenty-five persons more to the Communion, So that the number of our Communion now at Newtown, Reading, and places adjacent, is ninety-five. I preach frequently and administer the sacrament at Ridgefield, being about eighteen miles distant from the place where I dwell, where there are about fourteen or eighteen families of very serious and religious people who have a just esteem of the Church of England, and are very desirous to have the opportunity of worshipping God in that way. I have constantly preached one Sunday at Newtown—and the other at Reading, and after I have preached at Reading in the day-time, I perform divine service and preach at Newtown in the evening; and although I have not that success I could wish for, yet I do, and hope I always shall faithfully endeavor (as far as my poor ability will allow) to promote that good work that the venerable Society sent and maintained me for.

      I am, Reverend Sir, your most humble servant,

JOHN BEACH.

The following list of residents along the highways to whom "restitution" was made in 1740–1 gives the most reliable survey of those property holders :

Mr John Read
10. 08. 19. 23.

Mr Toucey.	1 11 & 3
John Lake	44
" Blackman	18
Dunnings heirs	43
Mr John Glover	21

Mr John Glover &
Shermans   26

Left Skidmore
John Glover   45

Mr Caleb Baldwin
Left Wheeler L Northrop   9

Morris Lyon John Shepard
Jno Bears. Jno Bristol
Nathl Briscoe
James Stilson
Jno Leavenworth   41

Bearses heirs   25

Mr Peter Hubbel
Jont Hubbel
Benjn Burit   38

Abm Kimberly
Sergt Booth   20

dec Peck heirs   47
Sert Jos Bots. Canfield   46
Cap Peck Ephm   16
Saml faris   42

Left Griffin John Hull   12

Mr John Gillet Jos Bristol   35
dec Jams Bristol Ser Stilson   13

Ebenr Johnson Roger Terrill   14

Ephr Bennit Stepn Morris
Matthew Sherman   17
Jeremh Turner. Saml Baldwin   7

Jos Sherman   6
Dec Botsford   28

Plat Josiah
Capn David Judson
Danniell Booth   39

Saml Camp & Datons heirs   15

Edd Agur. David
& Jonn Fairchild   36

Danniel foot Jno Booth   24

Cap Nathan Baldwin   37

Saml & David Summers
Jeremiah Baldwin   34

Abel Booth—Saml Turner   30

Sergt Nathl Nickols   32

Sert Nathl Nickols
Saml Sanfords heirs   40

Mr John plat
Jos Stilson & ben Stilson   29

Ben Curtice   33

ben & peter Curtice   42

Parmerly & Jabez Hurd   4

Mr Adams & benjamin
Northrop—John debill   22

Nettleton & Sum body
else   31
Thos Leavenworth
Jeremiah Northrop
Thom Sharp   48

Mr Henry Botsford   27

Capta T Bennits heirs   50

JOB SHERMAN CLARK.

In the winter of 1741 they meet in the "North School house" and appoint a committee, Joseph Bristol, John Gillet and Benjamin Curtice, "to take care & trie" if they can get

some of the proprietors to sign a paper giving up ten acres
"for ye use of ye Town Commons." And now there is some
dissatisfaction and jealousy between Newtown and "Reading"—as it was then spelled—about township lines, and John
Northrop, Ephraim Peck, John Bristol, Benjamin Curtice
and Joseph Bristol are deputed to "run & settel" the same
"from the south east corner of Danbury town ship to the
head line of Fairfield."

In 1743 we find the proprietors, or a part of them, greatly
exercised over the land which was "supposed to be Resigned
up to the Town by ye Rev^d Mr Beach" (this "resignation"
is fully given in the accompanying biography), and calling a
meeting to "Confirm to ye professors of the Church of England in said Town there proper honest Right in ye undivided
Lands for ye use of a Church meeting." . . . . This is signed
by Thomas Skidmore, John Glover, Matthew Sherman, Samuel
Camp, Nathaniel Nickols, John Bears, John Lake, Thomas
Leavenworth and Abner Hard. Consequently on March
13 of the same year, St. John Northrop, Junr, Caleb Baldwin and Mr. Henry Glover are a committee to "See how
many professors of the Church of England ther was that was
proprietors at the time of the Settlement of Mr Kent in the
work of the ministry in s^d Newtowne & so compute how
much land belongs to them to make & erect a proposition (or
perhaps proper-portion) with the lands that was supposed to
be given to the prisbeteren minister in Newtown, & to make
ther Report to the next ajurned meeting. Voted also that the
meeting shall be ajurned to next Monday" at which time
they vote a rate of 3 shillings upon "each Poll Right & So
the proportion to half or quarter or lesser Rights" and Serg^t
Botsford is appointed "Colector" for which he is to have
the sum of 1. 10. On the 19th of March the important
matter of church lands is settled. "Forasmuch as divers persons of ye presbeterean persuasion did formerly sign & subscribe to give to ye Rev^d Mr John Beach of s^d Newtown (as
apears on Records) . . . . divers peeces of land out of
ye thirty acre divisions & other divisions them to themselves
granted to be laid out in ye bounds of said Newtown as
apears on Record in Consideration of said Mr Beach settling
in ye work of ye ministry in ye said Town and Lands so
assigned to be given was laid out to Mr Beach & afterward s^d

Mr Beach declare himself to be of ye Church of England persuasion in Maters of Religion, & there upon did Resign up to
ye Town of Newtown all his right titel & interest in the lands
to him layd as aforesaid & there upon s^d Town by ye Com^{tee}
did execute a Deed in Due form of Law dated August ye 1st
1732 of one hundred & four acres & half of s^d land to Mr
Elisha Kent in consideration of his setteling in ye work of ye
ministry According to ye prisbeterian persuasion & s^d Signers
not having conveyed ye fee of s^d lands by any leagal deed or
deeds did afterwards lay out ther full rights in s^d Divition to
themselves & ther heirs & therefore s^d lands layd out to Mr
Beach as afores^d & supposed to be conveyed to s^d Mr Kent by
s^d deed did then of right belong to ye proprietors of ye common & undivided lands in sd Newtown Several of which said
proprietors was & did then profess themselves to be of the
Church of England persuasion & not willing to contribute
towards ye settlement of a presbeterien Minister & where as
part of said lands was layd out neare hom (nearer home) than
the limmits of ye thirty acre devition therefor to secure to s^d
Churchmen ye proportionable Rights in ye common and
undivided lands for ye use of a Church of England ministry
equal both (in) quantity and quallety to those of ye presbeterien persuasion whose rights are devoted to s^d Mr Kent his
heirs & assigns forever " (this is the *first* breathing space—take
time) "It is voted & agreed at s^d meeting that those proprietors of s^d common & undivided lands that were & doe profess
themselves to be of ye Church of England persuasion, two
acre & forty & three rods of land & so in proportion for half
Rights, etc., three eight parts to be laid out within one mile
from ye meeting house the remainder to be layd in ye Limmits assigned for ye Church of England clergy for ye use of
ye Rev Mr John Beach & his lawful successors forever.

Jobe Sherman."

Further petitioning to the Assembly of the North men, in
1743, reads : "Upon the Memorial of Benj Stephens Eben^r
Bostwick & others, inhabitants & dwelling in the North east
corner of Danbury township & in the north part of the Township of Newtown & the south part of the township of New
Milford praying for a committee to view the circumstances in
respect of there being set off & made a distinct Ecclesiastical

3

Society having liberty for a winter parish etc : Resolved by this Assembly—that Col Wm Preston, Mr Noah Sherman & Captn Thomas Knowles all of Woodbury be a Com^tee to repair to the Memorialists abode at their cost & after notifying all parties & haveing heard ther pleas & viewed ther circumstances in respect of their being a distinct Ecclesiastical Society or haveing liberty to hire preaching in the extreme season of the year & if s^d Com^tee think proper, to draw the line in each town for the bounds to s^d Society & make report of the opinion & doings there on to this Assembly in October next."

These many quotations on one all absorbing topic must be borne with, by the less interested reader, or the history of this town would not be written. So largely was it concerned in the establishment of the Episcopal Church in this part of the country that for many years its little band of followers were the centre of attack and defence, and had they not been withheld by the strong arm of their conservative but staunch leader, much bad blood would have been stirred and a veritable conflict inevitable. Fortunately also, many of the most influential persons both in Newtown and Redding were of that "persuasion," and where actual property holders are of a party, it has more than moral or physical support. That the Church of England men were at one with their Presbyterian brethren in the contest between them and the northern end of the town may be judged somewhat by the between lines of the following letter, written about this time by the new missionary, dated at Reading, to the secretary of his society :

"READING, IN NEW ENGLAND,
October 20th, 1743.

Reverend Sir :—I beg the venerable society's direction in an affair I am just now perplexed with. There are about twenty families professing the church at New Milford and New Fairfield, which are about fifteen miles hence. I preach to them several times in a year, but seldom on the Lord's day.

They frequently come to church at Newtown, but by reason of the distance they can't attend constantly, and their families very seldom, and when they can't come to church, they meet together in their own town, and one of their number reads some part of the common prayer and a sermon. They are now building a church, and hope in time to have a minister settled among them. But the Independents, to suppress this design in its infancy, having the authority in their hands, have lately prosecuted and fined them for their meeting, to worship God according to the common prayer, and the same punishment they are like to suffer for every offence in this kind, although it is the common approved practice of the same Independents to meet for worship in their own way when they have no minister. But what is a virtue in them, is a crime in our people. The same is like to be the case in many other towns, in which people professing the church are so far distant from a settled minister that they cannot constantly attend the worship of God with him. The case of these people is very hard: if on the Lord's day they continue at home they must be punished, if they meet to worship God according to the Church of England in the best manner they can, their mulct is still greater; and, if they go to the Independent meeting in the town where they live, they must endure the mortification of hearing the doctrine and worship of the church vilified, and the important truths of Christianity obscured and enervated by enthusiastic and 'antinomian' dreams.

Now, I should be thankful if the venerable society would direct me what course to advise these people to, and if I might receive a particular instruction to take care of those professing the church in New Milford and New Fairfield as part of my parish. I believe it would put me into a better capacity to protect them from the insults of their Independent neighbors. I have this half-year baptised eighteen children and admitted several more persons to the Lord's Supper. The enclosed is the state of my parish. I have this day drawn for my half-year's salary. I am, Reverend Sir, your's and the society's

Most obedient servant,

JOHN BEACH."

In 1743, also, Mr. John Glover sends in his account of the "Colloneys money" to the General Assembly, held in New Haven, 1741—£523.15.'/. In 1743, at the May Session, the northern inhabitants of the town, or some of them, move to the Assembly to be set off with part of Danbury and New Milford for a separate Ecclesiastical Society, "and whereas such a motion, should it succeed in such a very difficult Day as it now is with Newtown, must need be very unhappie. . . . Thos. Toucey, Esq., be and hereby is constituted agent for this Town of Newtown to ye Hon[l] General Assembly to oppose ye above s[d] motion, if any such shall be then made, and to manage that affair thoroughly as shall be needful."

At this trying time when members of the same household were often of different persuasions, and it was necessary to conduct public business with caution and to hold together for strength, they felt this defection of the northern residents keenly, and foresaw further weakening of their legislative powers in this proposed withdrawal. Such strong influence was brought to bear that it was over twenty years before Newbury was thus set off ; tho' continuous petitioning went on during the interval. The same year, 1743, at the last meeting in December, it was voted that "ye Inhabitants of Whisken - neare and known by that name, shall have Libertie to Cut and Clear ye underbrush in ye highway that leads to ye iron works from ye house of Francis Barlyes to ye Pond Brook, and yt Inhabitants of Zoar from ye house of Jos. Heard, and so to Potatuck Brook."

"Mr. Nathaniel Nichols and Thos. Leavenworth are appointed to secure a master for The South School and John Lake, Jeremiah Northrop and Ens^n Saml Summers was chosen and appointed tithen men to Take Care of Disorders in the Saboth and Sworn according to Law for ye yeare ensueing." Thus we see alas, that another evil of progress had followed the course of growing youth ; tithing men were now necessary to the proper observance of the Sabbath, and indeed if one may judge those early Christian Martyrs by any present Law of the one day in seven, great and fearful must have been their joy to escape punishment, doubtless deserved, by whatever methods easiest employed.

The "Saboth Day House" was intended for those who came from a distance to attend the Services, to meet and discuss their simple viands between sermons, if not indeed, these also. The interval was not long, and once in town they were expected to remain to both discourses.

They have now by the "sail of Job Sanfords house" a bolting mill on pototuck brook and John Lake is to collect the toll of Sanfords mill and has a "Bushill of Wheat" for reward. "A Sofishant Schoolmaster for ye north School" would carry its own appeal for such a functionary. This year the minister's rate is "seven pence in ye pound to ye Rev. Mr. Beach for the full yeare, and also ye Rev. Mr. David Judson Rate to be accordingly from ye 23d Day of May last past to ye first of January next ensuing, voted in ye Afermative.

Attest,   JOHN NORTHROP,
                                                       Town Clerk."

In March, 1746, they meet "to take measures for ye setting up a Publick meetinge house for the Church of England
so called in Newtown." This is more fully described in
another volume (4) of what is known as the Town Journal,
and is as follows: "At above s^d meeting $^e/_e$, held March 27
A D 1746, Jeremiah Northrop was chosen and appointed
moderator for the meeting. Test, John Northrop town clerk.
At above s^d meeting voted that whereas those of ye Church
of England in this place are now upon building a new meetinge house for the Publick worship of God that said People
of ye Episcopal Communion . . . . shall have Liberty to
Erect said house on ye west side of ye Town Street southerd
of ye Presbyterian Meeting House 28 Rods ye South End of
said Church of England Meeting house to be the termination
of ye 28 Rods said house to sett northward and southward
fronting to ye street & the Back or Westward side of said
house to be ten (10) feet distant from the front of ye home
Lott which it stands against and that they & their successors
shall never be molested by this Town from this Time forward
and forever in ye Employment of said place for ye use aforesaid.

Voted in ye afermative. Test,

JOHN NORTHROP,
Town Clerk."

The whole account of the Town's enactments and legislation on this subject, lends itself so completely to the impression desired, that it is given in detail : So, in April (the 12),
the Surveyor makes his report ; "I the subscriber being
assisted by $^e/_e$ $^e/_e$, proceeded with chain bearers to measure the
28 Rods southward and find said 28 Rods terminated 19 feet
southward of ye south side of ye Church of England meeting house, as they are now laid. The above work was performed at ye Request of ye Selectmen uf said Newtown By
me. Edward Lewis, County Surveyor."

Alas . . . but the apology follows, recorded on the same page
(23), "Newtown Ap. ye 12, 1746. We the subscribers members of the Church of England being sensable that we have
not fully complied with the vote of said Town in Respect to
Building the new church in that we did not Lay ye foundation of ye Church so far southward as it ought to have Been

By ye vote by twenty feet, & in so Doing have so far Done Contrary to Good order and ye agreement of ye Town by there said vote and hereby Desire those that we agreed to forgive us that rong. . . . .

We the Subscribers here
unto Rec^d of above ac-   JOHN GLOVER   ⎫
knowledgement and accept   THOS. SKIDMORE, ⎬ Comtee.
if it as we are concerned,   JAMES HEARD   ⎭
Day & Date above.

At the May session of the General Assembly in 1744, "Fayerfield Co." is given a probate Court, and "That the towns of Danbury, Newtown & New Fairfield be known by the name of the District of Danbury." The next year "The Town of Newtown is ordered to send in a list of polls and rateable estates at the session in October next," and the Secretary is ordered to "transmit a copy to the Selectmen of said Town," but in October we find that, " Whereas the Towns of Simsbury and Newtown have not sent in such lists, then the Town of Simsbury be doomed, & the same is herebye doomed at £15,300 in the public lists, and s^d Town is hereby required to pay rates accordingly, and s^d town shall receive their School money accordingly (which of course means no school money unless the rates are paid), and the town of Newtown is doomed at £12,000 in said list, who are required to pay accordingly and s^d Newtown shall receive the school money in proportion to s^d sum." So they send in a humble apology on account of their "Listers being disabled by sickness" to the May Session in 1747, and that august body resolves, "that the sum of £1183. 83^s & 5^d shall be abated out of ye said sum mentioned in said record, and "that the taxes granted in Octr last shall be levyed upon said Town of Newtown *exclusive* of the s^d £1183 83^s 5^d." Evidently "the Town of Newtown" had even then somewhat of a *political pull*. Returning to our more prolific town records, we read that in 1748 they decide to divide up the land which had been sequestered for town commons because "many grevious trespasses have been committed from time to time upon ye timber & fire wood growing upon s^d sequestrament, to ye grate Rong of ye Proprietors." So a "Devition" of six acres to the fifty "Rights" was ordered and the "said devitions are to be per^tikeler estate as to timber wood and stone lands, but in all other Respects town Commons," an adjournment of *one hour* is taken (probably the discussion had created a void which had to be filled before the actual business could be transacted), after which "Captn John Glover, Sergt Dan[l] Booth and Mr Jos Bristol are a com[tee] to lay out and number and size ye devitions. Captn John gets 18[s] a day, the others 13[s], while performing this task, but they are distinct in setting the time, for it is voted, that the work shall be begun on the first Day of March next, or as soon as the snow is off ye ground after, voted in ye A fermatif." The second division is ordered for November next. Finally, on February 15, it was voted "that Leiut John Northrup, should draw for the Rest of the Proprietors" and a draft of the decision is carefully entered in the records.

The "sarcumstances" of this or that highway or country road, would indicate the usual state of things even to this day. To those whose experience had been gained in English roads and lanes, there must have come moments of homesickness for the bright white glaring stoneless stretch, or the shady turf track under the hedge, and we may suppose that when a "Good Cart Bridge," all in capitals, is ordered to be Built over Pootatuck Brook, within the space of a year, that those whose farms lay on the other side felt encouraged to larger efforts and fresh activity. Schools began to be more frequent : "Newtown, Dec. 10, 1750, then voted that a school shall be kept in each of ye schoolhouses in ye Towne street in ye yeare ensuing, and in each of ye school houses of ye Several farms and that two thirds part of ye Interest of ye land money shall be expended in ye Mickalmust and winter season in ye two schools in ye Towne street, and the other third in ye spring and summer season of ye year, and that two thirds the money arising out of ye Countery Rate and also that arising out of ye two pence on ye pound out of ye Town, according to ye list of Rateable estates shall be expended in ye severall schools according to their Respective Lists, two thirds in Micklemust and winter season and the other third In Spring and summer, and if pariants, Masters or Mistresses of ye Schollers shall add and pay one third part so much money in each of ye above mentioned Seasons to ye soport of the Respectted Schools in ye limmits in which they Dwell— that is to say one third part of ye Respective schools shall be maintained by ye schollers—voted in ye affirmatif." In the record this is without punctuation, and it is doubtful if as now arranged it conveys the right impression. That schools were certainly *needed* goes without further comment. In 1748, " Then layd out to the people living at ye Northwest part of ye township of Newtown upon their Desier sixty Rod of land for a Bureing place to Bury ther dead in at a Place Northly off or from Benj^a Hawley's Dwelling House first Bounds is a heap of stones in the line of Caleb Baldwin's land then runs 11 rods westerly in s^d Baldwin's line to a heap of stones then Run southly 6 Rods to a heap of stones then Run westerly 11 Rods joyning to the Highway, then run northly 5 Rods to first bounds Land layd out by us.

> JOSEPH BRISTOL, } Comtee.
> LEMUEL CAMP. }

Recorded Dec. ye 18, 1747,
  per JOHN NORTHRUP, Clerk."

The first time prayer is used as chronicled is at the annual town meeting of 1750 : " The above s^d meeting being opened by prayer, Mr Amos Northrup is appointed to collect Rates for Rev Mr Judson, & Stephen Burril for Mr Beach ; for the schools, Abel Botsford and Eph^m Burrit for North School, & Daniel Beers and Matthew Curtis for South School. [These two will be frequently mentioned in the accompanying genealogy.] Caleb Baldwin Jr for Whisken-'er farms $^c/_c$ $^c/_c$ Jonathan Fairchild for Tantown School, Peter Lewis for ye school at ye farms called Palestine, John Plat for Zoar, and Jonathan Sanford to build a Saboth Day house at ye westerly end of Mr John Plat's, his house. Palestine bounds are North on Mr John Glover's Dwelling house, Easterly to include Noah Pamerly's House, and Eph^m Prindle's and Benjn Stilson's to Ab^m Bearses." Jos Smith, Danl Booth and Jon^u Botsford were appointed " Aigents in behalf of ye Town in the case of ye west farm Belonging to s^d Newtown making application to ye Honble General Assembly to be held at New Haven Oct 9th 1751, the professors of ye Church of England in Newtown shall be freed from any charg in that afaire above mentioned."

In answer to the petition for separate Ecclesiastical Society and the vote for its obstruction, Oct. 4, 1751, " Whereas in

May last .... by way of Barr, then appointed Deputy to
manage that afaire, viz, Thomas Toucey Esq who by Reason
of seerious sickness prevailing in ye place could not attend
ye Assembly (this was taken note of at the last mentioned
meeting of the Assembly), and whereas ye s^d writings ware
committed to ye other Deputy (viz Mr Nathl Nickols) who
nevere gaive them in owing probably to 2 Reasons, that Mr.
Nickols continually looked for Mr. Toucey's coming ; 2nd for
that Mr Nickols Returned home some considerable time before ye Conclusion of ye Assembly, and when he came home
found Distressing Sickness in his family and could not
Return again to ye Assembly and so ware unhappily prevented all plees, so things last to apeare to the Assembly
as that all parties ware easie with Relation to ye premises
that the Honble Assembly in this month to be held in New
Haven be made acquainted with these things. Voted in ye
afferm^tive." Here again no punctuation except at will of the
compiler. In this year but one collector is appointed for *both*
church rates, and the "Schollers shall find fire-wood."

Ferry fares underwent some changes—fares were raised
" man, horse and load 4^d, led horse 1^d, afoot man 1½^d, ox or
other such kine 3½^d, sheep, hog or goat ½ peney." About
this time the Church of England people refused to pay taxes
toward the support of the other church, and much trouble ensued. They cited the inhabitants of Newtown to appear
before the General Court at Hartford on the third Day of Instant May, (1752), if they please to show Reasons, if any they
have, why said Court should not grant said professors parish
priveleges, c/c, c/c, ...

"Pursuant to ye Citation ye Town meeting was legally
warned by ye selectmen of said Newtown to be held on Mun-
day ye 11th day of Instant May A D 1752, at six of ye clock
afternoon at ye North school house in said town street to do
what shall be thought proper in said afair and also to act in
all other Business as shall appeare needful to be Done in said
meeting." . . . Being met according to warning Captn John
Glover was chosen moderator of s^d meeting and the meeting
being opened by the moderator, "Put to vote at above s^d
meeting whether they would make choyce of any meet person to be an agant to appeare at Hartford on ye second
Thursday of Instant May of the General Corts sitting to op-

pose or give Reasons why ye professors of ye Church of England in Newtown should not have their prayers granted unto them. Voted in ye negative. Also, voted that . . . . we have no Reasons to offer against the motion of Professors of ye Church of England in Newtowns prayer to ye Assembly. Voted in ye afermative." The outcome was that the General Court " Resolved that the professors of the Church of England in Newtown who by the laws of this government are exempted from contributing to the support of the ministry settle^d and established by the laws of Government and for that Reason are Debare^d voting for raising such support, shall be, and they are hereby exempted from being taxed with the rest of the Inhabitants of s^d town in all such Rates and taxes as they shall make for the support of the Ministry established therein as afores^d. And the inhabitants of s^d town are hereby fully authorized and empowered exclusive of such professors therein, to grant such rates or taxes in the town meetings as they shall from time to time judge needful for the support of the minister and other society disbursements, as fully as other societies in this government are entitled to do." From the kindly manner with which the town meeting had previously acknowledged their claims and agreed not to oppose them, it would almost seem as if some expense and time might have been spared—not to mention *red tape*—but the sanction and indeed consent of the central ruling power had to be obtained in order to establish these privileges.

Very soon after this the town received a present of some law books—perhaps this may have been in order to teach them how to manage their affairs without so often coming to the Assembly, yet it must have been grist to the mill of the State to have so full a docket. " Dec. 12, 1754. At the Annual Town meeting voted and agreed, ℅, that ye law Books now sent to ye Inhabitants . . . shall be divided according to the List of Rateable Estates in ye year 1749," . . . . and follows the unmistakable favoritism of such preference.

" Mr Stephen Burwell was chosen & appointed to Draw the Law Books for ye several parts of ye town & they were drawn for in ye following manner : Tauton and West farmes called Whisken-ere, and olde Book, Up town an new Book, Down town a new Book, ye West part of ye towne a new book, the middle of ye town a new book, Zoar and Mild (mile-) hill an olde Book." Really, they might have let one "new Book " go to the dwellers *off* the "street" !

In this year also, the Newbury petitioners at last succeed in getting the Assembly to allow their claims for a separate Ecclesiastical Society and title. New Brookfield with a second Grist Mill, John Sanford paying ¼ part and the inevitable Committee of three—Glover, Skidmore and Curtis —to see fair play, and "John Lake to receive all yernings of s^d Mill," this eventful year's record closes. Some interesting details concerning lands bought and sold and given up by the Rev. John Beach, during these times of stress, are reserved for the story of his life in a later chapter.

Receipts for his "sallary," as well as those of the other ministers—the Rev. Mr. Kent and Mr. Judson—are sprinkled through the records, and show that Newtown piety was good for its debts, and rang true on the counters of its creditors. Apropos of this, here is an amusingly honest bit : "Newtown, May 21, 1756. Then taken up by Lt Jos Smith . . . a leathern pouch with 30^s of Silver and six Copers . . . entered by John Northrop, town clerk, May 28. The owners appeared *February 4th* for ye above s^d money and Received ye same at hand of Lt Jos Smith Before me John Northrop, town clerk, Rec^d by Ebeneezer Mills & John Mills, Sons in Law to ye man that lost s^d money."

It is difficult to draw one's lines of belief and admiration. Lt. Smith having apparently been accorded the safe keeping of the pouch, at the end of over nine months returns it to its belated claimants, *sons-in-law* to the man who lost it ! As nothing is said of the absence of one of those "30 silver shillins or six copers," it is presumed to have been returned intact. Captain Botsford is instructed to look up the school requirements of a place called Hanover, "and any person that shall kill a wild cat and bring the head thereof to the Selectmen shall be allowed 3^s pr head." It was then not always safe for young lovers to wander far from the protection of neighborhood ammunition, or the usual haunts of other strollers, and these hungry animals often visited farm yards at night and became so troublesome that a price was offered the expert marksman. Men went armed in those days, and all were taught to shoot straight.

Without going into the history of the country at large, we should recall the general condition of things as factors in legislation and influence. France and England had been almost incessantly at war from the first settlement of America, and whenever these conflicts occurred the two nations entered into the fray. Wherever weak, the Indians sympathized with the French. The colonies were put to great expense and kept in continual dread of both open and secret warfare.

In 1748, by the peace of *Aix la Chapelle*, the colonists saw their efforts of three years previous (the capture of Louisburg) put to shame, and it was not extraordinary that doubts began to suggest a change of government. When, in 1756, a fresh call to arms was sounded and the "old French war" entered upon, the colonists responded nobly, and from that hour until the close of the War of Independence, knew no peace. Newtown was not backward in filling her ranks and providing for her sons, as many commissions and tax lists show, but we concern ourselves more nearly with home affairs, and discover that the Stratford boundary lines, which were supposed to have been settled by our three "uninterested gentlemen" in 1725, are again in dispute, having never been put on record. Daniel Booth, Caleb Baldwin and Benjamin Curtice are a committee to look up the matter, so that "bickerings may be avoided or legal redress had." The Assembly recognizes the justice of this appeal and orders that the same be "confirmed and established . . . both as to jurisdiction and property." In some book of reference was found what is called "Newtown statistics for 1756 : 1230 whites, 23 negroes, no Indians." This may or may not be authentic ; certainly is *not* as to Indians. In the May of 1765, John Blackman, captain of the Second Company in the "train-band in s^d Newtown" presents a memorial to the Assembly, showing that "the setting off of Newbury Society and granting a Captain's Company there has very much broke the Co. of which the s^d Captain had the command, and also shewing to the Assembly that the 1st Co. or train-band in Newtown has near double the number of his, and thereupon desires the association to grant a new division of s^d Co., and that Col. John Read, Col^l of said regiment, be desired and impowered to make a new division of s^d Co. in s^d Newtown, and fix and ascertain the line between s^d companies, and make return thereof to the General Assembly for establishment. Resolved by this Assembly, that Col. John Read shall and is hereby, &c., &c.," in compliance with this request.

Military affairs take more room and begin to crowd out less important matter. For instance: "Oct., 1771. An Act entitled an Act for forming and regulating the militia and for the encouragement of military skill for the better defense of this Colony. . . . Be it enacted by the Governor, Council and Representatives in General Court assembled, and by the authority of the same, that the towns of Danbury, Ridgefield, Newtown and New Fairfield shall be one intire regiment, distinguished and called by the name of the Sixteenth Regiment, and shall be under the same rules and orders and have the same powers, privileges and advantages as other regiments of this Colony by law have."

The 16th regiment was finally officered as follows: Colonel, Joseph Platt Cooke, of Danbury; resigned in 1778; succeeded by Col. Nehemiah Beardsley, of New Fairfield, who had been promoted from lieutenant-colonel (1777), vice Col. Chandler, who was then colonel in the "Conn. Line." Lieut.-Colonel, Eli Mygatt, Danbury, previously major, promoted Feb. 7, 1878; and Major, Caleb Baldwin, of Newtown, promoted from captaincy at the same time. As will be seen later, these were finally selected after some trouble and discussion.

The town house is also decided on, and its dimensions, 32 ft. long, 24 ft. wide, and of the necessary height, and "Mr. Oliver Tousey shall build said town House at the prize of sixty-six pounds, and that the s^d Oliver Toucey shall give Bonds to the Committee for the Building s^d house. Voted at s^d meeting, that there shall be a Rate of 3 farthing half-penny on the pound to Rase and build s^d house. Voted at ye s^d meeting, that Mr. Jon^n Booth and Caleb Baldwin shall be a committee to obligate with s^d Toucey and take his obligation for the completing s^d house, and that the s^d Com^tee shall make and colect the s^d Rate. Voted, that s^d Toucey shall cause to be made in s^d town-house good seats as are generally made in form as in the State-House at Hartford, s^d house to be finished by the 1st Day of December, 1767. S^d Toucey shall Lite s^d house with 30 windows, 15 squars of glass in a window; size of glass, 7–9."

Whenever any expense was to be incurred, it was easy to vote a "Rate" accordingly, and this one does not seem exorbitant for the purpose. That "s⁴ house" was to be furnished with comfortable seats would lead us to suppose the schoolhouse *forms* had not given entire satisfaction to longer legs, and that they were a little tired of doubling themselves up into rows of figure *4's !* That Mr. Oliver Toucey was a man of his word and a chip of the old block, we have immediate evidence, for in "Dec., 1767, the annual town meeting is called," and is held in the town house, and Mr. Oliver Toucey is appointed one of the selectmen for the year ensuing. With him are Peter Nichols, George Terrill, Joshua Northrup, John Beach, Jun", Samuel Beers and Ebenezer Ford. Still others of the family are : "Surveyors of highways, Abner Hard, Jabez Peck and Abijah Curtis." James Glover is on the school committee, and the school district is laid out thus : "Deep Brook School, viz., from Lt. Samuel Griffin's to Eliphalet Hull's, Noah Pamerly, Jr., Benj" Stilson, Gideon Northrup and Eben Kimberly's," and at the second adjournment, "Voted, that all Inclosed in the Circle hereafter mentioned shall be a District for schooling known by the name of Sluts Hill, (viz.), James Baldwin's, Lemuel Sherman, Benj" Hawley, Jeremiah Turner, Jr., and all the Rest within s⁴ limnits." This locality is now known by the more agreeable title of Mt. Pleasant, so renamed by the late Simeon B. Peck, who built his house on the brow of the hill, where it now stands.

Capt" John Glover and Moses Plat are a com¹ᵗᵉ in 1768, to lay out a highway from potatuck Brook to parrock Sherwoods and through part of pine swamp to Stratford line toward the narrows. Lake George School District is next described ; it is easy to find the rather misleading nomenclature, for prominent among the dwellers in that district are George Smith and both Thomas and Nathan Lake. This same year they petition for a goal, and there is some agitation about changing the County Town from Fairfield to Norwalk, but whereas by actual measurement Reading is found to be the nearest to the centre of s⁴ County, "it is the very place meant by s⁴ vote," and whether they really meant it, or thought it sufficiently funny to be chronicled, they voted to order "a coppy of the above vote to be transferred to the agent of Reading for him to make use of at the General

Assembly." Probably this was to baulk the Norwalk choice. About this time the burying ground needs a new fence, and remembering the former inexpensive manner in this matter, they vote that "Mr. John Chandler shall have Libberty to fence the burying grounds for pasture, so long as he will keep it within good fence."

Mr. John Chandler very speedily became Col. John Chandler and was more occupied in adding a prefix to his *fences*. Zoar is "voted the olde buryinge cloath and the selectmen authorized to purchase a new one for ye use of ye town." On petition of Jon Booth, Lemuel Thomas, Abiel Botsford and associates the town house is lent for school purposes. The Town house stood just north of the present Episcopal Church and was afterwards removed to make way for the third church edifice, as will be shown in the account of that building. The next year, 1770, Daniel Beers and Moses Peck are a com^tee for South School, Ens Gideon Botsford and Eph^m Bennit for North School, Gideon Peck for Tinkerfield, Jonathan Fairchild for Tanton, George Smith for Lake George, Thos Wheeler, Hanover, Oliver Fairchild for Flat-swamps, Captn John Blakeman for Slutshill, Ab^m Beers for palestine (always spelled with a small p,) Nirom Hurd for Zoar, estermost, Hez Sanford for potatuck, Joseph Griffin for . . . . . Wm Hall for Curretuck." It would appear that education was paramount, and certainly no lack of districts, but regularity of attendance of teacher or scholar was not yet made compulsory ; probably many days beside those of wind and weather found the little school house door shut, and the teacher otherwise occupied than in imparting her slender stock of book-learning. Doubtless the few stragglers were as gleeful truants as would be rejoicing to-day over similar unexpected holidays.

The curfew is ordered rung thus : "Jabez Baldwin shall Ring the Bell of ye Meeting house at nine of ye clocke."

"Newtown Jan. 7, 1771. These are to caution ye Town Clerk not to Receive for Record nor Record any Deed or Return of any Land or any other estate, from ye Sherwoods to ye Parkers, or from any other persons to ye s^d Parkers cautioned and forbid.

JOHN BEERS	PETER NICHOLS
SAMUEL SHERMAN	JOHN BEACH
JOHN CHANDLER."	

In regard to Newbury settlement, 1772, Deac. Daniel Booth threatens to go to Law with the Town for "publick moneys" due him, and they finally come to terms by allowing a "note upon interest for the sum of 15 pounds lawful money upon condition that he withdraw his action now in Court."

The Susquehannah land troubles next occupy attention and legislation. Without going into all particulars we may notice that Oliver Toucey and Daniel Booth are sent to Middletown and a town meeting is called for "7 A. M. April 11th," to hear their report. The first record of revolutionary significance is at a town meeting Ap. 7, 1777, when "Oliver Toucey is appointed to take care of the excise money with the assistance of Mr Jon^n Booth and Mr Wm Burwell, and it is put to vote whether there shall be a com^{tee} put in by this Town to take the care of such money as shall be Remitted from time to time by any soldier agreeable to the Governor and Council of Safety bearing Date March 8, 1777; . . . . . voted in the negative : Put to vote whether we will adhere to the act of this State Respecting Regulating Trade; . . . . voted in the negative : Voted at s^d meeting that this town shall use their joint influence to Pervent the spreading of the small pox by Inoccolation or any other wise in this town." Feb 2, 1778 voted at s^d meeting that the salt belonging to this Town purchased by the State shall be transported from Bedford in Boston State to this place at the expense of the Town and that in a manner that the Selectmen shall think most expedient and safe either by land or by water," and a week later a meeting is called to receive the "Articles of Confederation as sent by Congress to the United States. Resolved that the Representatives of this Town Transmit the votes of this meeting to the General Assembly of this State approving of every Article of Confederation of the United States in Congress as the Sense of this town that the Delegates of this State be empowered By s^d Assembly to Ratify and Confirm the same in Congress." . . . . The sense is very apparent if the expression is somewhat involved.

In October, 1778, "Notice is herebye given to Newtown Inhabitants that there is to be a town meeting . . . . on Monday next at five o'clock afternoon to adopt some measures to Raise moneys to supply the Familyes of the Officers and soldiers belonging to s^d town now in Continental service Agreeable to a late Resolve of general Assembly. . . . by which each man pays Rates according to his proportion, and the government allows a pr cent after the same manner. " Voted at s^d meeting that they have no objections to the wives and familyes of Ep^{hm} Betts and Elias Skidmore Repairing to Long Island there to Tarry with their Husbands going under Direction and authority of the Selectmen. This meeting is Desolved." Military titles begin to frequent these peaceable pages, and "Lt. Matthew Curtis, Jr., with others is sent to Reding, to investigate and Report" on some doings there at a recent county convention. In Todd's History of Redding he says with only too much certainty, that many records are annoyingly incomplete. That is notably the case with a mysterious County Convention for the date of which we have only the following minute's word : At a meeting (town) held Sep. 6, 1779, " Voted to ratify the proceedings of the County Convention held Aug 10th, 1779, and to appoint a Committee to carry into effect what was Recommended in the first resolve of said Convention." Not a word is said as to its object nor is there any report of its proceedings. This is that Convention spoken of in the Newtown Records, in an equally vague manner ; they knew nothing of it until it was over, and sent their committee to inquire. Redding was a hotbed of toryism, and it may have been thought best to meet quietly, and without advertisement. Nathan and Calvin Turner return from the enemy and the town decides not to admit them as residents.

Apparently there are other delinquents, for shortly afterward the selectmen are authorized to prepare a memorial or a petition to the Assembly asking for instruction in regard to "those unfriendly persons in s^d Town together with the Reasons of the Friends of Liberty of America in this Town, entering their protest against the Town Clerk's entering those unfriendly persons in the list of those that have taken the Oath of Fidelity." . . . . Again, for lack of punctuation in the original, the evolution of this phrase is optional. Inspectors are soon appointed whose task,—not an easy or gracious one, seems to have been to discover such "unfriendly persons," and later, to take the supervision of provisions sent to the army, taxes are laid on flour, beef, pork, and even a Lottery is resorted to, a bounty is offered to volunteers, but

4

even this does not fill their quota ; and they, in Dec. 1780, vote
"that this Town will enable the Commanding officers of the
several military companies and the selectmen to procure by
hireing at the Town's cost if possible, the men now requested
by Preemptory Detachment and all other peremptory Detachments, Capt[n] Elijah Botsford Capt[n] Jabez Botsford Capt[n] Abel
Botsford Capt[n] Benj[n] Summers Capt[n] George Terrill Capt[n]
Rich[d] Smith Mr Richard Fairman Caleb Baldwin Jr and Mr
Joshua Northrup be a Com[tee] to class the Inhabitants of the
town for the purpose of filling up the Continental army."
With so many officers, it may have been just possible the
resources of the town had been already overtaxed ; however,
according to order they divide the town and find 8 classes,
upon whom the responsibility falls to raise their men for the
State "within six days." A special meeting is called on Feb.
25, 1782, to Raise the Town's Quota of men to serve at Horseneck, the scene of Putnam's great ride.

We note in the State records of the year 1778, the General
Assembly beginning its May session on the 14th of that
month continued its work until the thirteenth of June.
In the meanwhile, the Governor and his Council of Safety
began meeting on the 18th of May, at Hartford, June July
August and September in Lebanon, and the October General
Assembly was immediately followed by continued and frequent meetings of the Council. During this time some of
the most prominent men of Fairfield County were representing its interests. Elisha Sheldon resigned on account of ill
health ; he died the next year. In this year also the Continental Loan Office was established. They issued Certificates
for moneys invested arising from the sale of confiscated
estates, and many who were neutral fell into disgrace and
lost their homes, because it was made worth while to the
greedy informer to spy upon such, indeed committees of
Inspection were appointed whose duty it was to report all
persons inimical to the State. Here is an incident : "It being
represented to this Assembly by the selectmen of Fairfield,
that some persons in the western parts of this State are purchasing a large number of cattle under pretence of driving
them to State of New Jersey in order to be fattened, (though
in the apprehension of this Assembly it is most probable to
feed our enemies) : It is therefore resolved by this Assembly,

that the Commissary General of purchases be directed and desired and he is hereby authorized and fully empowered to seize and take all such cattle for the use of this and the United States."

"Upon a representation made to this Assembly that the three alarm list companies formed within the limits of the first society of Newtown in the 16th regiment have some time since made choice of persons for their officers, inimical to this and the other United States of America, who for that reason were refused commissions, and also that the officers of the third military company of said regiment in said town have either given in their commissions, or wholly neglect and refuse to execute their offices, whereby all the said companies are destitute of officers, and by that means not in a condition to be called upon to perform military duty for the defense of the country : Resolved by this Assembly, that the colonel or chief officer of said regiment be directed and he is hereby ordered and directed to cause legal warning to be given said companies as soon as may be, to meet for the purpose of choosing commission officers and lead or order them to be led to such choice for their respective companies, and in case they neglect or refuse to elect such persons as are qualified according to the laws of this State to execute such offices, that then the civil authority in and selectmen of said Newtown, with the advice of said colonel or chief officer, are hereby impowered and directed forthwith to nominate such officers as may be necessary, which choice or nomination shall by said colonel or chief officer be returned to this Assembly, or in the recess thereof, to his Excellency the Governor, who is desired to commissionate them accordingly ; which officers shall immediately proceed to detach their quota of men for the continental army as soon as the field officers of said regiment have proportioned them to the respective companies, which they are hereby directed to do."

Towns at this time were obliged to petition for right to use their own moneys. "Upon the memorial of the town of Newtown by the selectmen for said town, shewing to this Assembly the difficulty of repairing the public highways in said town at the present day in the way and manner directed by law, and praying that they may be authorized to tax themselves for said purpose, as per memorial on file ; Resolved by

this Assembly, that the said town have liberty, and liberty
and authority is hereby granted unto them from time to time
for the term of three years next coming, to tax the polls and
rateable estate of the inhabitants of said town, to raise such
sums as shall be necessary for the purpose of repairing the
public highways in said town ; and it shall be the duty of the
surveyors of highways in said town, within their peculiar
districts, to be set out and assigned them in such way and
manner as the town shall direct, to cause the public highways
within their respective limits to be well and sufficiently repaired, and to that purpose to hire and employ such and so
many persons from time to time for the abovesaid term of
three years, in proper seasons of the year, as they shall judge
necessary ; and the said surveyors shall keep a true and fair
account of the persons they shall employ for said purpose,
the time of service and the necessary materials procured, and
lay the same from time to time as may be expedient before
the selectmen of said town, who upon proper examination
shall draw on the Treasurer of said town in favour of the
person or persons who have done such service for such sums
as they shall judge reasonable and necessary to effect the purpose designed and promotive of uniformity through the various parts of said town."

Referring to the raising of further forces in Fairfield Co.,
in January of 1780, the Treasurer is ordered to "deliver as
soon as may be the sum of sixty thousand pounds in continental bills unto Colo. John Chandler, taking his receipt
therefor ; and the said Colo. Chandler is hereby appointed
and directed, with all convenient dispatch, to repair to the
army, consult with the officers of the Connecticut Line, and
thereupon, in conjunction with them, to use his utmost address and endeavor to recruit the Connecticut battalions by
engaging and re-inlisting such of the soldiers now in service
who are not already inlisted during the war, or any others,
and to pay to each recruit he may so engage the sum of three
hundred dollars in addition to the sum allowed by Congress
as a bounty, taking his receipt for the same ; and he is further
directed to make return of the number of men he may so engage, with the towns to which they respectively belong, to his
Excellency the Governor by the first day of April next, and
render an account to this Assembly in May next of his doings
and of the sums he may so lay out or expend as aforesaid."

Finding still great difficulty in securing men from an already depleted county, it is further Resolved, "That the Governor with his Council of Safety be and they are hereby authorized and impowered, to order such deficiency to be made up and completed by peremtory detachment after said first day of April next : such persons so detached to serve for a term not exceeding nine months, wherein repect shall be had as near as may be to the numbers that shall have been furnished by each town for continental service during the war to the number that may be estimated their true and just proportion. Such detachments to be apportioned and ordered accordingly, and that all such persons who may be detached for the service aforesaid, and who shall actually in consequence thereof go into the service, shall be entitled to the same wages, refreshments and allowances, and in having the same made good in equity during their continuance in service as aforesaid, as are allowed to the continental soldiers enlisted from this State. And the Governor and Council of Safety are hereby further authorized, if necessity require to fill up the number recommended by Congress, to allow such bounty as they shall pledge reasonable to such as shall voluntarily enlist to fill up said batallions for the said term of nine months."

In looking over the lists of "Connecticut men in the Revolution," it is evident that in spite of the large element of loyal sympathisers, Fairfield County responded nobly to the call of her adopted country. The 5th and 7th Regiments show many familiar names, especially so in Captain Dimon's 4th company of the 5th, under Col. Waterbury, first and second lieutenants Peter Hendrick and Wakeman Burr, Ensign Josiah Lacey ; the 7th Company, Captn Ichabod Doolittle, Ensign Ebenezer Banks ; 8th, Captn Joseph Smith (Newtown), Jabez Botsford and Nathaniel Blakeman lieutenants, Ebenezer Beach sergeant. In the 10th Company Col. Webb's regiment (the 7th), Captn Zalmon Read, Ezekiel Sanford and David Peck lieutenants, and Benjn Nichols, ensign. Among our friends on a list of individual record Simon Couch of Redding is authorized to raise recruits in '81 ; Thomas Nash made Captn of the Guards in '81 ; Jared Dunning of Newtown, trooper in Major Daniel Starr's Regiment of Horse, at Sand Pits in '80.

John Webb, Captn in Sheldon's Dragoons A D C to Genl
Greene in June '80.

Genl Silliman, captured by tories may 1 1779, held at L I
until April 28, 1780, exchanged for the Loyalist Judge Jones,
who was captured by the Americans in November 1779.

Apropos of this record we are brought into closer connection with this story than some are aware, for it was a *Glover*,
said to be of *Newtown*, who made the capture of the General.
Here is the tale : One Glover, previously employed (carpenter) by General Silliman and familiar with his house, was put
in command by Sir Henry Clinton of a band of eight Loyalists ; they rowed across Long Island Sound and approaching
the dwelling by night, Genl Silliman was awakened by them
and commanded to surrender ; he fired his musket, but the
assailants broke through the windows, seized and carried him
off.   On approaching the Long Island shore, Col Simcoe
of the Queen's Rangers, called out, " Have you got him ?"
" Yes !"   " Lost any men ?"   " No."   " That's well.   Your
Sillimans are not worth a man, nor your Washingtons !"

Now for the Jones side : Judge Thomas Jones was Judge
of the Supreme Court at the Revolutionary era ; he had married a daughter of Lieut. Gov. James de Lancey, and afterward lost his estates under the Confiscation Act.   In retalia-
tion for Glover's capture of Genl Silliman a party of Whigs
determined to seize upon Judge Jones at his country seat on
Long Island.   Twenty-five volunteered for the purpose under
command of Captain Daniel Hawley of Newfield (now
Bridgeport).   Captain Hawley and his men crossed the sound
on the night of the 4th of November, and on the evening of
the 6th reached Judge Jones' house—there was a ball and the
music and dancing prevented an alarm.   The Judge was
standing in his entry when the assailants opened the door,
seized and bore him off.   In passing near some Royalist
soldiers the Judge " hemmed " very loudly.   Hawley told
him not to dare to repeat it, but he did, and a rescuing party
captured six of the Whigs ; the rest got off safely.   It is
said that Mrs. Silliman breakfasted the Judge, and that he
remained at her house for several days.   After his exchange
he went to England, where he lived quietly and in retirement.
It is rather odd that the Glovers and the Hawleys, two such
prominent Newtown families, should have been thus repre-

sented. To continue our personal mention, "Aaron Hawley, Brig. Major to Gen[l] Silliman in March '81. William Edmond Newtown, volunteer wounded at Danbury raid . . . ."

In 1784, the Town Treasurer of Newtown, Mr. Richard Fairman, has left without settling his affairs with the town. A committee consisting of Mr. Daniel Baldwin, Henry Glover and Mr. Nehemiah Strong is appointed with full power to act. Nothing satisfactory being thus accomplished, in December the Selectmen for the time being are authorized to make "a compleat and final settlement with Richard Fairman late Town Treasurer of all matters of Dispute Controversy or accounts subsisting between the Town and s[d] Fairman, that all Difficulties with s[d] Fairman may be entirely put to an end." Alas, even this gentle ministration fails and a committee of arbitration, John Chandler, Wm. Edmonds and David Baldwin, is authorized to change notes of hand with Mr. Fairman. This seems to have produced some result, which is accepted, for in 1788, at the annual meeting they vote to make "use of the money due the town from Richard Fairman on execution in ye settlement of accounts with Capt[n] David Baldwin and to settle with him at their discretion."

"CONCERNING HIGHWAYS Dec. 13, 1790.
AND BRIDGE OVER POTO- Voted "that on condition John
TUCK BROOK. Beach Esq Messrs Abijah Curtis and John Beach Jun[r] will lay open a Publick highway from s[d] Curtises house to where Peter Hubbel formerly Dwelt in the most convenient place and give an authentick title to the same to the Town, that in such case the Town will build at their expense over Potatuck Brook where s[d] Road shall cross the same, a good Bridge, and support the same and that the Present Selectmen take such measures to build such Bridge as they shall judge cheapest and for the Best interests of the Town."

At the same meeting it was voted that the "People of the Episcopal Church and Society in this Town have liberty to erect a house for Publick worship at the place where the Town house now stands, placing the west part of the steeple in a line with the buildings on the east side of the Town street, they being at the expense of moving the Town house to some proper place that shall be agreed upon by the Town." This was the third church edifice, the second had stood immediately in front of Dick's Hotel (now rebuilt a little lower down and called "Newtown Inn.") Accordingly a notification of a Town meeting "to be held at the Town House on Thursday ye 29th Day of Instant March at 3 o'clock afternoon for the purpose of considering whether it will be advisable to sell the Town House," &c. &c.

EZRA BOOTH 〉 Select
GIDEON BOTSFORD 〉 men.
JOHN SANFORD JR 〉

March 23, 1792.

Such large movements can not be hurried, many opinions must be asked, and many more given, so it is not until the December of 1793 that they are ready to "put to vote whether the Town House shall be sold for the use of the Town or not," fully negatived, "an no vote at all, in favor." One would suppose it pretty effectually settled with *no vote at all*, in favor, but subsequent proceedings show the result of influence and do credit to a glorious minority. Again petitioned they vote "that this town will give Captn Solomon Glover £35 money for the purpose of Purchasing a tract of land to set the old church on, on condition that s^d Glover remove s^d Church on said land, s^d Town holding the Fee of s^d land and s^d Glover supplying the s^d Town with a sufficient Town House in some place between William Burwells and Deacon John Botsfords house, and also s^d Glover shall have for his own use the present old Town House. Voted at s^d meeting that s^d old church shall be removed by the 1st Day of June next: " s^d Glover must have made quite a good thing out of this business, in spite of the fact that s^d town rather hurried him in his moving. The Presbyterians at this time were feeling the depression of war time, and not able to do much, or to take their share of these expenses, so the Episcopalians moved their church for them to its present stand and built their own opposite. "April 3, 1797, Town meeting, Mr. Abijah Curtis, Moderator, voted that this meeting be adjourned and it is hereby adjourned to this place at 4 o'clock in the afternoon, next Monday." "10th April, 1797, The meeting opened by Mr. Abijah Curtis present and standing moderator, voted that this meeting be adjourned and is hereby adjourned to Captn Glover's old church to be attended forthwith. Old church

10th of April 1797, this meeting convened Mr. Abijah Curtis present is standing moderator, voted that the Selectmen contract with Captⁿ Solomon Glover for the use of a room in his Old Church house for 2 years for a Town House. Voted that the Selectmen sell the old Town House in the best manner they can and dispose of the money for the benefit of the Town." Again notice that s^d Glover is not as yet out of pocket. At the June meeting of that year they vote to "do something respecting the Inoculating the Small Pox."

Upon the application of Dr. Benjamin Curtis (son of Abijah, S^r, and brother to Major Abijah Birdsey Curtis) praying for "liberty to erect a Building for the reception of Patients for the purpose of communicating the small-pox by Inoculation. Put to vote that liberty be granted s^d Curtis to erect a Pest house for the purpose of carrying on the business of Inoculation for the Small Pox at some place and under such Limitations and orders as shall from time to time be prescribed by the authority and selectmen of Newtown, &c., &c." Negatived, but in 1800 it is allowed, "provided he Inoculate none other than those he shall have pronounced to have been through the operation of the Kine pox." It is not to be wondered at that the "authorities and selectmen" feared the cure almost as much as the disease. This year, also, there was some talk of moving the Academy from Cheshire to Newtown, but neither town took kindly to such a suggestion, and Cheshire never gave it a chance to become serious. When Dr. Dutton came to Newtown, the latter felt its educational cup quite full, and welcomed the first rusticated Yalensians with more ardor than it afterwards found advisable. Some tales might be told, were your historian so inclined, which would bear, with success, the ordeal and criticism of an alumni meeting. In regard to the Susquehanna affair, Newtown took its stand on high moral and financial grounds. In 1793, "In the opinion of this meeting the appropriation of the Western lands at the last session of the Assembly was an impolitic measure, . . . the sale of which would be injurious to true interests of State, being subversive not only of a sure resource of wealth when rightly managed in time of Danger, but of our great last resource, direct taxation excepted, and consequently destructive to general good. Voted, that this Resolution be published in the Farmer's Chronicle."

In closing this sketch of the planting and growth of the town of Newtown and the completion of its first century, I cannot more fitly leave it than with the following and last quotation from its town records :

"Dec. 15, 1800.   Voted, that two of the farewell addresses of the late President Washington be put in frames, and one of them be hung up in the Town Clerk's office, and the other of them, in the Town House."

"A FEW WORTHIES."

On the list of Representatives to the General Court from Newtown during this interval we find these four most prominent: Henry Glover, from 1751 to 1775 ; Daniel Booth, from 1751 to 1765, and again in 1770 ; Col. John Chandler, 1771-2 and 3, and from 1780 to 1789; and William Edmond from 1790 to 1798.   The Town Clerks were : Peter Hubbell, 1711 ; John Glover, 1712 and 1713; Joseph Peck, 1714 to 1738 ; John Northrop, 1739 to 1764 ; Caleb Baldwin, 1765 to 1799, and succeeded by his son, Caleb Baldwin, Jr., who held the position until 1843.

The Selectmen for 1799 were Abijah Curtis, Asa Chapman and Joseph Ferris.

A SHORT HISTORICAL SKETCH OF TRINITY CHURCH, NEWTOWN, CONN., SINCE THE DEATH OF THE FIRST RECTOR.

BY THE REV. GEORGE T. LINSLEY.

Newtown is one of the very few towns in the State of Connecticut where the Episcopal Church has been for many years the dominant religious body. Within the past half century, owing to the settlement of many of their people, drawn here by the factory interest, the Roman Catholics now number about one-half of the population.

But until this great industrial change took place Trinity Church was the leading Christian body in the town, and apart from the adherents of the Church of Rome still continues so to be.

Situated upon the crest of the ridge on which the village is built, the Church is the most conspicuous object in the landscape for miles around, a fitting type of what the parish itself has been through all its history as a strong center of influence for good and as a monument to the truth of pure religion faithfully taught in the reverent worship of Almighty God.

If it is true, as we read inscribed upon the tablet erected to his memory, that the Rev. John Beach was "of all most effective in laying deep and broad the foundation of the Church in the Colony of Connecticut," it is pre-eminently true that as the first Rector of the parish he was likewise most effective in laying firm and secure foundation for the parish itself. And to this day that early, persistent work of the "pastor untiring" and the "Christian hero undaunted" is producing fruit, and the members of the parish as well as his successors in office have enjoyed and are still enjoying the fruit of his labors.

The parish has had twelve rectors.

The Rev. Mr. Beach dying early in 1782, soon after the close of the Revolutionary War, there was an interim of about five years before his successor was chosen.

During this period the services were conducted by different

clergymen, but no permanent agreement was made with any of them until the Rev. Philo Perry was chosen Rector, January 9, 1787.

At this time the parish was in possession of Glebe lands, a library consisting of several large tomes of Theological works given to Mr. Beach by the Society for the Propagation of the Gospel, and delivered to the parish after his death (part having been given to Redding), also of ten pounds left in his will "towards settling a minister," and of ten pounds "for the purchase of Bibles to be distributed to the poor."

In the interval between the first two rectorships it should be remembered that the Rev. Samuel Seabury, D.D., was consecrated as the first Bishop of Connecticut, and indeed of the Church in the United States.

As the first Rector divided his attention chiefly between Redding and Newtown, the second served one-quarter of the time in Newbury, now Brookfield, which paid a due proportion of his salary.

During these years we find the parish acknowledging the authority of the Diocesan Convention, being represented at its meetings, and accepting its recommendations in regard to the offerings for the support of the Bishop. In the fall of 1790 a movement was begun with a view to building a new church. It was voted to apply to the General Assembly for permission to form a lottery for the purpose, but this scheme, we are glad to say, was abandoned, and about a year later £1000 was raised by subscription. This Church, 68x48 feet, finished in 1793 and formally named "Trinity Church," was consecrated by Bishop Seabury the following September.

The Rector's salary was increased, internal improvements were made in the new Church in the way of cushions and furniture, special attention was given to the subject of music, and there are many other evidences of activity and interest in the parish.

The Rev. Mr. Perry died October 26, 1798, having been for nearly twelve years, as in the words of the tablet in the present church, "The devoted and efficient Rector of this parish and a clergyman of eminence in the Councils of the Church."

On August 5, 1799, the Rev. Daniel Burhans, D.D., was offered the Rectorship and was present at the meeting and accepted.

The arrangement with Brookfield was continued for a time, as during the previous Rectorship.

An important movement was inaugurated in 1804 towards raising and augmenting the fund of the parish, this being the enlargement of that endowment, the nucleus of which was the original Glebe land belonging to the parish. This fund was further increased by a bequest in 1810 and has been similarly enlarged several times since ; in 1825 and in 1828, further and more general efforts were made throughout the town to increase this permanent endowment.

In 1818 the first organ was placed in the Church, and two years later the first stove was set up.

In 1824 the members of the parish coöperated with Churchmen throughout the State in raising money for Washington, now Trinity College.

The Diocesan Convention met in Newtown three times during this Rectorship, in 1801, 1806, and 1826.

In March, 1830, the subject of an Assistant Minister was considered, but owing to pecuniary and other embarrassments nothing was done.

In May the Rector, on account of infirmities of age, handed in his resignation, to take effect November 1, 1830.

With the resignation of Dr. Burhans the first century of the life of the parish ends, showing the remarkable record of having had only three rectors in that period. Bishop Brownell testifies to the "distinguished fidelity and zeal with which this venerable Father in the Church has performed the arduous duties of Rector for more than thirty years." And on the tablet to perpetuate his "beloved memory " may still be read these words : "The zealous and efficient Rector of this parish adorning his life with the fruits of the Spirit and his ministry with faithful diligence."

A new parish was established in Zoar, a district in the eastern part of the town, in 1830, and called St. James Church. But its location proved an unfavorable one, and it was soon found to be no longer needed, for in 1840 application was made to be received back into the mother parish. Services continued to be held there, however, under resident and nonresident Rectors, with some intermissions, until 1860, when Zoar surrendered its organization and became a chapel of Trinity Parish.

The Church building was afterwards torn down and removed.

The fourth Rector of Trinity Parish was the Rev. Samuel C. Stratton, being chosen October 1, 1831, and remaining eight years. During this Rectorship two libraries were established, each containing a goodly number of well-selected books, one for the Sunday School and the other for general parish use.

When we remember how much fewer were the facilities for good secular as well as good religious reading sixty years ago than they are now, we shall realize what an important work it was to establish these libraries and thus accomplish the task proposed some years before, in 1823.

The books still preserved on the same shelves prove that excellent judgment was shown in the selection of the parish library. At this time preparations were made for somewhat extensive repairs upon the church. And when owing to the feeble state of his health the Rector resigned his charge, his resignation was reluctantly accepted. A stained glass window to his memory has been placed in the present church.

He was succeeded by the Rev. S. Stebbins Stocking, who had officiated frequently in this interval, and was called to be Rector April 11, 1841. Further increase was made in the endowment fund from the sale of Glebe lands and other sources, and the subject of purchasing or building a rectory was agitated. The permanent fund at this time amounted to over $9700.

Mr. Stocking resigned September 24, 1848. The next Rector was the Rev. Horace Hills, who remained with the parish only a few months, from January 7, 1849, until November 11, 1849.

In the November of 1850, the Rev. William M. Carmichael, D.D., was called but remained only two years.

The eighth Rector was the Rev. Benjamin W. Stone, D.D., chosen November 29, 1852, with the condition, cautiously made by the parish, that the connection might be severed by either party upon six months' notice. He stayed about four years, until Nov. 15, 1856, when he resigned.

Important additions were made to the two libraries, and money was raised for a new organ which was built in 1853, and afterwards removed to the present stone church.

In the following January a call was extended to the Rev.

Newton E. Marble, D.D., who accepted the position February 23, 1857, and entered upon his duties at Easter. His is the third of the long Rectorships, for he remained twenty-three years.

Horse sheds were soon erected in the rear of the Church upon land purchased for the purpose, and the new Rectory, the one still in use, was built according to plans suggested by the Rector. But the great visible monument to his memory is the present dignified stone building, the Fourth Church Edifice, in the parish, located just south of the former site. The first service was held in the new Church on February 3, 1870, the old Church, used for the last time the previous Sunday, having stood seventy-seven years.

It has been estimated that the whole expense connected with building, furnishing and completing the new Church, with improvement of grounds, was more than $60,000.

A heavy debt remained upon the Church, $12,625 being paid off in 1872, and the rest, about $9000, in 1882.

It may reasonably be taken as the just conclusion that the zeal and energy of the Rector and the generous coöperation of his parishioners in accomplishing this great work, are a proof of corresponding faithfulness and devotion in those spiritual affairs " which can be brought to the test of no outward standard."

The simplicity of the inscription on the tablet erected to his memory will fittingly be reproduced here :

"This Church erected during his Rectorship stands as his monument, but a nobler and more enduring one will be found in the souls he won to Christ."

Owing to increased infirmities, Dr. Marble tendered his resignation April 22, 1878, to take effect September 1.

He was offered the position of Rector Emeritus with an annuity of $500 but declined.

He continued to reside in the parish until he fell asleep in Jesus, September 28, 1881.

Regular services had been started in Sandy Hook in 1858, by the Rector of the Zoar parish, and in 1861–1862, the work at both these places was under the immediate charge of the Rev. Jesse E. Heald, who was Assistant Minister in Trinity Parish.

In 1868 a Chapel had been built in the village of Sandy Hook, carrying out the conditions of a bequest left for that purpose by a parishioner, and in the first part of its history it was under the Rector of Trinity Church, who was helped by an Assistant Minister.

The Rev. William W. Ackley was the first of these assistants. He resigned in 1873, and was succeeded by the Rev. Thomas Mallaby. He was followed by the Rev. Francis W. Barnett, who remained till 1879.. In January, 1880, the Chapel was given into the charge of the Missionary Society of the Diocese, but soon after was made an independent parish and has recently become self-supporting.

The tenth Rector was the Rev. Thomas W. Haskins, who was chosen September 30, 1878. He instituted a parish day school, having Daily Morning and Evening Prayer in connection with it, and also a weekly celebration of the Holy Communion. This rectorship terminated October 1, 1880.

The next Rector was the Rev. Gouverneur Morris Wilkins, who was chosen March 26, 1881, and entered upon his duties at Easter. Under his vigorous administration and active leadership the balance of the debt resting upon the Church was paid off within a year, nearly $10,000 being subscribed for that purpose. If this work had not been accomplished at that particular time, it is plain that it would probably never have been done and the parish would be heavily burdened to this day. A beautiful marble font was placed in the Church, and four tablets erected to the memory of former Rectors.

The interior of the Church was also decorated in tasteful colors and in artistic and churchly designs.

Mr. Wilkins spent one year abroad, leave of absence being granted him. During that time, 1884–1885, the Rev. John Addison Crockett was minister-in-charge.

The Rector returning in the summer of 1885, spent four more years with the parish, until called to a larger work in New York City.

His resignation took effect December 30, 1889. The parish then testified that it was due to "his unceasing energy and perseverance that the debt was raised, and the church edifice improved and beautified," and here again we take these outward and visible achievements as evidences of corresponding fidelity in that higher work of the ministry which is invisible, the results of which we can not estimate.

The twelfth and present Rector is the Rev. George T. Linsley, who was called December 16, 1889, and entered upon his work February 6, 1890.

A floating debt of $600 was paid off within a year, extensive and expensive repairs have been made upon the exterior of the church, the old organ has been entirely rebuilt and modernized, being greatly improved, and placed in the northeast corner of the church by the chancel, new carpets have been laid, and important improvements made in the interior decorations. Early in this rectorship the parish came into possession of a most generous bequest of $20,000, thereby increasing the permanent endowment to more than $30,000, insuring its support for generations to come.

Trinity Church, Newtown, with this noble history of upwards of two centuries, has thus been one of the leading parishes of the Diocese.

Some of its Rectors have been eminent in the Councils of the Church, both within and without the Diocese, its influence upon the Church in other places can not be measured, and while in recent years it has lost many in numbers and much in financial strength, apart from its endowment, owing to industrial changes, yet it looks back with pardonable pride to the times when its first Rector preached to 600 people ; it remembers with satisfaction that three Diocesan Conventions have met as its guests, and less than fifty years ago a Rector of Christ Church, Hartford, declined a call to Newtown because it was a larger and more arduous work than he was then engaged in.

In the brief sketch of the history above given, it has not been possible to say much of the great work of saving souls, of preaching repentance, and of inculcating righteousness, nor to do more than allude to the important part which the members of the parish, the capable men and the faithful women, have had in all that has been achieved. But the signs of activity in the material interests of the parish and in things visible may here again be justly regarded as unmistakable evidences of similar activity in the things invisible and eternal ; and as abundant financial provision has been made for the maintenance of the preaching of the Gospel in Trinity Church, Newtown, for the future, let it be hoped that the venerable parish will endure through many, many generations, preserving the reverent and liturgical worship inherited from the past and witnessing to "the faith once delivered to the Saints."

5

THE CONGREGATIONAL CHURCH

These notes are taken from the very able historical address of the Rev. J. P. Hoyt, since whose ministry the church has had two pastors, Rev. Mr. Dalzelle and Rev. Otis W. Barker, the present incumbent. Quoting directly from Mr. Hoyt:

"The vote was taken Jan. 30, 1732, and is signed by sixty-four males, all apparently active members of the society, showing that notwithstanding the withdrawal of Mr. Beach and his party, the society was vigorous, large and strong. This is further shown by the fact that Mr. Kent's salary in 1740 was two hundred pounds, and his successor's, in 1744, three hundred pounds, or about fifteen hundred dollars,—a large sum for those days, even if paid in what were called bills of credit. The society, it appears, also gave Mr. Kent one hundred and four acres in settlement, provided (and here I quote from the record) that Mr. Elisha Kent shall give good security that if he shall see cause to alter his principles from ye foundation on which he shall be settled, he will pay ye above Presbyterian party ye sum of four hundred pounds lawful money, or about two thousand dollars. You will observe that those shrewd men did not intend to lose their minister again without making him pay roundly. But they did not foresee the trouble he would make in another direction. About ten years after his settlement certain charges were alleged against him, there was a long and tedious investigation on the part of the church and association and he finally was dismissed. I cannot but think that he was harshly judged and so misjudged. He appears to have lived a useful life ever after, and was much esteemed by his church in South East New York, where he died July 17, 1776. He was the grandfather of Chief Justice and Chancellor Kent, one of the most eminent men of his day, and great-grandfather of Elisha Kent Kane, the renowned Arctic explorer.

Mr. Kent's successor was Rev. David Judson, who was ordained in September, 1743. For many years the church and society were united and prosperous under Mr. Judson.

I note a few items of interest : In 1745 the church edifice
was repaired at an expense of two hundred and thirty pounds ;
glass was inserted in sashes, something new for those days ;
a bell of five hundred pounds weight was procured and
apparently was melted and recast and rehung on the 3rd day
of July, 1768. This bell cost twenty-seven pounds four shillings. It still hangs in the steeple, and for more than one
hundred years has summoned the people to the sanctuary and
tolled the knell of the departed. I saw it recently and read
upon it this inscription : "The gift of Cap. Amos Botsford
and Lt. Nath. Beriscoe ; John Witter, fecit 1768."

Mr. Judson died after a long ministry of thirty-three years,
Sept. 24, 1776, aged sixty-two, of a disease caught, as it is
said, while visiting the American camp in the Revolutionary
war. His grave is in our cemetery ; a cypress, evidently self-
sown, grows out of the heart, as if to keep his memory green.
There is among the records of the church a time-stained and
faded, but very valuable, record of the births, marriages, and
deaths for a quarter of a century, in Mr. Judson's handwriting ; the last entry is that of Mr. Judson's own death, made
by some friendly hand.

It is supposed that the church edifice of the Congregational
Society was occupied by troops during the war of the Revolution, and the vane now on the steeple bears the marks of
bullets then fired. This town was intensely loyal to the loving and loved Sovereign Lord, King George, as he was styled,
and in 1775 presented an able protest to the State Legislature against the action of Congress. (See town records, vol.
IV., pages 30–34.) The town, however, furnished its quota.
This society at the close of the Revolutionary war was in a
low condition, on account of the loss in men and means
occasioned by the war, and the parsonage, which must have
stood on or near the site of the present Episcopal Church
edifice, was sold to pay its debts.

Zephaniah H. Smith was the next minister. He, as well as
all his predecessors and most of his successors, was a graduate of Yale College. His pastorate began in 1783. A tax of
one penny on every pound was assessed in order to provide
him a settlement. A house on the main street was also built
for him in 1786 (the same now owned by Mr. George Stuart),
but he made the society a poor return for their generosity.

The records show that he tried to break up the church organization and to form a Sandemanian Church upon its ruins.
He caused those who opposed him to be excommunicated,
and finally abandoned his charge without being dismissed,
leaving the church almost a wreck, floating upon the troubled
sea without a pilot and almost without a crew. But a few
faithful souls remained in the ship, and, although discouraged,
they nobly stood at their post and rescued the Zion they loved
from utter destruction. Mr. Smith removed to Glastonbury
in this State, became a lawyer, and died in 1836, aged seventy-
seven. His daughters still reside there, and have become
known to fame by their refusal to pay taxes unless allowed to
vote. They are also known as accomplished scholars, and have
recently published a translation of the Bible from the original
Hebrew and Greek, for all of which Newtown can claim its
share of honor. The church edifice, which until 1893 had stood
in the middle of the street, nearly opposite its present location, was moved back to its present site, the Episcopal Society
(since it was for their accommodation) bearing the expense
and doing the work.

Jehu Clark was the next pastor. He resided just opposite the present parsonage. He was installed in 1799, the
services being held (by invitation) in the Episcopal Church.
The Congregational Church was now at the lowest ebb in
history; it was so completely demoralized that it was reor-
ganized, and comparatively few were found who were willing
to identify themselves with it. In 1808 an attempt was made
to build a new Congregational church edifice, and in order to
raise funds a public lottery was held, authorized, as was the
custom of the day, by the Legislature. As might have been
expected, this ill-advised course did more harm than good,
and during the war of 1812 the church was so deeply
involved in debt that a tax of seventeen cents on the dollar
was assessed to meet expenses. The church edifice was only
partly finished, and for want of support Mr. Clark resigned
in 1816; he died in 1839.

Several candidates supplied the pulpit from 1816 to 1825,
among them Rev. Lauren P. Hickok, D.D., since president of
Union College, and Rev. Mr. Burritt, whose labors were
blessed in the conversion of at least sixteen persons, who
united with the church and greatly strengthened it; but still

the membership was comparatively small, and many recorded
as members were absent from the place.

Mr. Mitchell was installed Jan. 14, 1825, and resigned and
was dismissed, May 31, 1831. He died in Corpus Christi,
Texas, Aug. 1, 1867.

Rev. Mr. Nemstron's pastorate began Dec. 5, 1832 and ended
April 1, 1838.

Mr. Atwater, like Mr. Mitchell, was a conscientious and faithful pastor. He resided where Mrs. Booth Terrill now lives;
indeed there is scarcely a building in Main street that does
not seem at some time to have been occupied by a minister of
this or some other church. The interests of the churches in
general and of this church in particular, were dear to Mr.
Atwater, and he labored hard and successfully in this his
chosen field.

After three years' effort twelve hundred dollars were raised,
and the church edifice, which had again become somewhat
dilapidated, was renovated, put in good repair, and dedicated
anew, Jan. 7, 1847. The congregation increased in members,
and a new life seemed infused into the church. But a decline
or reaction set in, and the question of abandoning the ground
and removing the church to Sandy Hook, was seriously agitated. A council, however, advised against it, and God set his
seal of approval upon the decision by graciously reviving his
work, and to His Church thirty-five members were added,
many of whom have been, and are now, the most valued and
useful of our number.

In 1852, the basement was fitted up and new seats and a new
pulpit provided for the audience-room of the church, at an
expense of five hundred dollars. Mr. Atwater accepted a call
to Southbury. He showed his continued love for and interest
in this church by leaving it a legacy of one hundred and fifty
dollars, at his death, which occurred in 1860.

The remaining pastors of this church, until the year
1874, Rev. W. H. Moore, Rev. W. F. Arms, Rev. D. W.
Fox, Rev. H. B. Smith, are yet among the living; their
work is not yet done, and of them and their work, therefore,
we will not speak at length. Mr. Moore's pastorate lasted
from 1856 to 1862, when he was dismissed to be a bishop over
our Connecticut churches. He still fills the responsible position of State secretary. Mr. Arms' pastorate was very short,

only about a year, from May, 1863, to Sept. 1864. He went
from here to Greenwich, Conn., then removed to Pennsylvania,
and is now in Sunderland, Massachusetts, pastor of a church
of more than three hundred members.   Mr. Fox was the first
minister who occupied your pleasant and commodious parsonage, which cost about two thousand dollars, but is now
worth more than twice that amount.   No society or individual loses by a generous act.   Mr. Fox, like his predecessor,
Mr. Moore, was the registrar of the Consociation ; his health
unfortunately soon failed and he was dismissed ; he is now
pastor of a church in New Jersey.

This church therefore had three pastors during the late
Civil War in striking contrast with the Revolutionary period,
when it had one pastor for a third of a century and until he
died.

Rev. Henry B. Smith was the next pastor, from 1867 to
1873.   From here he removed to Greenfield Hill, thence to
Staffordville, Conn.

"The present pastorate has been the longest this church
has had in more than one hundred years (with two exceptions).
Your minister (Rev. J. P. Hoyt) preached his first sermon in
this church Jan. 11, 1874.   The previous year the interior of
the church had been remodeled and beautified, as you see it
to-day, at an expense of two thousand five hundred dollars.
Since then seventy have been added to the church and fourteen hundred dollars to the fund (five hundred dollars being
donated by Miss Sarah Blackman of New Haven, a descendant of the first pastor, Rev. Thomas Tousey).   The debt resting on the Society has been paid ; we are at peace among
ourselves ; this church I am assured, numerically and finan-
cially, is now more prosperous than at any time for a century
past.   And yet it never needed the help of all its members and
friends more than now.   If this help is given, this church may
recover what it has lost, and be in generations to come what it
was in Colonial times, before the war for our liberty drained
it of its resources and members.   If so, we will be thankful ;
if not, we will be hopeful and still do our work."

REDDING

I shall attempt but a short sketch of this widespread little town, for the reason that its history has already been written by Mr. Charles Burr Todd, one of its own children. By his studies and this expression of them I am, by permission, about to profit largely in this sketch. Although Reading or Reding (it is spelled both ways in the records), was not in existence as a parish until 1729, or a town until 1767,—as early as 1687, its first grant was made to Cyprian Nichols for a hundred acres "where he can find it." Long after the oblong was surveyed to its original proprietors, the Indians were in possession, and not of a peaceful order, for they speedily showed fight and had to be much cajoled before they consented to allow any interference with their squatter rights. "Chickens" was their chief, " Chickens Warrup," to give him his full title, and that he was somewhat of a stickler for "above s⁴" rights, we shall shortly discover. Our old friend, Richard Hubbell, is a prominent first pur-chaser of "a grant of one hundred acres all in one peace." This and another early grant of two hundred acres in 1706, were bought in by Mr. John Read before they were even sur-veyed. But the great land speculator of Redding was Samuel Couch, and what he did not buy for himself he bought for Thomas Nash, and subsequently all the Couch sons married the Nash daughters, and vice versa for generations : Lone-town seems to have been the chosen locality in these days, for which Chickens gave his final deed "to the sᵈ Samuel Couch" in 1724, reserving "in the whole of the same lib-erty for myself to hunt fish and fowl upon the land and in the waters, and further reserving for myself my children and grandchildren and their posterity, the use of so much land by my present dwelling house or wigwam as the General Assembly of the Colony by themselves as a comᵗᵉᵉ indiffer-ently appointed shall judge necessary for my and their per-sonal improvement."

The other early settlers objected to these two magnates

gathering in the best farming lands, and sent in two petitions
or remonstrances, without effect—to the second there is also
a memorial for land with religious privileges, otherwise they
" will be soon as the Hathen are." This is signed by John
Read, Thomas Williams, Stephen Morehouse, Benjamin
Hambleton, Benjamin Franklin, Moses Knapp, Nathan Lyon,
Benajah Hall, William Hall, Dan'll Crofoot, Ebenezer Hull,
Asa Hall, Joseph Meeker, Dan'l Lyon, Thomas Hill, George
Hull. To this the "Longlots" contribute 25 more : Moses
Dimon, John Hide, Tho. Hill, Cornelius Hull, Elizabeth
Burr, Jona Sturgis, John Smith, Thad's. Burr, Andrew Burr,
Samuel Wakeman, Samuel Squires, Ezekiel Sanford, Robert
Turney, Jr., Joseph Wilson, John Wheeler, John Sturgis,
Joseph Wheeler, Thomas Sanford, John Morehouse, Joseph
Rowland, William Hill, Nathan Gold, John Gold, Robert
Silliman, Daniel Morehouse.

"According to tradition, the three first houses in the town
were built about the same time. One was in Boston district,
where Mr. Noah Lee's house now stands, the second in the
center, on the site of Captain Davis's present residence, and
the third in Lonetown, built by Mr. John Read, and which
occupied the site of Mr. Aaron Treadwell's present residence. ,
It is related of the lady of the house in the Boston district, that
becoming frightened one day at the conduct of a party of
Indians, who entered her house bearing an animal unmentiona-
ble to ears polite, which they ordered her to cook, she seized her
babe, and fled with it two miles through the forest path to her
nearest neighbor at the Centre, arriving there safely, though
breathless and exhausted. It is fair to assume, however, that,
erelong, neighbors were nearer."

"In 1723 they petition the Assembly again and ask that a
committee be appointed to measure out the 12 miles, first
laying out a farm of 200 acres for ye ministry, and 200 for a
school, and as much for the first minister that shall settle
there. Settling the bounds of the parish to comprehend so
much of the west end of ye long lots of Fairfield as may
make it near square at ye discretion of ye Com^{tee} upon ye
view of it when ye proprietors of the long lots shall settle
their end they may pay their dues there (if they will not be
so good as to fling up the west end to a public use, which
would doubtless be their private advantage also.)

"Yr. honr's most humble pet'rs, Nathan Picket, Gershom Morehouse, John Hall, Francis Hall, Robert Chauncey, Wolcott Chauncey, Daniel——, William Hill, Jr., Phillip Judd, Nathan Adams, Stephen Morehouse, Benjamin Fayerweather, Thomas Bailey, Thomas Williams, Asa Hall, Joshua Hull, David Crofut, Jno. Read, Isaiah Hull, Moses Knapp, Benjamin Sturges, Sam'l Hall, John Read, 2d, Burgess Hall, Isaac Hall."

"At a lawful town meeting in the November of 1730 'voted that we will build a meeting house in s^d Society for the worship of God in the Presbeterian way, and voted, that the meetinghouse shall be thirty feet long 28 foot wide & 2 stories high.' Voted, that Lemuel Sanford, Thomas Williams and Daniel Lyon (be) chosen a com^{tee} for s^d meetinghouse." That the "Presbeterian way," was a fairly good way, is evidenced by the following resolution passed in the February of that year. "You that are of the minds that all of those persons that do or hereafter may inhabit this parish which profess themselves to be of the Church of England shall have free liberty to come into this meeting house that is now in building, & attend the Publick worship of God there according to the articles of faith agreed upon by the laws of Divines at Seabrook (Saybrook) & established by this government & be seated in s^d hous according to their estates," and they were of "the minds," and an opportunity given to return to the fold, the door was to be "sat open" to them. The next year, for they builded slowly—Stephen Burr and Daniel Lyon promise to cart the stones and clay, to "underpin the meeting hous," and Theophilus Burr is to secure a parsonage.

Mr. Elisha Kent and the Rev. Timothy Mix had been invited, and declined, but in the January of 1732 the Rev. Nathaniel Hun was called and accepted; he was ordained in March, and the little meeting house became at once the common centre of interest. Mr. Hun's records were carefully compiled and have of late years become a veritable bible of faith to many doubtful searchers for the truth. His first congregation is liberally spread out in the pages of this little book, and many of them will be found in the genealogy accompanying these sketches. Mr. Hun remained in Redding until his death in 1749; his sixteen years pastorate seems to have been one of peace and comparative ease. He married Ruth Reed, the sister of one of his most influential parishioners, Col. John Reed, and was doubtless more favored with worldly goods than most of our early preachers. Before the first decade of his service had run its course, a new meeting house became necessary. This was built nearly on the site of the present one ; in the records we read : "& the old meeting house sold to John Burr for £34." In the seating of the new house of worship it was voted, not quite so widely as at first, "that s⁴ com¹ᵉᵉ shall seat those women whose husbands belong to the Church of England at their discretion." In the meanwhile a "schole" had been started, and a committee consisting of Mr. John Read, Joseph Lee, Joseph Sanford, John Hull, Nathan Lyon, Stephen Morehouse and Daniel Lyon, to see that their designs were carried out. School was kept in three places in succession, first five months at "The Ridge," five at the west side and two at Lonetown. This arrangement did not, as might be imagined, give entire satisfaction and it was not long before three schoolmasters and three accounts were kept. "Provided that each part of the Parish keep school three months in the year, otherwise the other two divide the assessment," and in case of two failures, "the one shall have it all." They are then designated as the school on the west side of the Aspetuck River, the school by Mill River, and the school by the Church.

In 1745 provision was added that "Each should Keep a school with a schoolmaster sufficiently capable to learn (?) children to Wright & Reade ! " The "old road" to Fairfield is the subject of much discussion ; this was laid out in 1734, under the charge of Mr. Stephen Burr and Mr. Thomas Williams, who were then chosen a committee "to repair to the County Court " in this interest. Mr. Todd says this was undoubtedly the first road from Chestnut Ridge to Fairfield, and that it led through the town, passing through Lonetown, the Centre and Sanford-town.

As early as 1738 they begin petitioning for an entire separation from Fairfield and town privileges and *twenty-nine* years afterward, it was granted them. The history of the Episcopal, or Church of England, life in Redding is so intimately connected with that of Newtown, that up to 1782, when the first rector, Mr. John Beach, fell asleep at the close of his labors, their interests and their stories were one.

The first church on Redding Ridge, which was built in
1733, and was quite small, was in 1750, replaced by another
on the same site, fifty feet long and thirty-six wide, sur-
mounted by a turret, which, in 1797, was replaced by a steeple
in which was placed the first bell. This church, according
to the style of the period, was furnished with square high-
backed pews, with seats on their four sides, so that some of
the occupants had to sit with their backs to the minister.
And though others doubtless besides Bishop Jarvis "could
see no necessary connection between piety and freezing,"
there was no heating apparatus in the churches until consid-
erably past the beginning of the present century. "Trinity
Church, New Haven, had no means of being warmed until
1822, and none of the rural churches were supplied with
stoves until a much later period." Many persons in these
districts were in the habit of walking several miles, bare-
footed, to church in summer, and probably did not feel the
lack of shoes a great privation. So common was it for men
to go to church without their coats, that the first time Bishop
Seabury preached in New Haven, a dissenting hearer reported
that " he preached in his shirt-sleeves." Often the family was
mounted, the parents with a child in arms to be christened,
upon one horse, and the older children upon another. Sometimes the whole family were clustered together upon the
ox cart or sled and thus they went up to the house of God."

One of the old landmarks of the family is the house built
and lived in by Isaac Beach. It is in the valley, beyond the
Ridge, and though still standing, is in a forlorn and abandoned
condition, and on the cloudy afternoon when I passed it last
summer, the brown timbers and broken windows made one
think of a weatherbeaten, begrimed, and homeless old dog,
and that night I read over the wedding list of Hannah Hill,
the daughter of Andrew L. Hill, who was as appears in her
father's combination diary and account book, " Borne Jan ye
7 1776 Mariade to Issac Beach Sepr ye 26, 1797 & Moved from
my House Dec 26th 1797. Took the following articles of
Household Furniture etc. which was delivered to her as part
of her portion, viz :

Item			
Two cows valued at	9	0	0
" Feather Beds bolsters and pillows at	13	15	0
One 4 ft cherry Table at	2	0	0
" set of Drawers at	10	0	0
" Common Dining table at	0	.18	.0
One small Round ditto (mahogany)	2	.5	.0
One Looking glass		6	.6
Six Windsor Chairs 3$^1/_6$	2	.11	.0
" Common Kitchen ditto 1-6	1	.7	0
One Red Chest		10	0
By Two Brass Kettles	2	.18	.5
59 yards of furniture Callico	6	.0	.0
8 pr Sheets at $^{20}/$	8	.0	.0
8 ditto of pillow Cases	1	.12	.0
14 Towels, Case of Diaper 15 yds	1	.10	.0
18 yards ditto Ditto in Table Linen	1	.16	.0
By sundries of Crockery boᵗ of Lemuel Sanford & Stephen Betts	2	.2	.1
3 tin milk pans at $^2/_4$	0	7	0
6 table spoons at $^1/$	0	6	0
6 Silver "	1	.8	.4
By one Brass Skimmer	0	3	.6
" two Dishes	0	2	.4
" " iron Candlesticks	0	1	.6
" Cash to Buy Crockery	0	3	
" Tin plate & other tin-ware	0	5	.11
1798 Pᵈ the Blacksmith for Bolling Kittles Iron etc.	1	.8	.0
Iron Pot & Kettle		9	.1
Copper Tea Kettle ¹⁸⁶	1	9	.3

Item				
Brass Candle sticks Warming pan $^{13}/_6$ Shovel & tongs 12	1	.5	.6	
Brasses etc. for Drawers	.1	3	.6	
Brass Andirons 2$^2/_6$ Common ditto & Gridiron	2	.0	.6	
Two Trammels (?)	12			
and 13¼ Pewter at $^1/_9$	1	.3	.2	
Block tin tea pot		.6	.0	
parc of small Bellows	3			
1 Bedquilt	1	.12		
3 Bed Carry (?) Blankets	3	.0	0	
1 Coverlid	1			
2 under Beds		.18	.0	
Case of washed Knives & forks	1	11	.10	
Two sets of China Cups & Saucers	1	.2	.0	
One Woman's Riding Saddle	6	.0	.0	
" pr Sugar tongs	2			
One hair sive	3			
By fulling Iron by Marchand	0	6	0	
" a Cedar tub made by Seth Wheeler	9			
" a Bedquilt	3	.0	.0	
By a great Spinning Wheel	0	.10	.0	
" a Churn made by Seth Wheeler	0	.8	.0	
Jan By a Flax Stretcher	0	8.	0	
99 Made by Marchant	0	.16	.0	
Nov By a Small 99 looking glass	0	.9	.0	
Freight ⁹/ pᵈ Henry Sturges for bringing the Looking glass etc. from New York.				

The above foregoing acct is carriade to the New Book page 80 !" [By permission of Miss Julia Hill Sanford, grand-daughter of Andrew Lane and Hannah (Lyon) Hill, to whom I am indebted for this and other quotations from the valuable papers in her possession, as well as for much immediate assistance and attention while in Redding.]

To return to our records. On the accomplishment of their long desired and often expressed wishes regarding town privileges May, 1767, they meet the next month, June 15, to choose officers. Col. John Read, moderator, and Lieut. Stephen Mead, clerk. The following are elected : " Ephraim Jackson and Daniel Hill (father to Andrew L., just mentioned), with Stephen Mead, selectmen ; David Lyon, Asahel Fitch, Dan¹ Hull, constables : Benjamin Hamilton, Zalmon Read, fence viewers ; Peter Fairchild, Lemuel Sanford, Jr., David Jackson, listers ; Thomas Fairchild and Jonathan Couch, grand-jurymen ; Gideon Morehouse, treasurer ; Paul Bartram, Thomas Fairchild, Eleazer Smith, Jr., tithing men ; Eben Williams and Eben Couch, pound keepers ; Benjⁿ Meeker and Jonathan Mallory, sealer of weights ; Ephᵐ Jackson, Gurdon Marchant, Captⁿ Henry Lyon, a committee to take all lawful and proper methods to clear the highways."

It now becomes necessary to set the bounds of the District ; a committee of seven is appointed for this purpose. Without going into detail and the repetition of the same names so frequently, we may consider the claims of those already mentioned to hold any office, quite settled, and indeed count on Mr. John Read, the Morehouse, Lyon and Hill families, to act their important parts in matters of legislation and town government.

The second Presbyterian minister, the Rev. Mr. Bartlett, who came to Redding in 1752, brought a wife with him, and so did not much concern the eligible ladies of the parish, tho' the gossips could mingle a dash of spice with their tea. This lady soon proved herself to have had some experience in such a position (having been the wife of the Rev. Mr. Russell of Branford), and met them on their own ground with the effect that she speedily assumed the privileges of her rank.

It was during his ministry that the Episcopal Church became a recognized " society," as we find. "To Seth S. Smith of Redding, in Fairfield Co., greeting : Whereas, by law the Episcopal Church in sᵈ Redding is become a distinct Society whereby the members of the Presbeterian Church in sᵈ Redding have become the first Society in sᵈ town.

These are therefore by the authority of the State of Connecticut to command you to warn and give notice to all the
members of s⁴ first Society and all others who by law are
obliged to contribute toward the support and the worship
of the ministry with the same to meet at the meeting house
in said Redding on Monday the 20th of December at 12
o'clock noon in order to have a moderator and necessary
officers." This was after the death of the Rev. John Beach,
and when the parishes of Newtown and Redding were separated.

The town was the scene of much dissension during the war,
families were divided and some of them forever. Those that
remained on their farms are now considered and spoken of as
true to their country, while the actual Loyalist was a renegade.
"The Redding Association," one of the strongest Loyalist
factions of the time, was largely representative of Fairfield
County's best blood, and it is curious to observe to-day, how
anxiously their descendants are trying to prove them traitors
to their oath; indeed, one author calls it an association
formed to assist the State Government! On the contrary
they were "pledged to defend maintain and preserve at the
risk of their lives and property, the prerogatives of the Crown
and the privileges of the subject from the attacks of any
rebellious body of men, any Committees of Inspection Correspondence, ⁰/ₑ ⁰/ₑ." Why any one to-day should regret
having had ancestors who were true to their birthrights,
oaths, and King, and still court an English line of descent,
as quite necessary to complete his "tree," seems incongru-
ous, but such little incongruities go to make new nations.
Quoting in part from Mr. Todd, while Squire Heron was
breakfasting the commanding officers of the British forces
(on that memorable morning of the 26th of April, 1777), "a
posse entered the opposite house and carried off brave old
Stephen Betts."

The Redding mothers were the chief sufferers, already
bereft of their husbands and grown sons, some on one side
and some on the other, and to invade a country at such a time
was not to conquer but to destroy. At the first hint, however, and there were those on both sides who could and
did give such, the absent regiments hurried in pursuit, led
by Brig. Gen¹ Silliman. Alas, they were too late; weary,

hungry and disheartened they had been marched from Fairfield but half prepared for the fray, and certainly not for the cold rain that came down with the night, and in the short hour's respite allowed, ran about in haste and confusion seeking the scant meal and dry clothing. Suddenly into the town dashed a body of cavalry headed by Major General Wooster and Brigadier General Arnold, their expiring energies were aroused—it is said Major Wooster made use of language which would have aroused the dead—and in a short time were on the road to Bethel. Had the Continental forces of that night been in any condition to make the immediate attack, a short march of three miles only, would then have brought them to where the enemy lay drunk with victory, but all the more at their mercy. Danbury was in ashes.

Of course General Putnam's encampment in Bethel, the winter of 1778-9 was, and is, the pride of the county. The site of the third settlement is now made into a beautiful park, " Putnam Park," and has a fine shaft to the heroes of his service. The vexed question of the execution of the spy, I shall not attempt to explain ; suffice it to say that it is not probable so dictatorial a General was softened in his distribution of strict justice by any interference. There are some queer tales afloat ; letters said to have been found, throwing suspicion on the military honor of this staunch old patriot. Whether true or false, time and the ceaseless eye of the searcher will discover.

Breaking up the grand camp at White Plains, Washington distributed the troops into winter quarters. The greater part he stationed under his immediate command at Middlebrook, N. J. West Point was garrisoned by Massachusetts men. The Connecticut Division with the New Hampshire Brigade and Hazen's regiment took post at Redding. Under orders of Oct. 22, '78, the division was to leave White Plains the next morning at 7 o'clock under the command of Maj.-Gen. McDougall. Nixon's Mass. Brigade marched with it, but kept on to Hartford. On Oct. 25, the division reached New Milford and was directed to go into camp "in the woods of Benjamin Buckingham." It was called "Camp Second Hill," and there the troops remained until Nov. 19, when they marched to Redding. About Dec. 1, Gen. Putnam assumed command (Gen. McDougall going to Peekskill) and the division settled into log huts for the winter.

From the camp at Redding detachments were occasionally
sent out to watch the enemy, and posts were kept upon the
Sound. On Dec. 5, '78, Gen. Parsons is reported with a party
at Horseneck, and in Feb. '79, he was there again looking
after the guards. In the latter part of the month Putnam
was at the same place endeavoring to repel a superior force
of the enemy under Tryon, and at this time occurred his
famous ride down the stone steps at Horseneck. An authori-
tative account of this and other incidents of camp life at
Redding appears in Humphreys' "Life of Putnam," Humphreys being Putnam's Aide-de-camp at the time. On the
30th of Dec., '78, the men of Gen. Huntington's Brigade
assembled under arms, determined to march to Hartford and
demand of the Legislature redress of grievances. Gen. Putnam immediately rode down to their quarters and demanded
by whose orders they were paraded. They replied that they had
been suffering for want of blankets and clothes, that their
pay was nothing, and that all engagements with them should
be made good. Putnam addressed them kindly and firmly
and they dispersed to their huts, remaining quiet through the
season. Putnam's report of the affair date Jan. '79, appears
in the MSS. "Trumbull Papers."

Before leaving quarters at Redding he issued the following order, May 27, '79 : "Maj.-General Putnam being about
to take command of one of the wings of the Grand Army,
before he leaves the Troops who have served under him the
winter past, thinks it his Duty to Signify to them his entire
approbation of their Regular and Soldier like Conduct, and
wishes them (wherever they may happen to be out) a Successful and Glorious Campaign."

While the Elder Bartlett was in charge of the Congregational church, the new Episcopal Society was not so settled;
doubtless it was passing through the usual course, after the
close of a long ministry, when, even if not altogether satisfactory to all, the aged missionary had received them into the
Church and held their babies in his arms, and when too, they
could criticise freely, and knew what to expect. With the
change came innovations and fresh personalities, more or less
disagreeable, and so we see them, in the following ten years,
with six ministers; the longest to remain was Ambrose Hull,
who was also the last, 1789–91. After that, until the pastorate

of Lemuel Beach Hull, from 1824 to 1836, none of the seven remained longer than six years, and most of them but three or four.

In 1789, the second Methodist Society in New England was organized at Redding by Jesse Lee, and the first members were Aaron Sanford, and his mother-in-law, Mrs. William Hawley. Mr. Sanford by this act became the first male member of the Methodist Church in New England ; he was at once appointed leader of the class thus formed and its meetings were held for years at his house. I think it was here that the partition of two of the rooms was made to draw up and hook to the ceiling in order to give sufficient space for these meetings.

Hezekiah Sanford, Isaac Sherwood, and S. Samuel Smith, joined in 1790, and from the church book of baptisms prior to 1794, we take the following names of those baptized : Children of Daniel and Anna Bartram, Silas and Hilda Merchant, Jonas and Lucy Platt, Paul and Mary Bartram, Jabez and Sarah Gorham, Elijah and Menoma Elder, Aaron and Mary Odle, John and Sarah Sherman, Uriah and Hannah Mead, Benjamin and Elizabeth Knap, Chester and Elizabeth Meeker, Charles and Lucy Morgan, Ezekiel and Easter Bertram, Jesse and Martha Banks, Isaac and Betty Platt, and Aaron and Eunice Hunt. Mr. Todd says we may safely reckon these as members of the church at that time. The first regular appointed minister was John Bloodgood. He preached in the school houses, under trees, sometimes in the barns, but always so fervently and with such native eloquence that multitudes flocked to hear him.

"The Rev. Aaron Hunt, while preaching in Redding in 1793, married Hannah, the daughter of Aaron Sanford, and shortly after located in Redding, where he continued to reside many years. Bishop Asbury, after a second visit in 1796, preached here with much satisfaction, as he remarks in his journal. ' The society in that village,' says Mr. Stephens, the historian of Methodism, ' had been gradually gathering strength. They assembled to meet him (the Bishop) at Mr. Sanford's, where he gave them an encouraging discourse from I Peter i, 13–15. From this time until 1811, the record of the church is one of continued growth and prosperity.' In this year the church was built on land purchased from Jonathan R.

6

Sanford, Esq. Quarterly meetings were the most important of all the institutions of the church, and those held in Redding were especially noteworthy. The first church was succeeded in 1837 by the present edifice. Twenty-five hundred dollars were speedily subscribed and the church was built that summer and dedicated in December of the same year. The names most familiar to the early membership perhaps, were those of the lay preachers, Aaron Hawley and Walter Sanford, and Rory Starr; the class leaders, John R. Hill, Abraham Couch, Urrai Meade, Sherlock Todd and Bradley Burr, and the official members, Thomas B. Fanton, David S. Duncomb, Aaron Sanford, Jr., Charles Gorham, Eben Treadwell and John Edmunds." In the meanwhile Mr. Bartlett was first assisted, then succeeded, by his son Jonathan, who, though delicate, continued to supply the pulpit of his father, and occasionally others, for some years after his withdrawal from active service. Bishop Davis speaks of him as a preacher "mighty in the scriptures," of native eloquence and so generous a disposition that in addition to the gratuitous services rendered, he left a legacy of three thousand dollars to the church of his choice. He died in the house in which he was born, at the age of 84 years. The town of Redding, during the last half century of which we have been reading, did not perhaps grow as rapidly in numbers as it did in size. The large farms and wide rolling country became prolific of food for man and beast, and the land records are a never-ending source of amazement; so much transferring of acres and rods, and such high prices paid for them too, show the wealth of the country to have been recognized and available. While, as we see by the long list of wedding outfit just quoted, Bridgeport provided some luxuries, and even New York was searched for a looking glass. Redding workmen there were who made tubs and spinning wheels, and churns were made by Seth Wheeler, "fulling irons as well as flax stretchers" by Marchant. Seth and Enos Wheeler had a saw mill, Enoch Marchant was a blacksmith. Others connected with this family record were Ezekiel Jackson and Co. traders, Eli and Stephen Lyon, joiners; Ezekiel Sanford and Ezekiel Jackson, inn keepers; and later, Comstock Forbes and Co. first woolen mill; Ephraim Sanford, carriage builder; Mr. James Banks, hat factory; Alanson Lyon, and the Fantons, father and son.

In 1842, Squire James Sanford built a foundry on the Aspetuck River in the Foundry district, and entered largely into the manufacture of agricultural implements. He had before invented an improved hay-cutting machine, in which the cutting was done by revolving cylinders furnished with knives, which he manufactured here, and which had an extensive sale throughout the country. This foundry is almost the only one of the old-time industries of Redding that remains in successful operation to this day. The Aspetuck River, dashing through a gorge in this district, furnishes abundant water power, and this the skill and energy of the Sanford brothers has utilized in the manufacture of buttons. Their three button factories have a capacity of between three and four hundred gross of buttons a day, employ twenty-eight hands, and have made this district one of the busiest and most prosperous localities in the town.*

January 2d, 1778. It was voted, "that the selectmen provide a Spade, Pick Axe, and Hoe to be kept for the use of digging graves." August 11, 1783, "Voted, that the town will set up a singing meeting. Voted to lay a tax of 1d. on a pound, to pay the Singing Master." March 13, 1787, "Voted not to admit Small Pox by innoculation : Voted to admit Small Pox by Innoculation next fall." October 19th, 1795. "Voted that the select men prosecute those persons that cut timber on the highways." September 19th, 1798 : "Voted that the district to which Silas Merchant belongs, shall pay him $2 for his dragg." In 1801 the town voted to relinquish to Enoch Merchant, the fine imposed on him by William Heron, Esq., for "admitting puppet shows into his house contrary to law." December 20th, 1802, John Read, Jr., was "excused" for admitting puppet shows into his house, "on said Read's paying the costs." In 1804 it was voted, "that this town will not remit to Ebenezer Robinson of Danbury, the fine imposed on him by William Heron, Esq., for breaking the Sabbath, which fine is now uncollected." The same year Aaron Read was appointed "Keeper of the Key to the Town House." In 1807, it was voted to remit the fines, $1.67 in amount, of Peter Bradley, and Nancy his wife, for Sabbath breaking : also voted, that William Heron, Esq., be paid $11.08, amount of costs in defending a suit brought by William P. Jones against him, for a fine collected and paid into the

* Since discontinued.

treasury of the town. In 1808, voted that the town will remit the fines of all those persons who labored on the Sabbath the 31st of July last past, in this town, on payment of costs. In 1817, Daniel Sanford and Aaron Burr were appointed a committee to procure the fish called pike, and put in Umpawaug Pond. In 1840, it was voted, that if any non-resident should kill birds within the limits of the town he should be fined and if he killed robins, except in case of sickness, he should be fined $5. In the records of a town meeting held December 8th, 1806, occurs the following curious entry : " Voted, that S. Samuel Smith, Lemuel Sanford, and Benjamin Meeker be a committee to write to William Crawford requesting him to name the person belonging to Redding to whom he delivered Mrs. Sarah Fleming's letter in May last, notifying him that in case of refusal, the Inhabitants of this town, will feel themselves authorized to declare to the world, that he never did deliver such a letter to any person belonging in Redding."

The following petition may not be uninteresting :

TROOP OF HORSE.

January, 1769.

On the memorial of John Hubbel and others, Inhabitants of the towns of Fairfield and Reading, being the westerly part of the fourth regiment of militia in this colony, praying that there may be a troop of horse made and formed in that part of said regiment, and that the memorialists may be formed into such troop, as per memorial on file ; Resolved by this Assembly, that there shall be a troop of horse made and formed in the westerly part of said regiment, viz : in said towns of Fairfield and Reading, and that the memorialists whose names are also signed to a certain subscription paper, dated on the 3rd day of October 1768, and with said memorial exhibited to this assembly, may and shall be, and they are here made, formed and constituted a distinct troop of horse by themselves, with all the powers and priviledges which the other troops of horse in this Colony by law now have, and that the Colonel of said regiment shall, as soon as may be, cause said troop to be warned to appear at such place as he shall think proper, and shall lead them to the choice of the proper and necessary officers, and shall make return thereof to this, or the next General Assembly. . . .

Elisha Sheldon was appointed Colonel.

"An Account of the Long Lots—Beginning on the East Side.

	Rods	Feet	Inch		Rods	Feet	Inch
Widow Wheelers	30	0	0	Meekers	14	4	8
Goodman Hall	28	12	6	Jennings	32	4	0
Whelpleys	10	12	6	Hendryx	5	0	0
John Dolls (?)	19	1	5	Highway Wilson	3	10	8
Saml. Treadwells	15	4	9	Wilsons	30	8	6
Isaac Wheelers	26	9	6	Geo, Squires	34	4	2
James Bennets	18	13	2	" " Jr.	6	1	7
Mother Sherwoods	22	10	1	John Bennits	10	8	2
Richard Hubbels	37	4	0	Jones Long Lot	11	9	9
Jackson's highway	4	14	0	Wheelers " "	40	14	0
Henry Jacksons	33	1	6	Wakeman	43	2	11
Michel Tryers	24	6	0	Thompson	14	12	7
Ezekiel Sanfords	17	7	0	Goold	44	5	9
Silamons	53	4	4	Wm. Hills	22	0	10
Wheelers	12	0	0	Wards	23	13	
Sealeys	35	1	10	Nath'l. Burr	26	0	11
Morehouses	42	6	0	Burrs Highway	6	0	0
Highway Morehouses	4	0	0	Danl. Burr	24	15	2
Turneys	24	0	6	Wilson or Hanfords	15	3	9
Adams	26	14	3	Sherwoods	4	7	9
Patchens	6	8	11	Parsonage	29	0	0
Benj. Turneys	9	14	4	Sherwood	29	4	6
Lyons	30	0	0	Bulkley	31	3	6
Stapleses	42	10	3	Bradley	17	7	0
Greenmans	24	15	10"				

Copied from account book and diary of Andrew Lane Hill.

BIOGRAPHY OF THE REV. JOHN BEACH

1700–1782

As we read, after so many similarly favored names, "born in Stratford," we recognize a happy and congenial birthright, a sort of Connecticut "hall-mark," as it were, of sterling qualification.

To that list of forty-one names—the first planters of Stratford—many a present Warrior and Dame owe existence.

There are still a few treasured landmarks to fill the souls of such quite full.

Along the two parallel streets of this charmingly situated village were born many children to those early planters and friends, and though the first burying ground had to give way to the demands of the living, some few of the rude stones can yet be seen and deciphered, in the new ground to which they were reverently removed. "E. B.–March 9–1652," for instance. Of this stone Mr. Orcutt, the historian of "Stratford," writing in 1886, says "Whom did men bear to his lowly rest beneath this monument two hundred and fifty-two years ago? Was it a stranger, or did he or she belong to one of the families of Blakeman, Burritt, Booth, Bostwick, Beardsley, or Beach?" The sentiment is good, the names correct, if necessarily alliterative, but alas for his *figures* (the italics are authorized). His ancestors must have attended that first school on Moses Wheeler's land in 1678 when "20 pounds of money" was voted for "maintenance of a school-master . . . . . to teach small children to read and rite" but not arithmetic. In 1712, however, two school houses were found necessary, and doubtless the rule of three was included in the curriculum.

"In this year was born John, the sonn of Isak," the very incompleteness lending an irritating charm to the old record. The date was "October 6th, AD 1700." He was the third 'sonn,' and so perhaps a disappointment to the mother's heart, for in all her husband's family of six married brothers, but five girls had come, and three of these to one father.

There were, however, seventeen boy Beach's in Stratford, surely enough to establish the succession.

At this time the Rev. Mr. Cutler was "settled in ye ministry" in Stratford, and soon became an intimate friend in the house of the tailor. Almost immediately his trained eye discovered special promise in the boy John, and by further investigation, that he himself had longings beyond the scope of ye village schule.

The parents, justly proud of the praise and encouragement of the minister, were nevertheless doubtful of possibilities; there were the other children to be educated, work for helping hands always ready—could they afford so great an outlay for one alone? On the other hand, what dreams of future happiness filled the mother's waking hours! Her son to go to College! To associate with the rising talent and meet on equal heights those dwellers of the intellectual world; and still higher and more beatific the vision, she might one day sit humbly before him and hear from his lips her soul's salvation! And when it was so decided, did she whisper this to father, or son, or guiding minister? Who knows? But surely, whether they knelt in prayer together, or each communed with heart alone, as we are told he was wont, that night was blessed to both.

Prepared by the advice and personal supervision of the kind Doctor himself, this 'sonn of Isak' went to his studies with his loins girded, and if—at college—life seemed strange and some of it distasteful, he soon learned where and how to apply himself toward the furtherance of those desires which had drawn him from the narrower circle of his village home.

We do not know if, among those left at parting, there was any special *other* woman's love than her's who bore him. Perhaps even at that early age, the hearts of the cousins had felt the 'mysterious pang.' Perhaps,—which is more probable,—the excitement of the entrance upon a new career, so filled that of the student that his, at least, knew not the answering flame, and her's—womanlike—bore enough for both in silence.

The clash of brain, new doors continually opening, the sudden spread of horizon, must have, to a never so well prepared mind, seemed little short of marvelous. It is not probable that at that early time, and while the classes numbered rarely over a dozen or fifteen, that class lines were drawn very closely—congenial spirits could meet and enjoy a mutual benefit. Our freshman could not have entered at a more momentous period. The College house had just been raised at New Haven, but the two Houses of Assembly at Hartford were still quarreling over the question of its settlement.

It was not until the August of 1718 that the handsome gift of books, a portrait of the King by Kneller and "goods to the value of two hundred pounds sterling," all sent from England by Governor Elihu Yale (Governor of India) to "the collegiate School at New Haven," settled the question once for all, and Yale College became a fixed fact. With this year also came that brilliant fellow star in the new firmament, Samuel Johnson, graduated in 1714. He had already taught, while part of the college was still at Saybrook, and now placed in charge of the new building (in which he lived), he entered upon his increased responsibilities with all the ardor of his buoyant nature.

Then began, what time but strengthened by every tie of blood and sympathy for two generations, that deep and enduring affection between these harmonious minds which was to exert so marked an influence on one of them, as to change his entire life. We can imagine them revelling together in the recently acquired library, for do we not read in that delightful exposé of the times in which not to be mentioned is oblivion indeed, the "Diary of President Stiles," that he (Dr. Johnson) "was a very indifferent writer but a very considerable reader all his days?"

It was due to this "indifferent writer" and his own religious doubts and changes, that John and his brother William eventually declared for the Church of England. In sophomore year, John's best and wisest counsellor and friend, the Rev. Mr. Cutler, accepted the call to the Rectorship of the College. It seems strange that they should have called, even temporarily, so well recognized a doubter to this position, but the college had sore need of a new rector. Several had declined, matters were becoming confused, the old trustees dying, the Rev. Mr. Samuel Andrew, who had served as a non-resident for years, wished to resign. He was over sixty years of age. Mr. Cutler was his son-in-law, he was a man of learning, dignified and eloquent. His wife had long known of his growing impatience under the restraint of the ministry, it is not improbable that her influence was largely concerned in the matter, and finally he was invited for a year's probation.

This may be the place to mention a still further relationship. The Rev. Samuel Andrew married twice. His first wife, Abigail Treat, the daughter of Governor Treat, died in Milford, December 5th, 1727. He married again in 1728/9, Abigail Beach, the widow of Samuel Beach of the same place. She survived him four years. (See No. 5 Milford Tombstones in the Vth volume of the New Haven Colony Historical Society papers.) Samuel Beach, the son of Thomas, brother to John and Richard the settlers, was born and died in Milford. He left no children, and before his will could be properly probated, his widow had married the recently bereaved Rector of Yale College. She thus had been by marriage cousin to our student, and became, also by marriage, step-mother to Mrs. Cutler. With the advent of the Cutlers, a new element entered upon the scene. At the head of the College was now a gentleman of extreme elegance and polished manner : a scholar by reputation, with a wife still young enough to attract, and remarked everywhere for a special charm of refinement and delicacy. In this cultivated atmosphere, young John found himself a welcome guest, and enjoyed the privileges of his former friendship and intimacy. Here he could once again hand a dish of tea to some other favored guest, and here, too, he could enjoy an unofficial special hour of argument and debate with his revered friend, for the cultivation of the art of expression, and the use of both Latin and English in conversation, were important and indeed necessary adjuncts to education.

Mr. Cutler was next year elected to the full and official rectorship, and it was then the title of *President* was introduced. President Cutler has been described as of a haughty, domineering nature, especially toward the young. This might have been so, generally, but the picture represented by what we know of him in connection with this young scholar of his adoption, does not tally with such outlines. Still it should be noted that his ideas were high, and the position which he occupied was but next highest to that of the Governor of the State,—nay, the highest,—for was not *the state* forced upon the Colony of New Haven after the most solemn promises of exemption? In 1722, he avowed himself for the Church of England. Naturally, to declare for Episcopacy in New England at that time meant to strike a blow at the actual foundation of the Colonies, founded on, and for, and by, Presbyterian rule. Great was the consternation and intense the excitement evoked by this defection in high place, and there were fanatics on both sides—unfortunately able men, who fanned the controversy to a personal issue.

John Beach was already graduated the year before this great crisis, and the autumn of 1721 found him back in Stratford, where all looked upon him with increased affection and respect. He had left them as the boy John, he returned as the man Beach, while it is not improbable that there was in a certain chosen sanctuary a small box or package labelled "Johnnie's curls." We have no portrait of him other than that drawn by the flattering pen of his great friend and admirer, Dr. Johnson, a character sketch which represents him in a recommendatory letter to the Bishop of London, dated April 5, 1732 : "The Church here has been happy . . . in the conversion (besides a number of good people) of the worthy persons who have all had a public education in the neighboring college (Yale) ; and two of them have had dissenting teachers ; two of them will go into other business, and one of them is Mr. Beach, the bearer hereof, whom I know by long experience of him (he having been heretofore my pupil and ever since my neighbor) to be a very ingenuous and studious person, and a truly serious and conscientious Christian,"—and the additional eulogies of the two historians of the Episcopal Church, the one at large and the other of Connecticut alone—Drs. Perry and Beardsley. Of course these speak of him after having accomplished his life and his work, and do not therefore picture him in his youth and early manhood.

The Presbyterian Church at Stratford had languished during the interval between Dr. Cutler's withdrawal in 1719 and Hezekiah Gold's coming in 1722. Several had been called but none chosen. The same feeble condition of things existed among the professors of the Church of England, though for a longer period. This year seems to have been a memorable one in Connecticut Church history generally. Confining ourselves to the localities of our immediate interest, we find that the First society in New Haven, under Mr. Joseph Noyes, was enjoying a monopoly of religious influence, for there was no Episcopal church or clergyman, and with the exception of Dr. Cutler, Dr. Samuel Johnson, tutor Browne, John Hart, Jared Eliot, Samuel Whittlesey, and James Whitmore, no professors (as they were called) of the Church of England. These speedily found spheres elsewhere, and it was thirty years before any actual impression was made in that city, and then, through the ministry of Ebenezer Punderson, formerly pastor of the Second Congregational church in Groton from 1728 to 1734.

In Stratford, the Rev. Hezekiah Gold (son of the Hon. Nathan Gold, Jr., of Fairfield) was pastor of the Church of Christ (Congregational) and sixty persons joined in his first year.

The Episcopal Church was first organized in this state at Stratford, indeed the first settlers of that town were from the Church of England. Rev. Adam Blakeman himself had been priest before he was a dissenter. The Rev. George Muirson, in 1706, first used the Church service in Stratford; he was a missionary from the Society for the Propagation of the Gospel in Foreign Parts stationed at Rye, N. Y., and the next year the parish was organized with wardens and vestrymen, and about thirty communicants. They were without a settled minister, however, with the exception of the passing of the Rev. Francis Phillips in 1712—a matter of five months only, until 1723; but it was in 1722 that the Rev. Mr. Pigot first arrived in Stratford, and it was certainly largely due to his enthusiasm and persistency that the Society allowed the claim of the Rev. Mr. Samuel Johnson to this field. In the interval, Dr. Johnson had been a Congregational minister at West Haven, which was but five miles from his beloved college library, from March 1720 to September 1722, when he declared for Episcopacy; thence to England, where he was ordained by the Bishop of Norwich. In his diary we read " 22 (March, 1723). This day in the morning, 10 of the clock, we waited on the Right Rev'd Thomas Lord Bishop of Norwich, and at the parish church of St. Martin's-in-the-Fields, after morning prayer, We were first confirmed, and then ordained Deacons ;

In the afternoon, I was at Prayers at St. Paul's, and then at Mr. Jonah Bonyer's, Bookseller." Thus simply does he record the first steps in the accomplishment of that great purpose of his life for which he had already sacrificed so much. And we also read between the lines, his reverent attendance at afternoon service to offer up his devout prayers of thanksgiving, and his solacing himself for the excitement of the day by a half hour among the treasures of learning which he loved. On the last day of the same month "at 6 in the morning " at the same church, and "at the continued appointment and desire of William Lord Abp. of Canterbury and John Lord Bishop of London, we were ordained Priests most gravely by the Right Revd. Thomas Lord Bishop of Norwich, who afterwards preached an excellent sermon from Rom. ii, 4 ; "Or despisest thou, etc." I dined with Mr. Murray in company with Mr. Godly and Mr. Bull, clergymen. Afternoon-I preached for Mr. Murray at St. Albans, Wood St. on Phil i. 27. We all spent the evening with Mr. Lord." This Diary, kept during the voyage out and his stay in England, is full of good things, but too long to give here. Quoting here and there, he writes " 26th We are safe by God's goodness after a storm. Just finished Mr. Nelson's "Practice of True Devotion." 5th, Finished "Dr. Taylor's Golden Guide" and "Hudibrass " 12th, This day we came to soundings. Finished reading "The Gentleman Interested in the Conduct of a Virtuous and Happy Life." Truly an excellent piece!'" Once in London, they began visiting and conferring, and seeking out each and every avenue of approach toward the great object for which they had come, and many a fruitless errand, and tiring day, and turning from doors, and all the disheartments of waiting upon the pleasure and convenience of lord bishops—ensued. Some dinners and social functions were given and held in their honor, and if the telling of a good dinner-table story was as powerful a lever then as now, doubtless Mr. Johnson's superior talent for elegant conversation produced its effect.

Mr. Johnson was the only Episcopal clergyman in Connecticut for years. He married, in 1725, Mrs. Charity (Floyd) Nicoll, widow of Benjamin Nicoll, and daughter of Col. Richard Floyd of Long Island. Mrs. Nicoll had three children, of whom the indulgent stepfather became very fond.

He prepared his sons (named William Samuel and William) for Yale, where they were both graduated in 1734. To a letter from Dean Berkeley, then in Rhode Island, and dated March 24, 1729–30, there is this postscript: "Pray let me know whether they would admit the writings of Hooker and Chillingworth into the library of the College in New Haven." This was the nucleus of that gift in 1733 of nearly one thousand volumes valued at about £500, "the finest collection of books ever brought to America," according to President Clap. That these, with the gift of his farm of 96 acres, came through Dr. Johnson is evidenced by a letter from Bishop Berkeley, dated London, July 25, 1732, in which he says: "The letter you sent by Mr. Beach (the Rev. John, of Newtown) I received and did him all the service I could with the Bishop of London and the Society. He promised to call on me before his return, but have not heard of him, so am obliged to recommend this pacquet to Mr. Newman's care. It contains the instrument of conveyance in form of law together with a letter for Mr. Pres't. Williams which you will deliver to him, [this letter has never been discovered by the way]. I shall make it my endeavor to procure a benefaction of books for the College library and am not without hopes of success." At first the Trustees were in doubt about accepting this donation, remembering previous consequences, but finally decided to do so, and the books and land were received, although President Stiles records that "Johnson persuaded the Dean to believe that Yale College would soon become Episcopal and that they had received his 'Immaterial philosophy.' This or some other motive influenced the Dean to make a donation of his Rhode Island farm in 1733. This donation was certainly procured very much through the instrumentality of Rev. Dr. Jared Eliot and Rev. Dr. Johnson." The latest lease of the farm was made in 1801 by President Timothy Dwight in favor of Paul Wightman, his heirs, and assigns forever, fixing the rent at $140 per annum from March 25, 1810, to March 25, 2761. It is now estimated to be worth $100,000.

Referring to the letter of the Lord Bishop where he says, in speaking of Mr. Beach, "he promised to call on me before his return but have not heard of him," one can see from whence comes the retiring disposition and repugnance to favor seeking of the latter-day saints in that family. Mr. Johnson was more worldly wise and had already some experience in the paths of preferment, but Mr. Beach had not then, or at any time in his long and often arduous church life, the faintest idea of self-seeking except before one throne. The words "ingenuous" and "ingenious" which Mr. Johnson and others of his time used so frequently in letters of moment, are synonymous, and meant well-balanced, competent, ready in debate or argument, and not at all what we should now convey by thus characterizing a young divine.

We have sought in vain for the marriage record of John and Sarah, though it was probably during the ministry of the Rev. Hezekiah Gold in Stratford, for we find on his record of church members that on "Aug. 5-1722, Mr. John Beach was taken into the church, ye 1ˢᵗ after my ordination, Hezekiah Gold." Previously in regard to date, but entered later, "March 24, 1722, Mrs. Beach after many years suspension from ye sacraments, restored to her former stand and privilege among us." This "Mrs. Beach" could not have been either the wife of Nathaniel or Isaac, for they are both mentioned later as will be seen : "July 29, 1723, were taken into the Church, Nathaniel Beach and his wife." "May 16, 1725, were taken into ye Church Mrs. Pittman, Nathaniel Curtiss with his wife, the wife of Joseph Birdsey, and Sarah Beach, daughter of Nathaniel Beach." "April 30-1727, Hannah Beach, ye wife of Isaac Beach."

Unfortunately there is no record of marriages in that church until 1754; presumably one of the books is lost or has been destroyed. That it took place in Stratford is evidenced by records showing their residence in that parish.

Reference has been already made in the Newtown history to the state of religious feeling there at the time of Mr. Toucey's resignation and espousal of secular and military honors ; and in the town records of 1724 we read :

"Articles of Agreement Concluded on and made this twenty-fifth Day of January, one thousand and seven hundred and twenty four or five, Between Mr John Beach of Stratford in ye County of Fairfield and Colony of Connecticut in New England on the one Part and Peter Hubbell, Samuel Beers and Jno. Leavenworth of Newtown in ye County and Colony aforesaid, on ye other part, witnesseth as followeth—Imprimis—The above said Mr. Beach doth Covenant with the above said Peter Hubbell, Samuel Beers, and Jno. Leavenworth as they are a Committee in ye behalf of the Town of Newtown abovesaid to Settle in the ministry of Newtown aforesaid, as soon as may be with conveniency conformable to providence only excepted and (al)" low " to continue during my life if ye providence of God shall allow the same, and furthermore, I, the said Mr. Beach Doe promise to find all the Iron work nails and glass for the Building me a house in Newtown this house after exprest. Item, Peter Hubbell, Samuel Beers, and Jno. Leavenworth as a Committee in ye behalf of ye town of Newtown abovesaid Doe Covenant with ye above said Mr. John Beach that upon his settling in the work of a ministry in Newtown aforesaid, therefore the said Mr. John Beach shall have paid him for his sallary the sum hereafter mentioning, sixty pounds per year for the two first years after the first Day of this Instant January and (al)low to Rise ten pound per year yearly, untill it make one hundred pounds per annum, and then to be Mr. Beach his standing sallory, all which payments are to be truly payd to Mr. Beach in provisions as they shall pass from man to man here in Newtown on the first Day of January, also to erect and finish a two story house for Mr. Beach, he finding glass and nails as above exprest; and to find Mr. Beach in his firewood yearly and also to give Mr. Beach ye improvement of four acres of pasture Land lying near Shay's home Lots as appears by Record dureing his Life, also we Peter Hubbell, Samuel Beers, and Jno. Leavenworth as a committee for the town of Newtown Doe make over unto Mr. John Beach sundry Parcels of Land containing one house and 23 acres and also four acres home Lott in Newtown abovesaid as may appear by Deed executed under our hands and seal Bearing Date with this Instrument in Confirmation of every of above articles the above mentioned parties have Enterchangably Sett to their hands and seals In Newtown the Date above mentioned.

John Beach { seal }

Signed Sealed & Delivered in presence of

   Thomas Bennit
   Joseph Peck.

This Instrument rec'd for Record January ye 25, 1724
   Recorded p⁵
     Joseph Peck, townclerk

Note that the above house is to be finished on or before the first Day of November next ensuing the Date above mentioned.

Peter Hubbell { seal }

Samuel Beers { seal }

Jno. Leavenworth { seal }

Mr. Samuel Beers dies shortly after and at a town meeting in May (14) 1725, Captain Bennit, Lieut. Northrop and Jos. Peck are added to the committee. Mr. Daniel Foot's deed of land is made out with no restrictions for the sum of forty pounds current money and "conveys and confirms unto Mr. Beach . . . . . and *to his heirs forever.*

Signed. Daniel foot."

In view of the later disagreements in regard to land holdings, it may be well to note this particular transaction. The next entry of importance is on page 77 :

"Att a lawful Town meeting held March ye 30ᵗʰ–1726, ye meeting is adjourned until Monday ye next, ye sixth day of April. Then agreed and voted by the Inhabitants of said Town that ye beforesaid Inhabitants would Pay a Tax or Rate of 10ᵈ per pound upon the List of ye said towne of ye year 1725 for to Defray ye Charges of Preaching and furnishing a house for the Reverend John Beach.

Jos. Peck town clerk."

In Vol. III, p. 109 :

"Newtown, April ye 12th 1726, then layd out for Mr. John Beach ten acres of land of ye 307 acre Devition given by Mr. Tousey , ... as deed will show. Lying westerly of Mr. Bennit's swamp, lying east, west and north on undivided land and south bounding ye Highway. ye Bounds are as followeth, ye first bound is a Read Oak bush with stones to it by ye highway, then we run northward forty rods to a rock with stones on't. Then 407 Rods westward to a rock with stones on't. Then we run 407 southward to a high rock with stones on't by a Highway. then we run by said Highway 40 rods to ye first mention road,
  pr. Record April ye 13–1726—by us—

	Daniel Foot
Recordᵈ by Joseph Peck	Joseph Bristol
Town Clerk	Committee."

With what satisfaction must he have seen this next item recorded :

"Received att Hand of Lieut. John Northrop Collector of Newtown, the full sum of my sallory for the year 1725, the full sum of sixty pound, I say—Received by me, dated Newtown this 8ᵗʰ day of December 1727—

John Beach."

Although it was thus late before the first year's "sallory" was paid, we can I think appreciate both the hardships which

prevented and the joy which accompanied, and once begun,
the little town was not again so backward, as the frequent
repetition of the above phraseology with its yearly increase is
regularly recorded. In 1728, they increased the rate to four
pence on the pound "for Mr. Beach his sallory" and "one
half penny upon ye pound on ye list to git Mr. Beach his
firewood." All at this time seemed favorable to a more settled condition in respect of religious affairs. Five families
were, however, withholding their interest and support, and
being occasionally ministered to in the Episcopal way by the
Rev. Mr. Johnson.

Mr. Beach was on friendly terms with these Church of
England professors, and it is not improbable that his intimacy
with Mr. Johnson brought upon him some criticisms. His
introduction of the Lord's Prayer into the service when recognized as such and a part of the English ritual, was thought to
lead at once to Rome and imperil souls forever.

Aside from rapidly growing doubts and self-examination,
his life at Newtown during this interval must have been comparatively happy. A newly built house, a tried, congenial
companion, little children to greet his home-coming, good
friends standing by him in all sincerity, and whatever his
decision ; and yet we have seen enough of him to know that
while this great thing was paramount, no lesser joys could
wean him to ease or forgetfulness. Finally, when the supreme
moment came and the step was taken which forever separated
him from this season of doubt, in spite of cavil or criticism
we see him once more serene and peaceful, ready to meet
both, and borne up with a great confidence, longing to begin
his work afresh.

Already he had begun to make plans for his journey to
England, and was in intimate correspondence with his friend
in Stratford whose recommendations in his behalf had been
long promised and now in process of fulfilment. We can not
surely tell if his wife had yet consented to give up her birthright and join her husband in word and deed, but we know
that she allowed him, in this month, to take their little son of
five years of age to Stratford with him, and that there he was
baptized by the Rev. Mr. Johnson. At the same time he himself was entered as a member of that church, and at Easter
partook of the Communion there. It must indeed have been

7

a solemn and wonderfully filled moment to both, when his kneeling form was reached, and firm as was now their mutual faith, the whispered prayer must have trembled between them.

It is odd that after this distinction we hear no more of the child, although in all the family records, Joseph is mentioned as " among those who lived to grow up and have children." Perhaps there may be some one who at this late day, reading this little record of that first Church service in the family, may recognize the ancestral honor, and so find his own way back to the fold. There were two children born to them at that time, Joseph in 1727, and Phebe in 1729. Joseph was the only one baptized before his father's voyage. This may have been because sons were then considered of more importance, or the mother may have wished it so. In Stratford, the brother William was either already a professor, or very soon after became a member of the church. Perhaps the dream of their mother had come true before this change in her sons' lives. It is more than probable that John had taken part in the worship of the meeting-house before going to Newtown. We find the name " Hannah the wife of Isaac Beach " on Mr. Hezekiah Gold's record in 1727, but that she must have been influenced to some extent in favor of the adopted church of two of her beloved sons, we must suppose, by her tombstone and grave in the Episcopal burying ground at Stratford, while that of her husband Isaac is in the old Congregational burying place, with those of his brother Nathaniel, his wife and others of the family.

Again to Town records :

"At a lawful Town meeting of ye inhabitants of Newtown held by adjournment February ye 28, 1731/2, Captain Thomas Bennit, Deacon John Botsford, Lieut. John Northrop, and Mr. Jno. Leavenworth by vote were chosen Committee in ye behalf of ye Town of Newtown, to to Discourige Mr. John Beach with Respect to his estate had by Lottment here and to know of him ye terms if any that he will be upon with Respect to the Resignation of ye whole or part of that above he hath received and to make Report to ye town at ye adjournment of this meeting."

The wording is suggestive of some doubt on their part whether their committee is going to accomplish the desired result, as well as some evident former experience with the

reverend gentlemen, . . . wherein he had not been entirely sub-
jugated, "to know of him ye terms *if any*" has an apprehensive
ring. We can be almost sure that the "Committee" as finally
composed was drawn with some difficulty from those present
at the meeting. The result follows :

" Whereas a committee appointed by the Inhabitants of the Town of
Newtown have made this proposal, viz. that if I will quit-claim all yt
land which I now possess by virtue of a deed from ye proprietors of ye
said Newtown, any of their acts, then I shall hold ye house and home
lot as my own estate and have ye use of yt lot near Nathaniel
Pammelees and yt under Mt. Tom, untill November next and be paid
by ye said Town for ye fines about ye above said lotts to ye above said
proposal I consent as witnesseth my hand this 8th Day of March,
1731/2. JOHN BEACH.

In presence of us,

THOS. BENNIT	JOHN BOTSFORD	} *Com.*"
JOHN NORTHROP	JNO. LEAVENWORTH	

The town's quit claim of same date, the same Com^tee, " for
& in consideration of ye past service of Mr. Beach of afores^d
Newtown in ye gospel ministry. . . . . Do by these presents
in ye stead Behalf & name of ye town of Newtown & their
successors forever unto the aforesaid Mr. John Beach his
heirs & assigns forever, Demise Releas, Relinquish & Quitt
Claim '_e, '/_o, with the House & Homestead on wh said
House is now Erected, containing four acres '/_e, east on ye
Main street, North on ye home lott of Daniel foot, South &
west . . . . heirs of Hugh Stilson Deceased." Recorded April
8, 1732, by Jos Peck—& signed by John Gregory Justice of
the Peace.

On the 17th day of the same month and year, he takes the
precaution to have this freshly laid out to him.

"3 acres of th^t Land Being two acres and half of it, of ye thirty
acre Division and ye other half acre of ye sizure of a twenty acre lott
the said land Lying on Mount Tom brook northwest from Nathaniel
Pammelee's house ye first bounds is a white tree being the south corner of Captn. Bennit's land, then we run 19 Rods northeasterly In
said Bennits line to his easterly corner there we run 36 rods in Prud-
dens line southeasterly to said Prudden's corner near ye Brook then
we run 9 rods westerly to a heap of stones and from thence to the first
station laid out by us.

Recorded March ye 17, 1732.

DAN'L FOOT	' Com."
JNO. SHERMAN	

April of that year found Mr. Beach in London, where, as
we have seen, he did not long tarry in court-yards or frequent
the gardens of dignitaries ; in fact one may criticise his inat-
tention to possible advancement, and suppose him, from letters of that season, even provokingly uncivil to proper
authority. But as is said of him in the address or sermon
already spoken of and shortly to be more fully introduced :
"With him religious truth . . . . became part of his life,"
and as often happens with those whose convictions come in
mid-career, causing the adoption of fresh exertions, and opening new paths of thought, every detail becomes important
and things which to the accustomed eye or ear carry no special
significance, assume legitimate and sometimes undue proportions. As soon therefore as the special business for which he
had crossed seas was accomplished and he had received his
appointment to Newtown and Reading, he came away home
to his new work in the old field. The Rev. Mr. Beardsley, in
his "History of the Church in Connecticut," thus speaks of
him at this time :

"No one went over from this country recommended to the Bishop
of London for Holy Orders with better testimonials than John Beach.
Johnson spoke of him, from a long acquaintance as 'a very ingenuous
and studious person, and a truly serious and conscientious Christian.'
Besides these testimonials, he bore with him a petition from Lemuel
Morehouse and others, members of the Church of England in Redding and Newtown, renewing their request for a share in the charities
of the Honorable Society, and particularly that Mr. Beach might be
appointed a Missionary in the town and vicinity where he was so well
known, respected, and beloved. The petition was granted, and the
usual allowance for salary appropriated ; but upon his return from
England, in September 1732, he found the affections of his old parishioners alienated from him, and himself and his plans for the church
opposed with increased rancor. A tribe of Indians three miles distant
from Newtown, to whom he was charged by the Society to extend his
ministrations had been stirred up to resist him and treat him with
indignity and violence, under the ridiculous plea that he was about to
rob them of their lands and draw from them money for his support.
But none of these things moved him from his godly work. Because
there was no suitable place for assembling, he invited the few professors of the Church of England to meet in his own house, where for a
considerable time he conducted the public services. 'He pressed on
with resolute and cheerful spirit ; conciliating many of the Indians,
and gathering around him large congregations of his own countrymen.'

In his first report to the Society, made six months after his arrival at his mission, he says 'I have now forty-four communicants, and their number increases every time I administer the Communion.' And of his flock he remarks: 'The people here have a high esteem of the Church, and are now greatly rejoiced that they have an opportunity of worshipping God in that way, and have begun to build two small churches, the one at Newtown and the other at Redding.' It is said that the frame of the building in Newtown, (twenty-eight feet long and twenty-four wide,) was raised on Saturday, the roof-boards put on the same evening, and the next day the handful of churchmen assembled for divine service under its imperfect protection, sitting upon the timbers and kneeling upon the ground. Johnson at Stratford, Caner at Fairfield, the elder Seabury at New London, Beach at Newtown and Redding, four missionaries, with five houses of worship, constituted the working clerical force of the Church in Connecticut down to the end of the year 1734."

In 1739, the celebrated case of the Rev. Mr. Arnold, as trustee in New Haven for the Church of England, was brought to the notice of the Society and seven clergymen signed the memorial of remonstrance ; Wetmore, Johnson, Caner, Beach, Seabury, Punderson, and Arnold. It would take an undue amount of writing and reading to enter at all into any description of this affair, but those interested in further inquiry can turn to Beardsley's or Perry's Histories of the Episcopal Church in this country, or the town records of New Haven, for fuller particulars. Mr. Johnson, in writing of this affair to the Secretary in the April of 1740, says : "The unsettled condition of some of our churches with respect to their ministers is also a great disadvantage to us. There is now a proposal that Mr. Beach should change with Mr. Arnold and go to Staten Island and Newark. He is indeed a very worthy and useful man, and nobody could do more good there than he, but then the loss of him would be an unspeakable damage to us here."

To quote further ourselves from the first authority :

William Beach of Stratford, a wealthy gentleman and brother of the Rev. John Beach, had been charged with the heinous sin of covenant-breaking, because he left the Congregationalists and entered into the communion of the Church ; and not willing to allow such a charge to go unnoticed, he persuaded Mr. Johnson, both for his own defence and as an antidote to the malicious ballad of Graham, to draw up and publish a tract, containing "Plain Reasons for Conforming to the Church." Replies and rejoinders followed, and the controversy reached down to the year 1736, when it was closed by Johnson; and Mr. Graham withdrew from a contest in which he had now no honors for himself and no advantage to his cause. The more the subject of Episcopacy was publicly discussed and the grosser the attacks upon it, the greater was the increase in the number of its adherents. Popular attention was drawn to the Church of England by the animated controversies in which her missionaries were involved, and the examination of her doctrines and worship softened or removed in many instances the prejudices of early education. A member of the little flock of Mr. Beach at Newtown, returning one day from service, accidentally dropped her Prayer Book, which was picked up, and pronounced by the person into whose hands it fell to be a Mass Manual, containing very wicked things. Curiosity was excited among his neighbors to see the heretical and extraordinary book, and several who looked over its pages were so far from agreeing in opinion with him that they found it contained a large portion of the Scriptures, besides several of the excellent prayers which Mr. Beach had been in the habit of using while serving them acceptably as a Congregational or Independent minister. The Society in England for the Propagation of the Gospel had furnished its Missionary in this place, as elsewhere, with a number of copies of the Book of Common Prayer for gratuitous distribution, and these were now put in circulation, and the result was, that, in the course of twelve months, eight families were added to the Church; and as the increased congregation rendered a private dwelling inconvenient to meet in, an edifice for public worship was called for and speedily erected.

In 1736 the communicants included in the mission of Mr. Beach were 105, but he was not permitted long to enjoy in quietness this measure of prosperity. The Rev. Jonathan Dickinson of New Jersey, the Presbyterian divine who had before appeared as a sharp assailant of Episcopacy, again took up his pen to attack the Church, and published in this same year a sermon entitled, "The Vanity of Human Institutions in the Worship of God." It was in the spirit and style of similar publications of that day, and evidenced that the author not only misunderstood or purposely misrepresented the nature and object of the Liturgy, but that he fixed the sin of schism, the guilt of rending the body of Christ, upon all who, from any motive, were led to conform to the Church of England. Copies were freely distributed in Newtown among all classes of people, and churchmen found them in their houses without knowing the source to which they were indebted for the singular gratuity. Mr. Beach was therefore compelled, in self defense, to enter the field of controversy, and wrote a little pamphlet called "A Vindication of the Worship of the Church of England" in which he met all the bold statements of the sermon, and maintained the utility of forms of prayer and their scriptural sanction without considering them as of special divine appointment. One hundred pages in reply followed from Mr. Dickinson, reiterating his former charges and adding some new "Misrepresentations and Slanders," with a zeal which would have done credit to the heart of a Puritan in the times of Oliver Cromwell. But scarcely had the printed sheets become dry before the Missionary was ready with an Appeal to the "Unprejudiced," in the course of which he made this personal allusion by way of justifying his own withdrawal from Independency: "I have evened the scale of my judgment as much as possibly I could; and, to the best of my knowledge, I have not allowed one *grain* of worldly motive on either side. I have supposed myself on the brink of Eternity, just going into the other world, to give up my account to my great Judge; and must I be branded for an Anti-Christ or heretic and apostate, because my judgment determines that the Church of England is most agreeable to the word of God?" . . . . . The immediate effect of this prolonged controversy was to double the number of churchmen in Newtown; . . . . . Mr. Beach often officiated and administered the sacraments at Ridgefield, distant from his residence about eighteen miles, where in 1735 there were nearly twenty "families of very serious and religious people, who had a just esteem of the Church of England, and desired to have the opportunity of worshipping God in that way."

There seemed to be no limit or set boundaries to the work which these first missionaries were called upon to perform, and so we find him assisting Mr. Johnson as far from his special cure as Waterbury. In Woodbury also as early as 1740 Mr. Beach was instrumental in gathering an "Episcopal Society," and a house of worship was soon afterwards erected "on the hill between a place called Transylvania and the present center of Roxbury." In 1743, chiefly through his influence, a church was built in New Milford, and in 1745, an organization was effected in Litchfield, where four years later a church was built by an Englishman, Mr. John Davis, who gave it the name of St. Michael's. The condition of the church in Newtown and Redding is fully described in the following letter:

"Reading in Connecticut—
in N. E. April 2ᵈ—1746.

Reverend Sir,

All that I have at present to acquaint the Venerable Society with, beside what is contained in the enclosed, is, that we have erected another church at Newtown which is forty-six feet long—thirty-five broad, and twenty-five up to the roof. It is a strong neat building, and though it be small, yet, considering the poverty of people in these new Settlements, and that the parish being sixteen miles in length, we must have two churches in it, it is a considerable charge to that part of the parish who have contributed cheerfully—some thirty—some fifty—and one man   two hundred pounds this currency; while our neighbors of the Independent persuasion have their meeting houses built by a tax laid by the government upon all the land in the parish. And in this parish, all who go to *meeting* are exempt from paying anything toward the support of the government—but as soon as any join in the worship of the Church of England they immediately lose that privilege. But the more we are oppressed, though there may be several professors of the Church of England, yet I hope, we shall be the more sincere in our profession; and it is very certain that our people generally expend more by far for the support of religion, than their neighbors of the dissenting persuasion. If the Venerable Society would think it reasonable to send me four dozen Common Prayer Books with Tate and Brady's version of the Psalms, and two dozen of the Whole Duty of Man—they should be carefully distributed among the poorer people—by

Reverend Sir, your's
And the Venerable Society's—
Most obedient and humble servant
JOHN BEACH."

This communication from the church wardens of Litchfield in 1747 will further emphasize his work there :

April the 4th, 1747.

. . . . Above two years past a great number of us declared our conformity to the Church of England, by subscribing a letter to the Reverend Mr. Beach inviting him amongst us, attending divine service with him, owing to the excellency of the doctrine and the manner of worship in the Said Church, and openly defending them to the utmost of our power; but even now the Dissenters have executions out against us for rates due long since, and daily threaten to take us to the gaol if we refuse to pay them; and this, notwithstanding we bring and offer them a discharge in full, under the hands of the Reverend Mr. Beach. . . . . . We are remote from all our Reverend Missionaries except the Reverend Mr. Beach and Mr. Gibbs—Mr. Gibbs being the nighest, who lives twenty-seven miles, and Mr. Beach between thirty and forty miles from us. . . . . .

In the Newtown Land Records of an earlier date we read, page 89 :

A vote passed by ye proprietors of the common and undivided land in Newtown, in ye county of Fairfield, at there meeting leagally warned and helded, by adjurnment on ye 19th Day of March A.D. 1743-4.

For as much as divers persons of ye presbyterian persuasion did formerly sign and subscribe to give to ye Rev. Mr. John Beach, Divers peaces of land of ye thirty acres divition and other divi ons then to themselves granted to be laid out in ye bound' of said Newtown as appears on Record, on Consideration of said Mr. Beach, setteling in ye work of ye ministry in said town and said lands soe signed to be given was laid out to Mr. Beach, and afterwards said Mr. Beach declared himself to be of ye Church of England persuasion in matters of Religion, and there upon did resign up to ye town of Newtown all his right titel and interest in the lands to him laid out as a fore said and there upon said town by ye com" did Execute a deed in due form of law dated August ye first 1732 of one hundred and four acres an half of said land to Mr. Elisiah Kent in consideration of his setteling in ye work of the ministry according to ye Presbyterian persuasion and said signers not having conveyed ye sec of said land to any legal deed or deeds did afterwards lay out their full right in said division to themselves and there heirs, and therefore said lands laid out to Mr. Beach as afore said and supposed to be conveyed to said Mr. Kent by said deed did then of right belong to ye proprietors as ye common and undivided land in ye said Newtown several of which said proprietors was and did profess themselves to be of the Church of England persuasion, not willing to contribute towards ye settlement of a presbyterian minister and where as part of said lands was laid out nearer th (hou') then ye limits of ye thirty acre division therefore to secure to said Churchmen ye proportionable right in ye common and undivided land for ye use of Church of England ministry, equal both in quantity and quality as ye presbyterian persuasion, whose rights are devoted to said Mr. Kent, his heirs and assigns for ever it is voted and agreed in said meeting that those proprietors of said common and undivided land y't were and did profess themselves to be of the Church of England persuasion two acres and forty and three rods of land, and so in proportion for half right etc. Three eights part to be laid out with in one mile of ye meeting house, ye Remainder to be laid in ye limits assigned for ye thirty acres division to be laid out for a parsonage for a Church of England clargy, for ye use of ye Rev. Mr. John Beach and his lawful successors for ever, Always provided that nothing in this vote shall be considered to break ye sequesterment Recorded ye day and date above

Per me JOBE SHERMAN prop" Clark

Voted in ye A
fermitive

Perhaps the best and most concise statement of his life and works is found in the Memorial Sermon already quoted and at the risk of some repetition these further extracts are given.

" At Reddi .g, he found a small band of Church people who had
been ministered to occasionally by Mr. Caner, of Fairfield, and for
whom it is .laimed that they were the first religious body organized
in that town.   At any rate, one hundred and fifty years ago John
Beach found the Church seated in quiet determination on the summit
of Redding Ridge, and there through storm and sunshine it lives unto
this day.

" There Mr. Beach ministered on each alternate Sunday to the
Church people gathered from far and near, some from a distance of
ten or fifteen miles.   Those who lived too remote to come and return
home on the Lord's day, came on Saturday, bringing their needful
supplies, and were given house-room by their brethren near the
church.   At Newtown, also, we learn that churchmen gathered for
worship, in those first years, from New Milford and other remote
places.   Ministering to such earnest people must have been one of
the chief alleviations in the hard lot of the lone missionary.

" His field was a very different country then and now.   Much the
larger portion was still covered with forest, the roads mere bridle-
paths or cart tracks; streams were oftener crossed by fords than by
bridges.   In one instance, at least, the missionary was near losing his
life in crossing an unbridged river."

The tradition is that every other plank in the bridge had
been removed presumably to prevent him from crossing, and
that not coming that way until evening his old horse had
carried him safely over without his perceiving anything
wrong.

" In twelve years from the erection of the first church another of
more than double its capacity was required and built.   Such growth
in such circumstances proves the missionary to have been of unusual
powers, as well as of unflinching purpose.

" Five years later still a like prosperity called for the erection of
the second and larger edifice at Redding Ridge.   At that place there
was then a more numerous and able population than now, the majority of whom became attached to the Church.   The building then
erected remained till 1832 unaltered, except that, near the close of the
last century, its bell-turret was replaced by a tall, gaunt steeple.

" Well do I remember that venerable building.   Like many another
old church in Connecticut, it was, as to the exterior, an imitation in
wood of St. Paul's, New York.   It was an honest church.   Its builders
offered to the Lord the best lumber their woods afforded, and they
did not by paint pass it off for stone.   Its interior was noble and
impressive in its simplicity.   Its high arched roof was sustained by
huge square pillars of white oak, on which the marks of those who
' lifted the axe upon the thick trees' were to be seen.   Through the

centre were ranged the benches, framed and pinned together with oak, and worn bright by generations of worshippers. Along the sides were ranged the square family pews, built of the fine white lumber of the tulip-tree—sheep-pens they were called, and each Lord's day they were full of sheep. Within the chancel-rail the three-decker arrangement of holy table, desk, and pulpit, and above all the sounding-board, all remaining as when John Beach ministered, come up in the mind's vision ; and in that full and devout congregation at that date here and there lingered a gray-headed worshipper who had listened to his stirring speech and been signed with the cross by his saintly hand. In how short a time have we passed on into a new and strange world !

" During about twenty years of his ministry he lived near that church, and within its shadow, in 1756, he laid the mortal remains of her who had shared the toils and trials of his early manhood and middle life. Soon after 1760 he appears to have resumed his residence at Newtown, which was thenceforth his home.

" Though devoted to his work as a missionary pastor, the exigencies of the times compelled him to engage in controversy to repel the attacks upon himself and upon the Church of his choice.

" The care with which he had investigated the claims of her polity, and the scriptural and primitive character of her doctrines and usages, admirably fitted him for this work. He knew every inch of the ground, for he had carefully surveyed it for the satisfaction of his own conscience. He knew the force and value of every objection for they had dwelt in his own mind till expelled by truthful investigation. He was patient with assailants and opponents, and allowed for their prejudices, for he had once shared them.

" As we read the pieces which remain of his controversial writings, we are surprised that amidst such a life of toil, in such a widespread field of pastoral work, and with attention to the cultivation of the soil to eke out his moderate income, he could have found time for a scholarship wide and accurate as he displayed. In this respect the scholarly Johnson was his only superior among our Connecticut clergy of his time ; and in his clear and popular way of putting things, so as to arrest and convince common minds, he had among them no equal.

" To store up rare learning till one becomes an encyclopædia, has been the achievement of many a man who has left the world neither wiser nor better than he found it ; but Beach had that gift by which a truly great mind makes its hard earned stores of learning the readily grasped possession of plain people.

" His freedom from bitterness and vituperation, his fairness in stating his own or his adversaries position, when contrasted with the tone and temper often shown by his opponents, all told in favor of his cause. There is in our Saxon make-up a love of fairness and justice, which was won upon by his style and method, and which the bitterness of his opponents turned in his favor.

"Nor was the purity of his personal character of small weight. When a pamphlet had been circulated in his parish traducing the Church and her ministers, it was remarked by a sage old man of the standing order: 'Mr. Beach is too good a man to be thus deceived. The king and parliament also are churchmen, and can they all be so wicked? I doubt it. Let us examine the subject a little more.' The result was that he and several others at that time came into the Church.*

" That was an age when pamphlets supplied, in a degree, the place now filled by the newspaper. In the scarcity of miscellaneous reading, and in the people's isolation from the great world, each of these little missives was read and re-read and carefully treasured up. The assailants of the Episcopal Church were diligent in circulating their pamphlets, and every few years there was a new issue of them. Several of these Mr. Beach answered, and his answers were diligently circulated and read. Copies of several of these were to be found in the old church homesteads of this diocese within the memory of persons still living. To these tracts is, in no small degree, owing the conservative and intelligent churchmanship which has distinguished our diocese from the beginning. And no individual of our colonial clergy wielded through this means so long-continued and so effective an influence as John Beach. ' He was a controversialist—able!'

"Many of Mr. Beach's publications on such topics were in the form of sermons, and belonged to the domain of the preacher as much as to that of the controversialist. These productions had their origin rather in the purpose of guarding the Church people from error, than in any love for polemics.

" The extreme doctrines of the standing order led to the errors of Antinomianism on the one hand, and to Socinianism on the other. These ill tendencies were quickened to new vitality on the coming of the Rev. George Whitefield. He shot like a meteor through the colonies, throwing society into a ferment. He had thrown off the restraints of his ordination vows in England, and had there denounced, without stint, the authorities of the Church of England, to which he belonged. Here he went to such lengths of extravagance as to draw forth, finally, protests from a considerable portion of the divines of the Congregational order, whom in turn he denounced as heartily as he had the Bishops. Division and disorder were still further increased by the preachers who followed in his wake. Many of the Congregational churches were rent in sunder, and the whole people were excited and disturbed with strange teachings and resulting controversies.

" Our Church people were in a degree affected by this state of things, and Mr. Beach and others of the clergy shaped their preaching in such wise as to guard their flocks. At the request of a convention

* Mr. Daniel Booth.

of his brethren, Mr. Beach prepared a sermon vindicating the funda-
mental principles of the Christian faith as against several heretical and
latitudinarian views which were becoming rife. This sermon was
published and circulated as a tract, with the endorsement of his
clerical brethren.

"Quite a number of his other sermons survive to attest his qualities
as a preacher. His style was clear and flowing, his words well chosen,
his matter well arranged. He had evidently drunk at the fountains
of English undefiled. His teaching was drawn from Holy Scripture,
and was in accord with that of the best divines of our mother Church.
He dwelt mainly on practical themes which have to do with conversion, a holy life, and salvation through Christ crucified. As we read
we feel that he is in earnest, and in passages he rises to an impassioned
eloquence. Moreover, tradition assures us that his delivery was in
keeping with his matter, and, says Dr. Mansfield, his was 'an unaffected
and commanding eloquence.'

"The estimation in which he was held is attested by repeated pro-
posals to him to remove to more desirable and less arduous fields in
this and neighboring colonies. But like Moses, 'he loved his people.'
For their good he lived, and with them he would die. The history
of the Church affords few more noble examples of life-long attachment
between pastor and people."

Dr. Johnson was now in New York City, having accepted
the presidency of King's College, and though his work was
congenial and made sufficiently light by the trustees, he
mourned his beloved Stratford without a shepherd ; both his
sons acted as lay-readers, the elder taking his place after
the younger had joined the father in New York to pursue
his theological studies. Mr. Beach had been thought of
for his successor, and all would have welcomed him to the
post, but he could not conscientiously leave his own church
vacant. In a letter to his son William Samuel, dated January
20, 1755, Johnson said : "The melancholy condition of my
poor destitute people is very affecting to me. I talked with
Ogilvie and Chandler to no purpose ; nor do I think there
is the least probability that Mr. Brown or Mr. Seabury, Jr.
would entertain the least thoughts of a removal, and since
there is no hope of Stiles (Ezra Stiles, afterwards president
of Yale College), I am sorry he should have had it in his
power to make a merit of his refusal. I am very sorry that
Mr. Beach cannot be prevailed upon to remove, and what
course you can now take, I cannot conceive. Methinks I
should be for trying Mr. Leaming . . . . . for Stratford or

Newtown. Can there be no thoughts of Sam Brown for
Newtown? Or is there no young man who would go for so
valuable a parish?"

Mr. Dibblee of Stamford is also thought of in case of Mr.
Beach's removal. Indeed there is a letter from him to the
Secretary in London, speaking of having received an invitation "from the good people of Newtown and Reading to
succeed the worthy Mr. Beach . . . . from him I am informed
that no one would give better satisfaction." But nothing
further came of it. This same Mr. Dibblee wrote in 1759 :
" The sound of the trumpet and the alarms to war, together
with the concern for the events thereof, principally engrossed
the attention of the people. Indeed the church of Stamford
is rather weakened than strengthened of late by enlistments
into public service, and through a very malignant disorder
that has prevailed among my people. . . . . ." In the same
letter, he mentions going to Salem, N. Y., "upon a special
fast appointed in that province to implore the smiles of
Divine Providence to attend his Majesty's arms the ensuing
campaign." "Arian and Socinian errors," writes Mr. Beach,
"by means of some books written by dissenters in England,
seem of late to gain ground a great pace in this country
among Presbyterians. . . . . . I have therefore adopted Dr.
Johnson's desire and advice and prepared a small piece for
the press, being an "attempt to vindicate Scripture Mysteries,
particularly the Doctrines of the Holy Trinity, the Atone-
ment of Christ, and the Renovation by the Holy Spirit ; also
of the Eternity of the Future Punishment, with some strictures upon what Mr. J. Taylor hath advanced on those points."
This he delivered in the shape of a discourse before the
clergy in 1760, and it was afterwards published with a preface
by Dr. Johnson recommending it as a fit corrective of the
latitudinarian spirit of the times. A previous sermon, called
"An Inquiry Concerning the State of the Dead," was so
misunderstood that the Rev. Mr. Wetmore felt obliged to
call a meeting of the clergy "to look into the affairs of Mr.
Beach's sermon and try to bring him to a better mind."
Dr. Johnson, writing to his son at this time, says : "Truly,
things are come to that pass that he must make some submission to the Society or be discarded, or at least severely
reprimanded, for Hobart [Noah Hobart, pastor of the Church

of Christ at Fairfield] has procured a complaint from their Association against him to the Society which has put them on these measures." Writing to his son a week later, he referred again to Mr. Beach, playfully, as one who "had always those two seeming inconsistencies, to be dying and yet relishing sublunary things." The reprimand, if given, seems not to have been very severe and Mr. Beach subsequently in a measure atoned for his mistake by the publication of a sermon on Scripture Mysteries which received the sanction of his brethren and was introduced to the public with a preface from the pen of Johnson himself.

In a letter from Mr. Beach this November he says:

"Reverend Sir, I beg leave to return my humble thanks to the venerable society for their instruction for our conduct in the late critical conjuncture, when we were in no small danger of becoming a prey to our barbarous enemies, which has had a good effect. Blessed be Almighty God, the snare which they had laid for us is broken, and we are delivered; the divine justice is very apparent in bringing off innocent blood, which in a most shocking manner they have been shedding for more than half a century."

And he cannot resist a little fling at the "train band:"

"My parish is in a flourishing state in all respects, excepting that we have lost some of our young men in the army, more indeed by sickness than by the sword, for this Country men do not bear a campaign so well as Europeans."

In an extract from a letter to the Secretary from the Rev. Mr. Winslow of Stratford, written July 14, 1760, we read: "At a late convention of the clergy of our church in the colony, at New Haven, a sermon was preached by the Rev. Mr. Beach, wherein much to his own reputation and I trust to the credit and advantage to the Church here he has with great zeal and faithfulness endeavored to vindicate and establish the important fundamentals of the Sacred Trinity." . . . [This is the sermon already spoken of.] "You will receive a copy from Dr. Johnson, who speaks of it in the following postscript to a letter to the Secretary from Stratford, the May of 1763: "It is unhappy that the Society's bounty to these Colonies should occasion such intense envy in any, as has of late appeared in two adversaries—as opposite to each other, as they are both to all sober dissenters here, and each to the Church of England. An answer to the first (which was sent to his Grace) done by Mr. Beach is now in press. The other, is Dr. Mayhew of Boston, a rough, ludicrous and audacious man equally disliked by most of the dissenters and us, and equally an enemy to the Trinity—to Loyalty—and to Episcopacy." . . .

Mr. Beach's letters for the next five years are largely descriptive of doctrinal and seditious troubles. In 1764, he writes that the building of small churches at Danbury, Ridgefield, North Fairfield and North Stratford have retarded the growth of the church at Redding. Nevertheless he is able to report an attendance there of three hundred, and in Newtown of from four to five hundred, and he thanks "that excellent gentleman to me unknown who has condescended to take so much notice of us in New England as to vindicate us from the reproaches of Dr. Mayhew in Boston." This was Archbishop Secher, and one of *his* criticisms was that "several members of the Church of England send their children to Harvard College and such a place of worship as their parents approve may be reasonably provided for them without any design of proselyting others. There is indeed a college in New England where students have been forbidden to attend Episcopal service, and a young man has been fined for going to hear his own father, an Episcopal minister, preach." This was young Punderson, the son of the Rev. Mr. Punderson, and the college referred to was Yale. (For particulars regarding these and other such publications prior to the Revolution, see Archaeologica Americana, Vol. VI, pages 307 to 661.) The next year Mr. Beach announces that he is engaged in a "Controversy with some of the Independent ministers about those absurd doctrines, the sum of which is contained in a thesis published by New Haven college last September, in these words, viz : '*Obedientia personalis, non est necessaria ad justificationem.*' They expressly deny that there is any law of Grace, which promises eternal life upon the condition of faith—repentance and sincere obedience ; and assert justification only by the law of innocence and sinless obedience. Though my health is small and my abilities less, I make it my rule never to enter into a dispute with them unless they begin, yet now they have made the assault, and advocate such monstrous errors as do subvert the Gospel, I think myself obliged by my ordination vow to guard the people (as well as I can) against such strange doctrines ; in which work I hope hitherto I have had some success, for the Church people here are very well fortified against both Antinomianism and enthusiasm, both of which rage amongst the Independents; neither are any of my parishioners afflicted in any degree with Deism . . . . "

At the risk of too much letter quotation, the following account is so much more satisfactory thus given in his own direct manner that no other apology is offered for so doing.

NEWTOWN IN CONN. April 22, 1766.

Rev Sir,—My congregations are in a peaceable and growing state, and very free from that seditious spirit which I must, with grief confess, is very epidemical in this country; the punishment of which, I hope, will not involve the innocent with the guilty. For sometime past I have not been without fear of being abused by a lawless set of men who style themselves the Sons of Liberty; for no other reason than that of endeavoring to cherish in my people a quiet submission to the civil government; neither am I yet without fear that we may be put to the dilemma, either to join with or suffer from them; . . . I thought it not foreign from my duty, *just to give a hint* of the anarchy and confusion we are in, but hope it may not be put into the Abstract, lest it should expose me to the rage and violence of the mob. For my part, I should be very thankful if it were agreeable to the wisdom of the Venerable Society, that they would be pleased to direct us how we ought to conduct (ourselves) in this new and melancholy affair.

NEWTOWN—Oct 6th, 1766.

Rev Sir, The death of my nearest neighbor, Mr. Davis, is a very great loss to the Church in Litchfield County, where, for the short time it pleased God to keep him—he gave uncommon satisfaction; he being very pious and prudent, zealous and laborious in the ministry. He was greatly beloved and is now much lamented. Here is one Mr. Sandeman, come from Scotland, who (as I fear) designs to propagate infidelity, libertinism, or no religion, under the mask of *Free Grace*, for, as I have heard him preaching in the Independent's meeting house in this town, I find that the sum and purport of his new doctrine is, that Christ has done all and everything for our salvation which God requires of us, and that mere assent to this report, is saving faith; and to have the least solicitude about anything *we* have to do to obtain Salvation, is that damning sin of unbelief in which all the Christian world, except his sect, is involved.

Where those monstrous tenets are received, there will remain a temptation to wicked men to turn infidels; . . . . Many of the Independents in these parts, both ministers and people, appear to be strongly captivated with this new fashioned Antinomianism, but none

8

of my people show the least inclination toward it, but the greatest detestation of it, and, instead of diminishing—it increases the number of my hearers—who as they continue in love, peace, and unity among themselves, so they steadfastly adhere to the doctrine and worship of the Church of England, while our Independent neighbors are in no small confusion and crumbling into mere parties.

I am Sir etc etc

JOHN BEACH.

April 14, 1768.

Rev Sir,—If I may presume to speak what falls under my observation, the Church people of these parts, are the best affected toward the Government of Great Britain; and the more zealous Churchmen they are, by so much stronger is the affection they discover for King and Parliament upon all occasions, but dissenters here—greatly exceed in numbers. It is very probable that if there were a Bishop among us to confirm and ordain, it would greatly increase the number of clergy and church people, and the fear and dread of the growth of the Church (if I mistake not), is the real source of the opposition which in these parts is made to it. If any of us of the clergy in America discover an aversion to it, it must be an additional argument for its necessity, because none but the disorderly decline Government.

I am Rev Sir etc etc

JOHN BEACH.

A better feeling between denominations is now apparent, and he may be pardoned if in his letters and thoughts this is largely due to his beloved church worship and influence, and in 1771 he rates the number of souls in the two parishes at twenty-four hundred, and a little more than half, under his care. The infirmities consequent on so arduous a life and the suffering therefrom cause him to feel his physical powers lessening. He says: "My most earnest desire is to answer the pious design of the Society, that at last I may be able to give up my account to my blessed Saviour and Judge with joy."

In the death of his first wife, and mother of his children, he found himself somewhat past middle life, bereft of that care and solicitude which had made it possible for him to give his entire attention to his calling. His eldest daughter had married and died; his two sons, John and Lazarus, were married and gone to homes of their own; Sarah and Hannah were dead also, and Lucy married. There was no one to lighten the burden of his declining years, but—without these reasons and explanations we should not be surprised at his re-marriage, for it was no uncommon thing in those days, when a house without a mistress was without its *raison d'être*. So—this second wife. Perhaps other eligible dames of his parish envied the rich widow of John Holbrook her own successful two marriages, and thought she might have been satisfied with wealth alone ; however that may have been, that she remained in Newtown solely on his account is evidenced by her immediate return to Derby after his death. At the marriage of his sons he gives each a farm and we find the deeds recorded in the Land Records of both Newtown and Redding. The stories told of his experiences during the Revolutionary war, had doubtless sufficient foundation, and a letter addressed to him by the justices and selectmen of Redding, speaks for itself. It was found in 1888 among the papers of the late Charles Beach, son of Isaac, son of John, son of Rev. John, and is preserved among the records of Christ church, in the keeping of John Close, Esq., parish clerk.

REDDING, Feb. 12ᵗʰ. 1778.

Rev. Sir, We have no disposition to restrain or limit you or others in matters of conscience, But understanding that you in your Public Worship still continue to pray that the King of Great Britian may be strengthened to vanquish, and overcome all his enemies, which manner of praying must be thought to be a great insult upon the Laws, Authority, and People of this State, as you and others, can but know that the King of England has put the People of these United States from under his protection, Declared them Rebels, and is now at open war with said States, and consequently we are his enemies.

Likewise you must have understood that the American States have declared themselves independent of any Foreign Power.—Now Sir, in order that we may have peace and quietness at home among ourselves, we desire that for the future you would omit praying in Public that King George the third, or any other foreign Prince or Power may vanquish etc. the People of this Land.

Your compliance herewith may prevent you trouble.

We are Rev'd. Sir, with due Respect your Obedient Humble Servants,

To the Revᵈ John Beach.

Justices { Lemˡ Sanford
{ Wᵐ Hawley

Select Men of Redding { Hezᵏ Sanford
{ Seth Sanford
{ Thad. Benedict
{ John Grey
{ Wᵐ Heron

That he went on thus praying and that a posse of soldiers was ordered out and commanded to fire into the church and upon him while so engaged and did so—seems very improbable and yet it is undoubtedly true that many years afterward on taking down the sounding-board a bullet was found embedded therein. This bullet is now placed in the corner of the tablet to his memory in the present church edifice at Redding. It had been in the work-basket of his granddaughter, Sarah Beach Sanford, wife to Squire James, whence by the persuasion of the Rev. Mr. Wilkins, who was rector at the time this tablet was placed, it was extracted and with the consent of the family, given its present honorable position. It is said that the reverend gentleman and staunch loyalist continued his customary prayers with an unfaltering voice. To quote from Bishop Williams (who at the request of the late Dr. Beardsley wrote out the following anecdote, which he related to the clergy assembled in Dr. Marble's study after the service at the opening of the present Trinity church, Newtown).

"In the early summer of 1848, I was travelling with the Rev Dr Rankine, who was at that time studying with me, in what we then called northern New York. Returning from Lake George, we passed down the banks of the Hudson river to visit the scenes of Burgoyne's surrender in 1777. Stopping for the night at an inn in the neighborhood of Schuylerville, perhaps in the place itself, I met an aged man, the father, I think, of the innkeeper, who told me that he was born and passed his early life in Newtown, Connecticut. He also told me he perfectly remembered being in the church at Newtown when soldiers entered, service being then in progress and threatened to shoot the officiating minister, the Rev John Beach, if he read the prayer for the King and the royal family. Mr Beach, he said, went on as usual with no change or even tremor in his voice and read the obnoxious prayers. My informant added that he believed (his recollection on this point was not quite positive) that they, struck with the quiet courage of Mr Beach, stacked their muskets and remained through the service."

This would imply a similar interference in the church at Newtown. Another anecdote may not be out of place. It is said that he was taken out of his house by either the military or some unauthorized enemies and escorted to the foot of the hill, where he was commanded to kneel down and make his last prayer, for they were about to shoot him. He knelt and prayed, not for himself, but for them, to such good effect that whether it was actually meant or not, they were ashamed to continue the scene, and left him, as usual, master of the situation. Mr. Todd says, in speaking of the occurrence at Redding : " The statement concerning the firing into the church is a mistake, and I am assured that the reverse is true. It is said that the church was not molested at all, except that a soldier, with a well directed ball, brought down the gilded weather-cock from the spire, and the fact that the pastor, the Rev. John Beach as well as several of its most prominent members, among them Squire Heron (above referred to), were most pronounced loyalists, strengthens the assertion."

The game old bird, a huge rooster, is still cock of the walk on the barns of the late James Sanford, Esq., son of "Squire James." Quoting in conclusion the closing phrases of Mr. Sanford's sermon :

"Such a life-work could not fail of abundant fruit. His ministry in the Church had now spanned the period between 1732 and the Revolutionary War, and he was a man of threescore and fifteen years. He was worn out with unremitting labors and the wearier endurance of an intolerance and hostility which never slept. He seems by some of his letters at this period to have stood, like Moses on Pisgah, looking back upon the course of his pilgrim-warfare, and wistfully forward to a rest in the heavenly Canaan. And, like Moses, he could justly feel a thankful satisfaction in the present and in the review of the past. Forty years before, he had begun a work here, to human view almost hopeless ; his flock but five families, with no church, and walled round with prejudice. He was alone in all the northwestern quarter of Connecticut, and with but three fellow-laborers in the whole colony, Now he has within his own cure one-half of its whole population, and more than three hundred communicants. All round him is a cordon of parishes ; and one in every thirteen of the population of the colony is a child of that Church for which he has toiled. But though the aged toiler may desire to depart, his work is not yet done ; he has run with *patience* his race, he must end it as a *Christian hero*.

"The time has come when we can afford to deal fairly by the actors on both sides of the strife which severed these colonies from Great Britain, that they might in God's Providence become greater than Britain. In the veins of many, if not most of us, flows commingled the blood of loyalist and patriot, and we may proudly claim that the true men on both sides were loyal to principle and lovers of their country. He was not the less so who looked upon severance from Great Britain as the sure ruin of the colonies, and revolt as grievous sin, than he who was ready to die for principles of free government, which were not universally admitted as correct till established and settled as the rich outcome of that fiery trial.

" Beach, like the most of his brethren, sought by peaceable means to secure concession to the demands of the colonies from the home government; but when war was precipitated his conscience compelled him to stand aloof from revolt against that government—a government to which he was bound at his ordination by a special oath, from which he knew no release but remission by the authority which imposed it.

" With a heart undismayed, though the flesh was tremulous with age, he entered into the storm. He was no hireling to flee, but stayed with his flock, and his flock, won by his love and labor, stood by him. Other pastors fled, and still others closed their churches when the colonies declared their independence, because they dared not use the Liturgy which required them to pray for the rulers they believed to be in legitimate authority. Beach alone quailed not. Though the bitterness which had followed him so long was intensified by the internecine war, he went his way ministering the comforts and counsel which so many sorely needed. Each Lord's day he kneeled in the house of God, ' and prayed as he did aforetime ;' the threat of death once and again blanched not his cheek nor hushed his voice. The crack of the rifle and the whirr of the bullet neither stirred nor stopped him as in the holy house he delivered his Master's message.

" At length, when those years of strife were almost done, at fourscore years and two, the poor worn out body could no longer retain the heroic soul. In truth and fitness, as he passed from earth, might *he* use the words, too high for *most* mortal lips : ' I have fought a good fight, I have finished my course, I have kept the faith : Henceforth there is laid up for me a crown of righteousness, which the Lord, the righteous judge, shall give me at that day.'

" The four tablets to the memory of Revs. John Beach and Philo Perry, and Drs. Burhans and Marble are very elaborate in design and detail. Each one has been made after a different design, conforming each to the character of the time in which the clergyman lived. They are the fitting consummation of all the work of the artist who has designed the whole, and, though occupying but a comparatively small space, are the most artistic and valuable decoration in the church. It is rarely that so costly tablets are placed in a church four at once, and it is interesting to notice the means that have been taken to have them of different appearance.

" In Rev. John Beach's tablet, most of the decoration is in the stone. The brasswork is simply a polished plate with the inscription, and but slight ornament. The letters of Rev. John Beach's tablet are in black enamel, in keeping with his times, but the others are in black, red, and blue."

It reads :

"To the blessed memory of Rev. John Beach, A.M. Founder of this parish. Born at Stratford, Conn., MDCC. Graduated at Yale College, A. D. MDCCXXI. At great sacrifice, upon thorough investigation and deep conviction, conforming to the Church of England, he was admitted to Holy Orders in England, A. D. MDCCXXXII, and appointed Missionary at Newtown and Reading, of the Venerable Society for the Propagation of the Gospel.

"He was a scholar thorough, a reasoner cogent, a controversialist able, a preacher persuasive, a pastor untiring, a Christian hero undaunted. He was of all most effective in laying deep and broad the foundation of the Church in the Colony of Connecticut. From the beginning of his ministry assailed by bitter intolerance and pursued by malicious plottings he patiently endured. In the added perils of a cruel war remaining with his flock, he continued his ministrations at the constant risk of threatened violence and death. Full of years and labors, he entered into rest, March 19, MDCCLXXXII, uttering, shortly before he ceased to be mortal, the words, ' I have fought a good fight.' "

EPITAPH ON HIS TOMBSTONE.

"Here lyeth interred the earthly remains of the Revd. John Beach, A. M., late Missionary from the Venerable Society for the propagation of the Gospel in foreign parts, who exchanged this life for immortality on the 19th day of March, 1782, in the 82d year of his age & 61st year of his ministry.

> The sweet remembrance of the just
> Shall flourish when he sleeps in dust.

Reader, let this tablet abide."

Extract from sermon delivered at Christ Church, Stratford, by Rev. Dr. Beardsley :

"BEACH! I have never thought, my brethren, that ample justice was done to his name on the pages of our history. He was scarcely inferior in strength of intellect, in knowledge of the church, in the toils and trials of his vocation, to him who has been justly styled the 'father of Episcopacy in Connecticut.' Indeed, after Johnson removed to New York, and served the church in the presidency of King's (now Columbia) college, Beach was our chief defender, and wielded the pen of controversy and exposed the schemes of his adversaries, both with skill and power. He kept his eye upon every rood of ground where the seed had been sown, and as fearless as faultless, traveled by night and by day, amid storms and snow drifts and across deep and rushing streams, to preach the word, to visit and comfort the sick, and to bury the dead. He remained at his post when the terrors of the Revolution came, and alone of all the clergy in the colony refused to close his church and pray the prayers of the liturgy."

Vol. I, p. 1.
"Rev. John Beach's Will. Probate Court records, Danbury, Ct.

"In the name of God Amen, I John Beach of Newtown in the County of Fairfield & Colony of Connecticut, New England, being of sound mind & memory and calling to mind my mortality, do make & ordain this my last Will and Testament.

"In the first place I resign myself to the infinite mercies of Almighty God, the blefsed author of my being, with an affurd hope of a resurrection to eternal life through Jesus Christ my only Saviour. My earthly remains I would have buried according to the Lithurgie of the Church of England. As to such worldly goods which it hath pleased God to betrust me with [after my just debts and funeral expenses are paid] I will give and bequeath in the following manner.

"Imprimis, I give to my beloved wife Abigail thirty pounds lawful money, one half of my linnen, all the Goods which fhe brought to my house, and what ever she hath since purchased, and one Silver Tankard marked A × B. a warming pan &c. The reason of my giving her no more is because fince our marriage I have given her a certain fum annually.

"*Item*, I give to my fon John Beach his Heirs and assigns forever, my house, barn, home lot and all my lands in Newtown, excepting my 150 acres at Hopewell.

"*Item*, I give to my son Lazarus Beach, his heirs and afsigns forever, all my land in Redding townfhip & my 150 acres at Hopewell with-in the bounds of said Newtown.

"*Item*, I give to each of my Congregations viz, at Newtown and Redding, ten pounds for the purpofe of settling another minister.

"*Item*, I give ten pounds to be laid out in Bibles and to be given to the poor of each of my said Congregations according to the difcretion of my Executors. The rest of my Estate I give to my fons John Beach, Lazarus Beach, my daughter Lucy Townsend, and my grand son Abel Hill to be equally divided between them. And I appoint my sons John & Lazarus to be executors of this my last Will and Testament; in which I have aimed to do right impartially to each of my Heirs and defire (if it may be) that my said heirs would agree to divide the little I leave them, with out calling in any foreign Afsiftance. In Confirmation of all which I have here unto set my hand and Seal this eleventh day of May 1772

Signed, sealed, pronounced and   John Beach { seal }
    declared in presence of
Henry Glover
Elias Glover
Sufanna Glover Jun'

THE
NEW YORK
PUBLIC LIBRARY

Aster, Lenox and Tilden
Foundations.
1901.

Newtoun January y 7th AD 1782 Thus are
to Inform all people to whom it may
Conceearn that sr John Beach of Newtou
In Fairfield County minister of the Gospel
in the Church of England in sd Town
Do By these present forever Discharge
all my parritimers & Every of them
from all Rates & Taxees that is or Ever
hath Bean due to me on acount of my
Preaching in sd Town to them or Either
of them and they are Hearby Discharge
from any demands from me or my heairs
on them or Eithier of them from the Begin-ing
of the world untill this Discharge
as witness my hand In Presenc off

Peter Nichols
Reuben Booth

John Beach
missionary

"At a Court of Probate held in Danbury for the District of Danbury, April 3ʳᵈ A. D 1782 —Present Joseph P Cook, Esqr.

Judge.

" Lazarus Beach one of the Executors named in the foregoing Will, exhibited the same for Probation, and accepted the Trust repofed in him by the Teftator : said Will being proved is by said Court approved and ordered to be recorded.   '

Test.   Joseph P. Cook Junʳ Clerk

"A true Record of the original Will

`   Test.   Joseph P Cook Junʳ, Clerk"

I have lately been presented with two pieces of the handwriting of the missionary. One a MSS. sermon, dated Sepᵗ 12, 1759, with the text from " Thess. 2, 12—That ye would walk worthy of God who hath called ye into his Kingdom," and is headed, " Wars, Advent, etc." The ink is faded and the paper brown with age, but the few leaves have been carefully pasted together by the loving hand of his descendant, Mrs. Elizabeth Sheldon Peck, among whose papers it was found. There is a little sprig of arbor vitæ pinned in the cover, evidently from the tree near his grave, and written in Mrs. Peck's own hand, " Buried at Newtown, Connecticut, near the monuments of Doctʳ Burhans and Rev. Joseph Perry." The other is the last receipt for his salary and is copied herein. This was given me by Mr. Charles H. Peck of Newtown, who though not a descendant, has been deeply interested and a valuable contributor toward the compiling of this book. The difference in the handwriting between 1759 and 1782 is not so marked as might be expected.

The Rev. G. Morris Wilkins, now of The Bible House, New York City, is in possession of a most uncomfortable high back chair which is said to have belonged to the Rev. John Beach. The late Mrs. David Johnson (Rebecca Beers) of Newtown, had collected many old family pieces which were unfortunately lost sight of after her death. Probably they are now scattered and beyond hope of special recognition.

Mr. Wilkins was at the time of his rectorship, very much interested in the parish, and its greatest advances of the last half century were made in that interval.

BEACH IN ENGLAND.

It is noticeable in many genealogies that branches of the same family often fail in establishing immediate connection. Throughout Burke, Dugdale, and others, such phrases as "probably descended from," and "this family is undoubtedly the same as" etc., seem to suffice for all purposes of claimants. Be that as it may, the few English notes and gatherings given here, are for the benefit of the Anglo-maniac who may wish to pursue them further. In Hoare's Modern Wilts we read, "This family of *Beche* or *Beach*, derives, according to tradition, its descent from the ancient and respectable family De La Beche, lords of Aldworth in the County of Berks, of which a particular account is inserted in Dugdale's Baronetage, Vol. II, p. 127 ; and in the visitation of the said county, taken by Elias Ashmole, Esq., Windsor Herald, 1664, there are drawings of the effigies of four knights of the family still extant in the parish church of Aldworth. The immediate ancestor of this branch of the family, seated at Warminster, in County of Wilts, was undoubtedly Robert Beche, of Warminster, of whose will, in Latin, a copy is preserved in Prerogative Court of Canterbury ; it is dated 19th May, 1519." The following quotations are copied from the admirably arranged MSS. of the late Dr. J. Wyckliffe Beach of New Haven, whose interested enquiries led him to make careful notes and to put together all such information. Dr. Beach was a descendant of Thomas of Milford, of whom further.

" From the Collectanea Tipographica et Genealogica, Vol. I, p. 368 & 9.
" From the Cartulary of the Abbey at Haghmon, co. Salop, England.
" Wm. De La Beche gave lands (to the Abbey) in Eaton Mascott, co. Salop. . . . . .
" Walter de Clifford gave the Church in Culminton, co. Salop, a virgate of land in Siditonia which Master Roger de Beche held, rendering him 5ˢ annually, and the deed was witnessed by Robert de la Beche " Master Roger his brother." Neither of these items is dated, but they are entered along with other matter dated variously from A. D. 1200 to 1400. Vol. V, p. 169—Elizabeth de la Beche daughter of William and Euphemia Comyne, married Sir Roger Elmerugge, son of Roger Elmerugge. Roger Jr. was aged 16 in 1328. [Then follows a little chart of Edmund Comyne of Sanscomb, Herts, and his two daughters, Euphemia and Mary, the former marrying William De La Beche, and having daughter Elizabeth.]

Vol. 7, p. 121, John de la Beche is recorded as an armed man, belonging in the Hundrith of Nedderfield, in a list of men returned as liable to serve the King under arms from the Pale of Hastings in the 13th year of Edward III, 1339-40. It was apparently in Sussex. Vol. IV, p. 144, Reginald de Beche as receiving land which had been property of his brother Walter, deeded him by Will de Hucha in consideration of his having paid 3 talents of gold.

From the age of Hugo de Londresford, who witnessed the deed and who died in 1203, we infer the age of the document. On p. 153, Reginald de Beche witnesses a deed of Thomas Aleyn owning fealty to Simon de Londresford who was by the pedigree, grandson to the above Hugo. This family was of Sussex county.

In Calendarium Genealogicum, Harv. Coll. Lib., giving the genealogical matters to be found in the Inquisitiones post mortem during the reigns of Henry III and Edward I, p. 764, appears the following " m—15—d [Roger de la Beche. Inquiry after his death, Galfridus son of said Roger is his next heir and is 15 years old (the Inquiry was made on the day of Mars after the feast of St. Peter in Cathedra in the 22nd year of Edward I, in Berkshire.)" This had been cancelled in the record and labelled "vacat quia est de anno 22 et ibi irraturlatur." " m—16. Thomas de la Beche, inquiry after his death—Galfridus, son of Roger, brother of said Thomas is next heir of said Thomas, and is of the age of 14 years and more." At Oxford—year 21,—Edward I.

From Burke—1847, p. 73,—"Thomas Beach of Warminster, Co. Wilts, who died in 1576, left by Agnes Stanlock his wife, a son William of Brixton Deverell, and Fittleton, co. Wilts, who married in 1657 Mary, sister of John Gifford, Esq. of Aldhampton and had a son and heir William who married in 1679. . . . was ancestor of Henrietta Maria Beach who married Oct. 7, 1779 Michael Hicks, the latter assumed the surname of Hicks-Beach by royal sign manual of June 23, 1790."

The present William Beach of Oakley Hall, Hants and Keevil House, county Wilts, who was born July 24, 1783, was a descendant of the latter, dropped the Hicks by sign manual in 1828, and is simply William Beach, Esq.*

Beach of Brandon Lodge, co. Warwick is described in Burke, 3rd and 4th edition.

* There is some error here, as the following taken directly from the Church records at Warminster will show.—Thomas and Agnes Stanlock—son William, born at Warminster, Oct. 5, 1567, buried at Brixton Deverell, Jan. 29, 1646/7, m. *Jane*, sister to Clement Adlam (same place)—son William of Brixton Deverell, Fittleton and Keevil, baptised at Warminster, July 30, 1603, buried at Fittleton (or Fitledean) 6 May, 1686, m Mary Gifford of Alhampton, co. Somerset, also buried at Fittleton, March 30, 1693, son William, b at Brixton Deverell, Jan. 4, 1655, died Aug. 24, 1741 at Keevil, m Anne, daughter of Rev. Gilbert Wither, who was buried at Keevil, April 9, 1742, a. 80. Daughter Henrietta, Maria, etc.

In Hoare's History of South Wilts 1825, it is stated that the Thomas Beach buried at Warminster in 1576 who was the ancestor of Hicks-Beach etc., etc. (as already quoted).

From Dugdale's Baronage 1676, Col. 2, p. 127—the family of De la Beche whose chief seat was at Aldworth in co. Berkshire, John is mentioned in 9th. Edward II, as having license free warren in all his demesne lands at Bastelden, Alhampton and Aldworth and in 11th Edward II, another for his lordships of Patingden, Everington, Hampsted, Woden-Hampsted, and Sumpton, all in the same County, and in 12th Edward II, had license for market, etc.

Contemporary with this John was Nicholas de la Beche who in 12th Edward II had charter for Free Warren, in his eight Lordships in Sussex co., and in 15th Edward II, governor of Montgomery Castle in the Marches of Wales, also of the Castle of Plecy in Sussex co. This Sir Nicholas was constable of the Tower of London in 13th Edward III, and incurred the displeasure of the King, but not long in disgrace.

Was in the wars of Brittany, and in 17th Edward III was made Seneschal Gascoine. Was summoned to Parliament in 16th Edward III, and died in 20 or 21 same reign, whereupon his widow married Sir Thomas de Ardene, Knight,—Brother, as Dugdale guesses, of this Sir Nicholas, was Philip de la Beche, to whom in 9th Edward III together with Nicholas, a charter for free warren was granted in their demesne lands in Co. Berkshire, but had no summons to Parliament."

Here the manuscript of Dr. Beach so far as English notes are concerned, ends. It may be interesting to quote from Agnes Strickland's "Queens of England" one or two stories of this Sir Nicholas de la Beche. (vol. 2, p. 133 and 183.)

" While the warlike Edward III was gaining the so far greatest naval victory of the English over France,—the battle of Blankenburg in 1340, Philippa, his queen, gave birth to her fourth son at Ghent (John of Gaunt, duke of Lancaster).

" The king hastened to embrace them and owing to this victory and the influence of the queen's mother, hostilities were in abeyance.

"They found themselves much in debt, however, and the king actually accepted the offer of his kinsman, the Earl of Derby, to surrender his person to the royal creditors, while he and his queen stole away to Zealand. Here he embarked with Philippa and the infant John of Gaunt, attended by a few servants. The ship was small, the weather stormy, and the royal passengers were in frequent danger of losing their lives; however, at midnight, December 2, 1340, they landed safely on Tower wharf. Here the king found that three nurses, and the rest of the royal children, constituted the sole garrison of his regal fortress of the Tower; the careless constable, Nicholas de la

Beche, had decamped that evening to visit a ladylove in the city, and his warders and soldiers, following so good an example, had actually left the Tower to take care of itself. The great Edward, who was not in the mildest of tempers owing to the untoward state of his finances, took possession of the fortress of his capital in a towering rage. As his return was wholly unexpected, the consternation of constable de la Beche may be supposed, when he had concluded his city visit. It was well for the careless castellan, that the gentle Philippa was by the side of her incensed lord, at that juncture."

And on page 133, on a list of presents when the king and queen kept Twelfth night, we read,—"To sir Nicholas de Becke, sir Humphrey de Luttlebury, and sir Thomas de Latimer, for dragging the king out of bed on Easter morning, Edward paid twenty pounds."

When in Wiltshire, in the summer of 1896, many local evidences of this branch of the family were found, both in church and state. The dates given in the footnote concerning Thomas and his descendants were copied from the old Minster records in Warminster, Wilts; In addition to those were :—Elizabeth, daughter to William Beach, born July 7, 1599, and John B. and William, sons to the same, born Aug. 16, 1601, and July 30, 1603.

BIRTHS OF BEACH'S IN CHURCH RECORDS.

John—June 22, 1557 } probably entered twice
"   "   2, 1558 } and a correction.
William—Oct. 5, 1567—Son of Thomas
Robert—May 28, 1567—married Mary Holbrook
Elizabeth—May 13, 1569—
Elinor—Nov. 28, 1571—died April 18, 1572.

The marriage of Thomas and Agnes Stanlock is entered as Jan. 27, 1562. Other marriages, probably all the same family, were :—

John Beach and Julian Stanlock (sister to Agnes), April 24, 1559.
Elizabeth Beach married (1603-Mar. 1) Henry Carsey.
Mary (Holbrook) Beach—widow of aforesaid Robert (referring to birth-date above), July 16, 1593—to John Smart.

DEATHS.

John—Jan. 24, 1559
Thomas—July 10, 1559
John"-gent—Apr. 24, 1573 (of whom further)
Thomas—Oct. 11, 1576
Julian (wife of John)—June 14, 1579.

In "The Poll of the Freeholders of Wiltshire for electing a Knight of the shire" in the room of Edward Popham Esq. taken at Wilton on 18th 19th 20th and 21st of August 1772, "William Beach lives in the Parish of Figledean." This little book is in the Library of the Archæological museum at Devises. In another magazine, shortly before published by Edward Kite for the Congress of the British Archæological Society held at Devises in 1880, on page 47, we find "The present manor house (Keevil) with its mullioned windows and gables belongs either to the Elizabethan or Jacobean period. It was built probably by some of the Lambert family, and has since for many generations been the property of the family of Beach of Netheravon and Keevil. The present lord of the manor is William W. B. Beach, Esq., M. P., of Oakley Hall, Hants." And again, page 83, "Netheravon, formerly a seat of the Dukes of Beaufort, has long been the property of the Beach family." The church, dedicated to All Saints, consists of chancel, nave, aisles, and a western tower. The west doorway is a fine specimen of Norman architecture. The Parish register commences 1582, and the two oldest bells were cast about the same date. One is inscribed "Oh man be meke, and live in rest;" the other, "In God is all my hope and trust." The remaining three belong to the next century.

In Daniel's History of Warminster, Harold's visitations (pg. 53)—"In the visitation of 1565, only the name of Perry, of Warminster, is recorded as one to whom his pedigree and arms were allowed by the Heralds; John Beche, having borne arms and taken on him the name and title of an Esquire or Gentleman, but not being able to show any good rights to either of those titles or to any arms belonging to him, appeared before the Clarenceux King-at-Arms, and promised to forbear the use of all such attributes, and disclaimed the name of a Gentleman." On pps. 39 and 40, however, speaking of lands at Newport and Portway, same county, the will of a Richard Middlecott is spoken of, and "He died 37 Elizabeth,

1595, when an inquest was taken on behalf of his son and heir, William, aged 37 : the Escheators were—Thomas Gifford, Gent., Christ. Eyer, Gent., W^m. Perye, Gent., *John Beche*, Gent.,—*cum aliis ignobilibus.*"

This is the "John Beach, sr. gent.," whose death is recorded in 1573. He may have been the husband to Julian Stanlock, whose death occurs five years later, not as *widow*, however, but *wife* of John Beach.

Attention is directed to the abstract of English wills, contributed to the New England Historical and Genealogical Magazine, continued at present by Mr. William Brigg of Harpenden, St. Albans, Herts, through whose kindness, when in England, I was enabled to secure information from sources not usually open to the uninitiated.

There were and are Beaches in Hertfordshire. A John and a Richard born in St. Albans, brothers, 1590 and 1601, and another pair, similarly named and related, 1625 and 1627. The first are too early and the second are too late for our dates. Richard was already married in New Haven in 1640 (to the widow Hull), and though John might be made to fit, it is hardly probable that at 16 years of age he was a full-fledged freeman. Mr. Brigg has, however, some notes of this family, if any one should wish to consult him. In a little publication called the Pilgrim Fathers of Nazing in Essex, I found the marriage in 1627 of a John Beech and Marye Curtiss, both of Waltham Abbey, and a Henry Beach as a freeholder in Nazing, Essex county.

These are, I think, all the odds and ends picked up in a rather desultory progress in the counties of Wilts, Shropshire, and Herts, together with some gleanings at the Library of the British Museum in London. They are presented in their crude condition and without apology, simply for reference.

BEACH IN RECORDS OF NEW HAVEN COLONY.

Of the traditional three brothers Richard, John and Thomas, Richard appears first on the New Haven Colony Records. "The 4ᵗʰ day of the 4ᵗʰ moneth called June 1639," Mr. Thomas Fugill writes: "All the free planters assembled together in a general meetinge to consult about settling Ciuill Governmᵗ according to God. . . . " This meeting was held in a large barn, which authorities have located on or near Temple street somewhere between Elm and Grove, and belonging to Mr. Robert Newman. Mr. Davenport "haveing propounded divers quæres" and carefully explained that what they were about to do would stand on record for posterity, Mr. Newman then stood up and read the same. To the first quæry—whether the "Scripturs doe holde a perfect rule for the directiō and gouernmᵗ of all men in all duet(ies) wᶜʰ they are to performe to God and men, as well in the gouernmᵗ of famylyes and comͫonwealths as in matters of the Chur" they all agreed. This being the groundwork of that simple and strict code of laws by which our early Connecticut fathers lived and died, it may be well to notice that one man—more bold or more experienced in such matters—dared to dissent. He agreed that "magistrates should be men fearing God"—that "the Church is the company where *ordinarily* such men may be expected." "Thatt they that chuse them ought to be men fearing God. Only at this he stuck, that the free planters ought not to give this power out of their hands." One trembles to think what might have happened to this colony, and what different records we might now be quoting, had the Rev. Samuel Eaton's advice then prevailed; he was, however, but one among the many, and so they voted, "that church members only shall be free burgesses, and that they onely shall chuse magistrates & officers among themselves to have the power of transacting all the public ciuil affayres of this Plantatiō, of makeing and repealing lawes, devideing of inheritances—decideing of differences thatt may arise—and doeing all things or businesses of like nature." Richard Beach came in at the second quæry and with "John Clarke Andrew Low Goodman Banister Ar(thur) Halbridge John Potter Robᵗ Hill John Brockett and John Johnson—these persons being not (ad)mitted planters when the couenᵗ was made, doth now express their consent to itt." The next mention of Richard is not until the following year, when his name appears on the list of fines : at "A court holden the 3rd of April 1640—"It is ordered that John Mosse, Timothy Forde and Richard Beach shall pay each of them 1ˢ fine for trees which they did fall disorderly."

At the "9th moneth" session of that same year (1640), a certain Arthur Halbidg—variously spelled—having been charged at a previous court with "falce" measure in lime, is again brought forward to prove his innocence, and Edward Adams, his accuser, testifies anew against him "wch when he had donne Arthur Halbidg excepted against itt, thinking to prove the said Edward Adams a pjured pson. Butt Goodman Pigge, Rich; Beach and John Wakefield affirmed the truth of what Edward Adams had testified (though the said Arthur Holbidg did conceive they would have contradicted Edʷ Adams his testimony), Itt was therefore ordered that the said Arthur should pay two folde for all the want of measure that is charged vpō him, and from henceforthe take noe work by the great, nor burn any lime to sell." Nevertheless two years later at "A court held the 5ᵗ Day of the 6ᵗ Moneth—1642, Richard Beach for nott perfor'ing covenant in the worke wch he undertooke to doe att the mill, wch he was to doe strongly and substantially, butt did itt weakely and sleightly as was *was* proved by the testimony of John Wakefield the miller, himselfe allso nott denyinge itt; Itt was ordered that he should make good the damage butt because the damage is not justly known what itt is, Mr Goodyeare and Mr Gregson are to ve (view) the worke, and consider off and sett downe the damage by his (defect)ive workmanship " . . . . So we find constantly through these pages—he who escapes *one* day lives but to come under the leash the next.

We first find John on these Records in the January of 1643, when he is fined " 2ˢ for twice late coming," and another 2ˢ for " defect' gun." He is in very good company, however, as " Isaac Whitehead, Richard Newman, Jonathan Marsh & others," as well as " Ric Beach" are likewise fined for similar offences. In the fourth month of the same year, we read the following story : " Joh. Beach haveing killed a cow of George Smyths wth the falling of a tree, the said George required satisfactiō, forasmuch as he conceiveth thatt the said John

9

Beach alleadged for himselfe, thatt he did nott doe itt negli-
gently, for he being falling a tree, there came some cowes
about him, and the tree in the falling did rest upon the bowes
of another tree thatt stoode neare, and then he left the tree,
and drave away the cowes as he did conceive wthout the reach
of the tree, and in the meane time some goates coming vnder
the tree, he retourned to drive them away allso, and then came
in haste to give 3 or 4 chops att the tree to hasten the falling
of itt before the cattell could come againe.   Butt itt was testi-
fyed by brother Andrews and brother Thompson (who were
intreated to *veiw* the cow and the place,) thatt he had nott
done whatt in reason he might and ought to have done to
pr'serve the cattell," . . . . and so on with much circumlocution, "vpon all of w'h testimony i(t) was ordered thatt the
said John Beach shall make good the damage to the vallue of
5¹, wch price Georg Smyth sett vpon his cow wth much mod-
eratiō, though she was really worth more."

The Court in those early days was not chary of its opinions, and in the distribution of its punishments gave much
incidental advice.

John and Richard both appear on the list of those to whom
Governor Eaton administered the oath of fidelity, at a meeting
.of the "Genˡˡ Court held att Newhaven the 1ᵗ of July 1644."

At the October session of the Court for 1645, "Michael
Palmer complayned that Richard Beach did promise to pay
him a debt of 35ˢ in beaver, but had fayled.   Richard Beach
acknowledged the debt & his promise to pay beaver, but pro-
fessed he could not gett beaver.

The court ordered that Richard Beach should pay the debt
in some other paye so as it maye equal beaver, to the said
Palmer's satisfaction (with damadges for forbearance) before
the next Courte, or elce an executeon shall goe forth agaynst
him" . . . .

We come now to an important crisis in the affairs of Richard, as the following item will explain:

"Richard Beach hath sould his owne howse to bro: Wᵐ
Pecke, & where-as the said howse was sugaged for the securetie of the portions of the children of Andrew Hull *(whose
widdow he marryed)* in lieu thereof he hath now *in*gaged his
howse, barne, cellar & well, vallewed at 40£ w'h the 7 acres of
land on wch it stands, the howse, barne, & cellar being com-

pleatly finished being built with bricke and stonne as he promiseth and so kept in repaire & the land in hart for securityc of the portions of the said children."

Later, added in the March of 1647, there is a "Thomas Beech" also. After several mentions of little moment, we find that *John* becomes a householder in 1647, when "Arthur Halbich passeth over to John Beech his house and home lott wth all his accomodations thereto belonging wthin New-haven." That same year, at a previous meeting, he had become suretie with Richard for five pounds worth of land in the interest of the Iles estate, which Richard was set-tling. It is accepted "wth this proviso thatt if John Beach should die or leave the town, Richard Beach put in other securetie to the Court's satisfaction." In connection with the settlement of this estate, Richard calls him "my *cousin* William Iles."

Thomas is twice fined 1ˢ for a defective gun. The Milford Records (of which later) give us more information of this brother.

In 1648 Richard becomes the owner of an additional shore lot. "John Moss passeth ouer to Richard Beech 1 acʳ, 1 quarter & 14 rod of meddowe lying in the West meddowe, one end abutting on the West River, the other end running into a cove in the vpland, betwixt the meddowe of Richard Beach and James Russell." . . . . . .

This is the "small pec." (piece) "of meddow in a cove on ye west side next his owne" which he had already tried to obtain from an earlier court, and been told was "lotted out alreadie." These meadow lands must have been much in demand, for very shortly we find him passing "ouer to Mathew Moulthrop one acʳ and a halfe of meddow lying 1 acʳ of it in ye West meddow on this sid ye river fronts vpon Mr Lam-berton's vpland, ye reare to ye river a highway through ye meddow to ye north, Mathew Moulthrop on ye south ½ acʳ in Sollatary Cove, nott laid out."

Matthew Moulthrop immediately passes this over to "Hen. Glover."

In 1649, "At a Generall Court for Newheven ye 12ᵗʰ of November, 1649, ... The orderes of the laste Generall Courte for ye Jurisdiction were reade. Mr. Thomas Yale and John Beech had libbertee to deppte the Court."

Last entry on New Haven Colony Records. Nothing in Vol. II.

"John Beach came to Stratford and bought his first land here May 21, 1660, of Ens' Bryan of Milford, one house lot 2 acres; he had then a wife and four children. In January 1671 he was made an auctioneer by the following vote: "John Beach was chosen Crier for the town, and to be allowed fourpence for everything he cries, that is to say for all sorts of cattle and all other things of smaller value, two years." This we read in Orcutt. Whether lost children were the "things of smaller value" does not appear.

"Benjamin Beach, son of Richard of New Haven, came to Stratford a single man."

John's name appears on both the first list of home lots in Stratford in 1660, and as an "inhabitant" on the list of 1668, which last was drawn up by the Governor's order, to straighten out church difficulties, and discover voting rights. Many on this list are "outlivers," and so not allowed a voice. In 1678, on the project of a new meeting house, five places were mentioned as suitable, "first in the street by the pond, 2ndly in the street by the northwest corner of widow Peat's lot; 3rdly in the street between Mr. Hawley and John Beach (their home lots); 4thly in ye street between Caleb Nichols and Daniel Beardslee; 5th upon the hill called 'Watch House Hill.'" Decided by lot, the choice of "Watch House Hill" is made, and Captn Wm. Curtis, Sergt. Jerema. Judson, John Curtis, Sergt. Jehiel Preston and John Birdsey, Jr., are a building committee. In 1699, another Proprietors' Rights list is ordered to be "Recorded for the future benefit and peace of the Town" (Stratford). On this John Beach is credited with 12 acres and "8 acres within five miles." That he was also a large land-holder in Wallingford we shall see later.

ANCESTRY IN CONNECTICUT.

John married in 1650 Mary, and had ten children.

1. ELIZABETH, b. March 8, 1652; m. Eliasaph Preston, the son of William Preston, one of the first settlers of New Haven.
2. JOHN, b. April, 1654; m. in 1679, Hannah Staples, the daughter of Thomas, of Fairfield.
3. MARY, b. Sept., 1656.
4. THOMAS, b. May, 1659; m. 1st, Ruth Peck; 2nd, Phebe Wilcoxson.
5. NATHANIEL, b. March, 1662; m. April 29, 1686 Sarah Porter.
6. HANNAH, b. Dec., 1665; m. 1st, Zechariah Fairchild; 2nd, John Burit.
7. SARAH, b. Nov., 1667.
8. ISAAC, b. June 29 (27 ?), 1669; m. 1693, Hannah Birdsey, b. Feb., 1671.
9. JOSEPH, b. Feb. 5, 1671; m. Abia Booth.
10. BENJAMIN, b. March, 1674; m. Mary Hitchcock.

The children of Elizabeth and Eliasaph Preston were : Elizabeth, b. Jan. 29, 1676 ; Hannah, b. July 12, 1678 ; Eliasaph, b. Jan. 26, 1679–80 ; Joseph, b. March 10, 1681–2 ; Esther, b. Feb. 28, 1683–4 ; Lydia, b. May 25, 1686 ; and Jehiel, b. Aug. 25, 1688, d. Nov., 1689.

The Prestons were early in New Haven. William was twice married ; his second wife, a Seabrook of Stratford, daughter of Robert, was the mother of Eliasaph and Hackaliah, twins, born April 7th, 1643. Eliasaph had been formerly married to Mrs. Mary (——) Kimberly, the widow of Thomas Kimberly, one of the first marshals of New Haven County. Eliasaph Preston removed to Wallingford about 1674. He was the first deacon of the Congregational church in that place.

John Beach, Jr., married Hannah Staples, the daughter of Thomas and Mary Staples, in 1679. Their children, recorded at Stratford, were : Mary, b. July 14, 1683, m. 1st, in June, 1704, Archibald Dunlap, and 2nd, —— Smith ; Ruth, b. about 1685, m. Samuel Fairchild in 1704; Mehitable, b. Sept. 30, 1690 ; Ebenezer, b. Sept. 14, 1692, m. 1715 ; Mehitabel Gibson and had eight children ; Hester, b. May 3, 1694.

John Beach, Jr., died in Stratford in 1712. Thomas Staples was one of the first five settlers of Fairfield, freeman 1669. By his wife Mary he had Thomas, John, and daughter Mary, who was the second wife of Josiah Harvey; Hannah, who married John Beach, and Mehitable, who married Rev. Jonathan Fanton. He was a man of remarkable energy of character and importance in the town of Fairfield. Resided on the southwest side of Ludlow Square and was a large landholder. He died before 1698. The Widow Mary, in her will dated 1696, mentions sons Thomas and John ; Mary, wife of Josiah Harvey ; Hannah, wife of John Beach ; granddaughter Hannah Harvey, grandchild Mehitable Fanton, loving friend Mary Hanson, and leaves a book to Ab^m. Gold by Dr. Preston. The Staples family appear to have largely settled at Green's Farms and Westport.

Thomas Beach, the second son was married twice, first to Ruth Peck, a sister of John Peck, second to Phebe Wilcoxson, daughter of Timothy. He had twelve children, four by his first wife. Their names were : Hannah, b. Feb. 26, 1680, d. Sept. 18, 1683 ; Ruth, b. Oct. 24, 1684, m. —— Fairchild ; Thomas, b. Dec. 9, 1685, d. Dec. 13, 1685 ; Benoni, b. Oct. 20, 1686, d. Dec. 5, 1686.

Mrs. Ruth Beach died Dec. 5, 1686. The eight by his second wife were as follows : Timothy, b. Jan. 11, 1689, m. Hannah Cook ; Nathan, b. Aug. 18, 1692, m. Jemimah Curtiss ; Moses, b. Feb. 19, 1695, m. 1st, Esther Tyler, 2nd, Susanna ——; Gershom, b. May 23, 1697, m. Deliverance How ; Caleb, b. ——, 1699, m. Eunice ; Thankful, b. Sept. 20, 1702, m. —— Baldwin ; Phebe, b. May 23, 1705, m. —— Tyler ; Joanna, b. Oct. 9, 1710, m. Abel (?) Royce.

Mr. Thomas Beach died in Meriden, where he was buried in the old cemetery May 13, 1741, aged 82 years. The sons were all Wallingford settlers.

Phebe Wilcoxson was the daughter of Timothy Wilcoxson and Joanna Birdsey. She was born in 1669. Her father was the son of William, an original proprietor of Stratford, whose house lot was situated about where Mrs. Turk's now lies (1863) and probably covered Mr. Wm. Benjamin's lot beside. Phebe's mother was Joanna, daughter of Deacon John Birdsey.

Nathaniel, the third son of Pilgrim John, married 1686 Sarah Porter, the daughter of Nathaniel and Sarah (Groves) Porter. They had ten children : Ephraim, b. May 25, 1687, m. 1712, Sarah Patterson, daughter of Andrew ; Elizabeth, b. Nov. 11, 1689 ; David, b. May 15, 1892, m. 1717, Hannah Sherman, daughter of Matthew, son of Samuel, senior ; Josiah, b.

Aug. 18, 1694, m. 1st, Patience Nichols in 1721, 2nd, Abigail Wheeler in 1750; Nathaniel, b. Dec. 22, 1696, m. 1720, Sarah, daughter of Solomon Burton; Sarah, b. Nov. 12, 1699, m. 1726, her first cousin, the Rev. John Beach; Daniel, b. Jan. 15, 1700, m. 1724, Hester, bap. 1706, daughter of Benj. Curtiss, son of John[2], son of John[1]; Anna, b. March, 1704, m. 1728, Elnathan Beers; Israel, b. May, 1705, m. 1731, Hannah Burrit, daughter of Joseph, son of John, son of William; James, b. Aug. 13, 1709, m. Sarah Curtis, b. Sept. 2, 1710, daughter of John, son of Benj., son of John[2].

Nathaniel's family settled mostly in Stratford. His will was probated in Fairfield County Court, and after years of search by many hands and through various records, it was my pleasant surprise and good fortune to find one of *his* children, Sarah, mentioned therein as "now the wife of Mr. John Beach of Reading." How many times those pages had been turned in vain! Yet it was all so simple when you had discovered it.

Hannah, third daughter of John and Mary Beach, married, first, Zechariah Fairchild, and then John Burit, as it is sometimes spelled on the records. All her children were by her first husband, whom she married Nov. 3, 1681. Mehetable, b. 1682–84; Hannah, b. 1685, m. 1706, Daniel Searles; David, b. 1688, m. Deborah; A(u)gur, b. 1691, m. 1712, Mary Booth; Caleb, b. 1693, m. ——, had two children; James, b. 1695; Mary, b. 1698, d. 1803, m. 1728-9, Samuel Adams; [their son Andrew Adams, b. Dec. 11, 1736 (Yale Col. 1760); was Representative, Assistant member of the Continental Congress, and Chief Justice of Connecticut. Mrs. Mary Adams died at their home in Litchfield in 1803, in her 106th year.] Zechariah, b. 1701; Abiel, b. 1703.

Isaac Beach, fourth son of John and Mary, married May 3, 1693, Hannah Birdsey, who was baptised Feb. 5th, 1671, and died Oct. 15, 1750. She was the daughter of John Birdsey, Jr., and Phebe Wilcoxson, son of John Birdsey (in Middlefield, Conn., in 1744) and Philippa Smith. Phebe Wilcoxson was the daughter of William and Margaret Wilcoxson, and Philippa Smith, the daughter of Deacon Henry Smith of Wethersfield. The children of Isaac and Hannah Birdsey Beach were six in number, three sons and three daughters. William, b. July 7, 1694, d. July 26, 1751, married Nov. 30, 1725, Sarah Hull, daughter of Joseph and Mary (Nichols)

Hull; Elnathan, b. July 7, 1698, d. Aug. 16, 1742, married
(1st) May 9, 1720, Abigail Ufford, 3rd daughter of Lt. Samuel
and Elizabeth (Curtiss) Ufford, b. ——, 1700, d. Dec. 2, 1738,
married (2nd) Feb. 8, 1742, Hannah Cook, the daughter of
Capt. Samuel and (——) Cook ; John, b. Oct. 6, 1700, d. Mar.
19, 1782 (see " Biography of Rev. John Beach ") ; Mary, b. Dec.
16, 1703 ; Hannah, b. May 26, 1709, m. Eliphalet Parker ;
Dinah, b. Oct. 14, 1713, d. 1714.

The three sons of Isaac and Hannah (Birdsey) Beach
became prominent and influential men. Of Isaac himself, it
is said he was a tailor in Stratford. In those days, his must
have been a very excellent and high-priced establishment, if
one may judge by the large estate which he left, and the
extravagance of educational advantages enjoyed by his
children. His wife also fell heir to no small fortune, as the
daughter of so rich a man as the second John Birdsey.

William married the daughter of Capt. Joseph Hull, of
Derby, Conn., a son of Dr. John and grandson of Richard.
Her mother was Mary Nichols, the daughter of Caleb and
Anne (Ward, daughter of Andrew of Fairfield) Nichols.
Caleb was the second son of Sergt. Francis Nichols, one of
the first settlers in Stratford, and was born in England. (For
a fuller account of this family see Nichols.)

William and Sarah (Hull) Beach had five children : Isaac,
b. 1726 ; Anne, b. 1729 ; Abel, b. 1731 ; Abijah, b. 1734 ; and
Henry, *baptised* in 1734. Abel and Abijah married into the
Lewis and Brewster families, and Anne, who married Nov.
5, 1749, William Samuel Johnson, was the mother of seven
children, one of whom, Samuel William, married in 1791,
Susan Pierrepont Edwards, granddaughter of President
Jonathan Edwards. Their present representatives are not
many, but feel themselves doubly honored in their descent
from the heads of both Church and Meeting ! This anecdote
is contributed by a descendant :

It is supposed that Mary Brewster was the daughter of James
Brewster and Faith Ripley. Thus, through her father she was descended
from Elder Brewster, through her mother she was descended from
Gov. Bradford and his second wife Alice (Carpenter, or Reyerer, widow
of Edw. Southworth ; (see Savage's Dec. Vol. I, p. 231.) The descent
being : Wm. Bradford I, and wife Alice ; Wm. Bradford II, and wife
Alice Richards ; Hannah Bradford, wife of Joshua Ripley ; Faith

Ripley, wife of James Brewster, (Orcutt's Hist. Stratford, pp. 420, 605, 112.)   See also Life of Wm. S. Johnson, LL.D., p. 179.

Mary Brewster was married when quite young to Mr. Abijah Beach,* whose sister, Ann Beach, was the first wife of Wm. S. Johnson, LL.D.† She was early left a widow with several children. She lived on a farm at Bull's Bridge, Litchfield County, where her husband and his brother-in-law Johnson had rebuilt an old bridge, spanning a gorge through which the Housatonic river runs. In consequence of this bridge the road across the farm became one of the great highways from Connecticut to Poughkeepsie, and thus to New York. When the troubles came between the colonies and the mother country Mrs. Beach had a hard time, for it was difficult to get money to buy necessaries, but the family lived from their farm produce, the mother and daughters spinning woolen and flaxen thread for weaving, and the boys helping in the work of the farm. So the trying days of 1776 passed by and the mountain farm was little disturbed. After the taking of New York, when the Continental troops were obliged to go by way of New Jersey, across the Hudson, through Connecticut, to Springfield and Boston, the road across the Beach farm became a common higway. Very soon it became the custom for the officers to halt their commands at "Madam Beach's," the great barns giving good shelter to the men, and the officers being sure of entertainment in the farm house. Gen. Washington was many times entertained there, he having a very high regard for Mrs. Beach. The Beach boys were too young to go into the army, but all were glad to do what they could for the Continental soldiers, and sick, or footsore men, were sure of kind care. There was almost always a disabled soldier hobbling about the place, waiting to join the first detachment of troops passing when he was well enough to be discharged by his kind hostess.

One day a company of soldiers came by having in their baggage wagon a poor man who had both his feet badly frozen. It was the bitter winter of 1779 and the men had come from Valley Forge. The commanding officer asked Mrs. Beach if she would take care of this man, who they feared would die, ere long, of pain and exhaustion. Mrs. Beach nursed the man for a long time, and indeed he staid for six months, going away at last on his own feet with his comrades in arms. One evening as all the family sat in the great kitchen, Madam Beach and her daughters spinning wool and flax by the light of the fire, Mrs. Beach lamented to her daughters the departure of their neighbor, the weaver, who fired by patriotism had gone to join the army. What to do they knew not, for they had quantities of thread, but could get no cloth made. Suddenly a feeble voice came from the

---

* Abijah Beach and Mary Brewster was joined in marriage April 15th, A. D. 1753. Benjamin, b. 1755, Sarah, 1756, and Elizabeth, 1758. Registered in Stratford early records. Copied by editor.

† (I Pres. Century Club at York, etc.)

chimney corner where the sick soldier was resting on the settee. He
said that he was a weaver and also a maker of looms, and that if they
would provide wood, etc., he would make a loom and after that weave
cloth. So he sat in the corner of the kitchen all day, working with his
hands, while his poor feet were useless, until, with the help of the boys
he made a loom. By this time he could use his feet a little and so
began to weave. He wove woolen cloth, coarse and fine linen and at
last damask. Some of the damask is now in the possession of a
Colonial Dame, a descendant of Mrs. Beach's step grandchild Elizabeth
Johnson-Devereux. Late in life Mrs. Beach married her late husband's
brother-in-law, Wm. Samuel Johnson of Stratford, living after that in
Stratford, where she died in 1827.

Should there be any descendant of William now living who
has his family honor at heart, he would do well to replace
the missing tablet on his tombstone in the old Stratford
Episcopal burying-place. That of his widow Sarah (who
afterward married June 18, 1761, the Rev. Samuel Johnson,
D.D.) still remains. The tombstone is table-shaped, and
much less hideous for so being than usual. The following
inscription is in good preservation :

"His worthy Relict | Mrs. Sarah Beach was | afterwards married to
the Reverend | Dr. Johnson President of King's | College at New
York: and died | of the small pox with much | Patience, Faith and
Resignation | Feb'y 9th-1763. Aetat. 61 : And lies | interred under
the chancel of Trinity Church there."

The Will of William Beach, dated July 4, 1751, gives his
wife "Sarah Beach £5000 Lawful money old tenor," and the
use of one-third of his dwelling-house. To his son Isaac
several pieces of land "and that part of my dwelling house
lot that now contains ye dwelling house and Barn that was
my Father's, with ye Chaise-house, and Ware-house, and flax-
house, and furnace-house, being near an acre." He mentions
"my four Children, Isaac, Abel, Abijah, and Anne Johnson,
wife of Wm Samuel Johnson."

"Item, for ye love I bear to that best of Churches, ye Church of
England, in which I have many years enjoyed great comfort and satisfaction, I give and bequeathe ye sum of £500 money old tenour,
towards purchasing a glebe lot for a pasture for ye use of sd Church
forever, the sd Sum to be lodged in the hands of the Rev. Dr. Johnson
or his son Wm Samuel Johnson, and laid out at his or their discretion
for ye purpose." "For ye love I bear to my very good friend and
pasture ye Reverend Dr. Samuel Johnson, I give and bequeath unto

him or his heirs ye sum of sixty pounds money, old tenor, for his and their use and benefit."

On a ground plan of the pews and occupants in the Episcopal church, Stratford, in 1745, William Beach has the large square pew on the left of the chancel, also the next pew on the side, which he sold (?) to Henry Davis. In 1756, when the organ was purchased, "Madam Beach" subscribes "a set of Curtains and fringes for the organ loft."

Stratford To all whom these presents shall come,
Feb. 11-1739/40 greeting;—

Know ye that we whose names are underwritten Do give unto the Episcopal Church of England in Stratford the several parcels of land affixed to our names . . . . . . for the only use, benefit, and behoof of ye s^d Church of England and their successors forever.

Wm Beach 3 acres
Saml. French 1 acre
" " Jr. ¼ "
" Blagge ½ " The land layd out next to
James Fairchild ¼ " Newtown line.
Caleb Beardsley 1 " April 4th-1743.
Joseph Sheldon 3 "
James Beers ½ "
Jonathan Curtis 60 rods

Stratford—

We whose names are hereunto subscribed, being convinced that it is our duty to contribute what we are able towards building a Church for ye honour and glory of God in this town, to be set apart for his worship and service according to the excellent method of the Church of England, Do hereby cheerfully and seriously devote to God the following sums (in the old tenor) annexed to our several names to be employed for the promotion of that pious undertaking.—

Samuel Johnson—a bell—£300		William Beach	750
William Beach	250	Abel Birdsey	60
James Beach	50	Ebenezer Hurd	30
Ephraim Curtiss	50	Edmond Booth	10
Abraham Blakeman	6	etc. etc. etc.	

A true copy.—
John Benjamin, Clerk.

Elnathan, the second son of Isaac and Hannah (Birdsey) Beach, married twice; first in 1720, Abigail Uffoot, Uffont, Ufford (thus variously spelled, the last correct), the daughter of Lieut. Samuel and Elizabeth (Curtis) Ufford, and was born in 1700. Lieut. Samuel was the son of John, who was the second son of Thomas and Isabel Ufford of Boston, Milford, and Stratford. Elizabeth Curtis was the daughter of Joseph and Bethia (Booth) Curtis, and was born in 1677. Joseph Curtis was a son of the first John of Stratford. (See Curtis family. See also Booth family for Bethia Booth.)

Elnathan and Abigail (Ufford) Beach had ten children; the first son, Isaac, died in 1724, the next Isaac born in 1725; 3 Elnathan, 4 John, 5 Samuel, 6 Sarah, 7 Hannah, 8 Abigail, 9 Lois, and 10 Esther.* Mrs. Abigail Ufford Beach died Nov. 2, 1738. Samuel (10th) was born Dec. 26, 1737, and (to quote from Yale Biographies, Vol. II, pps. 448-50) remained in his native town (now Cheshire) and became one of its principal inhabitants. . . . . In determining the part taken by Wallingford in the Revolutionary struggle, Mr. Beach was especially active. He was sent to the Legislature in May, 1775-76-77. From 1780 to 1788 he served as Representative in the General Assembly and also Town Clerk, and was a member of the State Convention which ratified the Constitution of the United States in 1788. He died in Cheshire, July 11, 1808. He married Aug. 30, 1759, Mary Hall, third daughter of the Rev. Samuel Hall (Yale Col. 1716), first pastor of the Congregational church in Cheshire. Mr. Beach was one of the deacons of that church from April 1766 until his death. Mrs. Beach died Aug. 8, 1768, at the age of 32, leaving two sons and two daughters, of these one daughter only lived. She married the Rev. Joel Bradley (Yale Col. 1789). Mr. Beach next married June 14, 1769, Esther, daughter of Aaron and Ruth (Burrage) Cook of Wallingford. The only son by this marriage was graduated at Yale College in 1793. Capt. Elnathan Beach married for his second wife Hannah Cooke, the daughter of Captain Samuel Cooke, Jr., a wealthy shipping merchant of New Haven and New Cheshire. The only child by this marriage, Abraham, born Aug. 29, 1740, was graduated at Yale College 1757. His father dying when he was but two years old, his mother married again, Dr. Jonathan Bull of Hartford. After graduation, Abraham Beach returned to Hartford, where he was Collector of Taxes in 1765. About this time he became a communicant in the Episcopal Church and afterwards pursued studies preparatory to ordination under the direction of his uncle, the Rev. John Beach of Newtown, and of the Rev. Samuel Johnson, who

*Children not in order of birth—Samuel was last child of Abigail. (Error in numbering in Orcutt.)

had married the widow of another uncle (William). He was ordained in England and appointed missionary to New Brunswick and Piscataway, New Jersey, with a salary of forty pounds. In the spring of 1770, he married Ann, the only child of Evart Van Winkle of New Brunswick. In 1784, at the particular request of the newly elected rector of Trinity church, New York City, the Rev. Dr. Provoost, he was appointed assistant Minister of that church with a yearly salary of five hundred pounds. He served with distinction in this office (with a change of title to Assistant Rector in 1811) until his resignation on March 1st, 1813, when in his seventy-third year. The vestry of the church then voted him an annuity during life of $1,500. One of the streets opened through the church lands had already been designated by his name. He then retired to the farm inherited through his wife on the Raritan River, about three miles from New Brunswick, where he died Sept. 10th–11th, 1828, at the age of 88, being as was supposed the oldest clergyman of his church in America. His wife died on January 24, 1808. Their eldest daughter married the Rev. Dr. Elijah D. Rattoone (Coll. of N. J. 1787), Professor in Columbia College and President of the College of Charleston ; the third daughter married the Rev. Thomas Lyell, D.D., and the youngest married the Rev. Abiel Carter (Dartmouth Coll. 1813). His daughter Cornelia married Isaac Lawrence, and became the mother of a most interesting family of six daughters and one son. The marriages of these children deserve mention.

Cornelia, married James Hillhouse ; Harriet, married John A. Post ; Isaphene, married Dr. Benjamin McVickar ; Julia Beach, married Thomas L. Wells ; Maria, married Rev. W. J. Kipp ; Hannah, married twice—first Henry, son of Stephen Whitney and second, Nathan Baldwin, of Milford.

William Beach Lawrence, the only son, married the daughter of Archibald Gracie of New York, and became Lieutenant Governor of Rhode Island. A sketch of Dr. Beach's life was written by his grandson, the Hon. William Beach Lawrence, for Sprague's Annals of the American Pulpit in 1852.

Joseph, fifth son of John and Mary, married Abiah Booth, eldest child of Ebenezer, son of Richard, the settler. (See Booth). Their children were :

Sarah, b. July 15, 1697 m. Jonathan Nichols ; Agur, b. Apr. 8, 1699, d. 1711 ; Abraham, b. Apr. 29, 1701, d. 1711 ; Hannah,

b. Feb. 12, 1702, m. Zechariah Tomlinson ; Joseph, b. and d. 1711 ; Abia, b. Jan. 12, 1712, m. Samuel Judson ; Bethia, m. Samuel Judson as 1st wife.

Benjamin, tenth and youngest, married in 1695, Mary Hitchcock, b. Dec. 10, 1676, daughter of John and Abigail (Merriman) son of Matthius and Eliz. Hitchcock. Benjamin and his wife Mary left Wallingford and settled in Hanover, Hunterdon County, West Jersey. This is shown by a deed from him dated at that place, relinquishing property coming to him through his wife. They had eight children : Peter, b. Sept. 14, 1696, Eunice, b. Aug. 3, 1698 ; Benjamin and Mary, twins, b. May 19, 1702 ; Noah, b. Nov. 15, 1705 ; Abner, b. Sept. 16, 1708 ; Tabitha, b. Feb. 12, 1712 ; Lydia, b. Aug. 27, 1713. The family of Nathaniel and Sarah (Porter) Beach, remained for the most part in Stratford, and their descendants still own the original property. A picture of the homestead erected in 1735, is given on page 1125, Vol. II of Orcutt's History of Bridgeport and Stratford. It would be pleasant to know if either of the two figures therein, represent any members of the family.

WALLINGFORD—(Davis.)—On a list of 38 signers to the Covenant, or original agreement of the first planters of Wallingford in 1669, we find Eliasaph Preston, John Beech, Samuel Cook, Samuel Street, Samuel Andrews, Simon Tuttle, Thomas Curtis, Isaac Curtiss, John Parker, senior, and Thomas Beach, and on a later property list, William Johnson has 12 acres, Simon Tuttle 8, Samuel Street 12, and William Curtis 8. On list of Patentees in the Charter—Richard Treat and Thomas Wells. On list of "Committee of New Haven for ye intended village as planters, (Wallingford) there are amongst others, the names of Eliasaph Preston, Samuel Cook, Samuel Whitehead, Daniel Sherman, Benjamin Lewis, Jehiel Preston, Thomas Curtis, and John Beach." These families intermarried with John's children and grandchildren. Other names soon added on the original proprietor list ; in addition to those already mentioned we find "John Parker, Daniel Mix, Doctor Hall, and Thomas Beach." John's name appears frequently on committees of Church and State, and as a purchaser of land, and on the "casting of Lotts for ye falls plaine." John, Thomas and *Isak* Beach have 64, 54 and 45 acres, respectively. Grand list for 1701—John Beach £50, Thomas Beach £79, Benjamin Beach £32.

"John Beach came from New Haven to Wallingford with the first company of Planters in 1670, and located himself in the southerly portion of the town, and I suppose him to be a brother of Thomas, of Milford. He was a man of some consequence in the settlement and was frequently elected to some of the offices in the gift of the people. His son Thomas was married to Ruth Peck, May 12, 1680. He located on the farm late the property of Cephas Johnson and built the old house that was taken down to make way for the present one built by Mr. Johnson on the old site. He died in Meriden, May 13, 1741, aged 82 years, and was interred in the old burying-yard hill, about a mile to the southwest of Meriden center."

On the north side of the Meriden monument—

Thomas Beach—May 14, 1741, aged 83.
Samuel Johnson—March 2, 1777, aged 28.

Moses Yale Beach was a descendant of Thomas by his second wife, Phebe Wilcoxson—through Moses,[1] b. Feb. 19, 1695, d. — m. Sept. 21, 1722, Esther Taylor; Moses,[2] b. Nov. 8, 1726, m. (1st) Mar. 19, 1756, Dinah Sperry, m. (2nd) Parthenia Tallman; Moses[3] Sperry, b. March 7, 1776, d. at Norwalk, Ohio, in 1826, aged 50 years; m. Lucretia Yale of Wallingford; Moses[4] Yale, b. Jan. 1800, d. July 1st, 1868. (Mr. Joseph P. Beach of Cheshire is of this line.)

I will not quote literally from this History, for there are many errors which time and further investigation would have corrected. John, Richard and Thomas of Milford were undoubtedly brothers, but Thomas of Wallingford was son to the first John, who owned land in New Haven, Stratford and Wallingford. Thomas of Milford was also in Wallingford for a while, but returned. The Benjamin who bought land in Stratford in 1669 was the son of Richard, his baptismal record together with those of his mother and his brother Azariah, and his sister Mercy, an infant, all the same date, 1648, being on the same record; these are given as born in 1644, 46 and 48 respectively. This is in "Baptisms in New Haven from 1639 to 1666, John Davenport's Record." It will be seen at a glance that in 1669 (not *1659*) when he was granted a home lot in Stratford he was sufficiently aged to be married. Richard bought land of Thomas Wheeler, who had previously bought of Robert Rice (the earliest grant recorded—Sept. 16, 1648) the lot where Mr. Meacham now lives (so says Davis' Wallingford in 1870). Wheeler moved to Derby. R. Beach sold it to Mr. Fenn of Milford, and he sold it in 1667 to Rev. Israel Chauncey, the second pastor of the Congregational church in Stratford. Part of this land with part of the land owned by John Brinsmade, one of the first settlers (on the river side), and the land owned by William Beardsley with a piece of Nicholas Knell's lot on the back street and now (1868) owned by Alfred E. Beach, son of the late Moses Yale Beach, of Wallingford, a lineal descendant of John, brother of Richard. Benjamin, son of Richard, as before shown, was in Stratford in 1669. From him descended Benjamin Beach, the merchant and owner of vessels, who was a man of property and built the old house that was taken down by Mr. Patterson some years ago, and which stood where Mr. Dutcher, in 1863, lived. Benjamin Beach senior's descendants settled in part in Trumbull. John Beach became one of the original proprietors of Wallingford, and is represented in the inventory of his estate as having property in Wallingford to the amount of £92.19s. and in Stratford to the amount of £312.13s. He seems to have bought in Wallingford with a view to the settlement of his sons there. John, Jr., Isaac, and Thomas removed to Wallingford, but the first two died in Stratford. Indeed Isaac in 1694 united with the Stratford Church, and is entered as of Wallingford. As John Beach senior's estate was administered in Fairfield County Probate Court, he evidently had not transferred his residence to Wallingford.

Will of Thomas of Wallingford, 1741, Jan. Wife Phebe ; sons Timothy, Nathan, Gershom (d), Moses, and Caleb ; grandson Thomas (son of Timothy) ; daughter Ruth Fairchild (d), Thankful Baldwin, Joanna Royce, Phebe Tyler.

ABEL ROYCE, Ex.

Thomas Beach of Milford, married Sarah Platt, daughter of Richard and Mary Platt, by whom he had five or six children, Sarah, John, Mary, Samuel, and Zopher. There is also a Thomas mentioned in the step-father's will (given later), and as *John's* will or settlement of his estate mentions also a "brother Thomas," we can but judge that he was either an older son, and of age, or the youngest, and born after his father's death, which seems more probable. I have seen somewhere the birth date of a Thomas. Thomas Beach, Sr., died 1662, and his widow married Miles Merwin. The two families became as one in the will of Miles Merwin. The children of Thomas Beach were very young when he died, and in the administration of his estate by Miles Merwin, "£30 to be paid to the children when of age." "Where-as I, Richard Platt have received two and twenty Lbs. and ten shillings of the s^d Miles Merwin, and doe hereby ingage to pay . . . . . . to the three sons of the sd. Beach when they shall come to age of 21 years. Dated April 12, 1674 ; Signed

RICHARD PLATT.

Witnesses : SAMUEL EELS
ROBERT PLUM."

This is the first estate administered on in the Court Records, June 13, 1666. Sarah Beach, daughter of Thomas, born 1654, John 1655, Mary 1657, Samuel 1660, and Zopher 1662. Of these, John goes to Wallingford, and marries Mary ——, dies 1709. Children : Thomas, John, Samuel, Lettis, and Hannah, *brother Thomas*, Executor, Eleazar Platt and John Hall, witnesses, John Sanford of New Haven, administrator. Mary goes to New Jersey and marries Samuel Lion. Samuel Beach marries Abigail ——, and dies in Sept., 1728, no children. His will is probated Oct. 11, and the estate distributed in February, 1729, when the court awards " one half to the widow, and the remainder to ye seven brothers and sisters, viz : Hannah Holbrook, only surviving sister ; the heirs of John Beach of Wallingford, Zopher and Mary Lion of New Jersey, heirs of Martha Prime and Deborah Burwell of Milford, and Mary Hurd of Derby—by which will—yields to ye widow £148. 5. 9, and to each brother and sister £21. 2. 10." Executors are John Fowler, Samuel and Josiah Platt."

Then follows a long inventory and before the business is concluded the widow marries the recently bereaved second Rector of Yale College, the Rev. Samuel Andrew, his first wife, Abigail Treat, daughter of Gov. Robert Treat, having died Dec. 5, 1727.

Miles Murwin dies in 1695, leaving four daughters by Sarah (Platt) Beach, Mary and Martha (twins), born 1666, Hannah, b. 1667, and Deborah, b. 1670. There is mention in his will of John, Thomas, Samuel, Elizabeth Canfield, Abegail, Martha Prime, Mary Hull, Hannah Holbrook, and Deborah Burwell ; and an Inventory of Sarah Murwin, widow, June 16, 1698. John, Thomas, and Samuel were the children of Thomas Beach ; Elizabeth Canfield and Abegail Ufford or

10

Trofford, unknown. Of the other four, Martha married in 1685, James Prime, son of James ; Mary married Mr. Hull of Derby ; Hannah married in 1683, Abel Holbrook, and Deborah married Samuel Burwell, Jr. N. G. Pond, Esq. of Milford, said the late Samuel Irenaeus Prime was a descendant of James and Martha (Murwin) Prime.

"Thomas Beach, Jr., married Feb. 19th, 1702-3, Sarah Sanford (by the Rev. Mr. Street of Wallingford)." After his death she married Jonathan Atwater, Jr., June 23, 1744-5. This Thomas was very prominent in Milford land dealings, and his transactions in this regard are numerous up to 1737. This is probably Thomas, son of John and Mary, and grandson of Thomas of Milford, about whose pranks as a young man we may read, and whose father, John, was obliged to give bonds for his good behavior ; his incidental divertisements were rather of the kind we should now call *hoodlum*,—such as shooting off muskets to frighten old ladies, kicking animals, and beating the watch. Wallingford was the scene of his frolics, but he was "bound in ye sum of ten pounds to the county treasury at New Haven,"—or his father was bound for him—before Thomas Yale, Justice. Later, he was a successful man of affairs. There is in the New Haven records the following : "I, John Beach, with the consent of my father Azariah Beach of New Haven ⁰/ₑ to John Hulls of Wallingford articles of apprenticeship from date until he is 21 years of age. Signed, John Hulls, Azariah and John Beach. Witnesses, Joseph and Mary Roys ; dated May 27, 1717.

"Sam¹ Lyon hath liberty to give Zopher Beach two acres of land to build on, Feb. 25, 1683. March 5, 1693-4, Zopher Beach is chosen by the town (Newark, N. J.) to be at the Court of Sessions according to act of General Assembly, in case John Browne is wanting at that time. Oct. 21-1709 he is appointed to draw up wholesome orders about the neck."

The foregoing from note book of the Rev. J. Wycliffe Beach, his descendant.

In 1778, John Beach of Morristown, New Jersey, yeoman, attorney for the heirs of Ezekiel Cheever, late of Morristown, deceased, conveys to Abner Cheever, Jr. of Lynn, certain estate set off to Ann Cheever, widow of Abijah Cheever of Lynn.

(p. 181, vol. 38, New England H and G—Register.)

DESCENDANTS IN THE LINE OF JOHN.

The Rev. John's children were all born in Newtown, as the records show. Of Joseph we have no further information than that already given. Phebe, the eldest daughter, married Captain Daniel Hill of Redding. This doughty officer was evidently a sort of free lance, for we find that "Dan¹ Hill of Reading is fined on compleint of Gen¹ Silliman for disobedience to orders." "Dan¹ Hill and David Hart of Stamford two of the officers thus complayned of fined 2—1—1 apiece." He was the son of William and Hannah (Morehouse) Hill. She was the daughter of Lemuel and Rebecca (Odell) Morehouse and was born in 1670. William Hill married three times—second, Rebecca Sanford (dau. Ezekiel and Rebecca (Squires) Sanford), and third Mary Ogden. He had by his first wife Daniel and Hannah, and by his second, Ezekiel, Abigail and Mary. "Daniel Hill son of Mr William Hill and Phebe Beach were married October 31, 1748." Abel, their only child, was born January 10, 1750. Phebe died the next year, and is buried on the Beach side of the old Christ church burying-ground; while her husband and his second wife, with their children, are all lying at the extreme opposite corner (TS). The second wife was Elizabeth Lane, by whom he had—but let us quote from the Town Records, vol. II, page 35 : "Daniel Hill's children—My son Abel was born Jany 10th A D 1750—My Daughter Hannah was Borne Feby 27th A D 1753. She Departed this Life Sepr 27th A D 1755. My son Andrew Lane was born Decr 14th A D 1764—My Daughter Sarah was Borne March 25th A D 1764 She Departed this Life June ye 19th 1764—A true Cop—Test Dan¹ Hill—Test John Couch Regist^r" After this he had two daughters, Hannah and Betty. Phebe's son, Abel Hill, married in 1773 Anna Lyon, the daughter of Peter and Abigail (Sherwood) Lyon. Peter was one of the three sons of Nathan (Joseph, David and Peter), and Abigail was the daughter of Captain Daniel and Anne (Burr) Sherwood. Abel and Anna had two children, Beach and Lucy ; Lucy died young and there is a curious tale of Beach, which has doubtless both lost and gained in all these years, but which—thanks to the kindness and memory of a distant connection—I am allowed to insert in its present only form. It comes from Ypsilanti, Michigan :

" Mr. Asahel Sanford, once of Reading, Ct., about thirty-five years ago wrote a long and graphic account of Beach Hill and published it in a western paper. I read the account at the time, the substance of which, as I now remember, was that Beach Hill left Charleston, S. C., unbeknown to his parents and located somewhere in England. After corresponding with friends a few years correspondence suddenly ceased. Sometime after this a woman came over from England bringing a small boy and claimed being the widow and son of Beach Hill. She was proved to be an impostor, and by the boy, too. He said that the woman was not his mother and no relation, that his name was William Sharp and he had been trained to tell his story. The boy and woman parted company and neither returned to England, according to the story. I do not now remember what became of them. The conclusion of the story was that Beach Hill was murdered and this woman had knowledge of the crime, but she never divulged anything in regard to it. Mr. Sanford died several years since, so nothing can be learned in that direction." . . . . . .

The writer, Mrs. Elizabeth Lyon Read, is a daughter of that Betty Hill, the youngest daughter of Daniel and Elizabeth (Lane) Hill, who married Eli Lyon. Whatever the true inwardness of the tale it is but too true now that there are no Beach Hills left in this otherwise lovely hill country. The families of Hill, Lyon, Beach and Sanford will be found almost inextricably involved, but patience will resolve doubts —and if it still seems chaos, would that you could have seen it before the hand of reconstruction arranged the pieces. Let us now take up the Johns—in succession. John the son was never the man his father had been ; this could hardly be expected of him—the shadow of such a mantle eclipses for a time. He was, moreover, a sympathiser with the cause of freedom from English rule ; tho' never a fighter, he was often on committees of advice, and was sent to the convention as a delegate in the place of Genl. Chandler when the Constitution was adopted. He owned much land in Newtown, partly by gift of his father and partly by purchase, as a consultation of the records will show. In marrying Phebe, a daughter of Matthew and Phebe (Judson) Curtis, he fell somewhat under the influence of this martial family. Of his children but two were boys—and one of these died young, so John the third

THE
... ORK
... ARY
... and Tilden
... ons.
1903

MABEL PEERY BEACH

was thus only brother to four sisters, and when he married
Mabel Beers, daughter to that Daniel (whom we shall bring
through two influential lines)—and took her to yet another
home—the girls and their mother knew the only thing to be
done was to fill in with good sons-in-law. Surely some such
arrangement must have been made, for they turned out so
remarkably well—Phebe married Zalmon Glover, a descendant of Henry of New Haven; Hannah married John Curtis,
son of the first Abijah, and so on to the good old stock; and
Sarah, the youngest, bided her time and thought the Booths
good enough for her. John and Mabel tarried for a while in
the old town, but the spirit of adventure was once again
revived and many were the stirring tales told of fine chances
and rich lands in a northern country; and, finally, after
many plans and much discussion, they betook themselves
with their little family to the wilds of Central Vermont.
Eventually, his daughter Ann having married Dr. Elisha Sheldon, who had named the town in which they dwelt, and the
Doctor, wishing to enlarge his practice as a family man, deciding to remove to Troy, Mr. Beach undertook the care of
the Sheldon farms and interests and remained there until his
death in 1830. His daughter Charlotte married there Epenetus H. Wead. His widow, who survived him twelve years,
removed to Coxsackie with her son David. It is her picture
which we have been able to reproduce from a very old and
faded daguerrotype, sent me by one of her great-grand-
daughters. The eldest son of John and Mabel, Matthew the
hermit as he was called, was, the story goes, crossed in love,
and being either a very weak or a very strong lover, went off
and lived by himself. To quote from a scrap of writing
pasted in the record leaves of the old Beers Bible: "Died,
in the township of Newcomb, State of New York (Essex
County), on the thirtieth of April, 1862, Matthew Beach, aged
about 86 years, great-grandson of the Rev. John Beach of
Newtown, Conn. A man of singular habits, having lived a
hermit's life nearly forty years in the vicinity of Rackett
Lake, Long Lake, and among the wild fastnesses of the Adi-
rondack mountains.—E. S. P." (Elizabeth Sheldon Peck.)
Time and the insatiate thirst for fresh experiences render this
description, even at so short an interval, rather amusing than
true. It may be that there was no romance to the pioneer

choice, or the longing for solitary communion with nature. Once I saw him, a grey-bearded, sweet-voiced old man, with piercing yet kind eyes, which smiled out at you from under shaggy eyebrows; he came, he said, to look at his people here before he died, but our life was not his, nor could any persuasion induce him to stay with us. He went again as quietly as he had come, and very soon afterwards, within two years' time, we heard that he had died. The next son, Boyle, became a New York State farmer, going out to New Baltimore to visit his sister Phebe, who had married Barent Houghtaling, a son of Andrew and Polly Van Benthuysen Houghtaling, and it was from her father Barent (or Bornt) Van Benthuysen that the curious name has come down to us. The Houghtalings have a widespread chart and influence, and both Phebe and her brother Boyle became instrumental in extending their scope. Boyle married Elizabeth, a daughter of John Staats of Staatsburgh, and had a family wherein the name John Staats is repeated to this day. The fourth John brings us to our own memories and the more intimate relations of personal intercourse. Born in Newtown, he alone did not accompany his family to their northern home, but remained in his native village as the adopted son of his uncle and aunt, Daniel and Naomi (Glover) Beers, who had no children : they gave him every educational advantage, and so well did he profit by it that when he decided to become a lawyer, their unselfish pride was equal to the parting and they sent him to New Haven to perfect his studies. He was admitted to the Bar in 1814, just 25 years of age. In 1821 he was made City Attorney, which position he held until 1824, when he became clerk of the Superior Court, and in this capacity served with honor for twenty years. A Judgeship in the City Court followed, but shortly after this he withdrew from active professional life. A man of great firmness of character, instinctive integrity and high ideals, his career as a lawyer, clerk and judge for half a century in New Haven was marked by continued expression of regard and deference, both during and after his years of public service. In an old Day book found among his effects there is an entry, "Sep. 29 (1813). To Captn Abijah B. Curtis, Dr. To Cash p^d for your Daut's Grammar " " 50." Was this the "Marcia" whom he afterwards married ? If so, what a field of inquiry

this might open ! Filled with thoughts of educational values himself, perhaps she may have longed to meet him on equal ground ! Again: "1816, Augt 20. To Danl Beers ^{Dr} To Cash sent you in a letter this day by Mr Hawley the Tavern-keeper, $100.00." 1871—Aug 2—Left I. & K. Townsend's room & Removed to Mr Leffingwells for which I am to give $50 p^r year rent." Mr.Townsend's offices were over the corner of Chapel and College streets, and "Mr. Leffingwell's" still stands on the N.E. corner of Court and Church streets. Some of the fees then charged would not have enabled higher rents. "David S Boardman, New Milford Dr To Drawing Writ agst Mr Gorham & D Fitch on notes in favour of Lem Can-dee (your property)–duty $^c\:$.—1- o. 2 — To going ^{to} New Haven to give endorser ^{c} T Painter Esq notice -1- To pay^g for Chaise hire there $\overset{cts}{50}$-". "March 23^d (1818) Henry Clark entered my office this day as Student at Law." There is no record from May 7 to the 28th of this year. On the 10th he was married in Newtown to Marcia Curtis [the daughter of Major Abijah Birdsey Curtis], whose grammar by this time was doubtless equal to demand, judging from the context. Their first home in New Haven was at a board-ing house kept by a Mrs. Jerusha Clark. In 1819 there is this entry : "Nov 1st—moved into Jno Scott's House in Crown st—c–$90 p^r year." At this time their first child—John—was just two months old. The names of Appollos Apple and Silvanus Biles—or Bills—occur more or less fre-quently, and many more familiar to to-day. The old Day book has been used as a scrap book also, and pasted in it there is a bit of yellow mummy-looking paper : "Aug 22, 1792—The Apprisal of the Homested of Mrs Daniel Beers viz—Dwelling House &c–with good well— 40–0–0
2 acres on the front— 56
8 Do. west from front . . . . . d7 . . . . 56 0 0
1⅝ Acre Little Meadow 18
                                                          _____
                                                          £114. 0. 0

Deed Recorded 26th May
   in Lib^r 12th page 163."

Another not so antiquated, a birthday round robin to Aunt Naomi, written by John S., Daniel and Annie E. Beach, children of John and Marcia. In the land records of New

Haven, vol. 71, page 495, after proper preliminaries : " Daniel
Beers, % Jno Beach of New Haven in consideration of one
dollar rec^d to my satisfaction %—I Daniel Beers of Newtown
in Fairfield C° remise—to Jno Beach his heirs %—certain
piece of land situated in the City of New Haven fronting
westerly on Temple st and Bounded as follows northwest-
erly corner Henry R Pyncheons—69 ft 5 inch—thence easterly on a line parallel with the north line of s^d Pyncheons
lot to the land of the widow Brainard—% % the same conveyed to me by James Brewster—Aug 8, 1821.

signed John Beach."

In those days and later indeed, it was considered absolutely necessary for elderly people to wear wigs or scratches
and old ladies' "fronts." I recollect very distinctly on
being sent one morning to call my grandfather to breakfast,
finding him with, apparently, his head in his hand, brush-
ing the dark curls thereof ; so fascinated by the wig that I
forgot to notice his bald pate, I came down to my own place
at table, where I sat in a kind of trance of silent curiosity.
No reference was made to the incident for years, and then I
was told that *he* was much embarrassed and shocked. In his
last illness, his own beautiful white hair so changed him,
that many looking upon him then for the last time hardly
recognized his noble head. It was due to the influence and
persuasion of our mother, his son John's wife, that he went
thus crowned to his honored grave. At a meeting of the
New Haven County Bar held on Tuesday, April 13, 1869, the
following resolution was unanimously adopted. " Resolved
that we have heard with deep regret of the death of John
Beach Esq., formerly and for many years Clerk of the Superior and County Courts, and though latterly from his
advanced age and bodily infirmities retired from active business, yet universally and deservedly honored and respected
as one of the most upright and exemplary of our professional brethren, and for his Christian virtues and private
worth as a citizen."

Among personal papers are letters from John and his wife
to their sons John and Daniel after graduation. While quotations would be interesting, time and the restraint due friends
equally forbid. One may be mentioned written by the mother
—begun on Sunday after church, all sermon—finished on

Wednesday after a 'quilting over the way,' all pure gossip.
This John, born in New Haven, was of a quiet and studious
disposition, perhaps somewhat encouraged thereto by the
buoyant spirits of a younger brother and a toy sister, whose
ringing laugh and noisy entrance ill prepared you—a stranger
—for the tiny perfect little figure. "How Annie does bang
that door !" said a near relative. "Well—and she *shall* bang
it ! do let her make all the noise she can !" was the mother's
quick reply ! Young men then, after graduation taught
school. John was graduated at Yale College in the class of
1839 and almost immediately accepted a position in a
school in Wilmington, Delaware. 'Master Eli's school' was
foremost in its curriculum and a college graduate was a
necessity. John, however, brought away more than he took
down to that mid-country city, where a larger hospitality and
freer impulse probably seemed to him as strange and attractive as the cooler reception and restraint seemed strange and
forbidding to his young classmates from the South. Shortly
after his arrival he fell in with a couple of congenial spirits
in matters educational and philosophic—the sons of a Quaker
Doctor of prominence, not unknown or unfriendly to the
world of letters. An intimacy destined to affect his entire
future speedily developed. His quietly observant figure
in the midst of this large family of irrepressibles—though
Quaker born and bred, must have and did give no small
entertainment to them, and many were the tales told of his
first coming and later wooing. With true discrimination,
however, his choice fell from the first on the loveliest of the
flock, and it was she who made his life the thoroughly happy
one it was. In the college catalogue for the year of his
graduation—1838-9, the students in the academic department
numbered 411, but 32 of whom were New Haven boys—
John T. and David F. Atwater, Eli Whitney Blake, David L.
Daggett, John M. Gilbert, Augustus R. Macdonough, Samuel J. Mills Merwin, Francis A. Olmstead, Horace C. Peck,
George Sherman and Levi D. Wilcoxson with himself
made 11 out of 95 seniors. In the Quarter Century Record of
the class we read of John Sheldon Beach that he was "born
July 23d, 1819, at New Haven. The first year after graduating
he was instructor in an academy in Wilmington, Del. He
then returned to New Haven, and went through a course of

legal study at Yale Law School; was admitted to the bar and
commenced practice in 1843. The next year he became partner with Gen. Dennis Kimberly and has ever since found in
his profession ample and well-rewarded occupation. Since
1852, when Gen. Kimberly retired from the profession, he has
been alone in business. He married September 15, 1847,
Rebecca, daughter of the late Dr. William Gibbons of Wilmington, Del., and has had six children, of whom are living
Rebecca, John Kimberly, Donaldson and Francis Gibbons.
The other two died in infancy." Donaldson died the next
year, and another son was born—Rodmond Vernon. I
recall a later meeting of the class, when the few members
gathered informally at the old house on Temple street
(where Thomas Trowbridge, Jr., now resides), and they were
left to recognize each other without being received by my
father; two came up the steps together—one very tall, the
other very short—an instant's hesitation at the open door,
and then—the short man was struggling in the arms of his
chum the " Major Bully "—and so they made their entrance.
My father was almost invariably recognized by his uncon-
trollable left eyebrow—which *would* smile all by itself! One
of his classmates, David L. Daggett, became a physician and
married Margaret Gibbons, a sister of Mrs. Beach.

Of this fifth John it may be truly said that his grasp of the
high water mark of his calling never relaxed; and we, his
children, might almost be pardoned for thinking him devoted
to his profession alone were it not for the occasional swift
revelation of his deep affection and solicitude for us.
Later in life—later than should have been—the faculty of
Yale College conferred on him the degree of LL.D. Innate
modesty struggled always with his forensic powers, and rich
in values and complete as were his arguments, he never rose
to address the court without the moment of stage fright and
trembling of the knees which in a less controlled nature
would have prevented speech. At his death from all sources
came expressions of sympathy and personal loss—Resolutions from the United States Court, the Circuit Court, the
Superior Court of New Haven, the Vestry of Trinity Church
and other official bodies, and many letters from private individuals in all walks of life, followed each other; but that
which expressed more nearly the highest mark of apprecia-

tion and seemed to recognize the full sense of our and his loss was the tribute of Governor Charles R. Ingersoll, a life-long friend, from which I copy a few phrases. It was in the shape of an address to the members of the bar at a session of the Superior Court for New Haven County September 30, 1887, and followed the Resolutions then presented by Tilton E. Doolittle as President. Mr. Ingersoll said : " It is not easy, Mr. President, is indeed impossible to express adequately by formal resolution, or I may say any words of man, the sentiments by which you and I are moved upon this occasion. . . . For more than forty years, in summer and in winter, we have been by his side in almost constant practice of our profession . . It is very hard to rupture such a tie. I look back upon this long life with which mine has been so connected, and it is luminous with qualities that sanctify friendships. . . . . As to his relations to this Bar—and our profession—I will add a word or two. John S. Beach was notably a lawyer. And he was thoroughly a lawyer. His element was the atmosphere of the law. His ambition and his delight was to be active in those places where justice is sought, and outside of his home, with its associations most cherished by him, his life duty was centered here among judges and lawyers. And, Mr. President, the zealous mistress of the law never found occasion to reproach him for any neglect or slight. No public honor ever allured him from her side. No phantom of popular fame ever led him away in its pursuit—no temptation of quick riches in other paths ever ensnared him ; but quietly, unostentatiously, industriously and conscientiously he has for forty-four years steadily fol-lowed the routine of the Connecticut lawyer. . . . . He had a broad nature and his way of life was a generous one. There was nothing cramped or narrow in his dealings with men or his judgments upon them. In argument simple, clear, without rhetorical or any other display, his conclusions were always artistically fitted and the whole structure polished by a pure and lucid diction, which not only commanded the attention but required the vigilance of him who had to hear another side." Mr. Ingersoll's eulogy was certainly not over-drawn, and he concluded : " I do not think any lawyer of this Bar ever had a larger clientage. There were few of the rep-resentative men of this community during the last thirty years who were not at some time familiar with his office. What secured this confidence? Not alone, Mr. President, the intellectual skill and professional experience I have pointed out, but underlying it all there was the primitive bed-rock of private virtue and moral strength, without which all the acquired accomplishments of the lawyer avail but little. Mr. President, let this Bar cherish his memory among its jewels. If one generation of its members has any legacy to leave to that generation just pressing upon us, I know no richer one than the example of John S. Beach."

John Kimberly, eldest son of John S. and Rebecca (Gibbons), named for his father's honored partner and friend—married Mary Roland, the daughter of the late Judge Charles Frederick Sanford of New York City, Y. C., 1847. Judge Sanford was doubly descended from the two early Milford planters Thomas and Andrew, and was the son of Hervey and Mary (Lyman) Sanford, old residents of New Haven. His sister, Mrs. Frank Armstrong and later Mrs. G. K. Billings, resided for many years at the old homestead on Temple street. John K. was graduated from Yale in the Class of 1877, and later from the Law School (1879), and was admitted to the Bar the same year. He had already entered upon his studies in his father's office : where very shortly his abilities obtained for him a partnership. Patent law—the specialty of both—became their almost exclusive practice, and although not by any means relaxing the pressure on himself, the older lawyer often invited the precedence of his junior, when nothing gave him so much delight as to attend court—a *silent* partner. Of late and since the death of his father he has taken a wider practice in general law, and he is to-day recognized by his older brethren as a fit representative of the third of his name in the profession. He has no family—and so the break in the line of Johns at the seventh generation. The ten-year-old son of his younger brother Francis G., John Francis Beach, while continuing the first name, does not of course qualify him for the full honor thereof. The careful reader will observe that the *first* break occurred over two hundred years ago—when John's son *Isaac* was born—and the line of Johns resumed with *his* son. For he was actually the third John, there having been none between him and his Uncle John, who had left no son of that name. The descendants of John the son of Thomas of Milford—have hitherto claimed this birthright.

Francis Gibbons Beach (Y. C. 1883), Law School 1885, next son of John S. and also a lawyer, has just served a term as postmaster in the New Haven Post Office (1898) very creditably—so it is said, and certainly in so far as manifestations of such an opinion can show—very successfully. He and his younger brother, Rodmond Vernon (Y. C. 1887), belong to the Connecticut National Guard, and as this is written the call to arms is not unexpected; and while our hearts quail at the thought, we would not have them do so or falter one instant in the path of honor.* The mother of John Francis, Elizabeth Charnley Wells, is herself of Connecticut descent—by many ancestors of known position ; her father was the Rev. Thomas Wells, D.D. (Y. C. 1859), late rector of St. Mark's (Episcopal) in Minneapolis, Minn. He was the son of Thomas and Jane Elizabeth (Bucklin) Wells, and her mother the daughter of the late William S. and Elizabeth B. (Atwater) Charnley—thus to the families of Atwater-Root-Strong, etc.

They have had three children, of whom John Francis alone survives and is the last and sole representative of his generation and the line of Johns—to whom this book is dedicated.

Daniel Beers Beach was a freshman while his brother John Sheldon was a senior : we can well picture the mingled respect and boon companionship with which he would season their home intercourse. Of a charming personality, quite unique in its New England setting, his was a nature most lovable, debonnair and impulsive ; welcomed everywhere, he succeeded in awakening an answering gayety, sometimes awkward in its expression. He also adopted the law as his profession, but much of his life was spent in Rochester and elsewhere, and the interval in New Haven, after the death of his father—when he was in the office of his brother, in the old Exchange Building, [now occupied by Judge Lynde Harrison]—seemed one of agreeably studious leisure rather than of close application at the shrine of the exacting goddess. It was certainly an interval of pleasant family intercourse, and brought together those who otherwise had not

---

* Captain Francis G. Beach, Battery C. United States Volunteer Connecticut Heavy Artillery.

Lieut. Rodmond V. Beach, Adjutant 1st Regt. United States Volunteer Engineers, Porto Rico.

had the opportunity to form those life-long attachments which in fresh separation draw hearts still closer.

He was married in 1853 in Rochester to Loraine Rogers, daughter of Levi and Loraine (Hart) Hosford Rogers, by whom he had six children, three of whom lived to grow up : three daughters, one still unmarried living in Rochester, where her musical talent and attractive personality have secured her a large circle of good friends. The daughters married are Annie L. and Mary D. The former married Edwin Arthur King of Troy, New York [the King genealogy is already in print], and the latter, Mary D., married George L. Swan of Rochester.* Ann Eliza, the sister of John S. and Daniel B.—before spoken of—whose small size made her so noticeable, was born in 1829 and died unmarried in 1862. She was of brilliant intellect and acquirements, and it was a great grief to her parents that she was thus handicapped. Of perfect figure and exquisite coloring, this dainty child-woman made herself a valued friend to many who can now recall her always bright and happy face. The tale is told—and it is a true tale—that when on a visit to Wilmington, Delaware, to act as bridesmaid for the new sister-in-law, one of the bride's tall brothers at a party dropped upon his knees, offered her his arm, and thus—taller than she—they made the tour of the rooms, to the delight of the company.

* Each has a son.

DESCENDANTS IN THE LINE OF LAZARUS.

Lazarus Beach was the fourth son of the Rev. John, and married Lydia, daughter of Lemuel and Rebecca (Squires) Sanford, of the Fairfield County branch of the name. A full account of her ancestry is given in the sketch of that family. Of Lazarus Beach it may be said, judging from town and land records of both Newtown and Redding, that he was prominent in public affairs and influential in their administration. Educational matters interested him largely, and we find him constantly petitioning for further school rights ; he was selectman in 1788 and 9, and took that opportunity to press the claims of Gregory's Orchard school district—for which he and Jarvis Platt, with others, were appointed a committee. This petition represents him as then resident "on a line between Newtown and Redding."

In May 1768 John Read of Redding deeds land to Lazarus Beach, as administrator on the estate of Ruth Hunn, "150 acres at a place called Hopewell," and in 1771 Lazarus deeds the same to his "honored Father John Beach." In 1778 he sells land to his son Lazarus. In 1789 John Beach deeds to his son John Beach Jun[r*] his "pieces of land in Potatuck which I bought of my brother Lazarus of Reading." Signed in the pressence of Hannah Beach and Jabez Botsford. [This is the land afterwards sold to Abijah Curtis.] In May 1787 John Beach Jun[r] obtains a 77 years' lease of water-ways through the land of Enoch and Comfort Hubbell at Potatuck brook. Lazarus becomes embroiled in the Tory interests, for in the Colonial State Records we read— "Lazarus Beach, Andrew Fairchild Nathan and Enos Lee and Abel Burr of Reading and Thomas Allen of Newtown of the County of Fairfield being tory convicts and sent by order of the Law to be confined in the town of Fairfield to prevent any mischievous practices of theirs having made their escape and being taken up and remanded back to his honor the governor and this Council to be dealt with—Resolved [c/e]—that the said Lazarus Beach Andrew Fairchild [c/e] [c/e]— be committed to the Keeper of the gaol at Wyndham within said prison to be safely kept until they come out thence by due order of the General Assembly or the Governor and his Council of Safety [c/]."

"Ap. 13, 1787 Lazarus Beach D[r]—For taking John Guyer

* John III.

and committing him to prison—cost of assistance expenses and fees upon execution—2. 12. ⌐." John Guyer was a member of the Loyalist Association and was one of a large family of Tories. Again :

"Aug. 1787—For going to the Records in Hartford and searching s^d Records for the survey of your Farm and cash paid for ye same—1. 6. o. . . . . April 1793—"Credit in a settlement made by s^d Beach at Esq. Bettses—1. 5. 6½." These items from Mr. Hill's Diary.

The children of Lazarus and Lydia were eight in number ; five married, as will be seen, into the families of Thompson, Sanford, Lyon, Hill and Winton. Lazarus Junior went early to Bridgeport, where he established himself in the printing and stationery business. The first newspaper published there (then called Newfield) was the "American Telegraph and Fairfield County Gazette," and was commenced in 1795— "issued weekly, by Lazarus Beach, who came here from Redding and carried on the business of printer, bookseller and stationer—on the corner of Wall and State streets opposite the old Washington Hotel ("Hinman's.") It was printed upon what would be called fair wrapping paper and circulated over 800 copies, which were distributed by post-riders throughout the whole of Fairfield County; the subscription price was $1.50 pr. annum, and it continued to be issued by Mr. Beach's successor for nearly ten years." Here is an advertisement from one of the old copies—

> " Take notice all who justly owe
> Curtis and Glover late in Co.
> Close y* accounts without delay
> Either by notes or ready pay
> For if by negligence you tarry
> Beyond the 1st of February
> Our books will all be put in suit
> And cost and trouble be the fruit.
> > Benjamin Curtis, Jr.
> > Ezra Glover.
> > Newtown, Jan. 12, 1804.

The American Telegraphe.

By LAZARUS BEACH, Newfield, Conn.

" Receive Instruction and not silver—and Knowledge rather than choice gold." Wednesday August 9th 1797. whole no. 123.

Fifth Congress of the United States, Monday May 15 1797 An Act laying duties on stamped vellum parchment and paper, [full account.] Signed Jonathan Dayton speaker of the House. Thomas Jefferson, Vice President of the U. S. and President of the Senate, and approved July 6 1797. John Adams. Deposited among the Rolls in the Office of the Department of State.

Timothy Pickering, Secretary of State.

The reading matter of these early newspapers seems to us now remarkably dry, but when we remember how uneducated public literary taste and discrimination was—owing largely to the infrequency of nourishment—we can, I think, imagine even the involved phraseology of the stamped vellum act, bearing a certain charm to hungry intellects. Mr. Beach was perhaps as good an editor as could be found ; he lightens his editorial column with some quizzical suggestions, and after inviting his friend, the reader, to sit down and crack a bottle with him offers the following toasts.—" 1, To the memory of John Lawrence Costars of Haarlem, Inventor of Printing ; 2. To the freedom of the press ; 3. May every just and liberal sentiment be nobly expressed and fully impressed, may no plan of public utility nor any plot against public peace and honor be suppressed, may every inclination to tyranny faction and disorganization and every opposition to the constituted authorities be repressed, may merit never be oppressed nor depressed and to compress all in one toast, may every useful thought be expressed and duly impressed—and neither depressed nor suppressed, nor may worth ever be oppressed or depressed." Then follows a sort of doggerel song with a refrain. There is an obituary of James Davenport of Stamford, and this shipping news : "Last Saturday arrived here the schooner Olivia, Thompson master, from Sullivan with upwards of 30 head of Oxen on board. The circumstance is novel, this being the first cargo of cattle ever landed at this place. Mr. Joshua Baily his lady and family came passengers in the Olivia." And ever so short a voyage in a schooner with 30 head of cattle must have been a trip to be remembered. His strictures on the English navy place Mr. Beach politically—" her navy system is sinking into insignificance. . . This puts an end to her tyranny over the Ocean." . . . . and he concludes " may we not from hence anticipate the time when men will no longer consent to shut themselves

11

up in floating boxes to shoot at each other—to gratify the malice, avarice, ambition or pride of Tyrants." Alas! what would he have written to-day?

These quotations are taken from a copy of the Telegraphe of that date, now in the collection of the New Haven Historical Society.

Lazarus Jun' was on a library committee for Danbury—probably his business enabled him to supply such societies on good terms; he was himself, however, no inconsiderable writer, and spent much of his time following a literary career. It is said that he was writing a history of his grandfather, the Rev. John, and had much material of value both in old papers and letters, and of his own compiling. When he found himself obliged to go to Washington, D. C., he took them with him in a valise, which was either mislaid or stolen. The loss was an ever-growing one, and with those papers *now* in hand there would be no apprehension of criticism in this work. In Washington he found himself in the midst of the great center of the opening life of a new and freed country. The charm of such society and spirit, and the enthusiasm of success prevailing everywhere, drew him into intimacy with other young and ready minds, and shortly introduced him into the admiring circle about young Lafayette, whose espousal of our cause and success in arms endeared him to young and old. The story goes—(and I have it from one of his descendants who has the chair referred to)—that the young French General took a fancy to our Connecticut editor, and showed him many marks of approval and friendship, ins o-much that when it came time to leave his adopted country and return to his waiting bride, he begged Mr. Beach to accept some souvenir of their intimacy. Allowed to choose, he greatly disappointed the General by picking out an old chair with desk and drawer attachment, in which he—the General—had been accustomed to sit and write and take his cup of tea; and despite protestations would take nothing else. The chair is covered with its time-honored green baize and studded with what remains of the nails. It is said that Mr. Beach never wrote at any other desk or table afterward. Lazarus married in 1797, Polly Thompson Hall, widow of Dr. John Hall of Goshen, and daughter of Hezekiah and Rebecca (Judson) Thompson, by whom he had three daughters, and no sons. There are two portraits of Mrs. Polly

Beach, as she was called, but I have not been able to learn
the artist nor to obtain any copy. They lived first in Bridgeport and afterward in New York, where both Lazarus and
his wife died. The marriages and descendants of the daughters are given. The only other son of Lazarus to marry
was Isaac—and with him we re-enter upon the Hill, Lyon
and Sanford complication. Referring to the former Hill
descent—Andrew Lane [half brother to Abel] and Hannah
(Lyon) Hill had two daughters, Hannah and Fanny;
Hannah married Isaac Beach and Fanny married Aaron Sanford, Jr. Isaac Beach built his house in the Valley, and
thereto went Hannah—with that long list of household furniture which we have already noticed in the Redding history. Of their children, the youngest son Isaac, who married
Mary B. Winton, was the only one to have descendants who
are still continuing the name. This is quite a different record
to that of the Sanfords, whose twelve children were many
and fruitful. I am told by a member of this family, that the
sisters—Hannah Beach and Fanny Sanford—were very attractive women, both in appearance and character, and that the
mother was so equally jealous that whenever she gave anything to one, she immediately presented its duplicate or equiv-
alent to the other; Hannah was also very proud, and it was
a great grief to her that two of her children were ' wanting';
and an added sorrow that she had to die and leave them to
other hands; they followed her very soon, however. The
daughters of Lazarus and Lydia, Sarah, Hannah and Eunice,
married respectively James Sanford, Philo Lyon and Jonathan Hull. The Sanford and Lyon families will give details;—
For the Hulls,—we must speak a word of that branch of the
Devonshire Hulls, which, starting at or about the same time
and with Gov. Winthrop's party, in the "Mary and John,"
Captain Squeb, sailing from Plymouth, March 30, 1629,
arrived thirteen days in advance at Nantasket—May 30.
This point was afterwards called Hull. George (born about
1590) was always called Mister or Master Hull, and was
one of the foremost men in the new plantation, which they
called Dorchester. He was deputy for that town to the first
General Court held at Boston, May 14, 1634. In 1635, his
brother Joseph, Rector of Northleigh, arrived with a large
company from Somerset and Dorset, and settled " Wessa-
gusset " (Weymouth). In 1636 George and his son-in-law,

Mr. Phippeny, came with many townsmen to Connecticut and founded Wethersfield. He was then deputy for that place to the first General Court at Hartford in 1637 and so continuously until 1646, when he purchased land in Fairfield and went there to live, after which he was elected similarly until 1656. A personal friend of Gov. Ludlow, he became "Assistant" and Lieut. of the military in 1645. In 1654 appointed "Associate Magistrate for the seaside towns." After Gov. Ludlow went to Virginia, Mr. Hull continued to be elected deputy, but was not again magistrate. His first wife and the mother of his children was Elizabeth, daughter of Henry Russell of Plymouth ; his second wife (whom he married in 1659) was Sarah, widow of David Phippeny. Mr. Hull died in 1659–60, having been foremost in establishing two of the New England commonwealths. Cotton Mather distinguishes him and Mr. Trumbull puts him on his list of worthies. Mr. Stiles, the historian of Windsor, speaks of him as "a citizen of worth and distinction." Bringing him down to our Jonathan—George and Sarah (Russell), Cornelius and Rebecca (Jones), Cornelius 2ᵈ and Sarah (Sanford, daughter of Ezekiel 1ˢᵗ), Deacon George and Martha (Gregory, daughter of Samuel and Rebecca (Wheeler) Gregory), Seth and Elizabeth (Mallory, daughter of John and Elizabeth (Adams) Mallory), Jonathan and Eunice (Beach) Hull. Seth—the father—was baptized July 29, 1733, and died April 5, 1796. We have not his marriage date, but his wife, Elizabeth Mallory, was baptized Dec. 17, 1738, and died Feb. 22, 1795. Among some papers found in an old desk belonging to the great-niece of Eunice Beach Hull, we may read to-day how this little family went in the early part of this century all the way to, and founded, New Haven, Illinois ; how they broke soil there and cleared a space for their needs, and how the unaccustomed toil and exposure brought grief and earthly parting ; and we may read, too, in those treasured yellow leaves how firm a tested faith can be, and to what heights the souls of good women ascend while yet in this world. Eunice Beach Hull was one of these. The son, the Rev. Lemuel Beach Hull, remained East and succeeded to the church of his great-grandfather in Redding, his ministry being the next in length. He then went out to Milwaukee, where he founded the Episcopal church which his descendants still attend.

BEERS.

JAMES AND RICHARD OF KENT.

Anthony, son of James, was born in Kent County. It is said that he came over with his Uncle Richard, who was one of the first men in Watertown, Mass. Anthony married and had seven children, five of them born in Watertown. In 1655 he removed to Roxbury, Mass., and in 1658 came to Fairfield, Conn. He was a mariner and was lost at sea in 1676. His wife Elizabeth survived him. Of his sons, John, born January 1652, married Mary ——. He united with the Stratford church in 1680 and died in 1682-3. He bought a house lott in 1667-8, "bounded east on the street, west on the burying-place, south by a highway 4 rods wide, and north on the common land." This highway now leads to the Stratford Congregational burying-place. They had but one child recorded, a son Samuel, born Nov. 9, 1679, who married in 1706 Sarah Sherman, the daughter of Samuel and Mary (Titharton) Sherman. The Shermans were from Dedham, England, this Samuel being fifth in descent from the first Henry : thus Samuel⁵, Samuel⁴, Edmund³, Henry², Henry¹. Mary Titharton was the daughter of Daniel and Jane Titharton. Marriage dresses must have cost a pretty penny in those days : in Daniel's will he leaves £10 apiece to his three daughters in addition to their inheritance for "wedding gowns." Daniel, son of Samuel and Sarah (Sherman) Beers, was born in Stratford, Nov. 23, 1714, and died in Newtown, Conn., Jan. 14, 1800. According to the old records, "Daniel Beers & Mabel Boothe was joyned in marage Decembʳ ye 27ᵗʰ-1744—there first Born a son named Cyrus was born March ye 23ᵈ A D 1746 ; there second child a Daughter named Jerusha Borne Sepʳ ye 29ᵗʰ 1747—the third a son named Amos Born May the 12ᵗʰ old stil A d 1750, their fourth a son named Daniel Born December ye 25ᵗʰ new stile in 1752, there fifth a Daughter named Ann Born november ye 1754." In another part of the book : "Daniel Beers & Mabel his wife three of there children entered here and the rest of there children entred in a nother place. there daughter Mabel Born Decʳ ye 12 A D 1756—there son Daniel Born march ye 15 A D 1759 there daughter named Easter Born on May 1ˢᵗ, 1761—there son

named Austen Born July ye 10th 1763." This Mabel married
June 13, 1779, John Beach, eldest son of John and Phebe
(Curtis) Beach. [See John III.] Samuel Beers, Jr., son of
Samuel and Sarah (Sherman) Beers and brother to Daniel,
born June 26, 1712, died Oct. 12, 1773, married Abigail Blackman, daughter of John and Abigail (Beers) Blackman; their
son Simeon, b. in 1750, d. 1813, married 1776, Phidema Nichols, daughter of Peter and Rebecca (Camp) Nichols. (See
Nichols.) Abel Beers, son of Simeon, was born Sept. 1st,
1777, and died February 18th, 1858; he married in September
of 1799, Mary Beach, fifth daughter of John and Phebe (Curtis) Beach. Their nine children will be found under Mary
(Beach) Beers. Apropos of this family an item on the town
records : Dec. 18, 1786—"Voted at s⁴ meeting that Mʳ Theophilus Hurd examine into the circumstances of the Country
road leading from the Town Street towards Redding by Cyrus
Bearses house and shift the same on the south side of s⁴
Bearses house in case the publick can be well accomodated
as where the road now lies."

In the Land Records of Newtown, Conn., Vol. 6, p. 10 & 11 :
Deed from Sarah Beers of Newtown to "my sons Samuel &
Daniel Beers of Newtown—for £750—the old farm." May
12, 1749.

On Land Records, Vol. 3 and 4 (one vol.), p. 464 : Nov A D
1740—the heirs of Samuel Beers—Moses and Mary (Beers)
Stillson for land Received of our Brethren John, Samuel
Daniel Nathan and Abraham all of above s⁴ Newtown sans
Nathan who is now of ye town of Norwalk . . . . . our hon-
oured father Mr Samuel Beers formerly of s⁴ Newtown and
now deceased—and that we Abner Hurd and Samuel (Beers)
Hurd for the sum of ℅ ℅—signed Mary Stilson Hannah
Hurd—John, Samuel Daniel Nathan and Abraham Beers.
Nov. 6, 1740.

Mr. James Beers of Brooklyn is engaged on a Beers book,
but he has told me there was nothing to be added to these
scant early facts.

THE BEERS BIBLE.

An old King James Bible—(1810)—contains these records :
"Marriages—1789—April 20ᵗʰ Daniel Beers married by the
Rev. Philo Perry to Naomi Glover. 1818—Newtown Conn

May 10 (Sunday) John Beach married (by the Rev. Mr. Burhans) to Marcia Curtiss." [A. foot note to the Beers–Glover marriage reads : " Entry made this 16th Day 1818 p^r Jno Beach—her account."] On the next page : Births— ".1764—October 3rd (Thursday) Naomi Glover (wife of Danl Beers) born. [With the same foot note.] 1789—Augst 28 (Friday) John Beach (born) entered the 14th of May, 1818. July 18, 1796 Marcia Curtis wife of John Beach, born—entered this 14th Day of May 1818 p^r Jno Beach. [The year of Marcia's birth is first entered as 1797, then as 1790, but corrected to 1796, and under it written " 1796 is the proper date D B B "] " John Beach died April 12th A D 1869—at ¼ past 12 A. M." On a scrap of white paper pasted in there is the notice of the death of Matthew the hermit, as before given, then follows : " Nathanel Fitch King (laborer) died April 17th 1810 aged 42 years 1. 16," and the next in order the Beers deaths.

"Daniel Beers died Jan^r 4th A D 1800, aged 85 years. Mabel Beers [his wife] died July 14 A D 1816, in the 94th year of her age." Cyrus Beers (son), died Nov. 7th 1825, in the 80th year of his age.

Austin Beers (son) died June 16, A D 1825, in the 62^d year of his age. [A foot note to this says, " on his monument 9th by mistake."] Saml Beers Junr (grandson) died June 8, 1813, aged 39 years. Esther Bennet (daughter), wife of Caleb, died April 22nd, 1796, in the 35th year of her age. Daniel Beers (son of Daniel and Mabel) died on the 2^d Day of March, 1839, at ¼ past 4 o'clock P M in the 80^{tn} year of his age (viz, he would have been 80 years of age on the 15th of March, 1839.) Naomi Beers (wife of Daniel Beers) died on the 5th Day of August, A D 1848, at 2½ o'clock P M (about 83 years of age.) James Glover died Oct. 28, A D 1821, aged 86 years 2 mos 25 days. Eunice Glover died Feby 18, 1795, aged 57. Ezra Glover (son) died Sep^t 4th, 1826, aged 54 years. Anna Glover (son's wife) died Feby 3rd, 1812, aged 37^{yrs} 11^{ms} 10^d. Ira Glover (grandson) died Decr 23rd, 1811, aged 15^{yrs} 2^{mos} 19^{ds}, " The above are taken from inscriptions on the monuments and entered here this 12th day of June A D 1841 by Jno Beach at request of Naomi Beers."

BIRDSEY.

Dea. John Birdsey came from Reading, Berkshire, England, to America in 1636, and to Wethersfield, Conn., where he married Phillipa, daughter of the Rev. Henry Smith and sister to Dorothy Smith, who married John Blakeman of Stratford, son of the Rev. Adam Blakeman. Tradition says Joseph Hawley, the first at Stratford, married a Birdsey at Wethersfield, Conn., and if so it was most probably a sister of this John Birdsey. John Birdsey removed to Milford in 1639, where his son was baptized in 1641. He removed to Stratford in 1649, where he was a prominent citizen and Deacon of the church, and where he died April 4, 1690, aged 74 years. He married 2d, Alice, widow of Henry Tomlinson. She died Jan. 25, 1698.

The two children of John and Phillipa were John Junr and Joanna. John was born in 1641 and died in 1697. He married in 1669 Phebe Wilcoxson, daughter of William and Margaret Wilcoxson. Of their children the oldest, Hannah, born Feb. 5, 1671, married May 3d, 1693, Isaac Beach son of John I.; their fourth child, Abel Birdsey, born Novr. 1679, married first, Comfort Wells (John^2, John^1, Thomas), and second, Mrs. Mercy Denton ; his daughter Elizabeth married Benjamin Curtis (q. v.).

" Voted—That Mr. Chauncey Whittlesey of Middletown be, and he is hereby appointed and directed to procure a warrant and seize the wheat in the hands of John Birdsey and his sons in Middletown for the use of this state,—leaving them enough for their own consumption, and cause the same to be floured as soon as may be, and deliver fifty bushels of wheat to the Selectmen of Saybrook, for the use of the troops in the fort there, paying said Birdsey and sons the lawful price for the same.

Oct—1777.

Hollister.

FROM "DESCENDANTS OF RICHARD BOOTH,

The following Genealogy of the New England Booths, or that part of them descended from Richard Booth (who descended from Richard Booth, of Cheshire, England), who settled in Fairfield County, Conn., U. S. A., is compiled from the town and church record of Stratford and Newtown, Conn., from records in family bibles, from inscriptions on grave stones, and from tradition. Tradition, the unwritten history of men and events, transmitted orally from father to son, or from ancestors to those of later generations, says, that three brothers, the sons of Richard Booth, of Cheshire, England, came to America between 1630 and 1640, their father having died in December, 1628. They landed at New Haven, Conn., and the oldest, Richard Booth, settled in Stratford, Conn., in 1640, one year after Stratford was settled. John settled at Southold, Long Island, N. Y., and the younger brother went North. History speaks of one Robert Booth at Exeter, New Hampshire, as early as 1645. The descendants of these brothers were aware of their English origin as told to them by their parents, and members of the Booth families visited their cousins in England and English cousins of the Booth family visited them at an early date.

Richard Booth, the progenitor of the Booth family of Fairfield County, Conn., emigrated from Cheshire, England, between the years 1630 and 1640, his father, as tradition has it, being Richard, the fifth son of Sir William Booth. Knight, who died and was buried at Bowden, Cheshire, September, 1578. Tradition says his two younger brothers emigrated to America with Richard, one of them settling on Long Island and the other elsewhere, Richard being the only one who settled in Connecticut. He married Elizabeth, sister of Captain Joseph Hawley, who was the first town clerk of Stratford, and settled in Stratford in 1640.

Richard Booth's name appears often in the town records of his day, as "townsman," or selectman, and in other commissions of office and trust. The prefix Mr., before his name, in the colonial records, indicates, under the rigid adjustment of social rank then observed, a position decidedly influential and respectable. His large landed property he divided in his time among his children. He left no will. The latest mention of him extant is in March, 1688-9, in his 82nd year. As the Congregational Burial Ground, west of Main street, was opened in 1678, he was doubtless buried there, and as his son Joseph, who outlived him not more than 12 or 15 years, would probably be interred at his side, the spot cannot be distant from the monument lately erected by William A. Booth, Esq., and other descendants of Joseph, over the grave of the latter.

Mr. Booth seems to have been twice married, for in 1689 (p. 16, vol. ii., Land Rec.) he speaks of "my *now* wife," a phrase commonly indicative, as then used, of a second marriage. His first wife, the mother of his children, was Elizabeth, sister of Joseph Hawley, the founder of that name, and the first recorder or town clerk of Stratford. This is another incidental proof of his being among the original proprietors of the town. Their daughter, Elizabeth, was born in 1641. A collateral evidence also of the marriage is the fact that his son Ephraim, in his will, styles Samuel Hawley, son of Joseph, " cousin."

Mr. Booth's home lot was in Main street, on the west side, the fifth in order below the Bridgeport road, and is No. 29, on the map of Stratford. Like the other proprietors, also, he had lands of considerable area in the aggregate, scattered through various parts of the town, where, in the divisions by lot, they chanced to fall. This disconnected state of one's farm lands is characteristic of such property in Stratford, even now. The children of Richard and Elizabeth Booth were : Elizabeth, Anne, Ephraim, Ebenezer, John,[2] Joseph, Bethiah, Johannah.

2. Sergeant John Booth *(Richard[1])* was born Nov. 6, 1653. His title of Sergeant was earned in the Pequot War. In 1675 King Philip incited a general Indian war against the whites, burning many villages, and killing men, women and children in the colonies of Massachusetts, Plymouth and Connecticut. The colonists made haste to defend themselves, and raised a thousand men to be placed under command of Col. Thomas Church for an expedition against the stronghold of the enemy in the swamps of Rhode Island, and to make active warfare upon them in their winter quarters there. The town of Stratford raised one company of troops for this purpose, among whose volunteers was John Booth, then but 22 years of age. The march to the seat of war was made in the winter,

on foot, through snow knee-deep, for nearly 100 miles and through an unsettled country, where they found the enemy entrenched in a fortress in a large swamp, difficult of access, on the island of a few acres in extent, surrounded by a broad ditch of water, the depth of which would reach to their armpits. Along this ditch was a barricade of logs, ten or twelve feet high, and an entrance was discovered at a place where a large tree lay across the ditch, capable of allowing only one at a time to pass out in single file between two block houses that guarded the entrance. There was no course to pursue but to press quickly forward and drive the Indians from the block house, and obtain possession.

Of the Connecticut troops to cross on the log, the first was another company from their colony ; the Indians sent forth a murderous fire from their muskets that killed a large number of them. The next company close behind was from Stratford, headed by their captain, who was shot down as soon as he began to cross the log, and most of the men next to him. John Booth, one of the soldiers, was in the center of that company. He pushed forward, and, while in the act of raising his low-crowned hat to cheer on the men behind, a musket ball passed through it, just grazing the top of the scalp, and would have pierced his skull had the hat been in its usual place.* This hat was preserved in the Booth family for upwards of half a century, after which it was unaccountably lost. By this time they had succeeded in driving the Indians from the block house, preventing the remainder of the troops from being obstructed by the fire of their guns in crossing to the fort. The tide had turned in their favor ; for sometime they fought desperately against the Indians, and before the close of the fight a portion of the Massachusetts troops effected an entrance in the rear—placing the Indians between two fires, killing and wounding numbers of them. The savages were completely routed, and soon disappeared. Their wigwams were fired, and the women and children that were in them perished with the structures. It was hoped that they could have got King Philip, but he escaped at that time, and was afterwards hunted down and shot dead in a swamp where he had fled for safety. The tribe having lost a greater part of their number, were completely broken up in their winter quarters.

* This statement rather involved—unless his skull rose with the hat.

Sergeant John married first, June, 1678, Dorothy, daughter of Thomas Hawley, of Roxbury. After her death, in 1710, he married, second, Hannah, widow of Robert Clark. She died in 1717. By his first wife, Dorothy, they had : Thomas, Jonathan, Ephraim, Mary, Ann, Sarah, John.

3. Jonathan Booth *(John² Richard¹)* was born at Stratford the winter of 1681-2, and married Hester, daughter of Samuel Galpin, 1703, and after the birth of his two oldest sons, he, with his cousin Ebenezer, journeyed to Newtown in 1707-8, following up the Housatonic River to where the tribe of Pohtatuck Indians lived, and purchased of them an extensive tract, about two miles west of the river, on that part of which the village of Newtown was afterwards laid out and built. They immediately commenced to clear the forests of the land for cultivation, returning next year to prepare dwellings before they moved their families.

From Jonathan and his cousin, Ebenezer Booth, all the Booths of Newtown have descended, and there is scarcely an old family name in the limits of the town but can (by intermarriage) trace their lineage back to them, as, for instance, the Beers, Nichols, Hawleys, Glovers, and many others. His youngest son, Jonathan, built a house on the old homestead lot, nearly in front of his father's, in 1740. This dwelling was covered with cypress shingles ; those on the roof lasted 80 years before renewal, and the bricks used in the construction of the chimney were brought from Holland. The plastering was done by an Indian and the ring composed of mortar in the ceiling of the parlor was considered a great piece of art in those days. This house remained until a few years ago ; it was removed to the opposite side of the street, to give place to the more modern structure, now on its site. These early settlers, brave in enduring hardships, with persevering industry and contented dispositions, laid the foundation of prosperity, which later generations of Newtown are now enjoying.

Jonathan Booth was buried near the center of Newtown Burying Ground, and his moss-covered, reddish gravestone reads as follows : " In memory of Mr. Jonathan Booth. He died February 8, A. D. 1755, aged 73 years." The grave of Hester, his wife, lies by his side, but the inscription on her gravestone is only partially legible. Jonathan Booth's children were : Daniel, Abel, Ann, Jonathan, Mabel.

4. Lieutenant Daniel Booth *(Jonathan², John², Richard¹)* was born at Stratford Jan. 12, 1704; removed with his parents, when four or five years of age, to their new home in New- town, Conn., where he spent a long, active and useful life. He was married to Eunice, daughter of Thomas Bennett, by the Rev. John Beach, then a Congregational minister, in 172–. By his marriage he had eight children, three sons and five daughters, all of whom lived to grow up, marry and have families, and settle around him. His father built him a house about half a mile east of his own, and gave him a deed of the same in March, 1728–9, with the orchard of young apple trees thereon, and two of them are still living at the present time. By his industry and management he acquired a large landed property, and was at one time the largest landholder in town. The inhabitants of the colony were sparsely settled within its limits, and looked to themselves to keep up a military organi- zation in defense of itself against any inroads of an enemy. Every able-bodied man was enrolled to duty, held himself ready in any emergency, and every town had its organized company. Daniel Booth was chosen a lieutenant in the com- pany at Newtown, and held a lieutenant's commission, and the numerous deeds on the town records give him the title of lieutenant.

Lieutenant Daniel Booth was a faithful and an honored member of the society to which he belonged, was a man of extensive reading, well versed in the Bible and had held the office of a deacon for thirteen years, diligently studying the Scriptures, continuing perusing their sacred leaves, until he became convinced of the errors of Congregationalism, and resigned his office of deacon and membership in the said society. The minister and members of said society expostu- lated and tried to dissuade him from his course, and called a day to meet them in the meeting house, and to discuss the subject of his resignation. In the month of September they met in the meeting house for the purpose of acting on his resignation. Deacon Daniel expressed his views on the sub- ject and the Rev. Mr. Judson followed him on the sub- ject of his resignation; they thus reasoned upon the matter together, but Deacon Daniel having thoroughly posted him- self, and brought forward so much Scriptural proof that he outreasoned the Rev. Mr. Judson, his minister, and the Rev. Mr. Judson told his people not to say one word against

Deacon Daniel Booth resigning. The members of the society recorded the following :

"Sept. 9, A. D. 1763 : Deacon Daniel Booth resigned of his own motion his office of deacon in this church, and also his relation as a brother, because he could not, as himself declareth, be easy under the Calvinistic doctrine therein taught."

The effect of the conversion of Rev. John Beach, and his faithful deacon, Daniel Booth, to the Church of England, brought a large number of followers from the Congregational Society to the Episcopal Church, and Trinity Church, Newtown, was from that time and continued to be one of the strongest Episcopal parishes in the diocese of Connecticut.

Lieutenant Daniel Booth was a man of broad views in his charities as well as in his religion. It was his custom to visit, in person, every poor family in town during the winter, carrying a grist of wheat or other provisions to the needy, and investigating the condition of each for the winter. If any did not have fodder enough to winter their cow, it must be brought and put with his cows till grass came. Of course, he never lacked for help in the coming harvest. Speaking of his sons, who complained that he gave away too much, he used to say : " My boys don't realize that for every pound I give away in charities there comes back ten pounds to me again." At a time when milch cows were scarce and he had cows to sell, he refused to sell to those who had money, because so many poor people needed cows, that had no money. Many instances of his liberal kindness are told, and the following inscription on his grave stone, near the center of Newtown Burying Ground, written by his beloved pastor, Rev. John Beach, sums it all up :

" The once well-respected Mr. Daniel Booth, here rested from the hurry of life the 8th of April, A. D. 1777, aged LXXIII. Could a virtuous, honest and amiable character, could blessings of the poor echoing from his gate, could the sympathetic grief of an aged partner disarm the king of terrors, he had not died.

> " What is life ? To answer life's great aim.
> From earth's low prison, from the vale of tears,
> With age incumbered and oppressed with years,
> Death set him free, his Christ had made his peace ;
> Let grief be dumb ; let pious sorrow cease."

Lieutenant Daniel was a tall man of a fine and commanding appearance, with a good physical constitution, far beyond one of his years. Reared in the midst of the Pohtatuck Indians, his every-day business bringing him in contact with them, they learned to both love and fear him, for he had a peculiarly fascinating influence over them. He taught them to cultivate the soil and many of the arts of civilization. He, in person plowed their corn, and they in turn hoed corn for him. Alone, in the dead of night, he would often leave his bed and go out in the darkness to their settlement, on what is now known as Walnut Tree Hill, one or two miles away, to still their "powwows" and settle their difficulties, and came home unharmed. Once his wife, after waiting and watching his return into the small hours of the night, was pacing the long hall, when the door opened noiselessly and a tall, straight form, like an Indian, confronted her in the gloom. She shrieked, and, fainting, was caught in her husband's arms —as she supposed he was killed and the stranger was on his murderous errand. He died universally respected and beloved. His children named in his will were: Esther, Anna, Daniel, Sarah, Abraham, Eunice, Naomi, Ezra."

Of the families to be specially noted in this connection, three of Jonathan Booth's children, Daniel, Ann and Mabel, married respectively into those of Bennett, Nichols and Beers. On the records "Daniel Booth was born January ye 12th 1704." He was married to Eunice Bennett by the Rev. John Beach, and had eight children as above. Of these, Eunice, born in 1738, married James Glover, son of John and Elizabeth (Bennett) Glover, and their daughter Anna married Major Curtis (q. v.). Ann, the daughter of Jonathan, born Ap. 15, 1710, married in 1732 Nathaniel Nichols (see Nichols). Mabel, born Dec. 13, 1722, married Daniel Beers (q. v.).

Deed of Jonathan Booth to his two daughters, Ann Nichols and Mabel Beers.

"To all present to whom, etc—Know ye that I Jonathan Booth of Newtown in ye County of Fairfield and Colony of Connecticut in New England—for & in consideration of ye Paternal Love good will & Affection that I have and Do bare towards my Daughter Ann—ye wife of Nathaniel Nichols—and Mabel ye wife of Daniel Beers all of said Newtown in ye County and Colony aforesaid, Do by these Pres-

ents give grant make over aliene & fully & absolutely convey one
certain tract of land lying in Newtown aforesaid upon walnut-tree hill
so called containing about 21 acres more or less, it being of a ten
acre Division & an old six acre Division with sizure Bounded westerly
& northerly by Daniel Booth's land, southerly & easterly by ye Highway and do hereby give unto my son Daniel Booth and his heirs ye
title and Privilege of having a cart Road through said land. And I
ye said Jonathan Booth Do likewise Divide ye said Lot to each of my
said Daughters in ye following manner & to be understood thus—My
Daughter Ann shall have eight acres & my Daughter Mabel thirteen
acres in equal proportion in quantity, that is to say—each one of said
eight shall be as good as each of thirteen acres—& likewise (vice
versa—) across & that either by alowance or Devision—to have & to
hold the above—etc, etc.

Signed JONATHAN BOOTH.

Dec 19, 1748."

1769—January.
Col Rec.
"Upon the memorial of Jonathan Booth of Newtown in the County of Fairfield representing to this
Assembly—that on the 5th day of December last as
he was paying away some money in Newtown, he
dropt a forty-shilling bill of 1762 date of this Colony emission, and
there being a great number of persons in the house it was trod upon
almost all to pieces, praying to this Assembly that they give him an
order on the Colony treasurer for the value of s^d bill, etc., etc."

—and such is their trust and confidence in his honesty that the

"s^d treasurer is ordered to pay him in the sum of fifty shillings being
the value of s^d bill accordingly."

CURTICE.

Whether this family name was originally and according to
Winter, "Courtoise," courteous, or "Courthoys," short-
hosed, in America it was certainly "Court-toise," short conclusions! stand and deliver! Much has been written of their
coming to this country, and the disentanglement of the various branches in so doing. We shall have the advantage of
the latest researches and thus enable ourselves to correct previous errors. In Nazing, County Essex, lived two brothers,
John and William. John married there, April 19, 1610, Elizabeth Hutchins. William married there Aug. 6, 1618, Sarah
Elliot, sister to John Elliot, afterward apostle to the Indians.
William and Sarah came to this country and settled in Rox-

bury, from whom are descended the Curtises of Boston and others. John's *widow*, Elizabeth, came with her sons John and William to Stratford, Conn. From these are descended the Curtises of Stratford, New Haven, Newtown and other Connecticut localities. In all early records the name is spelled Curtice, afterwards Curtis and Curtiss. Some of the family have preferred and still prefer to think it most incorrect to use more than one *s*, but others are as strongly convinced that the double final is necessary. I have used one only, for the reason that I have found it almost invariably so spelled in this particular branch of the family.

William, the son of John and Elizabeth (Hutchins) Curtis, was born in Nazing, Essex county. We find him taking a prominent part in Stratford as early as 1670. In the June of 1672, at the appointment of the General Court, he was "confirmed Captain, Joseph Judson Lieutenant and Stephen Burrit Ensign of the trainband." At the same Court and "until further orders be taken, Captn Nathan Gold (of Fairfield) shall be deemed chief military officer of the County . . . and Captn Wm Curtis his second." In August, 1672, he is with the Governor, Deputy Governor and assistants, as a war council against the Dutch in New York, appointed "to act as the Grand Committee of the Colony in establishing and commissionating military officers $^e/_e$ $^e/_e$." The next November, is Captain "for such forces as shall be sent from Fairfield County" in this cause. His Commission is renewed in 1675. In the meantime and afterward he is Deputy for Stratford to the General Court sixteen times. John was perhaps a less distinguished but an equally honored citizen.

The name of William's first wife, by whom he had all his children, has not yet been traced; he married second, Sarah (Morris) Goodrich; his family consisted of nine children, of whom the youngest, Josiah, born Aug. 30, 1662, is our ancestor.

Josiah married twice also; Abigail Judson, daughter of Joseph and Sarah (Porter) Judson, who was the mother of two children and died in 1697, when he married Mary Beach, daughter of Benjamin (son of Richard) and Mary (Peacock) Beach. To them were born eleven children. Two of the sons, Benjamin and Matthew, appear herein.

12

I. Benjamin was born Dec. 25, 1704, and died Sept. 4, 1776. He married first, Aug. 27, 1727, Elizabeth Birdsey, the daughter of Abel and Comfort (Wells) Birdsey. She died Feb. 24th, 1773, and he married, on June 2[d] of the same year, Bathsheba Ford. All his children by his first wife: Nehemiah, who married Martha Clark and had seven children ; Phebe, who married Daniel Morehouse : Eunice, who married Amos Hard; Elizabeth, who married Capt[n] John Glover ; Benjamin, who married first Phedima Nichols, second Mary Devine (de Vine), and third Phebe Ferris, (his ten children were born of his first two wives); Abijah, who married first Sarah Birdsey and second Mary ———, three sons ; Salmon, who lived but eleven years ; and Sarah, who married Nirom Hard.

II. Matthew, the son of Josiah and Mary (Beach) Curtis, was born 1712. He married June 2, 1730, Phebe Judson, daughter of Captain David and Phebe (Stiles, dau. Ephraim) Judson. She was born Feb. 9, 1717, and died Sept. 18, 1758. In a deed of land to his children in 1787, Matthew speaks of the following as then living : "Sons Nirom Matthew Josiah and Reuben, all of Newtown, Stiles Curtis of New Haven," and an "only daughter Pheby Beach." This Pheby was born Feb. 20, 1737-8, and married John Beach, Jun[r], in 1756, the son of Reverend John Beach.

Abijah Curtis, the fourth son of Benjamin and Elizabeth was born January 31, 1740, and died November 20th, 1817. By his first wife, Sarah Birdsey, he had three sons—John, Benjamin and Abijah Birdsey. John married Hannah, the daughter of John and Phebe (Curtis) Beach, about 1793. This family will be found under the head of John II.

Benjamin was born in 1766, and he died February 20th, 1825. His wife's name, mentioned in his will [one of the earliest probated in Newtown] was Mehitable ——— ; he left no children. This was the *Dr.* Benjamin Curtis spoken of in the sketch of Newtown as favoring inoculation.

Abijah Birdsey Curtis was born in 1772, and died in 1857. An account of his family and descendants follows in order.

Major Abijah Birdsey Curtis, called for brevity, " A B C," was a figure in Newtown remembrance. Farmer, as his people before him, he was of the order of Putnam—ready to leave the plow and grasp the sword. I shudder, as did my father before me, to speak that word, for was not that same sword afterwards made over to carve less dangerous but more palatable every day food ? There are several portraits of Major Curtis which show him to have been quite equal to the many tales told of his spirit and heartiness of enjoyment in things temporal. As a small child—or at least a very young one— I remember when in Newtown being taken to the Potatuck farm one day, to a twelve o'clock dinner. Grandfather Beach was delayed in catching the gray mare and therefore he—my grandmother, mother and myself, were late in arriving. It was not then the fashion, nor was it ever the habit of that house, to await guests, so they had already sat down in the big kitchen, and in spite of that locality our welcome was none too warm. As a child my attention was taken up with novel externals, and aside from the general stiffness I did not then appreciate the full situation. The occurrence was so often afterwards the subject of comment that I can now supply detail. The Major was furious and monosyllabic ; the rest of the household frightened ; the efforts of the guests to preserve their dignity, heroic ; and the as speedy as possible retreat after pie, when the pent up feelings burst forth and the homeward progress enlivened with such laughter as caused the sober villagers to stare and some less steady to join. On one of my last visits to Newtown I went down to the old place again. A very respectable Irish family now own it, and the old lady assured me with pride that the papers were made out in the names of Beach and Curtis. Somehow the kitchen did not look so large, or the well so far away. Grandfather Beach kept part of the old Beach farm and used to spend his summers there, and the grey mare, whose objections to anything in the way of harness or conveyance had occasioned us such lasting disgrace, is a prominent and fearful recollection ; he used to insist on driving her wherever she particularly disliked to go, and once, leaving Newtown, obliged us to sit in the wagon as the train approached the station, while the mare stood on her hind legs until our lives were in danger ; however, we had to sit and wait, and the train had to *stand* and wait until she was controlled, when he threw the reins on her back, got out slowly and deliberately, went to her head—but, *then* such a heavenly smile irradiated the scene that we came away in its glory. Major Curtis, of course, chewed :—and thereby hangs tale number two.

Persuaded to have his "daguerre" taken, he donned his Sunday blue and the finest of his ruffled shirts, and went off to the artist at Danbury, successfully posed and the picture in process—a critical moment for *both* arrived. He solemnly rose, walked over to a spittoon in the corner of the room, spit therein, and returning sat down and re-composed feature and limb to the former required angles. The artist threw up his hands: "My G— Major Curtis," he exclaimed—"you've spoiled one of the best things I ever did!" The Major glared a moment, then with great indignation he said, "D'ye mean to tell me, sir, that I can't spit?" "Why no, sir—of *course* you can't—why just . . . . " But the outraged officer waited for no explanation; he picked up his hat and riding whip, stalked out of the gallery, mounted his horse, and doubtless *galloped* home!

Major Curtis's military record is found not only in the intricacies of that large but incomplete volume called "Connecticut Men in the Revolution," etc., where it is wrongly placed as in the 'militia'—but in many family papers and legal records; his commissions were doubtless carefully preserved by some descendant, but I have not had the pleasure of seeing them. A pay roll of the 2nd company of the 1st Regiment, State Corps is however, presented here, with some corrections.

NEW HAVEN, Oct. 20, 1814.

1st Lt. Charles G. Curtis [probably Carlos G., his nephew, son of his brother John]. Ensign—Walter Brooks. Sergt⁸— Philo M. Wooster, Asa Sanford and Alfred D(evine) Curtis. Corporals—Amasa Washburn, Charles Judson, Sherman Hawley and Villeroy Glover. Fifers—Philo Dibble and Ira Shepherd. Drummers—Charles Sherman and Noble Pierce. Privates—Alanson Black (man?), Philo-Philo Jʳ and Amaranth Beers, Wheeler Bennit, Harry Blakeslee, Lyman Beecher, —— Barnes, Ebnʳ Booth, Smith Dunning, David Downs, Heber Frost, Lucius Gilbert, Thomas Green, Asa Griswold, Silas and Roswell Hurd, Reuben Hughes, Chauncey Isbell, Lucius Judson, Leverett Kneels (or Knevals), Ithama Merwin, Harman Northrop, Henry Nichols, Judson Platt, Jarvis Platt, Jacob Pardy, Lardner Peery, Ira Palmerly, Lewis Peet, John A. Peck, Marcus Ryan, Lemuel and David Summers, John Sherman, Jr., Francis Stone, Adoniram Squires,

Joseph Turner, Eli Wheeler, Amos Wells, David Williams, John Walker, Illsley Wyman, Abijah Wallace. Waiters— Horatio Nelson Curtis, John Beach Curtis and Ransom Bartlett.

Alfred Devine Curtis was the son of his Uncle Benjamin Curtis, while Corporal Villeroy Glover we shall meet again as the son of Zalmon and Phebe (Beach) Glover, and a Curtis on both sides of the house. Horatio Nelson and John (Abijah) Beach Curtis, his young son and nephew, were 15 and 16 years of age only. The old vexed question of rivalry and jealousy between State and Militia troops was then very strong, and we find among some old papers a copy of a remonstrance directed to his Excellency John Cotton Smith, wherein Captains Curtis, Butler, and Buckingham, as a committee, draft the petition containing complaints that the State troops are paraded to the left of the Militia, that militia officers are placed in command over them, and their officers obliged to lead the militia, that the same hold courts martial, etc. ; it is dated Oct. 19, 1814, and is sent in as an answer to unjust criticism of the State troops as "in a disgraceful state of disorganization." Military men will appreciate the situation. A Regimental Order sent to "Abijah B. Curtis Capⁿ 2nd Co. 1st Regt. State Corps," dated Ap. 7, 1814, commands quarterly instead of monthly reports. This is signed "Tim° Shepard, Col. 1st Regt. Infantry State Corps." Just when he was appointed Major I have not been able to ascertain, but probably at his discharge. Another story before we enter upon family matters. The boys and young men of the town were fond of firing off muskets to frighten old ladies and cutting up all such pranks as are natural to youth. The Major's well known fearlessness and fiery temperament made him a frequent butt. One night they planned to give him a scare : hid in the woods at a sudden dark turn of the road and waited with muskets loaded. He kept them in the cold and rain sometime, but finally the steady trot of old Bess was heard and all prepared for a grand burst ; "*bang*" went the guns. Bess shied a moment, but the Major drove in his heels and called out, "Hi ! there, you young scamps, go home and take some whiskey or you'll be sick to-morrow," and, plunketty plunk, on he went to his own waiting nightcap. It is just

possible that he had prefaced such with a nip at some hospit-
able house on the street, for there were many primitive and
unlicensed bars, where the weary friend or casual stranger
could alleviate thirst at regular rates. In Caleb Baldwin's
house [where the family of Charles F. Beardsley now live,
Mrs. Beardsley a great granddaughter of Major Curtis] there
was such a bar between the south parlor and the kitchen ; it
is now made over into a passage way and closets.

There were five sons and four daughters born to Abijah
Birdsey and Anna Glover Curtis, who were married in 1793
The eldest, a son, Elihu Starr, 1794–1850, was himself a militia-
man ; an old order dated Ap. 17, 1820, directed to Lieut.
Elihu S. Curtis, Newtown, contains his appointment as pay-
master of the 2d Reg' Riflemen Conn. Militia, and is signed
Lemuel G. Storrs, Col., accompanied by a personal note from
the Colonel, concerning such names as warrant its insertion.

Middletown Ap. 19, 1820,—Mr. Curtis, Dr. Sir, I annex you a rg'.
order of 17th Inst. and enclose you a warrant for the office of Pay
Master of the Regiment of wh you will make known to me as soon as
possible your acceptance or declension. I rec⁴ your letter pr. mail.
You will be expected to attend to choice of officers at North Milford, on
the 1st Monday of May next at 2 o'clock P. M. The order for choice
is sent to Leut. Alpheus Clarke. . . . I have sent reg' order to
Capt" Hawley and an order for choice of a Lieut in the room of Mr.
Nichols removed out of the State. I wish you to notify Capt" Hawley,
as he may not think to go to the Post office.

Yours "/o L. G. Storrs.

Elihu married in Rochester, and the death of a son Henry
is recorded in the old Curtis Bible, in 1864, "aged 29." Elihu's
death is given as "Jan. 1, 1850, aged 56." Marcia, the eldest
daughter of Abijah and Anna, married John Beach (q. v.)
Horatio Nelson, 1798–1871, was always spoken of as a most
attractive and elegant gentleman ; he early left home, went
first to Bridgeport, where he was in the business house of
Sigourney & Co., and thence to Rochester, New York State,
where he established himself in the manufacture of woolen
stuffs and the milling business. As children we used to hear
Uncle Nelson spoken of with the greatest affection and respect.
I suppose he must have visited us, indeed I know he did, but
there is no responsive mind-picture of a particularly superior
person. He married in Rochester and had several children ;

his wife was a daughter of Captⁿ Neafus ; his daughter
Sarah married her cousin, Carlos G., the son of Abijah
Beach Curtis, and their family will be found recorded.
The next child was a daughter Charlotte, 1800–1883, who
married in 1818, Nichols Booth Lake, of Newtown, the son of
Peter and Temperance (Thompson) Lake, another old New-
town family of note. Their children were Joseph Thompson,
Birdsey Curtis, Mary and Daniel Booth. Of these Joseph
married Hannah Rebecca Smith and had two daughters, Mary
Josephine and Nettie, who died young. Mary Josephine Lake
married Charles F. Beardsley and has two sons, Clarence
Lake and Paul Joseph.

Birdsey Curtis Lake married twice, first Jane Sherman of
Newtown, and second Phebe Warren Peck of New Haven
(q. v.). By his first wife he had two sons, one of whom, Levi
Ives Lake, resides in the West. Mary Lake married Robert
Peck and had one daughter, Charlotte, who married Eli C.
Barnum and lives in Danbury, Conn. The third daughter of
Major Curtis was Anna, 1802–1854 ; she married in 1829,
Simeon Blakeman Nichols of Newtown, son of Lemuel and
Alice (Blakeman) Nichols. They had one son and three
daughters. George Lemuel never married. Mary Alice
married in 1861 Dr. Alfred Starr of New York. [See Starr
Gen.] Charlotte Curtis married Henry Carrington Miles of
Milford ; one son, Henry C. Miles, Jr., married in 1895 Julia
Agnes Platt, daughter of George F. and Elizabeth (Addis)
Platt. Caroline Rebecca Nichols married in 1865 Ignatius
McKinnan, and died in 1869 at the age of 28. Joseph Beebe
Curtis—1805–1834—married Elizabeth ———— and had three
daughters ; one died an infant, and two, Sarah and Julia, said
to have been beautiful and lovely girls, died at the ages of 18
and 28. His widow remarried and is, I believe, still living.

Birdsey Glover Curtis—1807–1875—also went West. He
married in Beloit, Wisconsin, Louise Ketchum. I think there
were no children. Some of his letters from Canada and the
West seem to indicate a delicate state of health, but he lived
to the fourscore-and-ten limit.

Caroline, the fourth and last daughter, born in 1818, married in 1831 Simeon Peck of Newtown. She died in 1858,
leaving three sons, Abner, Henry, and David. Mr. Peck married again, the widow of Robert Peck and daughter of Gould

Curtis [Mr. Robert Peck's first wife being, as we have seen, Mary Lake]. Charles Gould Peck is the son of this marriage. David Peck is the only surviving son of Caroline.

Ira Lawrence Curtis, the youngest of Major Curtis' family, born in 1813, married his cousin Marietta Glover, and their family will be found in its order of descendants.

GLOVER, HUBBELL, MEIGS, HARD, &c.

The first records of our branch of this family open at once on an interesting early controversy and an intimate connection with some of New Haven's most notable colonists, Henry Glover, who was at once supporter and critic of the governmental system, and prominent in the growing business interests of the town. Dr. Bacon, in his "Historical Discourses," writes: "Concerning Henry Glover's seeking reconciliation with the Church, for the scandalous evils for which he was cast out, and the Church's receiving of him again, the 11th day of the 6th month 1644. Henry Glover having acquainted the elders with his desire of being reconciled °/. °/," a long and intricately worded setting forth follows, the gist of which being that his case is brought before the elders, and the next Lord's day he is appointed to speak before them. After morning service, the ruling elder rose and desired the rest of the elders would remain; this being done, the door was closed and the matter brought forward, and Henry Glover, who still stood without, was invited in to plead his cause; he "acknowledged the several facts for which he was cast out, and the rules he had broken, and showed also how many temptations he had been exercised with from Satan since he was cast out, ... and also expressed his earnest desire of being reconciled to the Church." So they conferred together as to whether his repentance was genuine and how he had borne himself, and neighbors were asked to testify. Goodman Chapman "spoke something tending to clear him," but no one accused him; however, they decided to wait over another week and see that everything was as it should be. The wisdom of this hesitation may be evidenced by the manner of its reception by the impatient sinner, for the report goes on to say: "Henry Glover, standing up by a pillar, went hastily down, when he saw it was deferred till the next Lord's day, and he let some words fall which had the appearance of discontent." However, he again apologized, and was finally received in full, an address, a long prayer, and the following absolution pronounced by the pastor, Mr. Davenport: "Henry Glover, I do in the name of the Lord Jesus Christ, and by power delegated from Jesus Christ to his Church, pronounce thee absolved and set free from the sentence of excommunication under which thou hast stood bound, and do restore thee to the liberties and privileges of this Church which thou formerly did'st enjoy." Dr. Bacon says: "I know not where to look for a more copious illustration of the duties performed by the ruling elder in the primitive New England churches." Doubtless it would now call a smile could we discover the catalogue of sins for which Mr. Glover was forced to make so complete a humiliation. The date of his marriage to Ellinor, Ellen, or Helena Wakeman, sister to John of Hartford, is not given, but the birth of his daughter Mary or her baptism is found in Mr. Davenport's records as in 1641. She marries Moses Mansfield. Hannah, b. 1646, marries David Ashley ; Sarah, 1655, marries John Ball ; Abigail, 1652, marries Daniel Burr ; and son John, 1648, marries Joanna Daniel, daughter of Stephen and Anna (Gregson) Daniel. These names need no introduction or explanation to many Connecticut families of to-day.

Henry and Elinor Glover appear frequently on Colonial records as responsible persons to sign wills, witness agreements and become trustees for various estates, guardians for minor children, etc., etc. In one of Mr. Davenport's letters to Gov' Winthrop, dated "New Haven this 14th day of the 2nd m—1655" (April 14), there is this phrase: "Sister Glover, newly returned from Long Island, puts us in fear that you are in some thoughts about transporting your family to the Bay or to Connecticut ; but I can not believe either, though I believe you may be inclined to both." By this it would seem that the breach was thoroughly healed and the Glovers reinstated, being once more in favor with God and man.

Henry's son John had also a son John, who was born Nov' 20, 1674, in New Haven, and died in Newtown, Conn., June 30, 1752. He married, Nov. 27, 1700, Margaret Hubbell, daughter of Lieut. John and Patience Hubbell. Lieut. John was one of the sons of Richard and Elizabeth (Meigs) Hub-

bell of New Haven, Guilford and Fairfield. Richard Hubbell was from Wales, and was on the fidelity list of 1647 in
New Haven, where he married, in 1650, the daughter of John
and Thomasine (Fry) Meigs [a son of Vincent Meigs]. The
Meigs came from Weymouth to Guilford and New Haven,
and John was at one time, 1648–58, second owner by purchase
of the Cutler lot [S.E. corner of Chapel and Church streets,
New Haven]. The deed of conveyance reads: " Wm Jeanes
passeth over to John Meigs his house and house lot lying at
the corner over against Mr. Gregson's—betwixt the house lot
of John Budd and the highway." Col. Return Jonathan
Meigs was a descendant, whose son became Governor of
Ohio and Postmaster-General of the United States. Margaret
Hubbell was born in 1681 ; her father, Lt. John, was interested in the settlement of· Derby, Conn. He purchased of
Samuel Sherman in 1683 a house and lot at "Old Mill" in
Stratford, " next west of Samuel Blakeman's house." John
Hubbell died of the small-pox in the Franco-Indian War,
near Schenectady. His widow married, as we shall see, into
the Hawley family. After the death of his first wife in 1704,
John Glover married the widow Bethia (Beach) Bickley,
widow of William Bickley, or Beckley, and daughter of Benjamin Beach, son of Richard of New Haven. By his first wife,
Margaret Hubbell, John Glover, Jr., had a son John, born
Dec. 30, 1701, who married, July 12, 1724, at Norwalk, Conn.,
Elizabeth Bennet, daughter of James and Sarah Bennett of
Stratfield. This was a runaway match, just why we do not
discover, for the families were intimate and friendly and no
reason except possibly some one else in the case, or indeed it
might have been as an old darkie Auntie of ours explained
an elopement in *her* family : " Dunno Missy—reckon Laure
done thought t'would save '*spense*." This was the John who
purchased land at Rye, 1742—" bought three acres of land on
Grachus street, near Hyatt's Cove—he was of Newtown,
Conn." And " in 1745, John Glover of Newtown Conn^t late
of Rye—releases to Joseph Haight his right as a descendant
of the ancient proprietors of the s^d Town of Rye by purchase
as that right was released to him by Robert Bloomer and
Joseph Kniffen."

James Bennet, his wife's father, was son of James and
Hannah (Wheeler) Bennet, who was from Concord, Mass.

and coming to Fairfield married Hannah, the eldest daughter
of Thomas Wheeler, one of the company coming with the
Rev. John Jones, residing first in Concord, Mass., and afterward a large proprietor in Fairfield, where in all deeds and
transfers he is written Thomas sen^r. He married Ann Smith,
said to be one of the daughters of Deacon Henry of Wethersfield.

John Glover IV was born Feb. 11, 1732, and died July 2,
1802. He married Elizabeth Curtis (daughter of Benjamin),
and is the John who figured in the midnight capture of Genl.
Silliman. Their 2nd son, Zalmon, born May 3, 1760, married
Phebe Beach, the daughter of John and Phebe (Curtis) Beach,
and of this branch Mr. Smith Peck Glover of Sandy Hook,
Newtown, is the only male descendant and last of his name.
John IV's brother, James, born Aug. 3d, 1735, married Eunice
Booth, the daughter of Daniel and Eunice (Bennit) Boothe,
and their daughter Anna Glover became the first wife of
Major Curtis ; her sister Naomi, as we have seen, married
Daniel Beers. Villeroy Glover, 2nd son of Zalmon and Phebe
(Beach), married in 1828 Susan Hurd, eldest daughter of
Benjamin and Mabel (Tomlinson) Hurd. This family de-
serves larger mention, both as to numerous intricate relationships and prominence in municipal affairs. "Abner Heard
(as it is first spelled in the old records) & Hannah Beers was
joyned in marage August ye 20th Ad 1740. The births of
their children are as followeth.

"Nirom Heard their first born a son born Decem^r ye 18th
1740." [Married Sarah Curtis, dau. of Benjamin and Elizabeth (Birdsey) Curtis.]

"Cyreneus ye second son Born January ye 5th A D 1742."
[Married Phebe Camp, dau. of Lemuel and Alis (Leavenworth)
Camp.]

"Ammon Heard—Born ye third son September ye 25th A D
1744,—John Heard ye fourth Son Born July ye 20th A D 1746."

"Abigail Heard a Daughter Born January ye 7th A D 1748.
Sarah Hurd Born January ye 9th Day A D 1751." [She married Alfred Divine (de Vine) Curtis, the son of Benjamin and
Mary (Divine) Curtis, and their daughter, Phebe Curtis, married Joseph Nettleton, q. v.].

"Currence Hard—Born the 21st Day of March A D 1753.
Ann Hurd Born the 9th Day of May A D 1755." [Ann married

Eben Beers, and their daughter Lucy was the first wife of John Glover (son of Zalmon).]

"Zilpha Hard Born the . . . . November A D 1756." Married or "was joyned in marage Covenant—to Zalmon Peck, on 12ᵗʰ of September 1781—their first born a son married Zerah Smith Ann Peck born on Wednesday December 18ᵗʰ A D 1782—"

"Abner Hard Born the 6ᵗʰ Day of September A D 1757." [He married Lavinah Nichols, dau. of Peter.] "Hannah Hard Born the 14ᵗʰ Day of May A D 1761—and Jabesh—or Jabeth—Born ye 9 Day of September A D 1763."

This is sufficient to indicate a rather numerous line of descendants, and is certainly confusing enough to the initiated, and although there is more of the same at hand, some consideration for the casual brain and its complement of grey matter induces to restraint.

HAWLEY.

The Hawleys, according to their own account of themselves, came from Parvidge, Derbyshire, in Old England, now called Parwich ("Parritch"), about nine miles from Derby and four from Ashbourne, the market town. Mr. Joseph Hawley came to America about 1629-30, but just where he located previous to our meeting him in Stratford in 1650 has not been revealed. His brother Thomas was in Roxbury, Mass., as early as 1639. Joseph purchased land in Stratford in 1650, was already married and had a son Daniel, born in 1647-8 Seven sons and three daughters are entered in the Stratford records [leaving out Samuel]. He was also one of the original proprietors of Newtown. Samuel Hawley Junʳ, in whom we are more interested, married Bethia Boothe, daughter of Ephraim ; he and his wife were second cousins, which anyone can discover by a sufficiently elaborate study of the "Hawley Record." This was the Samˡ Hawley who was one of the three purchasers of Newtown. The story of their first coming is traditional only, and *not* recorded. It is said they rode to the top of a high hill, at sunset, and seeing an impossible dip before them, stopped there and made their first settlement, calling it "Land's end." Hawley, Junos, and Bush were the historic three who made that wonderful bargain of coats, etc., with the

Indians. Our connection brings us by the way of Samuel Sr., who married two wives, Mary Thompson, daughter of Thomas of Farmington in 1673, and then Patience Hubbell, widow of John. Benjamin, the son of the second wife, born in 1697, married first in 1724, Mary Nichols, and 2d, Experience Dibble. Benjamin, Jr. married Catharine Hurd ; Jabez, son of Benjamin, Jr., married Parthenia Boothe (daughter of Daniel and Huldah (Thompson) Boothe, and their son Isaac married Avis Jane Shepard. Edson N. and Thomas A. Hawley, brothers, are sons to this Isaac.

Another connection is traced back from James Rogers Hawley, who married Lydia Beach (dau. of Isaac), and was the son of Joseph and Chloe (Rogers) Hawley, son of William and Lydia (Nash), son of Joseph and Hannah Walker, son of Captain John and Hannah, son of the first Joseph and Katherine Hawley. James Rogers Hawley was born in Redding, Sept. 18, 1797, and married March 28, 1822.—See his family Record.

LYON.

With patience and perseverance this branch of our ancestral tree was cleared of its dead wood and made to bloom again. Correspondence developed so much material and of so varied a character that personal research at the source became evidently necessary. The best part of a week in Redding Ridge last summer was spent in company with dust and spiders in the "town house," and in spite of inherent aversion to both these evils, self control and a forced, single-purposed application rewarded the attendant agony. In articulating these relationships, it was discovered that many bore similar surnames, both husbands and wives, as well as children ; the closest attention to dates should be given before questioning the accuracy of the following statements. Commencing with Anna Lyon, who married in 1773, Abel Hill. She was the daughter of Peter and Abigail (Sherwood) Lyon, and was born April 1, 1757. Peter was one of the three sons of Nathan, as found by an old land record, by which Joseph, David and Peter agree to a certain settlement according to the will of their "honoured father Nathan Lyon," but nothing further could be traced of Nathan. On the Sherwood side Abigail was the daughter of Captⁿ Daniel Sherwood and Anne Burr, who was a daughter of John Burr and Katherine Wakeman. Thus two first settler's families are indicated. Of course the Sherwoods need no "bush" to Connecticut genealogists. From these three sons of Nathan Lyon many descendants are now living.

David married in 1756 Harriet Sanford, and Joseph, in 1761, Lois Sanford, sisters and daughters of Ephraim and Elizabeth (Mix) Sanford. David had a son Nathan, as well as a son Cyrus, and two daughters "Betty Vreeland and Hannah Hill." With Betty we have no further connection. Hannah (born Feb. 10, 1758), married April 22d, 1725, Andrew Lane Hill. [For their family see Line of John.] One of their daughters married her cousin Asahel, the son of Peter Lyon. If not too confusing—please notice here—that Anna and her brother Peter Lyon married Abel and his half-sister Hannah Hill. Before further intricacies drive every sane idea from us, we will look up the military record of the family. At the October session of the Assemby in 1768, "this Assembly do establish Mr. Daniel Lyon to be Lieut. of the 16th Company or trainband in the 11th Regiment in this Colony." This is Daniel Lyon of Weston, whose children will be found mentioned further on. "May, 1771, this Assembly do establish Peter Lyon to be Lieutenant of the East Company or trainband in the Town of Redding." Peter had previously been Ensign. Beside Anna and Asahel, Peter had two sons, Walker and Zalmon, and another daughter Betty.

Now let us begin on the Daniel of Weston line. All we know of him is that he *was* of Weston and had three, perhaps four sons, Philo, David, Lemuel and Eli. Philo, born 1764, married Hannah Beach, one of the daughters of Lazarus and Lydia Sanford Beach ; Lemuel, born ———, married in 1787, Huldah Sanford, daughter of John and Anne (Wheeler) Sanford ; David married and had a daughter Eleanor, who married Thaddeus B. Reed of Redding ; and Eli married in 1795, Betty Hill. On the Redding records this marriage is entered on "Ap. 26, 1795, in presence of Abel Hill." Philo and Hannah Beach had seven children ; the two first died unmarried, and the five sons, Isaac Beach, Henry, Philo, Ziba and Philemon, all married. Lemuel and Hannah (Sanford) Lyon had six ; their children will be found in these records. Eli and this David's descendants do not further appear. By the kindness of Mrs. Julia Amelia Hawley Chase of Sharon, daughter to Lydia Beach Hawley, I have some valuable news-paper clippings, by which we may read of the deaths of the brothers, Ziba and Philemon Lyon, in Utica, New York. They were evidently pioneers and foremost in Church mat-ters. Quoting from the Utica Observer: "In the death of this highly esteemed man [Philemon] Utica has lost one of its most valuable citizens, and the Church one of its most con-sistent and devoted members. In every point from which Mr. Lyon's character can be viewed he was a good man." And of Mr. Ziba Lyon: "Some may have left a more dis-tinguished, none a more honest name . . . Mr. Lyon named the church (Grace) and was unanimously chosen senior warden, which position he held consecutively over forty years with universal acceptance. Mr. Lyon was a man of noted physique ; he strongly resembled in profile, George Washington. Of singular modesty and great kindness and liberality, indulging in no controversy, he was yet strong in the faith and a very bulwark to the weak."

It is to be deplored that these excellent men left no chil-dren to bear so enviable a name. In the probate records at Bridgeport the settlement of Levi Lyon's estate in 1839 con-tains this concluding clause, "The widow Larinda and Anna Lyon, widow of Nehemiah, to pass and repass thro' Orra's kitchen," Orra being the eldest son.

NICHOLS.

Although we have no exact data to establish the connec-tion, it seems more than probable that Francis and Sir Richard Nicoll, the first Governor of New York and Albany, were brothers, sons of Francis and Margaret, daughter of Sir George Bruce. Francis Nicholl is recorded as "of the Middle Temple one of the Squires of the Bath to Sir Edward Bruce and lyeth buried at Ampthill, County of Bedford." Beside Richard and Francis there was a third son, Edward, and a sister. Francis appeared in Stratford in 1639 with four children, Isaac, Caleb, John and a daughter. He married a second wife, Anne, daughter of Barnabas Wines of Southold, L. I., by whom he had one daughter, Anne. After Mr. Nich-

ols' death his widow married John Elton, also of Southold.
By order of the General Court on Oct. 10, 1639, "The Governor and Mr. Wells (are) to confer with the Planters at
'Pequannocke' (Stratford), to give them the oath of Fidelity, make such free as they see fit, order them to send one or
two Deputies to the General Courts in September and April,
and for Deciding of Differences and Controversies under 40ˢ
among them . . . . . . as also to assign Sergeant Nichols for
the present to train the men and exercise them in military
discipline." It is evident that he must have been some military officer at home. He died in 1650, leaving but a small
estate. His son Isaac became identified with Stratford, was
three times Deputy to the General Court ; he married Margaret, who died 1691-2 ; he died in 1695. His son Isaac, born
in 1654, married Mary and died before his father ; his son
Richard, born Novʳ. 26, 1678, in Stratford, married June 3,
1702, Comfort Sherman, daughter of Theophilus of Wethersfield, whose deed of 270 acres to Richard Nichols "my son
in law," is recorded at Newtown, May ye 15ᵗʰ 1736, although
dated August 24, 1711." There is also a deed from Josiah
Rossiter and wife, Sarah (Sherman, sister to Theophilus),
dated June 18, 1712, wherein Theophilus Sherman is spoken
of as "late of Weathersfield." This last is recorded in Newtown, June 10, 1731, in the presence of Samuel Beers and
Benjamin Sherman. Richard Nichols died Sepʳ 20, 1756.
Comfort died Febʸ 11, 1726, and he married a second wife,
Elizabeth. His third son, Nathaniel, was born April 8, 1707,
and settled in Newtown.

"Nathaniel Nichols and Ann Booth was joyned in marage
compact December ye 3ʳᵈ 1730 By ye Revʳᵈ Mr Jno Beach.

Peter Nichols, son of Nathaniel Nicholls by Ann his wife,
was born in Newtown on ye first day of March A D 1732-3,
Philo born Febʸ 27, 1734, Phodyma Feb 9, 1736, Richard
May 15, 1739, Austen July 2, 1741, Elijah Aug. 12, 1743. Ther
third daughter Ann Sepᵗ 1, 1845, Ester, eldest daughter Sep
25, 1731, Theophilus May 13, 1748, Joseph July 22, 1750.
Nathaniel died May 10, 1785—aged 78 ; Ann his wife died
Jan 5, 1780—aged 70. Austen (or Austin) died May 27, 1765
—Philo died Sep 19, 1776, æ 22. Theophilus died Oct. 23,
1785, and Elijah—Decr 25, 1813. Peter Nichols, the oldest
son, married April 29, 1753, Rebecca Camp ; his daughter

Phedima, born Dec 1st 1755, married Feby 7, 1776 Simeon Beers (see Beers) and died Jany 6, 1822. Their son Abel, born Sep 1, 1777—married 1799 Mary Beach, daughter of John and Phebe (Curtis) Beach.

Peter Nichols—called Captain—died Jany 15, 1799—Rebecca, his wife, died Oct 12th, 1793, in her 61st year." Whether the "one acre near Benty grass plaine, which he deeds to his daughter Phedima Beers, now the wife of Simeon Beers of sd Newtown" in 1788, represents her entire share of the property I have not been able to discover. Another child of Peter and Rebecca—"ther seventh son named Nathaniel" born July ye 11, A D 1769, married Grace Sherman, dau of Jotham, and had a son Harry, who married Sarah Blackman —and their son, Philo, married February 28th 1854 Sarah Esther Glover, daughter of Villeroy and Susan (Hard) Glover. (q. v.).

Richard Nichols the 2nd son of Nathaniel and Ann (Booth) Nichols, married Dec 2, 1760, Abigail Gold. To give it in the original: "Richard Nichols and Abigail Gold was marryed Dece 2d 1760 A D. Their first born a daughter named Ann— Oct 12, 1763—ther son Austin—July 24 A D. 1766—Huldah —Sep 22, 1769; Daniel June 21, 1773, Hannah Dec 23, 1775. Their servant Robbie, a Melatto boy, born January the 13 A D 1788." Abigail Gold was the eldest daughter of Captain Stephen Gold of Redding—and Grace Burr, daughter of Stephen and Elizabeth (Hall) Burr, all of Redding. Annie Nichols, daughter of Richard and Abigail (Gold) Nichols, born Oct 12th, 1763, married 1779 Jarvis Platt, son of Obadiah of Fairfield and Thankful (Scudder) Platt. [See Platt.] Their daughter Charlotte married in 1802 Lemuel Sanford, son of James and Sarah (Beach) Sanford—(q. v.).

To return to the family of Nathaniel and Ann (Booth) Nichols. Their son Theophilus, born May 13, 1748, married —or to quote again: "Theophilus Nichols and Sarah Meeker was joyned together in the mariage covenant on the first day of December A D 1771, and "their son James" born 9th of Sept' 1775, married Lucy Beach, the eldest daughter of John and Mabel (Beers) Beach. This family of Captain James and Lucy (Beach) Nichols, consisting of nine sons and at last one daughter, will occupy a large share in the genealogical portion of this book. The little portrait of Lucy Beach

Nichols is taken from an old picture, and while it has not the
colouring to add proper effect, is nevertheless extremely
well reproduced in the illustration. The oldest son of Lucy
and James Nichols, Theophilus Beach, usually called "Beach,"
was a sea captain, and there is a tale told of his tragic death
or rather disappearance while on a voyage homeward bound
from Vera Cruz. It seems that he had made up his mind to
settle down and give up the sea, but the company in whose
employ he had made many successful trips urged his taking
one more in their interest—and he went about Newtown taking his farewells and laughingly saying this was "positively
the last." It was at the time of the "Tippecanoe and Tyler
too" log hut campaign—and at Newtown they had one—
there the young people gathered and gave him a "send off."
He was right—it was indeed his last, for on the return passage, having transacted the business of sale and purchase at
that port, the crew mutinied, and neither the ship or its
cargo were every heard of again. A sister vessel sighted her
and made the customary signals, which being returned in a
curiously untutored manner, led the Captain to suppose
something was wrong, but night came on with a heavy storm
and in the morning nothing was to be seen. He reported the
circumstance to the owners, and from such evidence and the
non-appearance of any one concerned it was given out that a
mutiny had taken place, Captain Nichols either murdered or
in irons ; and that the ignorant crew had lost control of the
ship and all perished.

Another brother, the Rev. Abel, going out to the Bermudas
to take charge of a divinity school sailed on the "Silas
Marner." A most fearful storm came up, and the vessel
sprang a leak ; the life boats were lowered and the passengers and crew taken off—Mr. Nichols stood by the Captain
and assisted him to maintain order. At the last moment it was
found that there was room for but one more, and he insisted
that the Captain's life was of more value than his own,
beside his being responsible to the agents for his passengers,
and so—however it may have ensued—the fact remains that
the Rev. Abel Nichols was then and there translated to the
reward of his heroic self-sacrifice.

The fourth son, Drusus, went west and both he and his wife
died in Mongoquinong (now Mongo) Indiana. They were

LUCY BEACH NICHOLS

1908

brought to Lima, Indiana, by Charles G. Nichols, their son, who married into the Burnell family [as will be seen] and deposited in the Burnell Tomb there, as were others of the Nichols family who died in that State. Mr. Samuel Burnell and Drusus Nichols were settlers together and so warm an attachment sprung up that, at the death of Mr. Nichols, his son Charles, then a minor, chose him for his guardian. Mr. Burnell was himself an Englishman, having been born in Yorkshire in 1809. In 1829 he came to America, landing at New York with a capital of twenty-six dollars. He went west immediately and eventually became one of the richest land holders in the State. He was one of the earliest settlers of La Grange county, Indiana, and went through the days when meal and flour had to be ground in the coffee mill. His wife was also English, of London birth. By intermarriage with the Nichols, the families are to-day as one, both by such choice and friendly interests. There is an old haircloth trunk of historic value in their possession with this inscription written on a card which is tacked on the lid: "This trunk was brought from England by the Rev. John Beach, an Epis¹ Minister, Missionary to convert heathen, was brought from Conn. to Indiana by Philo Nichols, youngest great grandson of Rev. Beach."

SHELDON.

The earliest mention of this family is found in the settlement of Dorchester, when Isaac Sheldon (born in England 1629) was made freeman. In 1640 he was at Windsor, where he married in 1653 Mary Woodford, daughter of Thomas and Mary (Platt) Woodford of Hartford. The two families went to Northampton in 1655, where Mary died April 17, 1684. Isaac died there in July, 1708. His son Thomas, born Aug. 6, 1661, married Mary Hinsdale in 1685. She was the daughter of Samuel Hinsdale, who was killed by the Indians at Deerfield, Sept. 18, 1675. Deacon Thomas Sheldon's wife Mary was a grandaughter of Robert Hinsdale of Dedham, Medfield, Hadley and Deerfield ; he and his three sons were slain by the Indians. Mary's mother was Mehitable Johnson. Elisha Sheldon, son of Thomas and Mary, was born in Northampton, Sept. 2, 1709 ; he settled in Lyme, Connecticut,

as early as 1733, where he was appointed in October
of that year County Surveyor. He married Elizabeth Ely,
Oct' 7, 1735, the daughter of Samuel and Jane (Lord) Ely.
Richard Ely settled in Lyme as early as 1660; his son Richard
J' married Mary Marvin, daughter of Reynold and Sarah
(Clark) Marvin. And their son Lemuel married Jane, the
daughter of Richard and Elizabeth (Hyde) Lord. Elisha
Sheldon (Yale Coll. 1730,) was appointed a Captain in the
Militia in 1737 and was for five sessions representative for
Lyme to the General Assembly, from 1746 to 1749. In 1753
he removed to Litchfield, then newly settled, and was from
1754 to 1761, Associate Judge of the County Court. He represented Litchfield in the Assembly for six years, at seventeen
sessions. In 1761 he was elected to the Upper House, or
Board of Assistants, where he continued till his resignation,
the year before his death, which occurred in 1779. It is said
that owing to his patriotic determination to give credit to the
Continental Currency his estate was much diminished.

In the Colonial Records of Connecticut we read :

1768. "Upon petition of Benajah Douglas & others of Canaan,
against Asa Douglas of a place called Jericho in the Province of Massachusetts Bay, and Robert Livingstone, Jr., of the manor of Livingstone in the Province of New York— . . . . . . , whereupon Elisha
Sheldon John Williams and Increase Moseley were appointed a Committee . . . . . .

Oct. 1768. This Assembly do establish Mr Elisha Sheldon to be
Captain of the troop of horse in the fourteenth regiment this Colony.*

Oct 1769—The Ousatunuck Lottery settlement—Elisha Sheldon—
Increase Mosely and Daniel Sherman Esq—a committee of investigation.

May. 1770. With Benjamin Hall and Joseph Hull Esq—a com on
meeting house in Westbury.

May. 1770. On petition of Noah Wadhams of Goshen in the County
of Litchfield vs Elisha Sheldon of Litchfield in the County of Litchfield Esq—as he is treasurer of the County Litchfield aforesaid——"

Oct 1770. Committee on meeting house in Westbury report "that
they had affixed a stake in Mr Wait Scot's home lot on the west side
of the highway leading northward from the old meeting house, which
report is accepted by this Assembly . . . .

Oct, 1771. Personally appeared Lynde Lord Esq'—Sheriff of Litchfield County as principal—Elisha Sheldon of Litchfield Esq' and Mr
Enoch Lord of Lyme both of the Colony of Connecticut—as sureties"

* Elisha Sheldon, J'.

binding themselves to the amount of one thousand pounds—severally
—and joyntly,—   Signed

Jonᵃ Trumbull Govʳ.

Nominated—Oct 1768.   Oct 1769—
   " 1770.   " 1771.
Chosen Assistant May. 1768—May 1769—
     " 1770 .   " 1771.
     " 1772 .
Present . 1768—both sessions
   1769   "   "
   1770   "   "
   1771   "   "   & special August Session.
   1772—in May &   "   "   "
In May 1772—Appointed one of the Quorum in the county of Litchfield.

It was his son, Col. Elisha, who was appointed to the troop
of horse. Of him we may read in the history of Redding.
The second son Samuel, born Oct. 7, 1750, married Elizabeth
Baldwin, daughter of John and Sarah (Gun*) Baldwin. [See
Baldwin Gen.] They had a son Elisha, born July 15, 1782,
who married Ann Beach, the daughter of John and Mabel
(Beers) Beach.

Samuel Sheldon was the first man drafted on Litchfield
hills. It is his house which is now owned by Professor James
M. Hoppin. This Elisha was a physician and lived first in
Sheldon, Vt., a town founded and named by the family ; it is
probable that his marriage to Ann Beach took place there,
though his home after 1821 and professional studies and practice were made in Troy, New York State. He died Dec. 14,
1832, leaving a widow and two daughters.

Dr. Sheldon was foremost in his profession and held many
positions under the Government. He was one of the Trustees
of the village of Troy. Quoting from a letter written by his
daughter Elizabeth in 1822—" My Father's mother and father
spend the winter with us, but grandma stays with Aunt Leonard a part of the time." This daughter, Elizabeth, married
in 1827 Henry Edward Peck of New Haven, son of Nathan
and Mehitable (Tibbals) Peck. Their children will be found
duly chronicled, as well as those of the other daughter, Mary
Scribner.

   * Thus spelled in Baldwin.Gen.

TOWNSEND.

The Rev. Epenetus Townsend, Episcopal minister of Salem, New York, was graduated from Columbia (then King's College) in 1767, and went to England to take Holy Orders. He returned in 1768 and entered upon his pastoral duties. In 1776 he was sent to the Whig Committee, but was dismissed. Three weeks after the Declaration of Independence he abandoned his pulpit, and in October was a prisoner at Fishkill. In March, 1777, he was removed to Long Island, and shortly afterward embarked with his family for Nova Scotia; the vessel foundered and every one on board perished. As Lucy Beach is called "my daughter Lucy Townsend" in the Rev. John's will, made in 1772, it is evident that they were married shortly after his return from England. [See also mention of in " Biography."]

Rev'd John Beach and his Descendants

ABBREVIATIONS.

---

b. Born.

d. Died.

m. Married.

unm. Unmarried.

dau. Daughter.

bap. Baptized.

rec'd. Record.

p. Page.

T.p., Twp. Township.

Ts. Tombstone.

cem'y. Cemetery.

v. Verified record.

q. v. Which see.

Ed. Editor's note.

Rev'd John Beach and his Descendants

I.

Reverend John Beach.

[Third son of Isaac and Hannah (Birdsey) Beach, p. 135.]

b. October 6, 1700.
d. March 12, 1782. (Newtown Records.)
first m. 1726 : Stratford, Conn.

Sarah Beach.

[Second dau. of NATHANIEL BEACH and Sarah Porter.]

b. November 12, 1699, Stratford, Conn.
d. August 1, 1756. Buried at Redding Ridge.

second m. ABIGAIL (GUNN) HOLBROOKE.

[Widow of John Holbrooke ; dau. of Serg't Abel Gunn of Derby, and Agnes Hawkins.]

b. 1707, Derby, Conn.
d. 1783, Derby, Conn.

CHILDREN (of first marriage)

JOSEPH BEACH son of John Beach by Sarah his wife was born in Newtown, September y⁼ 26 at nine of y⁼ Clo'k at night Anno Domini 1727.

PHEEBE BEACH daughter of John Beach by Sarah his wife was born in Newtown, Sept y⁼ 30 5 of y⁼ clok in y⁼ morning anno of Domini 1729, page 202.

JOHN BEACH son of John Beach was born in Newtown, January y⁼ 19ᵗʰ 1731–32.

JOHN BEACH son of Jn⁰ Beach by Sarah his wife, Died Decemb. 31ˢᵗ 1733.

JOHN BEACH son of John Beach by Sarah his wife born September 5ᵗʰ, 1734 ; p. 148, 202.

LAZARUS BEACH son of fame Parents born September the 20ᵗʰ 1736 ; p. 159, 246.

SARAH BEACH of the fame Parents born January 24ᵗʰ 1738–9.

HANNAH dau. of Rev. Jno b. Jan. 24, 1741; died at Redding Jan. 7th, 1759, æ. 18 yrs.

LUCY BEACH, b. 1743; m. Rev⁴ Epenetus Townsend; p. 198.

II.

Phœbe Beach.

[Eldest dau. of Rev⁴ John Beach by his first wife, Sarah Beach.]

    b. September 30, 1729.   (Newtown Records.)
    d. May 9, 1751, T. S. Redding Ridge.
    m. October 31, 1748.   (Fairfield Families.)

CAPTAIN DANIEL HILL.

[Son of William and Hannah (Morehouse) Hill (m. Apr. 28, 1725).]

    b. January 26, 1726.
    d. July 11, 1805.

III.

Abel Hill.

[Only child of Daniel Hill by his first wife, Phœbe Beach.]

    b. Jan⁷ 10, A.D. 1750.   (Redding Rec., p. 35, Vol. II.)
    m. May 11, 1773.   Redding.

ANNA LYON.

[Dau. of Peter Lyon and Abigail Sherwood (m. May 10, 1753; dau. of Capt. Daniel and Ann (Burr) Sherwood).]

    b. April 1, 1757.
    d. January 22, 1827, T. S. Redding Ridge.

CHILDREN:

BEACH HILL, b. April 2, 1777, Redding, Conn.; d. abroad; p. 147.
LUCY HILL, b. March 4, 1783, Redding, Conn.; d. March 9, 1794.

———o———

II.

John Beach, Jr.

[Second son of Rev⁴ John Beach by his first wife, Sarah Beach.]

    b. September 5, 1734.   (Newtown Records.)
    d. May 15, 1791, Newtown, Conn.

JOHN BEACH & Phobe Curtis was joyned in yᵉ marrage Couvnant August yᵉ 3rd by Mr. John Beach, Clerk, A.D. 1756.

Mathew Curtifs & Phebe Judfon was married June ʸᵉ 2ᵈ Day in the yeare of our Lord Christ 1737. There firſt child a daughter named Phebe Born in February ʸᵉ 20ᵗʰ Day, A.D. 1737-8.—Died December 4, 1815.

(Newtown Records.)

CHILDREN:

There first Born a son Born December yᵉ 9ᵗʰ Day, named John A.D. 1757; p. 203.

There second a daughter named Phobe, born January yᵉ 29ᵗʰ A.D. 1760. p. 228. (Newtown Record, Vol. I.)

MATTHEW BEACH, b. February 22, 1763, Newtown; d. Sept. 10, 1766.

HANNAH BEACH, b. May 22, 1765, Newtown, Conn. p. 237.

LUCY BEACH, b. July 17, 1768; d. February 5, 1779.

SARAH BEACH, b. February 5, 1774, Newtown, Conn. p. 239.

MARY BEACH, b. August 4, 1778, Newtown, Conn. p. 243.

7 March child died 1762 at Birth; Sept. 17 child 1766 aged 3½ years.

—Mr. Isaac Beers' Note Book.

III.

John Beach, 3d.

[Elder son of John Beach, Jr., and Phœbe Curtis.]

b. December 9, 1757. (Newtown Records.)

d. June 10, 1830, Sheldon, Vermont.

m. June 13, 1779, Newtown, Conn.

MABEL BEERS.

[Third dau. of Daniel Beers and Mabel Boothe. (See Beers.)]

b. December ʸᵉ 12ᵗʰ A.D. 1756. (Newtown Records.)

d. January 5, 1844. (Beach Bible.)

CHILDREN:

LUCY BEACH, b. February 22, 1780, Newtown, Conn. p. 204.

ANNE BEACH, b. November 22, 1781; d. June 9, 1783, Newtown.

MATTHEW BEACH, b. November 5, 1782, Newtown, Conn.

ANN BEACH, b. December 25, 1783, Newtown, Conn. p. 211.

BOYLE BEACH, b. March 12, 1786, Newtown, Conn. p. 215.

PHŒBE BEACH, b. February 6, 1788, Newtown, Conn. p. 221.

JOHN BEACH, 4th, b. August 28, 1789, Newtown, Conn. p. 225.

CHARLOTTE BEACH, b. November 9, 1790, Newtown, Conn. p. 227.

DAVID BEACH, b. December 13, 1793, Newtown, Conn.; d. 1860; m. Mary Martin of *Coeyman's, Green Co., N. Y. One son, HENRY MARTIN BEACH, drowned in 1881.

MABEL BEACH, b. July 22, 1795, Newtown; d. Dec. 13, 1796, Sheldon, Vt.

* Possibly Coeyman's (Quoemen's), Albany Co., N. Y.

IV.
Lucy Beach.
[Eldest dau. of John Beach, 3d, and Mabel Beers.]

b. February 22, 1780, Newtown, Conn.
d. March 31, 1856, Newtown, Conn.

m. CAPTAIN JAMES NICHOLS.
[Second son of Theophilus Nichols and Sarah Meeker. (See Nichols.)]
Their son James b. 9 of September, 1775.   (Newtown Records.)
 ˙d. November 4, 1852, Newtown, Conn.

CHILDREN:

THEOPHILUS BEACH NICHOLS, b. 1800 ; d. 1840. p. 194.
ISAAC NICHOLS, b. April 19, 1802, Newtown,˙Conn. p. 204.
WILLIAM NICHOLS, b. November 6, 1803 ; d. December 24, 1824.
DRUSUS NICHOLS, b. March 2, 1805, Newtown, Conn. p. 209.
REVᵈ ABEL NICHOLS, b. May 25, 1807, Newtown, Conn.; d. December
    16, 1859, at sea ; m. Eliza Saunders (no children). p. 194.
THADDEUS HUBBELL NICHOLS, b. June 1, 1809.
    d. February 5, 1856, Newtown.
JAMES AUGUSTUS FERDINAND NICHOLS, b. June 10, 1812, Newtown,
    Conn.; killed by a fall in a warehouse at Ft. Wayne, Ind.,
    February 4, 1846, buried in the Burnell Tomb, Lima, Ind. ; m.
    Ann Green, d. 1851, buried Rome, Ind. One son, JAMES
    AUGUSTUS NICHOLS, b. Mongoquinong (Mongo), Ind. ; d. in
    the Civil War, 1861–1865.   (Mrs. E. B. N.)
JOHN NICHOLS, b. October 28, 1814, Newtown, Conn. p. 210.
PHILO NICHOLS, b. November 5, 1815, Newtown, Conn. p. 211.
SUSAN NICHOLS, b. December 24, 1818, Newtown, Conn. p. 233.
(Birth dates from a leaf from the old Nichols' Bible in possession of Mrs. Daniel Camp.)

V.
Isaac Nichols.
[Second son of Capt. James Nichols and Lucy Beach.]

b. April 19, 1802, Newtown, Conn.
d. September 17, 1853, Newtown, Conn.
first m. 1827–8 :

BETSEY PLATT.
[Dau. of Moses Platt and Anna Judson (m. 1770).]

b.   1798.
d. October 6, 1835, Newtown.
second m. March 20, 1838 :

LOUISA BARTLETT.
[Dau. of John and Sarah (Bennett) Bartlett.]

b. April 4, 1812.
d. October 21, 1894.

CHILDREN (of first marriage):

HENRY NICHOLS, b. May 8, 1829, Weston, Conn. p. 205.
JAMES NICHOLS, b. October 24, 1830. p. 206.
WILLIAM NICHOLS, b. February 11, 1833.
    drowned August 9, 1845, Newtown.
MARY BETSEY NICHOLS, b.   1835; d.   1853.

CHILDREN (of second marriage):

AUGUSTA NICHOLS, b. February 22, 1839, Newtown, Conn. p. 207.
SARAH NICHOLS, b. May 29, 1840, Newtown, Conn. p. 207.
MARGARET NICHOLS, b. March 20, 1842, Newtown, Conn. p. 208.
BEACH NICHOLS, b. February 8, 1844, Newtown, Conn. p. 208.
LOUISA BARTLETT NICHOLS, b. September 7, 1845, Newtown, Conn.;
    d. August 31, 1891, Newtown, Conn.
WILLIAM NICHOLS, b. Aug. 18, 1847; d. Jan. 7, 1866, Newtown, Conn.
ARTHUR NICHOLS, b. April 2, 1849; d. Oct. 5, 1853, Newtown, Conn.
GRACE NICHOLS, b. November 26, 1851, Newtown, Conn. p. 209.

VI.

Henry Nichols.

[Eldest son of Isaac Nichols by his first wife, Betsey Platt.]

b. May 8, 1829, Weston, Conn.
m. March 20, 1857, Greenfield, La Grange Co., Ind.

ELIZABETH SHARP.

[Dau. of Daniel and Ann (Cooke) Sharp.]

b. May 29, 1839, Sodus, Ontario Co., N. Y.

CHILDREN:

ARTHUR NICHOLS, b. June 6, 1858, Mongo, Ind. p. 206.
EMMA NICHOLS, b. January 16, 1860, Mongo, La Grange Co., Ind.;
    m. August 12, 1896, Orland, Ind.
        CHARLES M. CLARK.
        [Son of Noah and Anna (Mosely) Clark.]
    b. April 26, 1858, Burlington, Vt.
    d. September 8, 1897, Friend, Nebr.   (v. E. N. Clark.)
FRED NICHOLS, b. October 29, 1861, La Grange, Ind. (unm.)
ALICE NICHOLS, b. September 7, 1863, La Grange, Ind.
    m. November 8, 1893, Garret, Indiana.
        BENJAMIN FRANKLIN BARBER.
        [Son of William and Cidney (Slaybaugh) Barber.]
    b. May 21, 1862, Steuben, Ind.   (rec'd A. N. Barber.)
FANNY NICHOLS, b. September 9, 1864; d. May 26, 1894.
LIZZIE NICHOLS, b. May 8, 1866, La Grange, Ind. (unm.)
SUSAN NICHOLS, b. July 3, 1867, La Grange, Ind. p. 206.

JAMES NICHOLS, b. September 23, 1868 ; d. April 16, 1869.
WILLIE NICHOLS, b. August 1, 1871 ; d. September 4, 1871.
ANNA NICHOLS, b. June 7, 1875, La Grange, Ind. (unm.)
MARGIE NICHOLS, b. October 29, 1877, La Grange, Ind. (unm.)
BABE, 1879; 1879 (lived but three weeks). (v. Henry Nichols.)

VII.

Arthur Nichols.

[Eldest son of Henry Nichols and Elizabeth Sharp.]

b. June 6, 1858, Mongo, La Grange Co., Ind.
m. September 14, 1892, La Grange, Ind.

BELLE CANSE.

[Dau. of John and Hannah (Scripture) Canse.]

b. July 5, 1872, Orland, Ind.

CHILDREN :

CLARA NICHOLS, b. October 16, 1893, Orland, Steuben Co., Ind.
RAY NICHOLS, b. October 12, 1895, Flint, Jackson Township, Ind.
MABEL NICHOLS, b. July 18, 1897, Orland, Steuben Co., Ind.
(v. Arthur Nichols.)

VII.

Susan Nichols.

[Fifth dau. of Henry Nichols and Elizabeth Sharp.]

b. July 3, 1867, La Grange, Ind.
m. April 12, 1894, Orland, Ind.

JAMES A. TURNER.

[Son of James and Elizabeth (Rippey) Turner.]

b. Aug. 18, 1866, Fa'n river T'p, St. Joseph Co., Mich.

CHILDREN :

FANNY NICHOLS TURNER, b. July 30, 1895, Sturgis, Mich.
STANLEY RAYMOND TURNER, b. February 21, 1897, Sturgis, Mich.
(rec'd S. N. Turner.)

VI.

James Nichols.

[Second son of Isaac Nichols by his first wife, Betsey Platt. p. 204.]

b. October 24, 1830.
m. July 9, 1861.

ISABELLA M. STARKWEATHER.

[Dau. of Nathan and Cynthia (Loomis) Starkweather (m. Nov 7, 1838.)]

b. August 5, 1842.
d. October 9, 1895.

CHILDREN:

JAMES LOOMIS NICHOLS, b. February 20, 1863; d. June 29, 1871.
HELEN C. NICHOLS, b. December 24, 1870, Hartford, Conn. p. 207.
ISABELLA NICHOLS, b. October 23, 1874; d. June 28, 1875.

(rec'd Jas. Nichols.)

VII.

Helen Christine Nichols.

[Elder dau. of James Nichols and Isabella M. Starkweather.]

b. December 24, 1870, Hartford, Conn.
m. December 24, 1890, Hartford, Conn.

HARRY ALEXANDER SMITH.

[Son of Alexander and Charlotte (Smith) Smith.]

b. May 24, 1869, Springfield, Mass.

CHILDREN:

JAMES NICHOLS SMITH, b. October 2, 1891, Rochester, N. Y.
HARRIET HELEN SMITH, b. January 6, 1896, Rochester, N. Y.

(v. H. C. N. Smith.)

VI.

Augusta Nichols.

[Eldest dau. of Isaac Nichols by his second wife, Louisa Bartlett.]

b. February 22, 1839, Newtown, Conn.
m. November 23, 1859, Newtown, Conn.

DANIEL CAMP.

[Son of Dibble and Esther (Blackman) Camp.]

b. February 21, 1836, Newtown, Conn.

CHILDREN:

ESTHER LOUISA CAMP, b. January 27, 1862, Newtown, Conn.
GRACE CAMP, b. October 3, 1872, Newtown, Conn.
m. December 29, 1897, Trinity Church, Newtown, Conn.,
DOCTOR CLYDE OSCAR ANDERSON, Pittsburg, Penn.
[Son of Jacob H. and Elizabeth (McAlister) Anderson.]
b. October 17, 1870, Sardis, Penn.

(v. G. C. Anderson.) (v. Mrs. Daniel Camp.)

VI.

Sarah Nichols.

[Second dau. of Isaac Nichols by his second wife, Louisa Bartlett.]

b. May 29, 1840, Newtown, Conn.
m. October 15, 1860, Newtown, Conn.

SILAS NORMAN BEERS.

[Son of Charles and Mary (Glover) Beers.]

b. September 3, 1837, Newtown, Conn.
d. May 12, 1873.

CHILD:

SUSAN LYNNE BEERS, b. April 8, 1865, Newtown, Conn.

(v. S. N. Beers.)

VI.

Margaret Nichols.

[Third dau. of Isaac Nichols by his second wife, Louisa Bartlett.]

b. March 20, 1842, Newtown, Conn.

m. December 27, 1865, Newtown, Conn.

EDSON NICHOLS HAWLEY.

[Son of Isaac and Avis Jane (Shepard) Hawley. (Hawley Record.)]

b. November 3, 1839, Brookfield, Conn.

CHILDREN:

CLARA BERTHA HAWLEY, b. June 10, 1867.
   d. May 26, 1868, Brookfield, Conn.
ARTHUR SHEPARD HAWLEY, b. August 21, 1869, Brookfield, Conn.
JULIA NICHOLS HAWLEY, b. October 14, 1871, Brookfield, Conn.
CLARENCE BEACH HAWLEY, b. June 27, 1875, Brookfield, Conn.
JOHN BEACH HAWLEY, b. February 23, 1878, Brookfield, Conn.

(v. M. N. Hawley.)

VI.

Beach Nichols.

[Eldest son of Isaac Nichols by his second wife, Louisa Bartlett.]

b. February 8, 1844, Newtown, Conn.

m. December 27, 1865, Newtown, Conn.

ADELIA FAIRCHILD.

CHILDREN:

HARRIET G. NICHOLS, b. October 22, 1866, Newtown, Conn. p. 208.
JAMES BEACH NICHOLS, b. March 13, 1879, Newtown, Conn.

VII.

Harriet Gertrude Nichols.

[Elder child of Beach Nichols and Adelia Fairchild.]

b. October 22, 1866, Newtown, Conn.

m. September 16, 1891, Newtown, Conn.

HENRY SKIDMORE NICHOLS.

[Son of HENRY T. and Abby L. (Skidmore) NICHOLS (m. May 13, 1868).]

b. March 15, 1869.

CHILD:

JESSIE LOUISE NICHOLS, b. March 12, 1893, Newtown, Conn.

VI.

Grace Nichols.

[Fifth dau. of Isaac Nichols by his second wife, Louisa Bartlett.]

b. November, 1851, Newtown, Conn.

m. October 8, 1874, Newtown, Conn.

HOMER AUGUSTUS HAWLEY.

[Son of Isaac and Avis Jane (Shepard) Hawley. (Hawley Record.)]

b. July 20, 1843, Newtown, Conn.

CHILDREN:

WILLIS NICHOLS HAWLEY, b. August 9, 1875, Newtown, Conn.
SARAH LOUISA HAWLEY, b. June 21, 1879, Newtown, Conn.
JAMES SHEPARD HAWLEY, b. January 6, 1881, Newtown, Conn.

(v. G. N. Hawley.)

V.

Drusus Nichols.

[Fourth son of Capt. James Nichols and Lucy Beach. p. 204.]

b. March 2, 1805, Newtown, Conn.

d. October 16, 1850, Mongo, Ind.

m. May 30, 1832, Sherman, Conn.

REBECCA B. GRAVES.

[Dau. of Judge Jedediah Graves and Sally Northrop.]

b.   , near New Milford, Conn.

d. July 3, 1861, English Prairie, Ind.

CHILDREN:

CHARLES G. NICHOLS, b. September 13, 1836, Sherman, Conn. p. 209.
DAUGHTER, b. September 30, 1840, died in infancy.
SON, b. June 2, 1845, died in infancy.   (v. E. B. N.)

VI.

Charles Graves Nichols.

[Elder son of Drusus Nichols and Rebecca B. Graves.]

b. September 13, 1836, Sherman, Conn.

d. July 21, 1890, Lima, Ind.

m. June 21, 1860, English Prairie, Ind.

ELLA BURNELL.

[Dau. of Samuel Burnell (b. December 24, 1809, Yorkshire, Eng.), m. April 1839
Mary A. Mason ; son of Wm. and Ann (Halley) Burnell.]

b. May 8, 1840, English Prairie, Ind.

14

CHILDREN :

DRUSUS B. NICHOLS, b. March 9, 1861, English Prairie, Ind. p. 210.
MARY NICHOLS, b. August 12, 1864, English Prairie, Ind. (unm.)
CHARLES STUART NICHOLS, b. Nov. 14, 1865, Eng. Prairie, Ind. (unm.)
SAMUEL BURNELL NICHOLS, b. Nov. 10, 1867, English Prairie, Ind.
m. October 23, 1895, Homer, N. Y.
MARY SAMSON.
[Dau. of Isaac M. and Zelia (Nash) Samson.]
b. October 26, 1865, Homer, N. Y. (one child died in infancy).
FRANK MORSE NICHOLS, b. November 6, 1874, Eng. Prairie, Ind. (unm.)
GUNTHER C. NICHOLS, b. March 21, 1876, Eng. Prairie, Ind. (unm.)
(v. E. B. Nichols.)

VII.

Drusus Burnell Nichols.

[Eldest son of Charles Graves Nichols and Ella Burnell.]

b. March 9, 1861, English Prairie, Ind.
d. May 5, 1891, Chicago, Illinois.
m. October 25, 1882, Lima, Ind.

JENNIE LOUISE SHIPMAN.

[Dau. of Henry and Julia Maria (Holbrook) Shipman.]

b. March 10, 1861, Lima, Ind.

CHILDREN :

JAMES HOWE NICHOLS, b. July 12, 1883, Lima, Ind.
DRUSUS HOLBROOK NICHOLS, b. February 10, 1885, Lima, Ind.
MARION WILLIAMS NICHOLS, b. February 17, 1888, Albion, Ind.
(v. J. L. S. Nichols.)

V.

John Nichols.

[Eighth son of Capt. James Nichols and Lucy Beach. p. 204.]

b. October 28, 1814, Newtown, Conn.
d. September 7, 1857, Coldwater, Ind.

first m. JULIA ANN SHELDON.

d. July 28, 1841.

CHILD :

JULY SEELEY NICHOLS, b. (?) Orange Co., N. Y.
(rec'd E. B. Nichols.)

V.
Philo Nichols.
[Ninth son of Capt. James Nichols and Lucy Beach.]

b. November 5, 1815, Newtown, Conn.
d. June 28, 1886, East Springfield, Ind.
first m. March 23, 1848, Steuben, Ind. :

MELINDA CARR.
[Daughter of Daniel and Martha (Mason) Carr.]

b. December 19, 1828, Onondaga, N. Y.
d. June 25, 1851, East Springfield, Ind.
second m. March 17, 1857, East Springfield, Ind.:

ELIZABETH (MILLIS) STEWART.
[Widow of William Stewart ; dau. of Levin Millis.]

b. March 22, 1815, Talbot Co., Maryland.
d. January 5, 1893, La Grange, Ind.

VI.
Lucy Alice Nichols.
[Only child of Philo Nichols by his first wife, Melinda Carr.]

b. December 8, 1849, Steuben, Ind.
m. February 11, 1875, East Springfield, Ind.

JOSEPH WILLIAMS TALMAGE.
[Son of Elisha and Lucy (Williams) Talmage.]

b. January 20, 1841, East Springfield, Ind.

CHILD :

MARY NICHOLS TALMAGE, b. June 24, 1882, Ulysses, Nebraska.
(v. L. A. N. Talmage.)

———o———

IV.
Ann Beach.
[Third dau. of John Beach, 3rd, and Mabel Beers. p. 203.]

b. December 25, 1783, Newtown, Conn.
d. January 21, 1844, New Haven, Conn.
m. August 1, 1802, Newtown, Conn.

DOCTOR ELISHA SHELDON.
[Son of Samuel and Elizabeth (Baldwin) Sheldon.]

b. July 15, 1782, Litchfield, Conn.
d. December 14, 1832, Troy, N. Y.

CHILDREN:

ELIZABETH SHELDON, b. December 6, 1804, Harwinton, Conn. p. 212.
MARY SHELDON, b. June 7, 1809, Sheldon, Vt. p. 213.

V.

Elizabeth Sheldon.

[Elder dau. of Doctor Elisha Sheldon and Ann Beach.]

b. December 6, 1804, Harwinton, Conn.
d. August 1, 1893, New Haven, Conn.
m. September 19, 1827, Troy, N. Y.

HENRY EDWARD PECK.

[Son of Nathan Peck and Mehitable Tibbals.]

b. March 18, 1805, New Haven, Conn.
d. May 6, 1858, New Haven, Conn.

CHILDREN:

MARY HELENA PECK, b. October 9, 1828, New Haven, Conn. p. 212.
SAMUEL SHELDON PECK, b. Aug. 14, 1830.
     d. Jan'y 22, 1846, New Haven, Conn.
PHEBE WARREN PECK, b. October 29, 1832, New Haven, Conn. p. 213.
HENRY EDWARD PECK, JR., b. August 19, 1839, New Haven, Conn.
     d. November 4, 1864, Lawton prison, Milan, Georgia.

(v. P. W. P. Lake.)

VI.

Mary Helena Peck.

[Elder dau. of Henry Edward Peck and Elizabeth Sheldon.]

b. October 9, 1828, New Haven, Conn.
m. October 15, 1850, Trinity Ch., New Haven, Conn.

CYRUS STEBBINS CURTISS.

[Son of Cyrus and Lydia (Vanderberg) Curtiss.]

b. September 16, 1827, Hudson, N. Y.
d. October 8, 1853, New York City.

VII.

Mary Blandina Curtiss.

[Only child of Cyrus Stebbins Curtiss and Mary H. Peck.]

b. August 3, 1851, New Haven, Conn.
m. November 6, 1872, Trinity Chapel, N. Y. C.

JOHN H. CASWELL.

[Son of John and Mary (Haight) Caswell.]

b. December 27, 1846, New York City.

(v. J. H. Caswell.)

VI.
Phebe Warren Peck.
[Younger dau. of Henry Edward Peck and Elizabeth Sheldon.]

b. October 29, 1832, New Haven, Conn.

m. June 10, 1879, New Haven, Conn.

(2d w. of) BIRDSEY CURTIS LAKE.
[Son of Nichols Booth and CHARLOTTE (CURTIS) Lake.]

b. January 13, 1823, Newtown, Conn.

d. December 6, 1887, New Haven, Conn.

(v. P. W. P. Lake.)

V.
Mary Sheldon.
[Younger dau. of Doctor Elisha Sheldon and Anne Beach.]

b. June 7, 1809, Sheldon, Vermont.

d. February 23, 1897, Le Mars, Iowa.

m. January 26, 1836, Troy, N. Y.

JONATHAN FARMER SCRIBNER.
[Son of Benjamin and Mary Ann (White) Scribner.]

b. April 2, 1810, Andover, New Hampshire.

d. June 29, 1897, Le Mars, Iowa.

CHILDREN:

ELIZABETH SHELDON SCRIBNER, b. August 15, 1838, Sheldon, Vt.
m. November 3, 1881, Smithland, Woodbury Co., Ia.
DOCTOR CHARLES PAYNE ASHWORTH.
[Son of Charles and Mary Ashworth, Northfield, Vt.]
b. May 21, 1823, Northfield, Vt.
d. January 9, 1892, Leeds, Sioux City, Ia.
(v. E. S. S. Ashworth.)
ELISHA SHELDON SCRIBNER, b. November 27, 1841, Sheldon,Vt. (unm.)
MARY ANN SCRIBNER, b. Feb. 27, 1844, Sheldon, Vt. p. 214.
EMELINE RATHBONE SCRIBNER, b. Aug. 13, 1846, Sheldon,Vt. (unm.)
JONATHAN WHITE SCRIBNER, b. June 5, 1849, Elmira, N. Y.
m. January 25, 1883, Chicago, Ill.
ELIZABETH ADELAIDE GRIFFITH.
[Fifth dau. of Edward and Catherine Griffith.]
b. August 25, 1854, Boston, Mass.   (rec'd M. A. S. Jones.)
CHARLES STUART SCRIBNER, b. Sept. 25, 1851; d. March 15, 1852.
HELENA C. SCRIBNER, b. February 28, 1853, Elmira, N. Y. p. 215.
(v. M. A. S. Jones.)

VI.

Mary Ann Scribner.

[Second dau. of Jonathan Farmer Scribner and Mary Sheldon.]

b. February 27, 1844, Sheldon, Vt.

m. October 24, 1866, Janesville, Wisconsin.

CHARLES HENRY JONES.

[Son of Rowland and Hannah Jacobs (Kersey) Jones.]

b. January 16, 1842, Tamaqua, Schuylkill Co., Pa.

CHILDREN:

CHARLES H. JONES, JR., b. June 5, 1868, New Orleans, La. p. 214.
ROWLAND JONES, b. March 28, 1871, New Orleans, La. p. 214.
SHELDON SCRIBNER JONES, b. September 22, 1873, Le Mars, Iowa.
KERSEY JONES, b. December 3, 1876, Le Mars, Iowa.
JOHN WEBSTER JONES, b. November 29, 1879, Le Mars, Iowa.
MARION JACOBS JONES, b. March 13, 1882, Le Mars, Iowa.

(v. M. A. S. Jones.)

VII.

Charles Henry Jones, Jr.

[Eldest son of Charles Henry Jones and Mary Ann Scribner.]

b. June 5, 1868, New Orleans, Louisiana.

m. October 15, 1891, Chicago, Ill.

EMMA ELVIRA WILKINS.

[Dau. of Alfred Wilkins and Eliza Davies.]

b. September 20, 1871, Chicago, Ill.

CHILD:

LINDYL CHARLES JONES, b. April 25, 1893, Sioux City, Iowa.

(v. Chas. H. Jones, Jr.)

VII.

Rowland Jones.

[Second son of Charles Henry Jones and Mary Ann Scribner.]

b. March 28, 1871, New Orleans, Louisiana.

m. September 29, 1897, Sargeant's Bluff, Iowa.

BERTHA AMELIA DULÀ.

[Dau. of George Hamilton Dulà and Mary Amelia Woodford.]

(v. Rowland Jones.)

VI.

Helena Curtiss Scribner.

[Fourth dau. of Jonathan Farmer Scribner and Mary Sheldon.]

b. February 28, 1853, Elmira, N. Y.

m. March 11, 1875, LeMars, Iowa.

HARRY SWEEDEN COOKE.

[Son of Charles and Mary Elizabeth (Canby) Cooke.]

b. September 16, 1855.

d. April 29, 1894.

CHILDREN:

MARY SHELDON COOKE, b. October 15, 1876, Baltimore, Md. p. 215.
HARRY SCRIBNER COOKE, b. February 26, 1878, Le Mars, Iowa; d.
HELENA CURTISS COOKE, b. March 28, 1881, Smithland, Iowa.
CHARLES CANBY COOKE, b. April 5, 1886, Smithland, Iowa.

(v. H. C. S. Cooke.)

VII.

Mary Sheldon Cooke.

[Elder dau. of Harry Sweeden Cooke and Helena Curtiss Scribner.]

b. October 15, 1876, Baltimore, Md.

m. June 3, 1897.

RUTHERFORD BURCHARD SMITH.

[Son of Tomas Lawrance Smith and Martha Ann Mollatt.]

b. March 11, 1876, Newton, India.

(v. H. C. S. Cooke.)

————o————

IV.

Boyle Beach.

[Second son of John Beach, 3rd, and Mabel Beers. p. 203.]

b. March 12, 1786, Newtown, Conn.

d. December 8, 1861, Cleveland, N. Y.

m. February 16, 1822.

ELIZABETH STAATS.

[Dau. of John Staats.]

b. February 1, 1803.

d. December 1, 1837, New Baltimore, N. Y.

CHILDREN:

JOHN STAATS BEACH, b. February 16, 1823, New Baltimore, N. Y. p. 216.
ISAAC BEACH, b. December 16, 1824, New Baltimore, N. Y. p. 217.
MATTHEW BEACH, b. August 14, 1827, New Baltimore, N. Y. p. 218.
ANNE S. BEACH, b. April 20, 1830, Quœmens, Green Co., N. Y. p. 220.
CHARLOTTE BEACH, b. July 13, 1833; d. Feb. 1, 1837, New Baltimore.
JANE ELIZABETH BEACH, b. October 30, 1837.*

V.

John Staats Beach.

[Eldest son of Boyle Beach and Elizabeth Staats.]

b. February 16, 1823, New Baltimore, N. Y.
d. November 17, 1892, Cleveland, N. Y.
m. March 6, 1850, Cleveland, N. Y.

ANGELINE DICKINSON.

[Daughter of Jacob and Deborah (Fosdic) Dickinson.]

b. March 26, 1818, Carlisle, Scoharie Co., N. Y.

CHILDREN:

A. H. EATON BEACH, b. March 27, 1851, Cleveland, N. Y. p. 216.
ANSON CRAM BEACH, b. December 19, 1852; d. July 10, 1856.
MARY ELIZABETH BEACH, b. Sept. 5, 1857, Cleveland, N. Y. (unm.)
CHARLOTTE ANNE BEACH, b. Sept. 12, 1860, Cleveland, N. Y. p. 217.

(v. M. E. Beach.)

VI.

Alexander Hamilton Eaton Beach.

[Elder son of John Staats Beach and Angeline Dickinson.]

b. March 27, 1851, Cleveland, N. Y.
m. July 24, 1888, Cortlandt, N. Y.

ELIZABETH TUFTS.

[Dau. of John and Agnes (Hill) Tufts.]

b. July 14, 1860, West Vienna, N. Y.

CHILDREN:

JOHN ARTHUR BEACH, b. April 27, 1890, Cleveland, N. Y.
MABEL BEERS BEACH, b. April 5, 1892, Cleveland, N. Y.
MARY ELIZABETH BEACH, b. March 26, 1895, Cleveland, N. Y.

(v. A. H. E. Beach.)

* Married Frank Marble; had son Cyrus ———.

VI.

Charlotte Anne Beach.

[Younger dau. of John Staats Beach and Angeline Dickinson.]

b. September 12, 1860, Cleveland, N. Y.
m. October 7, 1886, Cleveland, N. Y.

REVᴰ JOHN ARTHUR, JR.

[Son of John and Elizabeth (Sessions) Arthur.]

b. April 1, 1862, Utica, N. Y.

CHILDREN:

JOHN BEACH ARTHUR, b. June 7, 1888, Cortlandt, N. Y.
MURIEL ARTHUR, b. May 26, 1890, Oneida, N. Y.
PAUL SESSIONS ARTHUR, b. October 6, 1893, Oneida, N. Y.
ALFRED HUNTINGTON ARTHUR, b. Jan'y 28, 1896, Oneida, N. Y.

(v. C. A. B. Arthur.)

V.

Isaac Beach.

[Second son of Boyle Beach and Elizabeth Staats.]

b. December 16, 1824, New Baltimore, N. Y.
m. September 2, 1852, New Baltimore, N Y.

MARY ANN BEDELL.

[Dau. of Jeremiah T. Bedell and Mary Bedell (third cousins).]

b. May 24, 1827, New Baltimore, N. Y.

CHILDREN:

AMBROSE BEACH, b. March 25, 1854, New Baltimore, N. Y. p. 217.
MARY MARTIN BEACH, b. Dec. 6, 1855, New Baltimore, N. Y. p. 218.
HENRY IRVING BEACH, b. December 11, 1859; d. March 30, 1880.
ANDREW N. BEACH, b. April 14, 1861 ; d. May 17, 1862.
JOHN STAATS BEACH, b. Dec. 4, 1864, New Baltimore, N. Y. p. 218.
CHARLES I. BEACH, b. Sept. 27, 1870, New Baltimore, N. Y. (unm.)

(rec'd Isaac Beach.)

VI.

Doctor Ambrose Beach.

[Eldest son of Isaac Beach and Mary Ann Bedell.]

b. March 25, 1854, New Baltimore, N. Y.
m. December 9, 1880, Coxsackie, N. Y.

JULIA CLEARWATER FITCHETT.

[Dau. of Gilbert F. and Elzada (Buckbee) Fitchett.]

b. February 26, 1859, Coxsackie, N. Y.

CHILD:

RICHARD BUCKBEE BEACH, b. May 28, 1884, Coxsackie, N. Y.
(v. A. Beach.)

VI.

Mary Martin Beach.

[Only dau. of Isaac Beach and Mary Ann Bedell.]

b. December 6, 1855, New Baltimore, N. Y.
m. September 4, 1878, New Baltimore, N. Y.

EDWIN EVERETT COLBURN.

[Son of Edwin Spaulding and Jane Elizabeth (Van Slyke) Colburn.]

b. June 4, 1854, New Baltimore, N. Y.

CHILDREN:

ELIZABETH VANDERPOEL COLBURN, b. Apr. 12, 1880, New Balto., N. Y.
MARY BEACH COLBURN, b. July 3, 1883, New Baltimore, N. Y.
(v. M. M. B. Colburn.)

VI.

John Staats Beach.

[Fourth son of Isaac Beach and Mary Ann Bedell.]

b. December 4, 1864, New Baltimore, N. Y.
m. June 9, 1886, New Baltimore, N. Y.

LIBBIE SCHERMERHORN COLVIN.

[Eldest dau. of John and Margaret Ann (Miller) Colvin.]

b. November 4, 1864, New Baltimore, N. Y.

CHILDREN:

FLORENCE BEACH, b. May 31, 1888, New Baltimore, N. Y.
LOIS MAY BEACH, b. October 19, 1889, New Baltimore, N. Y.
(v. J. S. Beach.)

V.

Matthew Beach.

[Third son of Boyle Beach and Elizabeth Staats. p. 215.]

b. Aug. 14, 1827, New Baltimore, Green Co., N. Y.
first m. March 26, 1851 (by Revd. Sam'l Thompson),
Vienna, N. Y.:

SARAH A. (GRISWOLD) THOMPSON.

[Dau. of Isaac Griswold.]

b. January 9, 1826, Buffalo, N. Y.
d. December 26, 1866, Northville, La Salle Co., Ill.

second m. November 2, 1867, Princeton, Bureau Co., Ill.:

SUSAN LOUISA BRITT.

b. December 16, 1835, Ashtabula, Ohio.

d. Nov. 9, 1896, Rockford, Winnebago Co., Ill.

CHILDREN (of first marriage):

SAMUEL THOMPSON BEACH, b. September, 18, 1852, Vienna, N. Y.;
  d. December 29, 1862, Northville, Ill.
GEORGE WALTER BEACH, b. Sept. 22, 1855, Dundee, Kane Co., Ill.;
  d. December 21, 1863, Northville, Ill.
ADAH ELIZABETH BEACH, b. July 18, 1857, Dundee, Kane Co., Ill.;
  d. December 6, 1863, Northville, Ill.
ANN AMELIA BEACH, b. February 17, 1859, Northville, Ill. p. 219.
SARAH ELIZABETH BEACH, b. July 10, 1862, Northville, Ill. p. 219.

CHILDREN (of second marriage):

NANNIE B. BEACH, b. June 13, 1869, Somonauk, Ill. p. 220.
JOHN MATTHEW BEACH, b. July 31, 1873, Polo, Ogle Co., Ill. (unm.)
EDITH NAOMAH BEACH, b. September 25, 1875, Polo, Ill. (unm.)
LETA MAY BEACH, b. July 13, 1883, Rockford, Ill.

(family rec'd S. E. B. L.)

VI.

Ann Amelia Beach.

[Second dau. of Matthew Beach, by his first wife, Sarah A. (Griswold) Thompson.]

b. February 17, 1859, Northville, Ill.

m. May 10, 1894, Beloit, Rock Co., Wisconsin.

HARRY CHARLES BURNSIDE.

[Son of Charles Rutledge Burnside and Ellen Armbrister.]

b. July 16, 1866, Nassau, New Provid'ce, Bahama Is.

CHILD:

GLADYS ELLEN BURNSIDE, b. October 23, 1895, Rockford, Ill.

(v. A. A. B. Burnside.)

VI.

Sarah Elizabeth Beach.

[Third dau. of Matthew Beach, by first wife, Sarah A. (Griswold) Thompson.]

b. July 10, 1862, Northville, LaSalle Co., Ill.

m. January 9, 1890, Janesville, Rock Co., Ill.

CHARLES LESLIE LOWE.

[Second son of Leslie William Lowe (b. November 13, 1842, St. Armands, Missisquoi Co., Canada) and Agnes Amelia Hollister (b. July 29, 1846, Osnabrook, Canada).]

b. May 30, 1865, Burlington, Ill.

CHILDREN:

BLANCHE DENETA LOWE, b. January 20, 1891, Rockford, Ill.
NINA KATHRYN LOWE, b. October 22, 1893, Galesburgh, Ill.
    d. May 2, 1896, Chicago, Ill.   (v. S. E. B. L.)

VI.

Nannie Blanche Beach.

[Eldest dau. of Matthew Beach, by his second wife, Susan Louisa Britt.]

b. June 13, 1869, Polo, Ogle Co., Ill.
m. February 10, 1890, Beloit, Rock Co., Ill.

JESSE LANE.

[Son of Isaac and Mary Adaline (Bibard) Lane.]

b. July 10, 1863.

CHILDREN:

GEORGE RANSOM LANE, b. July 26, 1891, Rockford, Ill.
MARIE LOUISA LANE, b. February 9, 1894, Rockford, Ill.
KYLE LANE, b. July 17, 1896; d. July 20, 1896, Rockford, Ill.
                                        (rec'd A. A. B. Burnside.)

V.

Anne Sheldon Beach.

[Eldest dau. of Boyle Beach and Elizabeth Staats. p. 215.]

b. April 20, 1830, Quœmens, Green Co., N. Y
m. September 11, 1858, St. Louis, Missouri.

CHARLES BRIGGS LEAR.

[Son of John and Ellen (Grant) Lear.]

b. December 10, 1824, Naples, Scott Co., Ill.
d. October, 23, 1871, Naples, Scott Co., Ill.

CHILDREN:

REGINALD HEBER LEAR, b. Dec. 25, 1859, Naples, Scott Co., Ill. p. 221.
WILLIAM FREDERICK LEAR, b. July 12, 1861; d. Oct. 14, 1861, Naples, Ill.
ELLEN ELIZABETH LEAR, b. Nov. 18, 1862; d. July 29, 1863, Naples, Ill.
CLARA ELLEN LEAR, b. Sept. 3, 1867; d. June 13, 1868, Naples, Ill.

VI.

Reginald Heber Lear.

[Elder son of Charles Briggs Lear and Anne Sheldon Beach.]

b. December 25, 1859, Naples, Scott Co., Ill.

m. June 8, 1891, " Ritenour Hill," St. Louis Co., Mo.

CARRIE MAIE BALDWIN.

[Dau. of Oscar Percival and Adeline Electa (Axtell) Baldwin.]

CHILDREN.

ETHEL ADELINE LEAR, b. Jan'y 5, 1893, Kirkwood, St. Louis Co., Mo.

MARY BALDWIN LEAR, b. Aug. 19, 1895, Kirkwood, St. Louis Co., Mo.

(v. A. S. B. L.)

————o————

IV.

Phœbe Beach.

[Fourth dau. of John Beach, 3rd, and Mabel Beers. p. 203.]

b. February 6, 1788, Newtown, Conn.

d. December 25, 1880, Coxsackie, N. Y.

m.   New Baltimore, N. Y.

BARENT HOUGHTALING.

[Son of Andrew Houghtaling and Polly Van Benthuysen (dau. of Barent Van Benthuysen).]

b. August   , 1785, New Baltimore, N. Y.

d.   , 1859, Coxsackie, N. Y.

CHILDREN :

ANDREW B. HOUGHTALING, b. Aug. 29, 1810, New Baltimore, N. Y.
   d. May 17, 1890, Coxsackie, N. Y.
   (Married twice : LYDIA BESSAC ; MARY HALLECK, no children.)

JOHN BEACH HOUGHTALING, b. March 14, 1812, New Baltimore, N. Y.
   d.   1863, New Orleans, La. (unm.)

ELIZABETH HOUGHTALING, b. Aug. 19, 1813, New Baltimore, N. Y.
   p. 222.

ELISHA S. HOUGHTALING, b. April 30, 1815, Coxsackie, N. Y. p. 223.

CHARLOTTE HOUGHTALING, b. July 30, 1818, Coxsackie, N. Y. (unm.)

GEORGE WASHINGTON HOUGHTALING, b. July 25, 1825.
   d. November 5, 1897, Coxsackie, N. Y. (unm.)

EDWARD HOUGHTALING, b. July 3, 1829.

JANE ANN HOUGHTALING, b. September 11, 1832; d. 1835.

(Houghtaling Bible.)

V.

Elizabeth Houghtaling.

[Eldest dau. of Barent Houghtaling and Phœbe Beach.]

b. August 19, 1813, New Baltimore, N. Y.
d. August 3, 1891, Coxsackie, N. Y.
m. November, 1832, Coxsackie, N. Y.

COLUMBUS LANE.

[Son of Jonathan and Sylvia (Ketchum) Lane.]

b. November 2, 1802, Johnstown, N. Y.
d. May 9, 1881, Brooklyn, N. Y.

CHILDREN:

JOHN EDWARDS LANE, b. October 27, 1834; d. December 26, 1834.
CHARLOTTE HOUGHTALING LANE, b. Dec. 2, 1835, New York City.
    m. June 18, 1873, Brooklyn, N. Y.
        WILLIAM BURNETT CLEMENTS.
        [Son of William and Eliza (Burnett) Clements.]
    b. December 5, 1847, New York City.
    d. May 5, 1876, Somerville, N. Y. (no children).
BARENT HOUGHTALING LANE, b. April 22, 1842, New York City. p. 222.
                                (v. C. H. L. Clements.)

VI.

Barent Houghtaling Lane.

[Younger son of Columbus Lane and Elizabeth Houghtaling.]

b. April 22, 1842, New York City.
m. December 10, 1867, Brooklyn, N. Y.

JULIA RICHMOND.

[Dau. of Robert and Elizabeth (Tenny) Richmond.]

b. February 8, 1844, Troy, N. Y.   (v. B. H. Lane.

VII.

Edna Elizabeth Lane.

[Only child of Barent Houghtaling Lane and Julia Richmond.]

b. February 18, 1871, Brooklyn, N. Y.

m. October 1, 1895, Yonkers, N. Y.

FRANK OTIS MELCHER.

[Only child of Francis Benjamin Melcher and Harriet Newell Harrington.]

b. June 14, 1864, Damariscotta, Maine.

(v. E. E. L. Melcher.)

V.

Elisha Sheldon Houghtaling.

[Third son of Barent Houghtaling and Phœbe Beach.]

b. April 30, 1815, Coxsackie, N. Y.
d. July 14, 1880, Albion, N. Y.
m. November 11, 1841, Stanton Hill, N. Y.

MARY EMILY POWELL.

[Dau. of Samuel and Patty (Lisk) Powell.]

b. December 28, 1822.
d. August 22, 1889, Albion, N. Y.

CHILDREN:

ELLEN B. HOUGHTALING, b. April 26, 1843, Cleveland, N. Y. p. 223.
LYDIA B. HOUGHTALING, b. July 16, 1848, Cleveland, N. Y. p. 224.
MARY L. HOUGHTALING, b. April 10, 1863, Cleveland, N. Y. p. 224.

VI.

Ellen Burroughs Houghtaling.

[Eldest dau. of Elisha Sheldon Houghtaling and Mary E. Powell.]

b. April 26, 1843, Cleveland, N. Y.
m. May 18, 1865, Albion, N. Y.

JOHN HENRY HOWELL.

[Son of Seth and Mary (Roberts) Howell.]

CHILDREN:

LOUIS S. HOWELL, b. May 22, 1870, B'klyn; d. July 23, 18, Albion.
CATHERINE L. HOWELL, b. September 16, 1872, Minneapolis, . in.

VII.
Catherine Ledlie Howell.
[Only dau. of Ellen B. Houghtaling and Jno. Henry Howell.]
b. September 16, 1872, Minneapolis, Minn.
m. February 28, 1896, Victoria, B. C.

CHARLES STUART TOURTELLOT.
[Son of Jeremiah and Helen (Miller) Tourtellot.]

CHILD:

ELINOR WRIGHT TOURTELLOT, b. Dec. 28, 1896, San Francisco, Cal.
(rec'd E. B. H. Howell.)

VI.
Lydia Bessac Houghtaling.
[Second dau. of Elisha Sheldon Houghtaling and Mary E. Powell.]
b. July 1, 1848, Cleveland, N. Y.
m. June 21, 1869, Albion, N. Y.

HORATIO WARNER STIMSON.
[Son of Nathaniel and Helen (Warner) Stimson.]
b. January 13, 1845, New York City.

CHILD:

SHELDON HOUGHTALING STIMSON, b. February 21, 1871, Albion, N. Y.
(v. L. B. H. Stimson.)

VI.
Mary Loraine Houghtaling.
[Youngest dau. of Elisha Sheldon Houghtaling and Mary E. Powell.]
b. April 10, 1863, Cleveland, N. Y.
m. June 30, 1886, Christ Church, Albion, N. Y.

CHARLES OLIVER FILKINS.
[Son of Morgan L. and Henrietta (Blackman) Filkins.]
b. November 1, 1856, Albany, N. Y.

CHILD:

ELIZABETH HOUGHTALING FILKINS, b. Sept. 21, 1893, Rochester, N. Y.
(v. M. L. H. Filkins.)

———o———

IV.
John Beach, 4th.
[Third son of John Beach, 3d, and Mabel Beers, p. 203.]

- b. August 28, 1789, Newtown, Conn.
- d. April 12, 1869, New Haven, Conn.
- m. May 10, 1818, Newtown (by Revd Burhans).

MARCIA CURTIS.
[Eldest dau. of Abijah Birdsey Curtis and Anna Glover. (Glover-Curtis.)]

- b. July 18, 1796, Newtown, Conn.
- d. August 6, 1861, New Haven, Conn.

CHILDREN:

JOHN (SHELDON) BEACH, 5th, b. July 23, 1819, New Haven, Conn.
  p. 225.
DANIEL BEERS BEACH, b. Nov. 14, 1823, New Haven, Conn. p. 226.
ANN ELIZA BEACH, b. June 30, 1829, New Haven, Conn.
  d. March 18, 1862, New Haven, Conn. (unm).

(v. R. D. Beach).

V.
John (Sheldon) Beach, 5th, LL. D.
[Elder son of John Beach, 4th, and Marcia Curtis.]

- b. August 28, 1819, New Haven, Conn.
- d. September 12, 1887, New Haven, Conn.
- m. September 15, 1847, "Vernon Place," Wilm., Del. (by Revd S. R. Wynkoop).

REBECCA GIBBONS.
[Third dau. of Dr. William Gibbons and Rebecca Donaldson of Wilmington, Del.]

- b. July 2, 1823, Wilmington, Del.
- d. September 5, 1893, New Haven, Conn.

CHILDREN:

JOHN HAMILTON BEACH, b. July 5, 1848, New Haven, Conn.
  d. April 14, 1849, New Haven, Conn.
REBECCA DONALDSON BEACH, b. Aug. 9, 1850, New Haven, Conn.
WILLIAM GIBBONS BEACH, b. April 24, 1852; d. April 24, 1852.
JOHN (KIMBERLY) BEACH, 6th, b. Oct. 18, 1855, New Haven, Conn. p. 156.
  m. April 15, 1890, Grace Church Chantry. N. Y. C.
    MARY ROLAND SANFORD.
  [Only dau. of Judge Charles Frederick Sanford and Elizabeth Looney.]

15

DONALDSON BEACH, b. April 6, 1858, New Haven, Conn.
d. December 15, 1864, New Haven, Conn.
FRANCIS GIBBONS BEACH, b. Feb. 28, 1861, New Haven, Conn. p. 226.
RODMOND VERNON BEACH, b. May 18, 1865, New Haven, Conn. (unm.)
(v. R. D. Beach.)

VI.

*Francis Gibbons Beach.

[Fifth son of John (Sheldon) Beach, 5th, and Rebecca Gibbons.]

b. February 28, 1861, New Haven, Conn.
m. June 1, 1886, St. Marks Ch., Minneapolis, Minn.
(Rector, Thos B. Wells, D.D.)

ELIZABETH CHARNLEY WELLS.

[Elder dau. of Revd Thos. Bucklin Wells, D.D. (b. Janʸ 1, 1839, Columbia, S. C.; d.
Aug. 4, 1891, at sea, S. S. Parthia, Pacific Ocean); m. 1st, Sept. 29, 1859, N. Y.
C.; Susan Fitch Charnley (b. Nov. 6, 1839, N. H., Conn.; d. April 4, 1868, Paines-
ville, O.), both buried Grove Street Cem'y, N. H., Conn.]
(Atwater b'k; Strong-Hart.)

b. November 21, 1860, Quincy, Ill.

CHILDREN:

JOHN FRANCIS BEACH, b. April 12, 1887, New Haven, Conn.
CHARNLEY WELLS BEACH, b. Dec. 26, 1889, New Haven, Conn.
d. July 7, 1890, New Haven.
REBECCA DONALDSON BEACH, b. Feb'y 22, 1892, New Haven, Conn.
d. Sept. 26, 1893, New Haven. (v. E. C. W. Beach.)

V.

Daniel Beers Beach.

[Younger son of John Beach, 4th, and Marcia Curtis.]

b. November 14, 1823, New Haven, Conn.
d. January 5, 1896, Rochester, N. Y.
m. June 1, 1853, Lockport, N. Y.

LORAINE ROGERS.

[Dau. of Levi and Lorana (Hart) Rogers.]

b. April 2, 1828, Troy, N. Y.
d. November 20, 1892, Rochester, N. Y.

CHILDREN:

JOHN HAMILTON BEACH, b. April 14, 1854, Rochester.
d. August 20, 1855, Lockport, N. Y.
FLORENCE LORAINE BEACH, b. May 8, 1856, Rochester, N. Y. (unm.)
ANNIE L. BEACH, b. March 12, 1859, Rochester, N. Y. p. 227.

* Captain, Battery C, Conn. Heavy Artillery, U. S. A. (1898).

DANIEL L. BEACH, b. Sept. 15, 1863; d. Aug. 31, 1864, Rochester, N. Y.
MABEL BEACH, b. Jan'y 3, 1866; d. Jan'y 7, 1866, Rochester, N. Y.
MARY DAISY BEACH, b. October 21, 1868, New Haven, Conn. p. 227.

(v. F. L. Beach.)

VI.
Annie Lottie Beach.

[Second dau. of Daniel Beers Beech and Loraine Rogers.]

b. March 12, 1859, Rochester, N. Y.
m. September 4, 1884, Rochester, N. Y.

EDWIN ARTHUR KING.

[Son of Harvey James King and Ellen Lowdon Blandina Bayeux.]

(King-Vanderheyden Book.)

b. June 9, 1857, Troy, N. Y.

CHILD:

ARTHUR BEACH KING, b. January 30, 1887, Troy, N. Y.

(v. A. L. B. King.)

VI.
Mary Daisy Beach.

[Fourth dau. of Daniel Beers Beach and Loraine Rogers.]

b. October 21, 1868, New Haven, Conn.
m. September 12, 1894, Rochester, N. Y.

GEORGE L. SWAN.

[Son of Theodore Talbot Swan and Julia Nash.]

b. August 27, 1869, Mt. Morris, N. Y.

CHILD:

HENRY BEACH SWAN, b. July 13, 1895, Rochester, N. Y.

(v. M. D. B. Swan.)

————o————

IV.
Charlotte Beach.

[Fifth dau. John Beach, 3d, and Mabel Beers. p. 203.]

b. November 9, 1790, Newtown, Conn.
d. April 1, 1874, Kirkwood, St. Louis Co., Mo.
m.   , Sheldon, Vt.

EPENETUS HOLMES WEAD.

[Son of Hezekiah Wead and his wife Rachel.]

d. at Montreal, Canada.

V.

Rachel Elizabeth Wead.

[Only child of E. Holmes Wead and Charlotte Beach.]

b. July 14, 1818, Sheldon, Vt.
d. January 9, 1875, Kirkwood, Mo.
m. July 6, 1843, St. Louis, Mo.

SPENCER SMITH.

[Son of Morris C. and Harriet (Spencer) Smith.]

CHILDREN :

REGINALD H. SMITH, b. Oct. 28, 1846; d. Feb. 20, 1847, St. Louis, Mo.
HARRIET H. SMITH, b. July 20, 1848; d. June 27, 1850, St. Louis, Mo.

(rec'd sent by Mrs. Lear, Kirkwood.)

———o———

III.

Phœbe Beach.

[Eldest dau. of John Beach, Jr., and Phœbe Curtis, p. 203.]

b. January 29, 1760. Newtown Records.
d. November 16, 1835, Newtown, Conn.

m. ZALMON GLOVER.

[Second son of John Glover, 4th, and Elizabeth Curtis. (Glover-Curtis.)]

b. May 3, 1760, Newtown, Conn.
d. October 21, 1827, Newtown, Conn.

CHILDREN :

LUCY ANN GLOVER, b. June 22, 1783, Newtown, Conn. p. 228.
JOHN GLOVER, b. November 1, 1787, Newtown, Conn. p. 232.
SARAH GLOVER, b. April 15, 1790; d. April, 25, 1790, Newtown, Conn.
VILLEROY GLOVER, b. June 17, 1794, Newtown, Conn. p. 236.
SARAH GLOVER, b. May 1, 1799; d. July 3, 1823, Newtown, Conn.

(rec'd S. E. G. Nichols.)

IV.

Lucy Ann Glover.

[Eldest dau. of Zalmon Glover and Phœbe Beach.]

b. June 22, 1783, Newtown, Conn.
d. February 15, 1864, Newtown, Conn.
m. April 7, 1802. Newtown Records.

ABNER ANSON NETTLETON.

[Son of Joseph Nettleton.]

b. June 22, 1780.
d. February 9, 1836.

CHILDREN:

PHŒBE BEACH NETTLETON, b. Nov. 1804; d. April 10, 1826, New-town, Conn.
JOSEPH NETTLETON, b. December, 1806, Newtown, Conn. p. 229.
ANN NETTLETON, b. Aug. 2, 1813; d. March 22, 1815, Newtown, Conn.

V.

Joseph Nettleton.

[Only son of Abner Anson Nettleton and Lucy Ann Glover.]

b. December 2, 1806, Newtown, Conn.
d. December 23, 1843, Newtown, Conn.
m. February 10, 1830, Zoar, Newtown.

PHŒBE CURTIS.

[Dau. of Alfred Devine and Sarah (Hard) Curtis. (See Curtis.)]

b. August 24, 1807, Newtown, Conn.
d. August 14, 1892, Shelton, Conn.

CHILDREN:

EDGAR A. NETTLETON, b. March 20, 1831, Newtown, Conn. p. 229.
CHARLES P. NETTLETON, b. Dec. 2, 1835, Newtown, Conn. p. 231.
JOSEPH F. NETTLETON, b. June 25, 1840, Newtown, Conn. p. 232.
PHŒBE BEACH NETTLETON, b. Feb. 8, '33; d. April 13, '36.
(v. Chas. P. Nettleton.)

VI.

Edgar Anson Nettleton.

[Eldest son of Joseph Nettleton and Phœbe Curtis.]

b. March 20, 1831, Newtown, Conn.
d. October 23, 1869, Branford, Conn.
m. October 4, 1859, Watertown.   (Newtown Record.)

ANN ELIZA ATWOOD.

[Dau. of Hinman and Eliza (deForest) Atwood.]

b. March 20, 1836, Watertown, Conn.

CHILDREN:

JOSEPH H. NETTLETON, b. June 11, 1861, Newtown, Conn. p. 230.
FLORA C. NETTLETON, b. May 9, 1863, Zoar, Conn. p. 230.
PHŒBE BEACH NETTLETON, b. Sept. 17, 1864, Zoar, Conn. (unm.)
FREDERICK H. NETTLETON, b. Oct. 14, 1867, Branford, Conn. (unm.)
MABEL B. NETTLETON, b. January 24, 1869, Branford, Conn. p. 230.
(v. Mrs. A. Nettleton.)

VII.

Joseph Hinman Nettleton.

[Elder son of Edgar Anson Nettleton and Ann Eliza Atwood.]

b. June 11, 1861, Newtown, Conn.

m. March 22, 1882, Brooklyn, N. Y.

HARRIET LEVINE.

[Daughter of Alexander Levine and Clara McNair (b. Oct. 3, 1834, Abington, Pa.).]

b. September 30, 1859, Philadelphia, Penn.

CHILDREN:

RHEA NETTLETON, b. Jan. 9, 1883; d. March 9, 1885, Brooklyn, N. Y.
ALEXANDER EDGAR NETTLETON, b. Aug. 16, 1886, Brooklyn, N. Y.
JOSEPH FOSTER NETTLETON, b. March 22, 1889, Parkville, L. I.
FLORA ROBERTA NETTLETON, b. September 25, 1892, Flatbush, L. I.
CLARA LEVINE NETTLETON, b. February 4, 1895, Parkville, L. I.
HARRIET FRANCES NETTLETON, b. November 26, 1897, Parkville, L. I.

(v. J. H. Nettleton.)

VII.

Flora Curtis Nettleton.

[Eldest dau. of Edgar Anson Nettleton and Ann Eliza Atwood.]

b. May 9, 1863, Zoar, Newtown, Conn.

m. December 19, 1883, Thomaston, Conn.

LOCKE AUSTIN LIBBY.

[Son of William Grant Libby and Jane S. Harvey.]

b. June 13, 1854, Magog, Pro. of Quebec, Canada.

CHILD:

BERTHA JANE LIBBY, b. August 22, 1886, Waterbury, Conn.

(v. F. C. N. Libby.)

VII.

Mabel Branford Nettleton.

[Third dau. of Edgar Anson Nettleton and Ann Eliza Atwood.]

b. June 24, 1869, Branford, Conn.

m. May 12, 1896, Bridgeport, Conn.

ANDREW KEITH THOMPSON.

[Son of John and Martha (Houston) Thompson.]

b. September 21, 1865.

CHILD:

MARJORIE NETTLETON THOMPSON, b. Feb. 11, 1898, New Haven, Ct.
(v. M. B. N. Thompson.)

VI.

*Charles Pulaski Nettleton.

[Second son of Joseph Nettleton and Phœbe Curtis, p. 229.]

b. December 2, 1835, Newtown, Conn.
m. July 12, 1861, Derby, Conn.

FRANCES ANN HALLOCK.

[Dau. of Israel and Rosannah (Easton) Hallock.]

b. February 6, 1839, Albany, N. Y.
d. February 4, 1897, Shelton, Conn.

CHILDREN:

CHARLES SUMNER NETTLETON, b. October 22, 1862, Derby, Conn.
m. May 1, 1886, Bristol, R. I.
EMILY ESTELLA BROTHERTON.
[Dau. of Walter Ezekiel and Charlotte Ann (Mitchell) Brotherton.]
b. March 28, 1868, Bristol, R. I.
ALBERT I. NETTLETON, b. June 2, 1866, Ansonia, Conn. p. 231.
ERNEST CLIFTON NETTLETON, b. January 9, 1869, Shelton, Conn.
REBECCA H. NETTLETON, b. January 2, 1872; d. August 2, 1872.
ROSA A. NETTLETON, b. March 10, 1873; d. August 10, 1873.
FRANCIS IRVING NETTLETON, M.D., b. Oct. 23, 1874, Shelton, Conn.
RUTH E. NETTLETON, b. Apr. 4, 1878; d. Mar. 20, 1893, Shelton, Conn.
(v. Chas. P. Nettleton.)

VII.

Albert Israel Nettleton.

[Second son of Charles P. Nettleton and Frances A. Hallock.]

b. June 2, 1866, Ansonia, Conn.
m. October 31, 1886, Hannibal, Mo.

ANNA MARGARET JOHNSON.

[Dau. of Walter and Sarah Francis (Watts) Johnson.]

b. Oct. 12, 1868, Montpelier T'w'p, Muscatine Co., Ia.

CHILDREN:

HOWARD ALBEE NETTLETON, b. September 18, 1887, Hannibal, Mo.
CLYDE HARRISON NETTLETON, b. Aug. 18, 1889, Pleasant Prairie, Ia.
(v. A. I. Nettleton.)

* 1st Conn. Heavy Artillery, Co. B, from 1862 to 1865.

VI.
Joseph Foster Nettleton.
[Third son of Joseph Nettleton and Phœbe Curtis. p. 229.]

b. June 25, 1840, Newtown, Conn.
m. April 29, 1861, Branford, Conn.

AMZETTA BARKER.
[Dau. of Eliphalet and Martha (McCoy) Barker.]

b. April 12, 1842, Columbus, Ohio.

CHILD:

LUCY BEACH NETTLETON, b. March 21, 1862, Branford, Conn.
(v. L. B. Nettleton, Cal.)

———o———

IV.
John Glover.
[Elder son of Zalmon Glover and Phœbe Beach.]

b. November 1, 1787, Newtown, Conn.
d. May, 1828.

first m. LUCY BEERS.
[Dau. of Eben Beers and Ann Hard. (See Hard).]

second m. POLLY CURTIS.
[Dau. of Philo and Huldah (Hubbell) Curtis.]

third m. BETSEY (HARD) WHITNEY.
[Widow Benj. Whitney; dau. Cyrenus Hard and Phœbe Camp. (See Hard.)]

CHILD (of first marriage):

WILLIAM BEACH GLOVER, b. Feb. 4, 1811, Newtown, Conn. p. 232.

CHILDREN (of second marriage, none by third)

MARIETTA GLOVER, b. March 27, 1814, Newtown, Conn. p. 233.
JULIETTA GLOVER, b. February 13, 1816, Newtown, Conn. p. 235.

V.
William Beach Glover.
[Only child of John Glover, by his first wife, Lucy Beers.]

b. February 4, 1811, Newtown, Conn.
d. March 18, 1864, Sandy Hook, Conn.
first m. November 7, 1832, Newtown, Conn. :

HARRIET ANN PECK.
[Dau. of Zerah Smith Ann Peck and Clara Smith. (See Hard.)]

b. September 1, 1810, Brookfield, Conn.
d. September 30, 1843, Sandy Hook.

second m. September 25, 1848, Newtown, Conn. :

SUSAN NICHOLS[V].

[Only dau. of Captain James Nichols and LUCY BEACH, p. 204.]

CHILDREN (of first marriage, none by second)

ESTHER SOPHIA GLOVER, b. September 23, 1833, Newtown.
d. January 4, 1860, T. S. Sandy Hook.
JOHN E. GLOVER, b. Dec. 10, 1835; d. Feb. 5, 1872, T. S. Sandy Hook.
SMITH PECK GLOVER, b. August 16, 1837, Newtown, Conn. p. 233.
BEACH B. GLOVER, b. June 9, 1838; d. April 5, 1841, T. S. Sandy Hook.

VI.

Smith Peck Glover.

[Second son of William Beach Glover and Harriet Ann Peck.]

b. August 16, 1837, Newtown, Conn.
m. September 30, 1861.

MARIE ANTOINETTE TOMLINSON.

[Dau. of George Albert Tomlinson and Eliza Antoinette Judson.]

b. March 7, 1838.

CHILDREN :

WILLIAM TOMLINSON GLOVER, b. October 13, 1862.
d. September 5, 1863, Newtown, Conn.
LORENA TOMLINSON GLOVER, b. May 6, 1865, Newtown, Conn.
m. December 11, 1895, Newtown, Conn.

GEORGE FRANCIS TAYLOR.

[Son of Edward and Susan (Botsford) Taylor.]

b. November 3, 1864, Newtown, Conn.   (v. S. P. Glover.)
HARRIET PECK GLOVER, b. May 30, 1870, Newtown, Conn.
m. January 12, 1898, Sandy Hook, Newtown, Conn.

CHARLES LAWRENCE WARNER.

[Son of Austin and Belle T. (Lawrence) Warner.]

b. July 16, 1868, Vicksburg, Miss.   (v. H. P. G. Warner.)

V.

Marietta Glover.

[Elder dau. of John Glover, by his second wife, Polly Curtis.]

b. March 27, 1814, Newtown, Conn.
d. August 30, 1887, Bedford, Ind.
m. January 18, 1835, Newtown, Conn.

IRA LAWRENCE CURTIS.

[Son of Abijah Birdsey Curtis and Anna Glover. (Curtis-Glover.)]

b. November 19, 1813, Newtown, Conn.
d. January 1, 1843, Newtown, Conn.

CHILDREN:

ELIZABETH CURTIS, b. October 19, 1835, Newtown, Conn. p. 234.
JULIETTE CURTIS, b. July 9, 1837, Newtown, Conn.
m. September 16, 1858, Newtown, Conn.
WINTHROP ALVIN FOOTE.
[Son of Winthrop and Cynthia Childs (Barlow) Foote.]
b. December 25, 1832, Bedford, Ind. (no descendants).
(rec'd J. C. Foote.)

VI.

Elizabeth Curtis.

[Elder dau. of Ira Lawrence Curtis and Marietta Glover.]
b. October 19, 1835, Newtown, Conn.
m. September, 19, 1860, New Haven, Conn.

DANIEL WEBSTER PARKER.

[Son of Woodbridge and Harriet M. (Thornton) Parker.]
b. June 3, 1831, Salem, Washington Co., Ind.

CHILDREN:

CORA PARKER, b. July 5, 1861, Bedford, Ind.
m. October 15, 1885, Bedford, Ind.
THOMAS JEFFERSON LEONARD.
[Son of Joseph and Saphronia (Lyon) Leonard.]
b. March 15, 1853, Owensburg.
ALFRED CURTIS PARKER, b. March 26, 1868, Bedford, Ind. p. 234.
(rec'd J. C. Foote.)

VII.

Alfred Curtis Parker.

[Only son of Daniel Webster Parker and Elizabeth Curtis.]
b. March 26, 1868, Bedford, Ind.
m. July 12, 1892, Bedford, Ind.

GERTRUDE BOWDEN.

[Dau. of Doil Riley and Harriet (Laforce) Bowden.]
b. June 26, 1868, Bedford, Ind.

CHILD:

MABEL PARKER, b. May 18, 1893, Bedford, Ind.   (rec'd J. C. Foote.)

V.

Julietta Glover.

[Younger dau. of John Glover, by his second wife, Polly Curtis. p. 232.]

b. February 13, 1816, Newtown, Conn.
d. March 13, 1864, Danbury, Conn.
m. November 5, 1837, Newtown, Conn.

ISAAC HERSON HAWLEY.

[Son of Sherman Hawley and Hester Hurd.]

b. February 22, 1811, Newtown, Conn.
d. January 28, 1883, Oxford, Conn.

CHILDREN:

MARY JOSEPHINE HAWLEY, b. Feb. 6, 1839, Newtown, Conn. p. 235.
HELEN SOPHIA HAWLEY, b. Sept. 30, 1844, Newtown, Conn. p. 236.
(v. M. J. H. Osborn.)

VI.

Mary Josephine Hawley.

[Elder dau. of Isaac Herson Hawley and Julietta Glover.]

b. February 6, 1839, Newtown, Conn.
m. March 18, 1860, Danbury, Conn.

*THOMAS SMITH OSBORN.

[Son of Thomas Clark and Nancy (Smith) Osborn.]

b. February 2, 1839, Oxford, Conn.

CHILDREN:

HERSON CLARK OSBORN, b. August 27, 1861, Danbury, Conn. p. 235.
ARTHUR RAY OSBORN, b. August 1, 1866, Oxford, Conn.
m. October 5, 1892, Ansonia, Conn.
MARY JOSEPHINE QUINLIN.
THOMAS ELMER OSBORN, b. July 5, 1869, Oxford, Conn. (unm.)
(v. M. J. H. Osborn.)

VII.

Herson Clark Osborn.

[Eldest son of Thomas Smith Osborn and Mary Josephine Hawley.]

b. August 27, 1861, Danbury, Conn.
m. October 28, 1882, Brooklyn, N. Y.

CALISTA JOHNSON CRANE.

[Dau. of Stephen Crane and Calista Jane Johnson.]

b. January 18, 1862, Ansonia, Conn.

* 20th Regt., Conn. Vol., Civil War.

CHILD:

FLORENCE JOSEPHINE OSBORN, b. May 15, 1888.

(rec'd H. C. Osborn.)

VI.

Helen Sophia Hawley.

[Younger dau. of Isaac Herson Hawley and Julietta Glover.]

b. September 30, 1844, Newtown, Conn.
m. December 25, 1872, Oxford, Conn.

ORIN DELOS WARNER.

[Son of Orin and Susan (Gardner) Warner.]

b. March 23, 1839, North Haven, Conn.
d. September 3, 1896, North Haven, Conn.

CHILD:

RUTH JULIETTE WARNER, b. March 4, 1880, North Haven, Conn.

(v. H. S. H. Warner.)

————o————

IV.

Villeroy Glover.

[Younger son of Zalmon Glover and Phœbe Beach, p. 228.]

b. June 17, 1794, Newtown, Conn.
d. October 2, 1841, Newtown, Conn.
m. March 5, 1828, Newtown (Hard Bible).

SUSAN HARD.

[Eldest dau. Benj. Hard (b. Feb. 1779; d. May 1, 1836), m. Dec. 17, 1801, Mabel
Tomlinson (b. Dec. 25, 1783; d. Jan. 29, 1864.]   (Hard.)

b. October 13, 1806, Newtown, Conn.
d. January 13, 1847, Newtown, Conn.

V.

Sarah Esther Glover.

[Only child of Villeroy Glover and Susan Hard.]

b. February 25, 1833, Newtown, Conn.
m. February 28, 1854, Newtown, Conn.

PHILO NICHOLS.

[Son of Harry Nichols (Nathaniel, Peter, Nathaniel and Ann Boothe) and Sarah
Blackman.]   (Nichols.)

b. April 27, 1832, Newtown, Conn.

CHILDREN :

FRANK B. NICHOLS, b. Jan. 17, 1855; d. M'ch 17, 1857, Newtown, Conn.
GRACE NICHOLS, b. June 16, 1863; d. Aug. 17, 1864, Newtown, Conn.
RUTH AMELIA NICHOLS, b. August 17, 1865, Newtown, Conn., p. 237.

(v. S. E. G. Nichols.)

VI.

Ruth Amelia Nichols.

[Younger dau. of Philo Nichols and Sarah Esther Glover.]

b. August 17, 1865, Newtown, Conn.

m. October 1, 1895, Newtown, Conn.

HOBART H. CURTIS.

[Son of Benjamin Curtis and Laura Lewis.]

b. November 13, 1859, Newtown, Conn.

CHILD :

MARION NICHOLS CURTIS, b. May 14, 1897, Newtown, Conn.

(v. S. E. G. Nichols.)

———o———

III.

Hannah Beach.

[Second dau. of John Beach, Jr., and Phœbe Curtis. p. 203.]

b. May 22, 1765, Newtown, Conn.

d. May 11, 1816, æ. 51 yrs.   (Newtown Record.)

m. JOHN CURTIS.

[Son Abijah and Sarah (Birdsey) Curtis. (See Curtis.)]

b. June, 1764, Newtown, Conn.

d. Oct. 19, 1820, æ. 56 yrs., 5 mo.   (Newtown Record.)

CHILDREN ;

CARLOS G. CURTIS, d. October 16, 1817, æ. 23 yrs.   (Newtown Record.)
CHARLES CURTIS, d. July 27, 1820, æ. 21 yrs.   (Newtown Record.)
RUSSELL CURTIS, d. October 12, 1820, æ. 19 yrs.   (Newtown Record.)
LUCY CURTIS, d. November 9, 1820, æ. 17 yrs.   (Newtown Record.)
DAVID B. CURTIS, d. Oct. 11, 1820, æ. 14 yrs. & 10 mo.   (Newtown R'd.)
JOHN CURTIS, JR., d. Sept. 29, 1820, æ. 11 yrs.   ⎫
BETSEY CURTIS, d. in Rochester, æ. about 46 yrs.   ⎪ (Mr. Isaac
*BEACH CURTIS, d. in Rochester, æ. about 40 yrs.   ⎬ Beers' rec'd,
SARAH CURTIS, d. in Huntington, Jan. 11, 1815, æ. 19 yrs.   ⎭ Sandy H'k.)

IV.

*Abijah Beach Curtiss.

d. November 26, 1829, æ. 30 yrs., Rochester, N. Y.

m. ABIGAIL SHELDON.

d. December 9, 1830, æ. 33 yrs., Rochester, N. Y.

CHILDREN:

ELIZABETH SHELDON CURTISS, b. August 12, 1823, Rochester, N. Y.
  d. October 25, 1843, æ. 20 yrs., Brooklyn, N. Y.
JOHN BEACH CURTISS, b. March 3, 1826, Rochester, N. Y.
  d. August 8, 1858, æ. 32 yrs., N. Y. C.
  m. CLARA J. FISHER.
  d. March 28, 1852, æ. 20 yrs., Rochester.
JACOB S. CURTISS, b. December 28, 1827, Rochester, N. Y. p. 238.
CARLOS G. CURTISS, b. November 8, 1829, Rochester, N. Y. p. 238.

(v. E. M. C. Meyrueis.)

V.

Jacob Sheldon Curtiss.

[Second son of Abijah Beach Curtiss and Abigail Sheldon.]

b. December 28, 1827, Rochester, N. Y.

m. May 27, 1851.

LAURA S. CHAMPION.

CHILDREN:

PLINY ALLEN CURTISS, b. July 7, 1853; d.
CARLOS C. CURTISS, b. August, 1856; m.
LOUISE CURTISS, died unmarried. (rec'd E. M. C. Meyrueis.)

V.

*Carlos Grandison Curtiss.

[Third son of Abijah Beach Curtiss and Abigail Sheldon.]

b. November 8, 1829, Rochester, N. Y.

d. July 30, 1871, Rochester, N. Y.

m. September 25, 1855, Rochester, N. Y.

*SARAH ELIZABETH CURTIS.

[Second dau. of HORATIO NELSON CURTIS and Maria Neafus.]

b. February 14, 1836, Rochester, N. Y.

d. June 12, 1860, Detroit, Mich.

* Here is an instance of the ss in the marriage of second cousins. Mme Meyrueis attributes it to an early difference of opinion in the family.

CHILDREN :

ELIZABETH M. CURTISS, b. July 25, 1857, Rochester, N. Y. p. 239.
EDWARD GRANDISON CURTISS, b. Oct. 13, 1859, Detroit, Mich.
    d. Feb'y 15, 1879, Detroit, Mich. (unm.) (v. E. M. C. Meyrueis.)

VI.

Elizabeth Mumford Curtiss.

[Only dau. of Carlos Grandison Curtiss and Sarah Elizabeth Curtis.]

b. July 25, 1857, Rochester, N. Y.
m. June 14, 1883, Grand Rapids, Mich.

JULES ANDRÉ MEYRUEIS.

[Eldest son of Charles Meyrueis and Constance Hollard.]

b. September 16, 1852, Paris, France.

CHILDREN :

ELSIE ANDRÉE MEYRUEIS, b. Oct. 11, 1884, Paris, France.
CONSTANCE SARAH MEYRUEIS, b. Dec. 12, 1885, Paris, France.
CECILIA ANDRÉE MEYRUEIS, b. Nov. 22, 1890, Paris, France.
(v. E. M. C. Meyrueis, Paris, France.)

————o————

III.

Sarah Beach.

[Fourth dau. of John Beach, Jr. and Phœbe Curtis, p. 203.]

b. February 5, 1774, Newtown, Conn.
d. July 9, 1859, buried at Zoar, Conn.

first m. JOEL BOOTH.
[Son of Ebenezer Booth, 4th, and Olive Sanford. (m. Nov. 20, 1766.) (Booth.)]

second m. (2nd wife of) ZALMON PECK.
[Eldest son of Henry Peck and Ann Smith "was joyned in marage December y* 23ʳᵈ,
A. D., 1755."]
There first Born a Son born of Ann his wife named Zalmon.
Born March yᵉ 10ᵗʰ, A. D. 1758.

CHILDREN (of first marriage, none by second) :

PERSEUS BOOTH, b. 1794; d. June 16, 1812, æ. 18 yrs., Zoar Cemetery.
JOHN BEACH BOOTH,   p. 240.

IV.

John Beach Booth.

[Younger son of Joel Booth and Sarah Beach.]

m. September 13, 1813, Stratford, Conn.

JULIA BROOKS.

[Dau. of Capt. Benj. Brooks of Stratford and Rebecca Sherman.]

b. February 13, 1793, Stratford, Conn.
His widow m. 2nd, JOHN PEABODY of Fayetteville, N. C. (son Charles, died young).
d. 1827, Fayetteville, N. C.

V.

Catherine Ann Booth.

[Only child of John Beach Booth and Julia Brooks.]

b. March 3, 1815.
d. October 11, 1873, New York City.
m. November 28, 1833, Bridgeport, Conn.

STARR BEACH.

[Son of RICE EDWARDS BEACH, b. M'ch 1780; d. July 24, 1860 (Ephraim, Jr.; Ephraim; David; NATHANIEL and Sarah Porter) and Betsey Booth, d.   ]

b. July 18, 1811, Trumbull, Conn.

CHILDREN :

EMELINE AUGUSTA BEACH, b. Nov. 14, 1835, Bridgeport, Conn. p. 240.
SARAH CATHERINE BEACH, b. Nov. 25, 1838, Bridgeport, Conn. p. 241.
JOHN MILES BEACH, b. September 15, 1840, Bridgeport, Conn. p. 242.
JULIA F. BEACH, b. June 3, 1842; d. June 5, 1844, Bridgeport, Conn.
JULIA BROOKS BEACH, b. July 31, 1844, Bridgeport, Conn.
d. July 28, 1875, Jersey City, N. J.
m. December 7, 1870,
CHARLES GALBRAITH of Galveston, Texas.
EDWARDS STARR BEACH, b. March 20, 1850, Bridgeport, Conn. (unm.)
MARY ELLA BEACH, b. September 6, 1851, Bridgeport, Conn. p. 243.
(rec'd J⁰⁰ M. Beach.)

VI.

Emeline Augusta Beach.

[Eldest dau. of Starr Beach and Catherine Ann Booth.]

b. November 14, 1835, Bridgeport, Conn.
d. June 28, 1889, Lakewood, N. J.
m. December 4, 1855, Bridgeport, Conn.

GEORGE W. BURRITT.

CHILD:

GEORGE STARR BURRITT, b. July 14, 1857, Bridgeport, Conn.

(rec'd Jno. M. Beach.)

VI.

Sarah Catherine Beach.

[Second dau. of Starr Beach and Catherine Ann Booth.]

b. November 25, 1838, Bridgeport, Conn.

d. October 10, 1894, Orange, Conn.

first m. November 25, 1857, Bridgeport, Conn.:

DAVID FREDERICK WELLS.

[Son of Levi Curtis and Mary (Hawley) Wells.]

b. April 18, 1836, Huntington, Conn.

d. March 1, 1870, Jersey City, N. J.

second m. May 22, 1873, New York City:

CHARLES A. MARKLEY.

[Son of Jacob Fry Markley (b. July 25, 1800, Strausburg, Lancaster Co., Pa.; d. May 25, 1854, Phœnixville, Pa.) Ann Hamilton (b. May 29, 1799, Lacock, Lancaster Co., Pa.; d. March 27, 1885, Hatboro, Montgomery Co., Pa.)]

(P. H. Markley, M.D.)

CHILDREN (of first marriage, none by second):

IDA WESTERN WELLS, b. May 10, 1860, San Antonio, Texas; p. 241.

HELEN HOLMES WELLS, b. June 18, 1861, Waterbury, Conn.; p. 242.

(rec'd H. H. W. Day.)

VII.

Ida Western Wells.

[Elder dau. of David Frederick Wells and Sarah Catherine Beach.]

b. May 10, 1860, San Antonio, Texas.

m. October 17, 1882, Orange, Conn.

JOHN JULIAN MERWIN.

[Son of Alpheus Newton and Mary (Alling) Merwin.]

b. June 31, 1859, Orange, Conn.

CHILDREN:

HELEN WELLS MERWIN, b. August 16, 1884, Orange, Conn.

MARION MERWIN, b. July 31, 1892, Orange, Conn.

JOHN JULIAN MERWIN, JR., b. October 31, 1897, Orange, Conn.

(v. I. W. W. Merwin.)

16

VII.

Helen Holmes Wells.

[Younger dau. of David Frederick Wells and Sarah Catherine Beach.

b. June 18, 1861, Waterbury, Conn.

m. July 6, 1892, New York City.

AMASA THAYER DAY.

[Son of John William Day and Frances Bradford Thayer.]

b. Oct 10, 1864, Brooklyn, N. Y.

d. ....   (v. H. H. W. Day.)

VI.

John Miles Beach.

[Elder son of Starr Beach and Catherine Ann Booth.]

b. September 15, 1840, Bridgeport, Conn.

m. December 17, 1863, Bridgeport, Conn.

JENNIE CHARLOTTE HIGGINS.

[Dau. of Amos and Susan (Beardsley) Higgins.]

b. April 1, 1844, Bridgeport, Conn.

CHILDREN:

FREDERICK F. BEACH, b. November 4, 1864, Bridgeport, Conn. p. 242.
SUSAN EDITH BEACH, b. July 8, 1877, Bridgeport, Conn.
NATALIE ELIZABETH BEACH, b. Sept. 27, 1886, Bridgeport, Conn.

d. July 19, 1888, Bridgeport, Conn.   (v. J. M. Beach.)

VII.

Frederick Frank Beach.

[Only son of John Miles Beach and Jennie C. Higgins.]

b. November 4, 1864, Bridgeport, Conn.

m. April 20, 1887, Bridgeport, Conn.

MINNIE REBECCA NORTHROP.

[Dau. of George W. and Julia (Pollard) Northrop]

b. May 2, 1864, Bristol, Conn.

CHILD:

DOROTHY MARIE BEACH, b. April 11, 1892, Bridgeport, Conn.

(v. F. F. Beach.)

VI.
Mary Ella Beach.
[Youngest dau. of Starr Beach and Catherine Ann Booth. p. 240.]
b. September 6, 1851, Bridgeport, Conn.
m. September 6, 1871, Jersey City, N. J.

PHILIP HENNY WHEELER.

VII.
Véra Jennie Wheeler.
[Only child of Philip H. Wheeler and Mary Ella Beach.]
b. September 19, 1874, Rockford, Ill.
m. February 6, 1894, San Francisco, Cal.

THOMAS JEFFERSON EDWARDS.
[Son of John Cummins and Emma Jane (Richard) Edwards.]
b. December 12, 1864, Stockton, Cal.

CHILD:
DARRELL BEACH EDWARDS. b. January 30, 1896, Stockton, Cal.
(v. Thoʼ J. Edwards.)

————o————

III.
Mary Beach.
[Fifth dau. of John Beach, Jr., and Phœbe Curtis. p. 203.]
b. August 4, 1778, Newtown, Conn.
d. October 19, 1846, Newtown, Conn.
m. September, 1799, Newtown, Conn.

ABEL BEERS.
[Son of Simeon Beers (b. July 20, 1752; d. Dec. 11, 1813), m. Feb. 7, 1776, Phidema
Nichols (b. Dec. 1, 1755; d. Jan. 6, 1822).] (Beers–Nichols.)
b. September 1, 1777.
d. February 18, 1858.

CHILDREN:
SYLVIA BEERS, b. June 24, 1800, Newtown, Conn. p. 244.
JOHN BEACH BEERS, b. September 11, 1802, Newtown, Conn.
ISAAC BEERS, b. March 10, 1805, Newtown, Conn.
d. May 25, 1890, Newtown, Conn.
first m. October 28, 1837:
MARIA (NICHOLS) GLOVER.
second m. January 4, 1871:
ANN ELIZA BOSWICK.

CHARLES CURTIS BEERS, b. Sept. 2, 1808, Newtown, Conn. p. 245.
MARY BEERS, b. April 10, 1811 ; d. May 27, 1829, (T. S., Newtown, Ct.)
ESTHER BEERS, b. December 31, 1813, Newtown, Conn.

> d. November 28, 1863,   (T. S., Newtown Cemʸ.)
> m. November 1, 1835, Newtown, Conn.
> > DAVID H. JOHNSON.
> > [Son of John and Clara (Peck) Johnson.]
>
> d. February 24, 1874, aged 59 years, T. S.

PHŒBE BEERS, b. August 4, 1816; d. January 3, 1835.
SARAH BEERS, b. September 6, 1819; d. November 27, 1830, T. S.
REBECCA BEERS, b. April 27, 1822.

> June 3, 1890, " Entered into rest." T. S.
> m. (Second wife of)
> > DAVID H. JOHNSON.

[Son of John Johnson (d. March 9, 1845, æ. 63), widow of John Johnson (d. Aug. 29, 1845, æ. 63.)]

IV.

Sylvia Beers.
[Eldest dau. of Abel Beers and Mary Beach.]

> b. June 24, 1800, Newtown.
> d. January 8, 1870, aged 69.   (T. S., Newtown Cemʸ.)
> m. SINCLAIR TOUCEY.
> > [Son of Donald and Betty Toucey.]
>
> July 24, 1855, aged 58.   (T. S., Newtown Cemʸ.)

CHILDREN :

EDWARD TOUCEY, October 17, 1846, aged 12.   (T. S., Newtown Cemʸ.)
HENRY SINCLAIR TOUCEY, March 27, 1870, aged 43. (T. S., Newtown.)
MARY E. TOUCEY,

IV.

John Beach Beers.
[Eldest son of Abel Beers and Mary Beach.]

> b. September 11, 1802, Newtown, Conn.
> d. March 3, 1860, Council Bluffs, Iowa; buried Newtown Cemʸ.
> m.   1857, Bellevue, Sarpy Co., Nebr.
> > ELIZA DUNN.

V.

Sarah Beach Beers.

[Only child of John Beach Beers and Eliza Dunn.]

b. August 6, 1859, Council Bluffs, Iowa.
m. September 11, 1877, Council Bluffs, Iowa.

MILLARD FILLMORE ROHRER.

[Son of Judge George C. Rohrer and Sophia E. Deaner (formerly Rohrersville, Washington Co., Md.).]

b. August 30, 1850, Rohrersville, Md.

CHILDREN:

JOHN BEACH BEERS ROHRER, b. December 31, 1878.
    d. February 8, 1880, Council Bluffs, Iowa.
ISAAC BEERS ROHRER, b. August 16, 1881, Council Bluffs, Iowa.
CARRIE TEST ROHRER, b. April 4, 1884, Council Bluffs, Iowa.

(v. M. F. Rohrer.)

IV.

Charles Curtis Beers.

[Third son of Abel Beers and Mary Beach.]

b. September 2, 1808, Newtown, Conn.
d. November 28, 1843, aged 35 years, 2 mo. 26 da.

m. HARRIET PECK.   (Mr. Beers' Note Book.)

[Dau. of Isaac and — (Botsford) Peck.]

b.   1807.
    November 20, 1877 ; died aged 70.

(Isaac Beers' Note B'k.)

CHILDREN:

SARAH ESTHER BEERS, b. Dec. 31, 1832 ; d. Sept. 13, 1857.
ISAAC BEACH BEERS, b. Nov. 29, 1840 ; d. May 27, 1856.

(Isaac Beers' Note B'k.)

II.

Lazarus Beach.

[Fourth son of REVᴰ JOHN BEACH, by his first wife, SARAH BEACH. p. 201.]

    b. September 20, 1736.   (Newtown Records.)

    d. January 20, 1800, Redding.

    m. June 20, 1756.

LYDIA SANFORD.

[Dau. of LEMUEL SANFORD and Rebecca Squires (Sanford).]

    b. May 17, 1738 O. S.

    d. November 28, 1796/7.

CHILDREN:

SARAH BEACH, b. Sept. 27, 1758; d. Nov. 21, 1759, Redding, Conn.
LAZARUS BEACH, Jr., b. December 1, 1760, Redding, Conn. p. 246.
LEMUEL BEACH, b. March 31, 1763, Redding, Conn.
SARAH BEACH, b. November 19, 1764, Redding, Conn. p. 255.
HANNAH BEACH, b. April 11, 1767, Redding, Conn. p. 289.
EUNICE BEACH, b. September 23, 1769, Redding, Conn. p. 293.
ISAAC BEACH, b. May 19, 1773, Redding, Conn. p. 296.
ABIGAIL BEACH, b. Sept. 13, 1778; d. Dec. 17, 1837, age 59.

                           (Redding Records.)

III.

Lazarus Beach, Jr.

[Eldest son of Lazarus Beach and Lydia Sanford.]

    b. Dec. 1, 1760, Redding, Conn.   (Redding Record.)

    d. June 28, 1816, New York City.

    m. August 19, 1797, Bridgeport, Conn.

POLLY (THOMPSON) HALL.

[Widow of Dr. Chas. A. Hall (m. 1783); dau. of Hezekiah and Rebecca (Judson) Thompson.]

    b. February 15, 1764.

    d. August, 1824.

CHILDREN:

A son, b. November 29, 1798; d. November 29, 1798.
FANNY BEACH, b. March 30, 1800, Bridgeport, Conn. p. 247.
CAROLINE BEACH, b. December 20, 1801, Bridgeport, Conn. p. 251.
CATHERINE BEACH, b. October 12, 1805, Bridgeport, Conn. p. 254.

IV.

Fanny Beach.

[Eldest dau. of Lazarus Beach, Jr. and Polly (Thompson) Hall.]

b. March 30, 1800, Bridgeport, Conn.
d. March 14, 1868, Brooklyn, N. Y.
first m. April 8, 1818, N. Y. C. (by Rev'd Jas. Milnor.)

JAMES LADD.

b. November 7, 1792, Plymouth Dock (later Davenport), Devonshire, England.
d. April 15, 1852, Throgg's Neck, N. Y.
second m. June 14, 1854, Throgg's Neck, N. Y.

WILLIAM WHITEHEAD.

b. December 17, 1786, Touch Place, Sterling Co.,
Scotland.
d. May 22, 1866, Throgg's Neck, N. Y.
(Merchant in N. Y. C.)

CHILDREN (of first marriage)

FANNY SOPHIA LADD, b. March 24, 1819, N. Y. C.; d. May 29, 1840,
Tarrytown, N. Y.; m. April 8, 1839, St. Peter's Ch., N. Y. C.
(by Rev'd H. Smith, D.D.)
JAMES LAW, M.D., of Perth, Scotland, res. N. Y.
JAMES LADD, Jr., b. Dec. 20, 1820; d. Oct. 21, 1823, New York City.
MARY CAROLINE LADD, b. March 1, 1823; d. January 6, 1834, N. Y. C.
WILLIAM WHITEHEAD LADD, b. November 1, 1825, N. Y. C. p. 248.
SAMUEL DENTON LADD, b. Feb'y 29, 1828; d. Jan'y 13, 1834, N. Y. C.
CATHERINE MEDORA LADD, b. M'ch 22, 1831; d. Jan'y 5, 1834, N. Y. C.
Infant son b. December 27, 1833; d. December 27, 1833.
{ JAMES BEACH LADD, b. October 19, 1834; d. Oct. 19, 1834, N. Y. C.
{ SAMUEL BEACH LADD, b. October 19, 1834, New York City (umm.)
CAROLINE MEDORA LADD, b. June 25, 1837, New York City. p. 249.
ELLEN LOUISE LADD, b. October 30, 1839, New York City. p. 250.
FANNY BEACH LADD, b. Dec. 28, 1841; d. Jan'y 11, 1844, N. Y. C.
CATHERINE LADD, b. June 12, 1844, Throgg's Neck, N. Y. p. 249.

(certified copy F. G. Van Wyck.) (Ladd's Bible, Wm. W. Ladd, Jr.)

V.

William Whitehead Ladd.

[Second son of James Ladd and Fanny Beach.]

b. November 1, 1825, New York City.
m. June 11, 1851, St. Peter's Church (Rev'd W. Canfield), New York City.

SARAH HANNAN PHILLIPS.

[Dau. of Thomas Phillips, res. N. Y. C. (b. in Maine), and Mary Ann Hannan, N. Y. C.]

b. April 28, 1826, New York City.
d. August 9, 1884, Brooklyn, N. Y.

CHILDREN:

WILLIAM W. LADD, Jr., b. Sept. 24, 1852, Throgg's Neck, N. Y. p. 248.
WALTER G. LADD, b. September 20, 1856, Throgg's Neck, N. Y. p. 248.
HENRY M. LADD, b. June 7, 1858, Throgg's Neck, N. Y. p. 249.
JAMES B. LADD, b. June 27, 1860, Throgg's Neck, N. Y. p. 249.

(W. W. Ladd, Jr.)

VI.

William Whitehead Ladd, Jr.

[Eldest son of William Whitehead Ladd and Sarah Hannan Phillips.]

b. September 24, 1852, Throgg's Neck, N. Y.
m. May 22, 1876, New York City.

ELIZABETH ADELAIDE ROWE.

[Third dau. of Griffith Rowe (b. Apr. 18, 1814, Carnarvon, Wales; d. Apr. 10, 1895, N. Y. C.) m. Dec. 13, 1838, N. Y. C., Cornelia Jane Rodgers (b. June 26, 1819, N. Y. C.; d. Dec. 10, 1887, N. Y. C.) dau. of Jas. Forrester Rodgers, London, Eng., and Mary Lynch.]

b. January 12, 1852, New York City.

CHILD:

ELIZABETH LADD, b. February 25, 1881, New York City.

(W. W. Ladd, Jr.)

VI.

Walter Græme Ladd.

[Second son of William Whitehead Ladd and Sarah Hannan Phillips.]

b. September 20, 1856, Throgg's Neck, N. Y.
m. December 5, 1883 (Rev'd Jno. Hall, D.D.), N. Y. C.

KATE EVERIT MACY.

[Dau. of Josiah Macy, Jr., and Caroline L. Everit.]

b. April 6, 1863, New York City.

(v. W. G. Ladd, Cal.)

VI.

Rev'd Henry Manchester Ladd.

[Third son of William Whitehead Ladd and Sarah Hannan Phillips.]

b. June 7, 1858, Throgg's Neck, N. Y.

m. October 25, 1887, Hartford, Conn.

MARTHA WILLIAMS COIT.

[Dau. of Samuel Coit and Mary Elizabeth Gladding.]

b. April 5, 1862, Hartford, Conn.

CHILDREN:

COIT LADD, b. May 7, 1890, Cincinnati, Ohio.

HENRY MANCHESTER LADD, Jr., b. Sept. 3, 1892, Norwood, N. J.

(v. Rev'd H. M. Ladd.)

VI.

James Beach Ladd.

[Youngest son of William Whitehead Ladd and Sarah Hannan Phillips.]

b. June 27, 1860, Throgg's Neck, N. Y.

m. Oct. 9, 1889, Darby, Delaware Co., Pa.

REBECCA SERRILL.

[Dau. of William Daniel Humphreys Serrill and Fanny Pascall Lloyd.]

b. March 10, 1867, Darby, Delaware Co., Penna.

CHILD:

FRANCES SERRILL LADD, b. Feb. 28, 1894, Baltimore, Balto. Co., Md.

(v. J. B. Ladd.)

V.

Caroline Medora Ladd.

[Fourth dau. of James Ladd and Fanny Beach, p. 247.]

b. June 25, 1837, New York City.

d. July 2, 1878, Brooklyn, N. Y.

m. November 15, 1859, St. Peter's Church of Westchester, Westchester Co., N. Y.

*DOCTOR WILLIAM GILFILLAN.

[Son of Alexander Gilfillan, R. N., and Eliza McCutchens, b. 1808 ; d. 1897.]

b. May 25, 1834.

* m. as second wife CATHERINE LADD, seventh dau. of James Ladd and Fanny Beach, b.
June 12, 1844, Throgg's Neck, N. Y.; d. Nov. 10, 1895, Brooklyn, N. Y.

CHILDREN (of first marriage, none by second):

FANNY GILFILLAN, b. July 1, 1862, Brooklyn, N. Y. p. 250.
WILLIAM WHITEHEAD GILFILLAN, b. Dec. 4, 1869, B'klyn, N. Y. (unm.)
(v. F. G. Van Wyck.)

VI.

Fanny Gilfillan.

[Only dau. of William Gilfillan, M.D., by his first wife, Caroline M. Ladd.]

b. July 1, 1862, Brooklyn, N. Y.
m. November 3, 1890, Brooklyn, N. Y.

ALBERT VAN WYCK.

[Son of Samuel Van Wyck, Huntingdon, L. I. and Eliza A. Ketcham, Huntingdon.]

CHILDREN:

KATHERINE LADD VAN WYCK, b. March 5, 1892, Brooklyn, N. Y.
SAMUEL BEACH VAN WYCK, b. July 29, 1893, Brooklyn, N. Y.
(v. F. G. Van Wyck.)

V.

Ellen Louise Ladd.

[Fifth dau. of James Ladd and Fanny Beach.]

b. October 30, 1839, New York City.
m. October 22, 1867, Brooklyn, N. Y.

WILLIAM WALLACE, M.D.

[Son of Rev⁴ Henry and Mary Simpson (Kennedy) Wallace.]

b. May 15, 1835, Cork, Ireland.
d. December 22, 1896, Brooklyn, N. Y.

CHILDREN:

HENRY WALLACE, M.D., b. July 11, 1868, Brooklyn, N. Y. p. 250.
WILLIAM WALLACE, Jr., b. April 28, 1873, Brooklyn, N. Y. (unm.)
(v. E. L. L. Wallace.)

VI.

Henry Wallace, M.D.

[Eldest son of William Wallace, M.D. and Ellen Louise Ladd.]

b. July 11, 1868, Brooklyn, N. Y.
m. October 14, 1896, Brooklyn, N. Y.

CARRIE LOUISE BOSTWICK.

[Dau. of Cyrus Benjamin Bostwick and Sarah J. Riblet.]

b. February 25, 1870, New York City.
(v. E. L. L. Wallace.)

IV.

Caroline Beach.

[Second dau. of Lazarus Beach, Jr. and Polly (Thompson) Hall, p. 246.]

b. December 20, 1801, New York City (?)
d. April 9, 1837, New York City.
m. July 12, 1825, New York City.

*AUGUSTIN AVERILL.

[Son of Col. Perry and Dorothy (Whittlesey) Averill.]

b. August 30, 1795, Washington, Conn.
d. July 9, 1857, New York City.

CHILDREN (of *his* first marriage) :

LUCY CAROLINE AVERILL, b. June 17, 1826, New Utrecht, L. I. p. 251.
PERRY BEACH AVERILL, b. February 28, 1828 ; d. Oct. 9, 1829, N. Y. C.
JOSEPH OTIS AVERILL, b. Oct. 22, 1830, New York City. p. 253.
AUGUSTIN GURLEY AVERILL, b. Oct. 30, 1832, New York City.
    d. Dec. 17, 1833, New York City.
                            (rec'd Miss Dixon and E. C. R. Moffat.)

V.

Lucy Caroline Averill.

[Only dau. of Augustine Averill, by his first wife, Caroline Beach.]

b. June 11, 1826, New Utrecht, L. I.
d. July 7, 1856, Cozzen's Hotel, West Point, N. Y.
m. July 28, 1847, Woodbury, Conn.

WILLIAM CHURCHILL, JR.

[Son of William and Mary Elizabeth (Haden) Churchill.]

b. February 4, 1825, Boston, Mass.
d. June 7, 1873, Montclair, N. J.

CHILDREN :

MARY CAROLINE CHURCHILL, b. July 16, 1849, New York City. p. 252.
FLORENCE CHURCHILL, b. April 21, 1851, Brooklyn, N. Y. p. 252.
WILLIAM CHURCHILL, 3d, } b. May, 1854 ; died in early infancy.
LUCY CHURCHILL,   }
                            (rec'd Miss Dixon and E. C. R. Moffat.)

* Augustine Averill, m. 2d. May, 1837, Margaret Fraser, dau. of Simon Fraser and Amy Thompson (dau. of Hezekiah Thompson); b. Sept. 22, 1812; d. Dec. 29, 1888. Ch: Mary Frances, b. Oct. 24, 1840, unm.; Margaret Fraser, b. May 10, 1843, m. Nov. 25, 1879, Thomas Hooker; Louise Edelsten, b. Nov. 22, 1844; d. July 7, 1893; m. March 24, 1870, Charles Meigs Charnley. Ch.: Chas. M., James, Louis E., and Constance Charnley: Heman and Augustin Averill died.   (rec'd M. F. Averill.)

VI.

Mary Caroline Churchill.

[Eldest dau. of William Churchill, Jr., by his first wife, Lucy Caroline Averill.]

b. July 16, 1849, New York City.
m. November 9, 1870, Brooklyn, New York.

GEORGE HURLBUT RIPLEY.

[Son of George Clinton Ripley and Hannah Bass Penniman.]

b. February 3, 1848, Brooklyn, New York.

CHILDREN:

ELIZABETH C. RIPLEY, b. April 11, 1872, Montclair, N. J. p. 252.
EDITH CHURCHILL RIPLEY, b. November 26, 1873.
FLORENCE CHURCHILL RIPLEY, b. June 23, 1875.
ANNAH CHURCHILL RIPLEY, b. April 25, 1877.
GEORGE CLINTON RIPLEY, b. June 8, 1878.
RUTH RIPLEY, b. June 4, 1882; d. March 21, 1884.

(v. E. C. R. Moffat.)

VII.

Elizabeth Churchill Ripley.

[Eldest dau. of George Hurlbut Ripley and Mary Caroline Churchill.]

b. April 11, 1872, Montclair, N. J.
m. April 11, 1896, San Mateo, San Mateo Co., Cal.

FRASER MUIR MOFFAT.

[Son of David Moffat (Musselburgh, Scotland) and Susannah Lundie (Kelso, Scotland).]

b. January 8, 1868, Brooklyn, New York.

CHILD:

FRASER MUIR MOFFAT, Jr., b. August 8, 1897, Brooklyn, N. Y.

(v. E. C. R. Moffat.)

VI.

Florence Churchill.

[Second dau. of William Churchill, Jr., by his first wife, Lucy Caroline Averill.]

b. April 21, 1851, Brooklyn, N. Y.
m. Oct. 19, 1875, Montclair, N. J.   (rec'd E. C. R. M.)

WILLIAM LAWRENCE GERRISH, JR.

[Son of William Lawrence Gerrish.]

b. September 10, 1846.

CHILDREN:

WILLIAM CHURCHILL GERRISH, b. November 13, 1877.
THORNTON GERRISH, b. July 17, 1879.
{ JOHN BROWN GERRISH, b. December 26, 1885; d. April 7, 1886.
{ FLORENCE GERRISH, b. December 26, 1885.

(rec'd Mrs. W. L. Gerrish.)

V.

Joseph Otis Averill.

[Second son of Augustin Averill, by his first wife, Caroline Beach, p. 251.]

b. October 22, 1830, New York City.
d. September 29, 1889, Brooklyn, N. Y.
first m. May 11, 1852.

SARAH E. JONES.

[Dau. of John H. Jones of Cold Spring Harbor, L. I.]

d. March 19, 1853.
One daughter, b. March 19, 1853; d. July, 1853.
second m. June 17, 1855, Commack, Long Island.

MARY ELIZABETH SMITH.

[Dau. of Caleb Smith, Smithtown, L. I., and Harriet Atwood Bailey.]

b. January 25, 1834, Commack, N. Y.
d. March 21, 1894, Bay Ridge, N. Y.

CHILDREN (of second marriage):

HEMAN AUGUSTIN AVERILL, b. May, 1856; d. April, 1857, New York.
JOSEPH OTIS AVERILL, Jr., June 4, 1857, New York City. p. 254.
ELLEN MILLS AVERILL, b. July 11, 1859, New York City.
   m. September, 1895.
         (2d wife of) CHARLES MEIGS CHARNLEY.
[Son William Slater Charnley and Elizabeth Bates Atwater (New Haven, Ct.).]
HENRY RUSSELL AVERILL, b. August 20, 1861, New Haven, Ct.;
         d. July 7, 1894, Brooklyn, N. Y.
CHARLES SMITH AVERILL, b. November 24, 1863, Brooklyn (unm.)
MARY AVERILL, b. March 28, 1866, Brooklyn, N. Y.
WILLIAM JUDSON AVERILL, b. May 22, 1870, Smithtown, L. I.;
         d. Sept. 1895, New York.   (v. Chas. S. Averill, Japan.)

VI.

Joseph Otis Averill, Jr.

[Second son of Joseph Otis Averill, by his second wife, Mary E. Smith.]

b. June 4, 1857, New York City.

m. December 13, 1886, Yokohama, Japan.

JULIA CAMMANN BLAKE.

[Dau. of Alexander Veits Blake and Maria E. Whitehouse.]

CHILDREN:

DOROTHY AVERILL, b. June 22, 1888, Yokohama, Japan.

OTIS AVERILL, b. January 15, 1891, Yokohama, Japan.

NORMAN WHITEHOUSE AVERILL, b. Jan. 20, 1892, Yonkers, N. Y.

(v. Chas. S. Averill, Japan.)

—————o—————

IV.

Catherine Beach.

[Third dau. of Lazarus Beach, Jr. and Polly (Thompson) Hall.]

b. October 12, 1805, Bridgeport, Conn.

d. November 3, 1866.

m. April 21, 1825.

THOMAS SMITH UNDERHILL.

[Eldest son of Peter and Hannah (Smith) Underhill. (Direct descendant of Lord Underhill of Warwickshire, Eng., otherwise Capt. Jno. Underhill, famous in the history of Long Island.)]

b. February 3, 1803, Great Neck, Long Island.

d. February 17, 1852.

CHILDREN:

CATHERINE SOPHIA UNDERHILL, b. May 20, 1826, New York. p. 255.

GEORGE FREDERICK UNDERHILL, b. Nov. 3, 1833; d. May 1834,

HANNAH SMITH UNDERHILL, b. March 2, 1835, New York City. p. 255.

{ AUGUSTIN AVERILL UNDERHILL, b. Sept. 28, 1836, New York;

            d. Oct. 18, 1854, New York City.

{ CAROLINE AVERILL UNDERHILL, b. Sept. 28, 1836, New York.

            d. Nov. 27, 1897, Brooklyn. (unm.)

EMMA BEACH UNDERHILL, b. Nov. 1839; d. Jan. 22, 1841, New York.

THOMAS SMITH UNDERHILL, Jr., b. March 12, 1842, New York;

            d. April 30, 1843, New York City.   (v. Miss Dixon.)

V.

Catherine Sophia Underhill.

[Eldest dau. of Thomas Smith Underhill and Catherine Beach.]

b. May 20, 1826, New York City.
d. January 22, 1863, New Canaan, Conn.
m. Nov. 16, 1853, Ch. of the Holy Communion, N.Y.C.

JOHN DIXON, JR.

[Son of John Dixon and Ann Hargrave.]

b. 1824, Bradford, England.
d. November 10, 1869, Bradford, England.

CHILDREN:

AUGUSTIN UNDERHILL DIXON, b. July 16, 1855, New York.
d. February, 1856, New York City.
ANNIE DIXON, b. August 10, 1856, New York City. (unm.)

(v. Miss Dixon.)

V.

Hannah Smith Underhill.

[Second dau. of Thomas Smith Underhill and Catherine Beach.]

b. March 2, 1835, New York City.
m. April 25, 1866, St. Matthews Ch., B'klyn, N. Y.

WILLIAM ASHLEY RUMSEY.

[Son of Joseph Elicot and Lucy Matthews (Ransom) Rumsey.]

b. November 4, 1833, Stafford, N. Y.

CHILDREN:

{ WILLIAM ASHLEY RUMSEY, b. June 13, 1867, Helena, Montana.
{ LOTTIE M. RUMSEY, b. June 13, 1867, Helena, Montana.

(v. H. S. U. Rumsey.)

————o————

III.

Sarah Beach.

[Second dau. of Lazarus Beach and Lydia Sanford. p. 246.]

b. Nov. 19, 1764, Redding, Conn.
d. May 10, 1828.
m.   , 1780.

JAMES SANFORD.

[Eldest son of JOHN SANFORD and Ann Wheeler. (Sanford.)]

b.   , 1758, Redding, Conn.
d. April 14, 1842, bur'd Redding Ridge, Conn.

CHILDREN :

LEMUEL SANFORD, b. November 20, 1781, Redding, Conn. p. 256.
LYDIA ANN SANFORD, b. August 1, 1782, Redding, Conn. p. 269.
ISAAC SANFORD, b. April 23, 1786, Redding, Conn. p. 281.
ALANSON SANFORD, b. January 20, 1789, Redding, Conn. p. 282.
LAZARUS SANFORD, b. Dec. 8, 1791, Redding; d.——(unm.)
SALLY SANFORD, b. February 14, 1794, Redding, Conn. p. 285.
JOHN BEACH SANFORD, b. October 10, 1796, Redding, Conn.
    John Beach and Anna Sanford's children George and Cathe-
    rine, bapt. June 4, 1821.   (Christ Ch. Rec'd.)
JAMES SANFORD, Jr., b. June 10, 1799, Redding, Conn. p. 285.
CHARLES SANFORD, b. January 7, 1801, Redding. (Rec'd, Vol. II., p. 112.)
CHILD, b. October 1, 1804, Redding, Conn.
HARRIET SANFORD, b.   ; d. April 29, 1840.
MARIA SANFORD, b. April, 1811 ; d. March 28, 1824, æ 13 yr.
                                    (p. 56, Vol. II, R. R.)

IV.

Lemuel Sanford.

[Eldest son of James Sanford and SARAH BEACH.]

b. { November 20, 1780.
   { November 20, 1781.   (Redding Rec'd.)
d. April 26, 1826, Redding, Conn.
m.   , 1802.

CHARLOTTE PLATT.

[Dau. of Jarvis Platt and Annie Nichols.]   (Nichols-Sanford.)

b. November, 1785.
d. January 14, 1846, æ. 60 yrs. 3 ms.

CHILDREN :

*PHILLIDA SANFORD, bapt. Oct. 27, 1817 " Felida."
                (Christ Ch. Rec'd, Redding Ridge.)
   m. December 15, 1822.   (Redding Rec'd.)
   NORMAN T. MIDDLEBROOK of Weston (one ch. died.)
*SARAH ANNE SANFORD, bapt. Oct. 27, 1817.   (Christ Ch. Rec'd.)
*ABBY SANFORD, b. June 26, 1808, Redding, Conn. p. 257.
*PHILO SANFORD, bapt. October 27, 1817.   (Christ Ch. Rec'd.)
*ISAAC PLATT SANFORD, b. November 22, 1811, Redding, Conn. p. 259.
*BETSEY SANFORD, b. June 16, 1815, Redding, Conn. p. 262.

(*On records—baptized at Redding Episcopal Ch., October 27, 1817.)

*HANNAH BEACH SANFORD, b. 1816; d. 1841;
   m. Newtown, Conn., EDMUND WHEELER; d. Sept. 29, 1895.
   Child: JAMES SANFORD WHEELER, b. Feb. 23, 1840; d. May
   28, 1868, N. Y. C.
DAVID PLATT SANFORD, b. Jan. 29, 1819, Redding, Conn. p. 266.
EUNICE LOUISA SANFORD, b. June 4, 1824, Redding, Conn. p. 268.

V.

Abby Sanford.

[Third dau. of Lemuel Sanford and Charlotte Platt.]

b. June 26, 1808, Redding, Conn.
d. June 19, 1893, Saint Paul, Minn.
m. April 2, 1827, Redding, Conn.

HARRY WARNER.

[Third son of Hermon Warner (b. April 16, 1769) and Rebekah Camp (b. April 20,
   1771) joined in marriage January 20, 1793. Vol. II, p. 11.]

b. October 16, 1798.   (Newtown Record.)
d.

CHILDREN:

JOHN MORRIS WARNER, b. September 7, 1828, Redding, Conn. p. 257.
REUBEN WARNER, b. July 14, 1831, Redding, Conn. p. 258.

VI.

John Morris Warner.

[Elder son of Harry Warner and Abby Sanford.]

b. September 1, 1828, Redding, Conn.
m. September 20, 1862, Saint Paul, Minn.

ROSA SCHAUER.

CHILDREN:

ANNIE H. A. WARNER, b. September 25, 1865, St Paul, Minn.
GEORGE WARNER, b. September 12, 1870, St. Paul, Minn.
ROSA D. C. WARNER, b. Oct. 1, 1873; d. Jan. 4, 1876, St. Paul, Minn.
                         (rec'd Jno. M. Warner.)

17

VI.

Reuben Warner.

[Younger son of Harry Warner and Abby Sanford.]

b. July 14, 1831, Redding, Conn.

m. April 22, 1869, St. Cloud, Minnesota.

MARY ROBERTSON.

[Dau. of J. W. and Ann M. (Langing) Robertson.]

b. September 23, 1848, Fredericton, St. Johns, N. B.

CHILDREN :

REUBEN WARNER, JR., b. October 15, 1870, St. Paul, Minn. p. 258.
ABBY SANFORD WARNER, b. December 27, 1871, St. Paul, Minn.
} HARRY FLANDRAU WARNER, b. March 27, 1874, St. Paul, Minn. p. 258.
‹ GRACE ALICE WARNER, b. March 27, 1874, St. Paul, Minn. 259.
SIDNEY ALEXANDER WARNER, b. Sept. 15, 1877, St. Paul, Minn.
EUGENE FREDERICK WARNER, b. May 16, 1879, St. Paul, Minn.
ARTHUR HOBART WARNER, b. December 23, 1881, St. Paul, Minn.
LESTER A. B. WARNER, b. Jan. 5, 1886, St. Paul, Minn.
     d. May 19, 1891, St. Paul, Minn.
CHARLES DUDLEY WARNER, b. November 14, 1892, St. Paul, Minn.
                              (v. Reuben Warner.)

VII.

Reuben Warner, Jr.

[Eldest son of Reuben Warner and Mary Robertson.]

b. October 15, 1870, Saint Paul, Minn.

m. June 1, 1892, Minneapolis, Minn.

GABRIELLE HUTCHINS.

[Dau. of Dr. E. A. Hutchins and Elizabeth Jane Thickens.]

b. March 7, 1873, Canton, N. Y.

CHILD :

ELIZABETH SANFORD WARNER, b. February 24, 1893, St. Paul, Minn.
                              (v. Reuben Warner, Jr.)

VII.

Harry Flandrau Warner.

[Twin child of Reuben Warner and Mary Robertson.]

b. March 27, 1874, Saint Paul, Minn.

m. April 7, 1896, Saint Paul, Minn.

MARY DOUGHERTY.

[Dau. of F. I. Dougherty and Elizabeth S. Smith.]

b. October 4, 1876.

CHILD:

GRACE EUGENIA WARNER, b. January 25, 1897, St. Paul, Minn.

(v. H. F. Warner.)

VII.
Grace Alice Warner.

[Twin child of Reuben Warner and Mary Robertson.]

b. March 27, 1874, St. Paul, Minn.

m. February 17, 1897, St. Paul, Minn.

GEORGE DAKIN COCHRANE.

[Son of Robert Henry Cochrane and Mattie Dakin.]

b. January 31, 1868, St. Clairesville, O.

CHILD:

GEORGE DAKIN COCHRANE, JR., b. Dec. 7, 1897, St. Paul, Minn.

(v. G. A. W. Cochrane.)

————o————

V.
Isaac Platt Sanford.

[Eldest son of Lemuel Sanford and Charlotte Platt. p. 256.]

b. November 22, 1811, Redding, Conn.

d. March 10, 1887, Lake Forest Cem'y, Grand Haven, Mich.

m. October 27, 1834.

MARY JENNINGS ROYALL.

[Dau. of Timothy and Christina (Cranse) Royall.]

b. December 1, 1814.

d. October 6, 1883, Grand Haven, Mich.

CHILDREN:

TIMOTHY R. SANFORD, b. June 13, 1835, Elmira, N. Y. p. 260.

ISAAC HULL SANFORD, b. September 27, 1836, Elmira, N. Y.;

m. September 30, 1874, Grand Haven, Mich.

MARY (MILLER) OSGOOD.

[Widow of Lieut. George Osgood; d. of Capt. Harry and Elizabeth D. (Really) Miller.]

b. May 14, 1836, Detroit, Mich.

LIEUT. JOSIAH BENNETT SANFORD, b. April 30, 1838;

d. April 22, 1887, Grand Haven. (unm.)

MARY FRANCES SANFORD, b. March 4, 1840, Dunkirk, N. Y. p. 260.

GEORGE DAVIS SANFORD, b. January 7, 1842, Kent, Ohio. p. 261.

*DAVID PLATT SANFORD, b. December 18, 1844, Akron, Ohio.

m. September 10, 1870, Grand Haven, Mich.

ANNA DIKEHOUSE (DYKEHUIS.)

b. April 19, 1849.

*Sergt. Co. B, 1st Mich. Sharpshooters.

HENRY CARLTON SANFORD, b. June 14, 1846, Akron, Ohio. p. 261.
EMMA MARETTA SANFORD, b. August 6, 1849, Akron, Ohio.
   m. January 24, 1884, Lansing, Mich.
           JAMES PEASE BRAYTON.
]Son of James Colgrave Brayton and Julia Barnard. "Swain and Allied Families."
                                                    (See Brayton.)
       b. Nov. 23, 1847, Aztalan, Wis.
ADELINE WHEELER SANFORD, b. Sept. 7, 1851; d. Nov. 15, 1852.
CHARLES EDMON NEWELL SANFORD, b. June 1, 1858;
       d. July 28, 1884. (unm.)   (Rec'd E. M. S. Brayton.)

VI.

*Timothy Royall Sanford.

[Eldest son of Isaac Platt Sanford and Mary Jennings Royall.]

   b. June 13, 1835, Elmira, N. Y.
   d. March 16, 1886, Grand Rapids, Mich.
   m. May 11, 1858, Akron, Ohio.

       MARY E. MACDONALD.

VII.

Harry Royall Sanford.

[Only child of Timothy Royall Sanford and Mary E. MacDonald.]

   b. May 31, 1859.
   m. November 18, 1886.

       CEDELLA L. ROWAN.

           CHILDREN :

CHESTER CHRISTIAN SANFORD, b. April 16, 1888.
MARY ELLEN SANFORD, b. August 9, 1892.   (rec'd E. M. S. Brayton.)

VI.

Mary Frances Sanford.

[Eldest dau. of Isaac Platt Sanford and Mary Jennings Royall.]

   b. March 4, 1840, Dunkirk, N. Y.
   m. December 23, 1868, Grand Haven, Mich.

   † GEORGE HENRY SAXTON.

[Son of Jonathan Ashley Saxton and Miranda Wright. (Deerfield History.)]

   b. May 21, 1831, Deerfield, Mass.

       * Serg't Konklin's 4th Ohio Battery. ⎫ Civil War.
       † Co. B, 1st Michigan Sharpshooters. ⎭

CHILDREN:

ISAAC ASHLEY SAXTON, b. July 27, 1870, Grand Haven, Mich.
EDMUND LUKE SAXTON, b. July 29, 1872, Grand Haven, Mich.
MARY EMMA SAXTON, b. September 23, 1874, Grand Haven, Mich.

(rec'd E. M. S. Brayton.)

VI.

George Davis Sanford.

[Fourth son of Isaac Platt Sanford and Mary Jennings Royall.]

b. January 7, 1842, Kent, Ohio.
m. May 1, 1873, Grand Haven, Mich.

FRANCIS STONER.

[Dau. of Jacob and Anna (Webb) Stoner.]

b. June 24, 1852, Ripley, New York.

CHILDREN:

GRACE ROYALL SANFORD, b. Nov. 22, 1874;
d. Jan. 31, 1876, Grand Haven, Mich.
LILLIAN WEBB SANFORD, b. July 7, 1876, Grand Haven, Mich.
GEORGE DEROY SANFORD, b. February 29, 1880, Grand Haven, Mich.
MARY FRANCIS SANFORD, b. November 26, 1881, Grand Haven, Mich.
CHARLES GUY SANFORD, b. June 26, 1883;
d. Feb. 20, 1884, Grand Haven, Mich.
FRANCIS STONER SANFORD, b. Oct. 22, 1890, Grand Haven, Mich.

(rec'd E. M. S. Brayton.)

VI.

Henry Carlton Sanford.

[Sixth son of Isaac Platt Sanford and Mary Jennings Royall.]

b. June 14, 1846, Akron, Ohio.
m. February 14, 1870, Grand Haven, Michigan.

EUGENIA BECKWITH.

[Dau. of Edward Mertimer and Helen M. (Boughman) Beckwith.]

CHILREN:

ISAAC HULL SANFORD, b. November 8, 1870, Grand Haven, Mich.
CARLTON WHEELER SANFORD, b. August 21, 1872;
d. July 24, 1873, Grand Haven, Mich.
HENRY CARLTON SANFORD, Jr., b. Nov. 18, 1875, Grand Haven, Mich.
EUGENIA BECKWITH SANFORD, b. Mar. 12, 1882, Grand Haven, Mich.
JAMES BRAYTON SANFORD, b. September 9, 1883, Grand Haven, Mich.

(rec'd E. M. S. Brayton.)

————o————

V.

Betsey Sanford.

[Fourth dau. of Lemuel Sanford and Charlotte Platt. p. 256.]

b. June 16, 1815, Redding, Conn.
d. October 27, 1856, Bethel, Conn.
m. May 15, 1835, Bethel, Conn.

GEORGE BARNUM.

[Son of Asahel and Lucy (Grey) Barnum.]

b. May 11, 1812, Bethel, Conn.
d. March 6, 1864, Bethel, Conn.

CHILDREN :

CHARLOTTE AUGUSTA BARNUM, b. Mar. 31, 1837, Bethel, Conn. p. 262.
HANNAH SANFORD BARNUM, b. Dec. 2, 1839, Bethel, Conn. p. 263.
ADALINE AMELIA BARNUM, b. April 28, 1842, Bethel, Conn. p. 264.
SARAH ELIZABETH BARNUM, b. Oct. 19, 1845, Bethel, Conn. p. 264.
BETSEY LOUISA BARNUM, b. Sept. 8, 1847 ; d. Feb., 1866, Bethel, Conn.
GEORGE W. BARNUM, b. February 22, 1849, Bethel, Conn. p. 264.
HENRY TAYLOR BARNUM, b. May 14, 1850, Bethel, Conn. p. 265.
LUCY JENNETTE BARNUM, b. February 27, 1852, Bethel, Conn. ;
    m. January 12, 1890, Chicago, Ill.
          PETER GEORGE.
        [Son of James and Mary George.]   (v. L. J. B. George.)
CHARLES LEMUEL BARNUM, b. October 21, 1855, Bethel, Conn.
               (Rec'd Family Bible, Mrs. Benedict.)

VI.

Charlotte Augusta Barnum.

[Eldest dau. of George Barnum and Betsey Sanford.]

b. March 31, 1847, Bethel, Conn.
m. November 24, 1859, Bethel, Conn.

DAVID OSBORNE, JR.

[Son of David and Hannah (Griffen) Osborne.]

b. February 20, 1835, Danbury, Conn.
d. August 19, 1874, Redding, Conn.

CHILDREN :

CORA BARNUM OSBORNE, b. July 16, 1862, Danbury, Conn.
BESSIE LOUISE OSBORNE, b. November 4, 1874, Danbury, Conn.
               (v. C. A. B. Osborne.)

VI.

Hannah Sanford Barnum.

[Second dau. of George Barnum and Betsey Sanford.]

b. December 2, 1839, Bethel, Conn.
m. November 23, 1865, Bethel, Conn.

LEWIS B. BENEDICT.

[Son of Joseph and Nancy (Hempstead) Benedict.]

b. September 7, 1842, Newtown, Conn.

CHILDREN :

ALIDA E. BENEDICT, b. November 22, 1866, Bethel, Conn. p. 263.
JEANNETTE B. BENEDICT, b. March 23, 1870, Bethel, Conn. p. 263.

(v. H. S. B. Benedict.)

VII.

Alida Elizabeth Benedict.

[Elder dau. of Lewis B. Benedict and Hannah Sanford Barnum.]

b. November 22, 1866, Bethel, Conn.
d. April 5, 1894, Rock Valley, Iowa.
m. August 18, 1892, Centreville, South Dakota.

WILSON HINKLEY.

[Son of Gideon and Mary Ann (Wilson) Hinkley ; (nephew of Jacob Hinkley.)]

b. May 15, 1865, Wisconsin.

CHILD :

IRMA SANFORD HINKLEY, b. Oct. 22, 1893 ; Rock Valley ;
d. Sept. 13, 1894, Rock Valley, Ia.   (v. Mrs. Jacob Hinkley.)

VII.

Jeanette Barnum Benedict.

[Younger dau. of Lewis B. Benedict and Hannah Sanford Barnum.]

b. March 23, 1870, Bethel, Conn.
m. November 9, 1892, Bethel, Conn.

CLIFFORD BENEDICT MORGAN.

[Son of Jerome and Cornelia (Benedict) Morgan.]

b. July 13, 1870, Bethel, Conn.

CHILD :

ETHEL CELESTE MORGAN, b. August 25, 1893, Bethel, Conn.

(v. J. B. B. Morgan.)

VI.

Adaline Amelia Barnum.

[Third dau. of George Barnum and Betsey Sanford. p. 262.]

b. April 28, 1842, Bethel, Conn.
d. February 21, 1898, Centreville, South Dakota.
m. November 11, 1884, Centreville, S. D.

JACOB HINKLEY.

[Son of Jesse and Eliza H. Hinkley.]

b. January 18, 1842, Lisbon, Maine.
d. July 1, 1897, Centreville, South Dakota.

EDDY HINKLEY, b. December, 1875 (was living with his step-mother
on the farm, at the time of her death.)

(v. by S. E. B. Norvell for her sister.)

VI.

Sarah Elizabeth Barnum.

[Fourth dau. of George Barnum and Betsey Sanford.]

b. October 19, 1845, Bethel, Conn.
m. September 25, 1883, Centreville, South Dakota.

REV^D JOSEPH ELGIN NORVELL.

[Son of George W. Norvell and Luvicy Parrott Boyd (b. Aug. 27, 1822, Mo.; d. Oct.
28, 1897, Hillsdale, Iowa).]

b. May 1, 1859, Waubousey, Iowa.
(Member of Dakota M. E. Conference.)

CHILDREN :

GEORGE WHITFIELD NORVELL, b. May 25, 1885, Hartford, S. D.
GRACE EDITH NORVELL, b. November 5, 1886, Beresford, S. D.
} PHILIP DAVID NORVELL, b. August 9, 1888, Lodi, South Dakota.
{ JULIA SANFORD NORVELL, b. Aug. 9, 1888, Lodi, South Dakota.

(v. S. E. B. Norvell.)

VI.

George Washington Barnum.

[Eldest son of George Barnum and Betsey Sanford.]

b. February 22, 1849, Bethel, Conn.
d. October 20, 1883, Centreville, S. D.
m. March 14, 1875, Centreville, S. D.

NORA BELL KOONS.

[Dau. George Bowman Koons (b. Jan. 15, 1818, near Pittsburg, Pa.), m. M'ch 22,
1854, Delmar, Clinton Co., Iowa, Eunice Lucinda Decker (b. June 14, 1822, Albany,
N. Y.), (are still living near Haram, S. D., 1898).]

CHILDREN:

ADDIE BELL BARNUM, b. June 10, 1877, Sioux City, Iowa,
SADIE ELIZABETH BARNUM, b. October 18, 1879, Haram, S. D.
BERTRAND ANDREW BARNUM, b. December 29, 1882, Haram, S. D.
(v. H. T. Barnum.)

VI.

Henry Taylor Barnum.

[Second son of George Barnum and Betsey Sanford.]

b. May 14, 1850, Bethel, Conn.
m. October 15, 1884, Haram, Lincoln Co., S. D.

NORA BELL (KOONS) BARNUM.

[Dau. of George Bowman Koons and Eunice Lucinda Decker.]

b. April 2, 1858, Delmar, Clinton Co., Iowa.

CHILDREN:

LUELLA MAUD BARNUM, b. July 18, 1885, Haram, S. D.
GEORGE KOONS BARNUM, b. November 6, 1889, Haram, S. D.
ROYAL CHARLES BARNUM, b. May 17, 1893, Haram, S. D.
FRED CLIFFORD BARNUM, b. October 17, 1895, Haram, S. D.
(v. H. T. Barnum.)

VI.

Charles Lemuel Barnum.

[Youngest son of George Barnum and Betsey Sanford.]

b. October 12, 1855, Bethel, Conn.
m. November 25, 1884, Delaware, South Dakota.

HELEN SITGREAVES.

[Dau. of Martin H. and Sarah (Iding) Sitgreaves.]

b. July 14, 1862, Waymart, Wayne Co., Penna.

CHILDREN:

ILBA SITGREAVES BARNUM, b. August 23, 1889, Delaware, S. D.
d. March 3, 1891, Lead City, S. D.
SHELDON CHARLES BARNUM, b. July 6, 1891, Lead City, S. D.
(v. Chas. L. Barnum.)

V.

Rev'd David Platt Sanford, D.D.

[Third son of Lemuel Sanford and Charlotte Platt. p. 256.]

b. January 29, 1819, Redding, Conn.
d. April 3, 1883, Thompsonville, Conn.
first m. April 3, 1847, Newtown, Conn.

CAROLINE HAMLIN.

[Dau. of Ancillus and Jerusha (Botsford) Hamlin.]

b. April 7, 1822, Newtown, Conn.
d. July 7, 1851, St. Louis, Missouri.
second m. November 18, 1852, Brooklyn, N. Y.

EMMA BARTOW LEWIS.

[Dau. of Rev'd William H. Lewis and Emmeline Julia Bartow.]

b. June 14, 1829, Flushing, L. I.

CHILDREN (of first marriage) :

GRACE HYDE SANFORD, b. February 19, 1848, Newtown ;
    d. December 7, 1894, Nebraska City, Nebr.
ALICE SANFORD, b. October 16, 1849, Wolcottville, Conn.;
    d. September 21, 1850, St. Louis, Mo.

CHILDREN (of second marriage) :

CAROLINE HAMLIN SANFORD, b. Feb. 11, 1854, B'klyn, N. Y. (unm.)
HARRIET E. SANFORD, b. November 21, 1855, Brooklyn, N. Y. p. 266.
DAVID L. SANFORD, b. September 6, 1857, Brooklyn, N. Y. p. 267.
CHARLOTTE BEACH SANFORD, b. Feb. 3, 1860, Long Hill, Trumbull;
    d. July 30, 1864, Wolcottville, Conn.
WILLIAM HENRY SANFORD, b. March 31, 1862, Long Hill, Trumbull ;
    d. April 15, 1862, Long Hill, Trumbull, Conn.
EDGAR L. SANFORD, b. June 24, 1864, Wolcottville, Conn. p. 267.
AMELIA SANFORD, b. April 26, 1868, Torrington (Wolcottville), Conn.
FREDERICK H. SANFORD, b. July 5, 1874, Thompsonville, Conn. p. 268.
(v. Mrs. D. P. Sanford.)

VI.

Harriet Emma Sanford.

[Second dau. of Rev'd David Platt Sanford, by his second wife, Emma Bartow Lewis.]

b. November 21, 1855, Brooklyn, N. Y.
d. November 19, 1885, Salisbury, Conn.
m. September 8, 1875, Thompsonville, Conn.

REV'D JAMES HARDIN GEORGE, JR.

[Son of Rev'd James Hardin George and Martha Ann Taylor.]

b. March 29, 1853, Albany, Georgia.

CHILDREN:

THEODORA GEORGE, b. June 28, 1876, Thompsonville, Conn.
HARRIET EMMA GEORGE, b. September 28, 1877, Pittsfield;
   d. October 12, 1877, Pittsfield, N. H.
DAVID SANFORD GEORGE, b. November 8, 1878, Pittsfield, N. H.
BERTHA NILES GEORGE, b. September 5, 1880, Pittsfield, N. H.
KATHERINE LOUISE GEORGE, b. January 16, 1882, Windsor Locks;
   d. August 13, 1882, Windsor Locks, Conn.
CAROLINE ANNA GEORGE, b. June 17, 1883, Salisbury, Conn.
JAMES HARDIN GEORGE, 3d, b. November 21, 1884, Salisbury, Conn.
(rec'd Rev'd J. H. George and Rev'd D. L. Sanford.)

VI.

Rev'd David Lewis Sanford.

[Eldest son of Rev'd David Platt Sanford and Emma Bartow Lewis.]

   b. September 6, 1857, Brooklyn, N. Y.
   m. April 20, 1882, St. Andrew's Church, Thompsonville, Conn.

ANNA TRAVER BRISCOE.

[Dau. of Hon. Charles Henry and Anna (Traver) Briscoe.]

   b. December 5, 1858, Thompsonville, Conn.

CHILDREN:

HELEN TRAVER SANFORD, b. March 21, 1883, Thompsonville, Conn.
ALICE AMELIA SANFORD, b. September 4, 1884, Thomaston, Conn.
CHARLES BRISCOE SANFORD, b. January 10, 1887, Thomaston, Conn.
EDGAR LEWIS SANFORD, b. October 31, 1889, Bellows Falls, Vt.
JOHN BEACH SANFORD, b. June 22, 1891, Bellows Falls, Vt.
ARTHUR HALL SANFORD, b. March 15, 1895, Bellows Falls, Vt.
DAVID PLATT SANFORD, b. September 20, 1896, Bellows Falls, Vt.
(v. Rev'd D. L. Sanford.)

VI.

Rev'd Edgar Lewis Sanford.

[Third son of Rev'd David Platt Sanford and Emma Bartow Lewis.]

   b. June 24, 1864, Wolcottville, now Torrington, Ct.
   m. October 16, 1889, Winsted, Conn.

ANNA EUGENIA MUNSON.

[Dau. of Eugene Miller Munson and Sarah Moses Squire.]

   b. Jan. 6, 1866, Winsted, Conn.

CHILDREN :

VÉRA SANFORD, b. October 1, 1891, Douglaston, Queens Co., N. Y., (Greater N. Y.)

EVA MATTHEWS SANFORD, b. July 6, 1894, Nebraska City, Nebr.

(v. Rev'd E. L. Sanford.)

VI.

Frederick Harriman Sanford.

[Fourth son of Rev'd David Platt Sanford and Emma Bartow Lewis.]

b. July 5, 1874, Thomsonville, Conn.

m. November 10, 1897, Danbury, Conn.

EVA STARR BATES.

[Dau. of Joseph Taylor Bates and Abbie Starr Taylor.]

b. April 16, 1874.   (v. F. H. Sanford.)

———o———

V.

Eunice Louisa Sanford.

[Sixth dau. of Lemuel Sanford and Charlotte Platt. p. 256.]

b. June 4, 1824, Redding, Conn.

d. September 11, 1881, Kent, Ohio.

m. June 17, 1847, Akron, O.

THOMAS MELVILLE.

[Son of John and Irme Melville.]

b. February 9, 1814, New Mills, Scotland.

d. September 14, 1877, Kent, Ohio.

CHILDREN :

FRANK I. MELVILLE, b. October 2, 1848; d. March 30, 1852.

MINNIE M. MELVILLE, b. July 4, 1854, Kent, Ohio.

(v. M. M. M. Babbitt.)

VI.

Minnie M. Melville.

[Only dau. of Thomas Melville and Eunice Louisa Sanford.]

b. July 4, 1854, Kent, Ohio.

m. June 18, 1882, Kent, Ohio.

DOCTOR GEORGE A. BABBITT.

[Son of Simeon and Emily (McKinstry) Babbitt.]

b. December 30, 1852, Bethel, Vermont.

CHILDREN:

G. MELVILLE BABBITT, b. June 7, 1883, Western Star, Ohio.
LOUISA E. BABBITT, b. August 2, 1886, Western Star, Ohio.
PAUL K. BABBITT, b. December 13, 1889, Western Star, Ohio.

(v. M. M. M. Babbitt.)

————o————

IV.

Lydia Ann Sanford.

[Eldest dau. of James Sanford and SARAH BEACH. p. 255-6.]

b. August 1, 1782. (Redding Rec'd.)
d. April 22, 1824, Redding, Conn.
m. August 16, 1801.

WILLIAM SHEPARD.

[Prob. son of Capt. Moses Shepard (d. April 25, 1809, Newtown Rec'd).]

b. March 30, 1780. (Newtown Rec'd, p. 59.)
"Said to have fallen at *Battle of New Orleans*, Jan'y 8, 1815."

CHILDREN:

ELVIRA SHEPARD, b. January 15, 1802, Redding, Conn. p. 269.
WILLIAM MC SHEPARD, Jr., b. April 15, 1803, Redding, Conn. p. 274.
SALLY SHEPARD, p. 280.

V.

Elvira Shepard.

[Elder dau. of William Shepard and Lydia Ann Sanford.]

b. January 15, 1802, Redding, Conn.
d. April 29, 1878. (Sanford Burial Ground.—T. S.)
m. , Redding, Conn.

WILLIAM B. CABLE.

b. October 7, 1801, Weston, Conn.
d. April 19, 1873.

CHILDREN:

HARRIET MARIA CABLE, b. 1822, Redding, Conn. p. 270.
MARY E. CABLE, m. left no descendants.
CHARLES CABLE, said to have been living in 1850, Albany, N. Y.
{ MARGARET CABLE (died young at Albany).
{ JAMES CABLE, b. 1837; m. 1861, Bridgeport, Conn., two children.
JENNIE CABLE; AGNES CABLE.

(Rec'd Mrs. Henry Sanford.)

VI.

Harriet Maria Cable.

[Eldest dau. of William B. Cable and Elvira Shepard.]

b. 1822, Redding, Conn.
d. June 16, 1891, Chicago, Ill.
m. February 23, 1839, Albany, N. Y.

STEPHEN HANNAFORD.

[Son of William and Agnes Hannaford.]

b. May   , 1807, Stoke, Devonshire, England.
d. July 18, 1866, Bridgeport, Conn.

CHILDREN:

{ GEORGE W. HANNAFORD, b. Nov. 23, 1839, Albany, N. Y. p. 270.
{ WILLIAM H. HANNAFORD, b. Nov. 23, 1839; d. —— Albany, N. Y.
*WILLIAM H. HANNAFORD, b. June 13, 1841, Albany, N. Y.
STEPHEN HANNAFORD, b. February 7, 1844; d. ——, Albany, N. Y.
ELIZABETH HANNAFORD, b. February 2, 1845, Albany, N. Y. p. 272.
STEPHEN HANNAFORD, b. November 20, 1846; d. ——, Albany, N. Y.
MARGARET HANNAFORD, b. August 3, 1849, Plattsburg, N. Y. p. 273.
EMMA HANNAFORD, b. August 11, 1853; d. 1855, Bridgeport, Conn.
CHARLES G. HANNAFORD, b. September 24, 1854, B'p't, Conn. p. 273.
SAMUEL HANNAFORD, b. Jan'y 20, 1856; d. Jan'y 25, 1856, B'p't, Conn.
HARRIET M. HANNAFORD, b. Feb'y 26, 1857; d. July, 1858, B'p't, Conn.
ROBERT H. HANNAFORD, b. Sept. 8, 1858, Bridgeport, Conn. p. 273.
HARRIET L. HANNAFORD, b. Dec. 3, 1860, Bridgeport, Conn. p. 274.
†ANNA L. HANNAFORD, b. Dec. 18, 1863, Bridgeport, Conn.
HENRY ——   (Hannaford Bible.)

VII.

George W. Hannaford.

[Twin son of Stephen Hannaford and Harriet Maria Cable.]

b. November 23, 1839, Albany, N. Y.
m. January 19, 1860, Bridgeport, Conn.

HARRIET STILES.

[Dau. of Walter J. Stiles and Harriet A. Wilson.]

b. November 6, 1843, Bridgeport, Conn.

CHILDREN:

EMMA J. HANNAFORD, b. September 28, 1861, B'p't, Conn. p. 271.
KITTIE HANNAFORD, b. Dec. 12, 1864, Bridgeport, Conn. p. 271.
GEORGE S. HANNAFORD, b. November 18, 1867, Chicago, Ill. p. 272.

* d. Feb'y 18, 1898, Boston, Mass., left one child—a daughter.
† m. James Spooner.

WALTER M. HANNAFORD, b. February 24, 1870, Chicago, Ill;
 d. August 14, 1880, Chicago, Ill.
HARRIET A. HANNAFORD, b. June 2, 1874, Chicago, Ill. p. 272.
FREDERICK J. HANNAFORD, b. March 16, 1876, Chicago, Ill;
 d. May 25, 1876, Chicago, Ill.
IDA M. HANNAFORD, b. September 1, 1877, Chicago, Ill. (unm.)
FRANCIS J. C. HANNAFORD, b. February 18, 1882, Chicago, Ill.
MYRTLE I. HANNAFORD, b. September 14, 1885, Chicago, Ill.

(v. Geo. W. Hannaford.)

VIII.

Emma Jane Hannaford.

[Eldest dau. George W. Hannaford and Harriet Stiles.]

b. September 28, 1861, Bridgeport, Conn.
m. January 19, 1885, Chicago, Ill.

SIMEON JAMES SMITH.

[Son of Charles and Caroline (   ) Smith.]

b. May 24, 1857, Kingston, Canada.

CHILDREN:

CARRIE MAY SMITH, b. November 19, 1885, Chicago, Ill.
AMY AUGUSTA SMITH, b. June 8, 1889; d. June 10, 1892, Chicago, Ill.
LULU IRENE SMITH, b. May 10, 1893, Chicago, Ill.

(v. E. J. H. Smith.)

VIII.

Kittie Hannaford.

[Second dau. of George W. Hannaford and Harriet Stiles.]

b. December 12, 1864, Bridgeport, Conn.
m. August 26, 1882, Chicago, Ill.

JAMES ARCHIBALD McLEAN.

[Son of Archibald and Eliza (Ferris) McClean (original spelling).]

b. December 4, 1860, Chatham, England.

CHILDREN:

HARRIET AUGUSTA McLEAN, b. Apr. 12, 1884, Wyandotte, Kansas;
 d. Aug. 31, 1891, Chicago, Ill.
GEORGE ARCHIBALD McLEAN, b. Nov. 30, 1887, Wyandotte, Kansas.
GERTRUDE EMILY McLEAN, b. March 22, 1891, Kansas City, Kansas.
JAMES HERBERT McLEAN, b. Dec. 11, 1892, Kansas City, Kansas.
 d. June 28, 1893, Kansas City, Kansas.
ELEANOR CORA McLEAN, b. July 22, 1897, Chicago, Ill.

(v. K. H. McLean.)

VIII.

George Stephen Hannaford.

[Eldest son of George W. Hannaford and Harriet Stiles.]

b. November 18, 1867, Chicago, Ill.

m. December 18, 1887, Chicago, Ill.

MARGARET REBECCA JEFFREY.

[Dau. of William Wallace Jeffrey and Margaret Spantou.]

b. December 18, 1866, Toronto, Canada.

CHILDREN :

MILDRED LOIS HANNAFORD, b. Jan'y 3, 1889, Chicago, Ill.

MARION ESTELLA HANNAFORD, b. Nov. 22, 1890, Chicago, Ill.

EDNA HARRIET HANNAFORD, b. Sept. 3, 1897, Chicago, Ill.

(v. Geo. Stephen Hannaford.)

VIII.

Harriet Augusta Hannaford.

[Third dau. of George W. Hannaford and Harriet Stiles.]

b. June 2, 1874, Chicago, Ill.

m. October 2, 1895, Chicago, Ill.

HENRY HAVELOCK BERRY.

[Son of William D. Berry and Joanne F. Lawrence.]

b. Jan'y 28, 1864, West Sumner, Oxford Co., Maine.

CHILD :

ORA RUTH BERRY, b. July 11, 1897, Chicago, Ill.   (v. H. A. H. Berry.)

VII.

Elizabeth Hannaford.

[Eldest dau. of Stephen Hannaford and Harriet M. Cable. p. 270.]

b. February 2, 1845, Albany, N. Y.

d. December 4, 1877, Bridgeport, Conn.

m. January 16, 1864, Bridgeport, Conn.

WILLIAM H. LOCKWOOD.

CHILDREN.

WILLIAM H. LOCKWOOD, b——

ELIZABETH LOCKWOOD.

JESSICA LOCKWOOD.

VII.

Margaret Hannaford.

[Second dau. of Stephen Hannaford and Harriet M. Cable. p. 270.]

b. August 31, 1849, Plattsburg, N. Y.
m. November 30, 1882, Redding, Conn.

HENRY SANFORD ⱽ.

[Sixth son of JAMES SANFORD, JR. and Eliza French. p. 285.]

b. January 29, 1846, Redding, Conn.

ONE CHILD ; d —— (v. M. H. Sanford.)

VII.

Charles G. Hannaford.

[Sixth son of Stephen Hannaford and Harriet M. Cable.]

b. September 24, 1854, Bridgeport, Conn.
m. August 14, 1875, Chicago, Illinois.

Seven ch.: EDITH; MARION GRACE; FLORENCE; LILLIAN (d.) ; EVA BUNKER; RALPH STEPHEN (d) and RUTH, twins.

(rec'd from Mrs. M. H. Sanford.)

VII.

Robert H. Hannaford.

[Eighth son of Stephen Hannaford and Harriet M. Cable.]

b. September 8–⁽⁰⁾, 1857, Bridgeport, Conn.
d. August 3, 1892, Chicago, Ill.
m. October 6, 1891, Holland City, Michigan.

MARTHA BLOM.

[Dau. of William and Elvira (Ellis) Blom.]

b. June 5, 1866, Holland City, Mich.

CHILD :

LAURA ELVIRA HANNAFORD, b. May 17, 1892, Chicago, Ill.

(v. Mrs. M. B. Hannaford.)

18

VII.

Harriet Louisa Hannaford.

[Fifth dau. of Stephen Hannaford and Harriet M. Cable.]

b. December 3, 1860, Bridgeport, Conn.
d. July 31, 1891, Bridgeport, Conn.
m. May 15, 1880, Bridgeport, Conn.

ALEXANDER WATT, JR.

[Son of Alexander Watt and Isabella Leith, of Aberdeen, Scotland.]

b. June 7, 1850, Astoria, Long Island.

CHILDREN:

ALEXANDER HANNAFORD WATT, b. February 21, 1881, B'p't, Conn.
LOUISA HANNAFORD WATT, b. August 3, 1882, Bridgeport, Conn.
ROBERT BRAISTEAD WATT, b. March 6, 1884, Bridgeport, Conn.
GRACE LEITH WATT, b. December 12, 1885, Bridgeport, Conn.
FREDERICK HOWARD WATT, b. September 1, 1887, Bridgeport, Conn.

(v. Louisa Hannaford Watt.)

V.

William (Mc) Shepard, Jr.

[Only son of William Shepard and Lydia Ann Sanford. p. 269.]

b. April 15, 1803, Redding, Conn.
d. October 6, 1873, Sheffield, Ohio.
first m. December 1, 1824, Newtown, Conn.

ANNA GRIFFIN.

[Dau. of Andrew Griffin and Mary Rowland.]

b. February 21, 1808, Newtown, Conn.
d. September 4, 1833, Newtown, Conn.
second m. November 10, 1833, Newtown, Conn.

LUCY STILSON.

[Dau. of Lazarus Stilson and Bessie Johnson.]

b. June 24, 1806, Newtown, Conn.
d. February 9, 1871, Sheffield, Ohio.

CHILDREN (of first marriage):

WILLIAM SHEPARD, 3rd, b. October 28, 1825, Newtown, Conn. p. 275.
ANDREW SHEPARD, b. November 6, 1827, Newtown, Conn. p. 276.
MARY SHEPARD, b. October 19, 1829, Newtown, Conn. p. 278.

CHARLES SHEPARD, b. Oct. 9, 1831 ; d. Nov. 30, 1831, Newtown, Conn.
SUSANAH SHEPARD, b. November 21, 1832, Newtown, Conn.
  m. June 29, 1879.
  ARCHIBALD CUNNINGHAM, of Columbus, Ohio.
  b. April 10, 1820, Beaver Co., Penna.
  d. August 25, 1897, Columbus, O. (no children.)

(rec'd Horace Shepard.)

CHILDREN (of second marriage):
JOHN SHEPARD, b. Oct. 15, 1834, Newtown, Conn.;
  d. Dec. 26, 1856, Sheffield, Ohio. (unm.)
HORACE SHEPARD, b. July 3, 1836, Sheffield, Ohio. (unm.)
GEORGE J. SHEPARD, b. September 24, 1838, Sheffield, Ohio. p. 279.
JAMES SHEPARD, b. March 27, 1842, Sheffield, Ohio. p. 279.

Church Record : " Nov. 1, 1832, I reported to the Baptist Church, Gods special dealings with me, and the 15th I was baptized. `
April 1835, myself and wife received a letter of dismission and recomend from Weston, Conn.
June 1835, I handed in our letter to the Conference in Sheffield, Ohio, July 6th, we received the right hand of Fellowship from the Church."

(Rec'ds, fr. Wm. F. Boynton and Horace Shepard.)
(v. Wm. McShepard's Bible.—C. R. S.)

VI.

William Shepard, 3rd.

[Eldest son of William (Mc) Shepard, Jr. (by his wife) Anna Griffin.]
  b. October 28, 1825, Newtown, Conn.
  d. October 30, 1895, Kingsville, Ohio.
  m. October 4, 1859.

SAPHRONIA E. JARVIS.

[Dau. of Sidney Sylvester and Clarissa (Boynton) Jarvis.]
  b. March 18, 1836, Otisco, Onondaga Co., N. Y.
  d. September 15, 1888, Kingsville, Ohio.

CHILDREN :

FRANKE L. SHEPARD, b. February 7, 1861, Denmark, O. p. 276.
EMMA E. SHEPARD, b. March 9, 1863, Denmark, O. p. 276.
LIDA VIOLA SHEPARD, b. May 20, 1866, Denmark, O.
  d. June 6, 1888, Kingsville, O.
NELLIE GERTRUDE SHEPARD, b. April 4, 1869, Denmark, O.
  d. March 12, 1895, Kingsville, O.
MARY E. SHEPARD, b. January 4, 1871, Denmark, O. (unm.)
(v. F. L. S. Kingsbury.)

VII.
Franke Lillian Shepard.
[Eldest dau. of William Shepard, 3rd, and Saphronia E. Jarvis.]

b. February 7, 1861, Denmark, Asht. Co., O.

m. June 18, 1880, Kingsville, Asht. Co., O.

GUILFORD G. KINGSBURY.
[Son of Munson I. Kingsbury and Hulda A. Davis.]

b. June 22, 1861, Kingsville, Ohio.

CHILDREN:

LELIA IVA KINGSBURY, b. March 14, 1881, Kingsville, Ohio.
   d. October 3, 1881, Kingsville, Ohio.
PAUL SHEPARD KINGSBURY, b. November 23, 1885, Kingsville, Ohio.
GUILFORD G. KINGSBURY, JR., b. July 13, 1891, Kingsville, Ohio.
(v. F. L. S. Kingsbury.)

VII.
Emma Shepard.
[Second dau. of William Shepard, 3d, and Saphronia E. Jarvis.]

b. March 9, 1863, Denmark, Asht. Co., O.

d. December , 1892, Madison, Conn.

m. HORACE HUNTER.

CHILD:

WILLIAM SHEPARD HUNTER, b.

VI.
Andrew Shepard.
[Second son of William (Mc) Shepard, Jr., by his first wife, Anna Griffin. p. 274.]

b. November 6, 1827, Newtown, Conn.

*d. June 14, 1869, Bristol, Conn.

m. March 22, 1858, Bristol, Conn.

†LEONTINE MARIA TUTTLE.
[Only child of Abner Tuttle and Hannah (Hall) Parker.] (Tuttle B'k.)

b. September 30, 1841.

* In Shepard Bible: " My son Andrew died Jan. 15, 1869, æ. 41 yrs. 2 mos. 15 da."
† Mrs. Andrew Shepard remarried Feb'y 4, 1891, DR. HENRY AUSTEN CARRINGTON, 2nd
son of Abijah and Anna (Austen) Carrington ; b. Sept. 2, 1826, Milford, Conn.

CHILDREN :

CHARLES ROLLS SHEPARD, b. October 14. 1859, Bristol ; May 21, 1868 (drowned in the river).
ANNIE MAY SHEPARD, b. January 24, 1862, Bristol, Conn. p. 277.
WILLIAM TUTTLE SHEPARD, b. Jan'y 1, 1865, Bristol, Conn. p. 277.
GEORGE ANDREW SHEPARD, M.D., June 6, 1868, Bristol, Conn. (unm).

(v. Mrs. H. A. Carrington.)

VII.

Annie May Shepard.

[Only dau. of Andrew Shepard and Leontine Maria Tuttle.]

b. January 24, 1862, Bristol, Conn.
m. March 11, 1885, Bristol, Conn.

LORA WATERS ROBINSON.

[Son of Timothy B. Robinson and Sophie E. Wells.]

CHILDREN :

PAULINE SHEPARD ROBINSON, b. December 26, 1885, Bristol, Conn.
ARCHER WATERS ROBINSON, b. Aug. 12, 1887; d. Aug. 15, 1887, Bristol, Conn.
LYLE WELLS ROBINSON, b. May 1, 1889, Bristol, Conn.
KENDALL SHEPARD ROBINSON, b. June 20, 1894, Buffalo, N. Y. d. April 8, 1895, Bristol, Conn.
WELLS HALL ROBINSON, b. September 15, 1896, Buffalo, N. Y.

(rec'd Mrs. H. A. Carrington.)

VII.

William Tuttle Shepard.

[Second son of Andrew Shepard and Leontine Maria Tuttle.]

b. January 1, 1865, Bristol, Conn.
m. December 7, 1887, New Haven, Conn.

JULIA ISABEL CARRINGTON.

[Dau. Henry Austen Carrington, M.D. and Grace Tomlinson.]

b. June 18, 1866, Lansingburgh, N. Y.

CHILDREN :

MARGARET GRACE SHEPARD, b. October 12, 1890, Buffalo, N. Y.
DONALD CARRINGTON SHEPARD, b. October 8, 1891, Buffalo, N. Y.
CHESTER DEWITT SHEPARD, b. September 24, 1893, Buffalo, N. Y.
ALAN AUSTEN SHEPARD, b. November 19, 1897, Bristol, Conn.

(v. Wm. T. Shepard.)

VI.

Mary Shepard.

[Elder dau. of William (Mc) Shepard, Jr., by his first wife, Anna Griffin. p. 274.]

b. October 19, 1829, Newtown, Conn.
d. Sept. 17, 1863, Saybrook, Ashtabula Co., Ohio.
m. February 11, 1855, Kingsville, Ohio.

LYMAN BOYNTON.

[Son of Ezra and Hannah (Walkup) Boynton.]

b. March 26, 1817, Vermont.
d. April 11, 1869, Saybrook, Ohio.

CHILDREN:

ANNA BOYNTON, b. May 29, 1857, Saybrook, Ohio. p. 278.
WILLIAM E. BOYNTON, b. April 10, 1861, Saybrook, Ohio. p. 278.

(v. Wm. E. Boynton.)

VII.

Anna Boynton.

[Only dau. of Lyman Boynton and Mary Shepard.]

b. May 29, 1857, Saybrook, Ohio.
m. October 1, 1878, Ashtabula, Ohio.

EUGENE MAURICE PACKARD.

[Son of Sidney and Lydia (Ives) Packard.]

b. July 25, 1852, Milton, Wisconsin.

CHILD:

ROBERT BOYNTON PACKARD, b. March 14, 1890, Chillicothe, Mo.

(v. A. B. Packard.)

VII.

William Ezra Boynton.

[Only son of Lyman Boynton and Mary Shepard.]

b. April 10, 1861, Saybrook, Ohio.
m. May 5, 1886

KATIE CROWELL.

[Dau. of James Crowell and Roxie Durkee.]

d. December 9, 1894, Ashtabula, Ohio.

CHILDREN:

RUTH THERESA BOYNTON, b. January 15, 1888, Ashtabula, O.
LYMAN CROWELL BOYNTON, b. November 4, 1893, Ashtabula, O.

(v. Wm. E. Boynton.)

VI.

*George Johnson Shepard.

[Third son of William (Mc) Shepard, Jr., by his second wife, Lucy Stilson. p. 274.]

b. September 24, 1838, Sheffield, Ohio.
d. March 12, 1897, Erie City, Erie Co., Penna.
first m. September 9, 1858.

JULIA A. STURDEVANT.

[Dau. of Edward Sturdevant and Yubia Cooley.]

second m. March 3, 1866, McKean, Erie Co., Penna.

CHARLOTTE REBECCA GRANT.

[Dau. of Aaron Grant and Charlotte Dennis.]

b. April 25, 1842, McKean T'p, Erie Co., Penna.

CHILD (of first marriage):

CHARLES A. SHEPARD, b. May 29, 1860, Denmark, Ohio.
d. May 17, 1896, Temple, Michigan.
m.; two ch. (both died) elder named GEORGE J. SHEPARD.

CHILDREN (of second marriage):

IDA SHEPARD, b. January 30, 1867, Denmark, Asht. Co., Ohio.
d. May 22, 1886, æ. 19 yrs. 3 mo. 23 d., Erie City, Pa.
FRANK ARTHUR SHEPARD, b. July 4, 1870, Denmark, Ohio. (unm.)
STELLA SHEPARD, b. Nov. 14, 1872, Erie City, Pennsylvania.
d. August 6, 1873, æ. 8 mo. 23 d., Erie City.
EDITH SHEPARD, b. September 7, 1874, Erie City, Penna. (unm.)

(v. Mrs. C. R. Shepard.)

VI.

James Shepard.

[Fourth son of William (Mc) Shepard, Jr., by his second wife, Lucy Stilson. p. 274.]

b. March 27, 1842, Sheffield, Ohio.
first m. December 24, 1868, Denmark, Asht. Co., O.

SARA E. KNAPP.

[Dau. of Harmon and Mittie (Barker) Knapp.]

b. August 16, 1846.
d. February 12, 1886.
second m. January 22, 1887, Ashtabula, O.

ELIZA ASKEW.

[Dau. of Thomas and Mercy (Archer) Askew.]

b. August 28, 1859, Ellington, Huntington, Eng.

* George J. Shepard enlisted in Co. F., 2nd Ohio Vol. Cav., Aug. 20, 1861, was Honorably Discharged Oct. 10, 1864, at Ft. Cochran, Va.

CHILDREN (of first marriage) :

ROLLIN W. SHEPARD, b. June 22, 1874, Ashtabula, Ohio. p. 280.

EDWARD C. SHEPARD, b. September 28, 1885, Ashtabula, Ohio.

CHILD (of second marriage) :

JAMES B. SHEPARD, b. January 12, 1888, Ashtabula, Ohio.

VII.

Rollin W. Shepard.

[Elder son of James Shepard, by his first wife, Sara E. Knapp.]

b. June 22, 1874, Ashtabula, Ohio.

m. November 29, 1893, Ashtabula, Ohio.

GRACE V. ROOT.

[Dau. of Clarkson L. Root and Frances Laskey.]

b. November 20, 1873, Ashtabula, Ohio.

· CHILD :

JAMES CLARKSON SHEPARD, b. June 30, 1895, Ashtabula, O.

(rec'd Wm. E. Boynton.)

————o————

V.

Sally Shepard.

[Younger dau. of William Shepard and Lydia Ann Sanford. p. 269.]

m. BURTON THORPE.

HIGHLAND, May 12, 1850.

Dear Aunt:

* * * * my Father, Mother and Sister were all taken from us in three short weeks, Father and Sister dead and buried before I knew that they were sick and Mother lay at the point of death. They died one year ago last February, there is five children alive now, the youngest nineteen months the next eleven years next Nov. Henry is the oldest son he is 23 year and is married. Charles Sanford the next 20 years old next Oct. Harriet Maria thats my humble self is the oldest one of all as you know I suppose and 26 next July if I should be spared till that time.

* * * * we received a letter from Uncle William last spring but neglected to answer it he was alive and well he complained that he had not heard from you in a long time that you did not get his last letter, his letter is post marked North Sheffield, Ohio. I wish you would write to him as soon as you receive this and give him the particulars of the deaths as received by you. Now I will write a few lines about myself. I am married and have been for eight years last April

and have two Children one six years old the other 1 year. My husband's name is Nathaniel Burnham he is from Hillborough County New Hampshire we expect to go to N. H. on a visit to his relatives the first of June nothing prevents. We shall go the northern route and pass through Albany and you may expect to see us. How glad I shall be to see my Mother's Sister and my Cousins. I don't think we shall go to see Uncle William can't be gone not over five weeks at the most and it would take some to go where he lives. If I knew the street that Aunt Laura lives on I should like to go and see her. I have heard Mother talk so much about you and her that I almost know you as well as though had seen you give my love to all of my Cousins and Uncle C.

Yours respectfully,

HARRIET MARIA B.

please to direct your letters to

Highland P. O. Madison County, Ill.

From letter addressed to Mrs. Elvira Cabel, Orange Street 159, Albany. New York. (In possession of her g'd-dau. Mrs. Henry Sanford.)

(Letters addressed to Highland, Ill., have been returned.—R. D. B.

——o——

IV.

Isaac Sanford.

[Eldest son of James Sanford and SARAH BEACH. p 256.]

b. April 23, 1786, Redding, Conn.

d. March 30, 1832, Catskill, N. Y.

first m. BETSEY CHAPMAN.

[Dau. of William and Amy (Lovell) Chapman.]

b. August 22, 1784, Sharon, Conn.

d. December 16, 1816.

second m. MARILLA CHAPMAN.

[Dau. of William and Amy (Lovell) Chapman.]

b. October 24, 1793, Sharon, Conn.

d. August 21, 1849, Palmyra, N. Y.

(rec'd Mrs. Chase.)

CHILDREN (of first marriage):

*MARILLA SANFORD, b. June 7, 1813; d. Sept. 30, 1896, Palmyra. (unm.)

*JAMES WILLIAM SANFORD, b. July 23, 1815, Redding, Conn.

d. June 30, 1895, Buffalo, N. Y.

m. Susan (   ) McKnight. (no children.)

* Bapt. Jan'y 19, 1818, Christ Church Rec'd, Redding Ridge, Conn.

CHILDREN (of second marriage):

AMOS C. SANFORD, b. July 2, 1820—married, lives at Palmyra, N. Y. Three sons (one married), CAPT. JAMES C. SANFORD, U. S. A., eldest son.

DAVID P. SANFORD, b. Nov. 12, 1827; d. April 19, 1872, leaving seven children, four sons and three daughters, five of whom are married and four have children.

ISAAC SANFORD, JR., died at or near Chattanooga, Tenn. (he was paymaster in Grant's Army), March 19, 1863-4; buried at Buffalo, N. Y. Left a widow, but no children.

(Amos C. Sanford, further correspondence, without result.)

————o————

IV.

Alanson Sanford.

[Third son of James Sanford and SARAH BEACH. p. 256.]

b. January 20, 1789, Redding, Conn.

m. January 30, 1815.   (Cong. Rec'd, Redding, Conn.)

SALLY GORHAM.

CHILDREN:

ELIZA SANFORD, b. 1816. p. 282.
*POLLY SANFORD, bapt. June 4, 1821.

(Christ Church Rec'd, Redding Ridge.)

JOHN BEACH SANFORD, bapt. June 4, 1821.

(Christ Church Rec'd, Redding Ridge.)

V.

Eliza Sanford.

[Elder dau. of Alanson Sanford and Sally Gorham.]

bapt. June 4, 1821.   (Christ Church Rec'd, Redding Ridge.)

d. August 27, 1857, Ridgefield, Conn.

m. August 7, 1836, Norwalk, Conn.

JAMES BUTLER SMITH.

b. December 11, 1816.

d. April 17, 1891, New York City.

CHILDREN:

MARY VIRGINIA SMITH, b. Aug. 12, 1838, Ohio City, now Cleveland, O. m. May 27, 1888.

(2nd wife of) AMOS GALLOUPE.

[Son of Benjamin and Ruth A. (Mills) Galloupe. p. 284.]

(v. Mrs. A. G.)

* m. —— Luther.

SARAH E. SMITH, b. June 13, 1840, Ridgefield, Conn. p. 283.
LOIS G. SMITH, b. April 1, 1842, Ridgefield, Conn. p. 284.
WILLIAM HARVEY SMITH, b. April 7, 1844.
    d. February 28, 1854, Ridgefield, Conn.
JAMES SANFORD SMITH, b. Dec. 1, 1846.
    d. Mar. 3, 1888, N. Y. C. (unm.)   (rec'd Mrs. Edw. Trowbridge.)

VI.

Sara Eliza Smith.

[Second dau. of James Butler Smith, by his wife, Eliza Sanford.]

b. June 13, 1840, Ridgefield, Conn.
first m. December 11, 1862, Ridgefield, Conn.

JULIAN MAIN.

[Son of Sylvester and Susan (Rashite) Main.]

d. November 21, 1865, Ridgefield, Conn.
second m. December 11, 1867.

HENRY WINNER.

[Son of Septimus and Susan (Logan) Winner.]

b. February 18, 1844.

CHILDREN (of first marriage):
HELEN MAIN, b. May 1, 1863; m. 1882; d. August 3, 1884.
JULIAN MAIN, JR., b. March, 1865. p. 283.

CHILDREN (of second marriage):
MARY FRANCES WINNER, b. June 6, 1869, New York City. p. 284.
WILLIAM SEPTIMUS WINNER, b. July 1, 1870, Norwalk, Conn. p. 284.
HARRY LOGAN WINNER, b. November 21, 1871, Norwalk, Conn.
AUGUSTA WINNER, b. August 9, 1873, East Orange, New Jersey.
RAYMOND BUTLER WINNER, b. December 9, 1878, East Orange, N. J.
EDWIN RECKAFUSS WINNER, b. January 28, 1881, East Orange, N. J.
MABELLE WINNER, b. February 28, 1883, East Orange, N. J.
    (rec'd Mrs. Winner.)

VII.

Julian Main, Jr.

[Only son of Julian Main and Sarah Eliza Smith.]

b. March, 1865.
m.   (correspondence, no result.—R. D. B.)

VII.

Mary Frances Winner.

[Eldest dau. of Henry Winner and Sarah E. (Smith) Main. p. 283.]

b. June 6, 1869, New York City.
m. January 11, 1882, East Orange, N. J.

THERWALD UNNEVER, JR.

[Son of Therwald Unnever.]

CHILD:

OLGA UNNEVER, b. January 21, 1883. (rec'd Mrs. Henry Winner.)

VII.

William Septimus Winner.

[Eldest son of Henry Winner and Sarah E. (Smith) Main.]

b. July 1, 1870, Norwalk, Conn.
m. ANNICE TWOMBLEY, of Lindrey, Ont., Canada.

CHILDREN:

ALICE MARY WINNER, b. July 13, 1890, East Orange, N. J.
CHARLES NOBLE WINNER, b. Feb. 12, 1892, East Orange, N. J.
HARRY LOGAN WINNER, b. April 19, 1897, East Orange, N. J.
ANNICE ADELAIDE WINNER, b. January 16, 1898, East Orange, N. J.
(rec'd Mrs. Henry Winner.)

VI.

Lois Gertrude Smith.

[Third dau. of James Butler Smith, by his first wife, Eliza Sanford. p. 282.]

b. April 1, 1842, Ridgefield, Conn.
d. January 13, 1885, Charlestown, Mass.
m. October, 1867.

AMOS GALLOUPE.

[Son of Benjamin Galloupe and Ruth A. Mills. p. 282.]

b. December 20, 1836, Bangor, Maine.
d. March 17, 1890, Chicopee, Mass.

CHILDREN:

JAMES BUTLER GALLOUPE, b. August 19, 1868, New York City.
d. August 6, 1888, Charlestown, Mass. (unm.)
EDWARD TROWBRIDGE GALLOUPE, b. 1870, Charlestown, Mass.; d. 3 mo.
(v. Mrs. Amos Galloupe.)

———o———

IV.

Sally Sanford.

[Second dau. of James Sanford and SARAH BEACH. p. 256.]

b. February 14, 1794. (Redding Record.)
d. November 5, 1820, Redding, Conn.
m. November 12, 1815. (Redding Record.)

ALDEN WINTON.

CHILDREN:

ELINOR HULL WINTON, bapt. June 19, 1818. ⎱ (Christ Ch. Rec'd,
ELIZA ANN WINTON, bapt. June 4, 1821. ⎰ Redding.)

————o————

IV.

James Sanford, Jr.

[Sixth son of James Sanford and SARAH BEACH. p. 256.]

b. June 10, 1799. (Redding Record.)
d. May 26, 1883, Redding, Conn. (old age).
m. January 27, 1822. (Redding Record.)

ELIZA FRENCH.

[Dau. of John Turney French and Mercy Senah Perkins.]

b. February 28, 1802.
d. February 28, 1896, Redding, Conn.

CHILDREN:

JOHN TURNEY SANFORD, b. March 23, 1823.
    d. Sept. 24, 1824, Redding, Conn.
TURNEY SANFORD, b. January 23, 1825, Redding, Conn. p. 286.
SENAH SANFORD, b. February 24, 1828, Redding, Conn. (unm.)
JAMES SANFORD, 3RD, b. October 19, 1830, Redding, Conn. p. 286.
SARAH SANFORD, b. June 7, 1833, Redding, Conn. p. 287.
STEPHEN SANFORD, b. March 28, 1835, Redding, Conn. p. 288.
BETSEY SANFORD, b. September 13, 1838, Redding, Conn. p. 288.
PERKINS SANFORD, b. February 24, 1841, Redding, Conn.;
    d. February 28, 1868, Redding, Conn. (unm.)
ABBY SANFORD, b. July 21, 1843, Redding, Conn.
HENRY SANFORD, b. January 29, 1846, Redding, Conn.
    m. November 30, 1882, Redding, Conn.
            MARGARET HANNAFORD, [VII] p. 273.
CHARLES SANFORD, b. February 5, 1849, Redding, Conn. p. 289.
                    (v. Mrs. S. S. Duncombe).

V.

Turney Sanford.

[Second son of James Sanford, Jr., and Eliza French.]

b. January 23, 1825, Redding, Conn.
m. May 21, 1862, Southport, Conn.

MARY ROE.

[Dau. of Elijah Woolsey Roe and Ruth Ketchen.]

b. July 23, 1841, New York City. (v. Turney Sanford.)

VI.

George Turney Sanford.

[Only child of Turney Sanford and Mary Roe.]

b. March 16, 1864, Westport, Conn.
d. December 31, 1894, Mississippi.
m. October 17, 1888, Norwalk, Conn.

FLORENCE HILL.

[Dau. of Stephen John Hill and Victoria Pool.]

b. May 28, 1868, New Orleans, Louisiana.

CHILD:

BEULAH SANFORD, b. October 18, 1889, Redding, Conn.

(v. Turney Sanford.)

V.

James Sanford, 3rd.

[Third son of James Sanford, Jr., and Eliza French.]

b. October 19, 1830, Redding, Conn.
d. June 10, 1896, Redding, Conn.
m. December 20, 1853, Redding, Conn.

SARAH MEEKER.

[Dau. of Arza Meeker and (m. Oct. 11, 1818, Ch. Ch. Rec'd) Adelia Gorham.]

(Sanford.)

b. January 8, 1837, Redding, Conn.

VI.

William Clinton Sanford.

[Only child of James Sanford, 3rd, and Sarah Meeker.]

b. July 7, 1859, Redding, Conn.

m. January 25, 1881, Weston, Conn.

EDITH COLE.

[Dau. of William and Mary Jane (Brown) Cole.]

b. August 27, 1862, Weston, Conn.

CHILD:

JAMES HAROLD SANFORD, b. May 11, 1891, Redding, Conn.

(v. W. C. Sanford.)

V.

Sarah Sanford.

[Second dau. of James Sanford, Jr., and Eliza French.]

b. June 7, 1833, Redding, Conn.

m. November 9, 1858, Redding, Conn.

WILLIAM EDGAR DUNCOMBE, VIII.

[Sixth son of David Duncombe and RUTH SANFORD, VII.] (Sanford.)

b. February 17, 1830, Redding Centre, Conn.

(v. S. S. Duncombe.)

VI.

Emma Eliza Duncombe.

[Only child of WILLIAM E. DUNCOMBE, by his second wife, SARAH SANFORD.]
(Sixth gen. Revd John Beach ; ninth gen. Thomas Sanford.)

b. June 1, 1864, Redding Centre, Conn.

m. November 11, 1886, Redding Centre, Conn.

GEORGE BENJAMIN BEERS.

[Son of Benjamin and Eliza (Wheeler) Beers.]

b. November 15, 1861, Easton, Conn.

(v. E. E. D. Beers.)

V.

Stephen Sanford.

[Fourth son of James Sanford, Jr., and Eliza French. p. 285.]

b. March 28, 1835, Redding, Conn.

m. November 23, 1864, Fairfield, Conn.

Mary Sophia Banks.

[Dau. of Francis Bradley Banks (2nd son of Abram and Eunice Banks of Fairfield) and Almira Sherwood.]

b. July 3, 1842, Redding, Conn.

children:

Emory Perkins Sanford, b. May 14, 1871, Redding Ridge, Conn.
Stephen Ernest Sanford, b. January 4, 1877, Redding Ridge, Conn.

(v. Stephen Sanford.)

V.

Betsey Sanford.

[Third dau. of James Sanford, Jr., and Eliza French. p. 285.]

b. September 13, 1838, Redding, Conn.

m. January 1, 1862.

George Botsford Sherwood.

[Son of Philo Botsford Sherwood (son of Jno. and Eliza (Botsford) Sherwood) by his first wife, Julia Silliman. p. 289.]

b. August 28, 1839, Easton, Conn.

(v. Mrs. B. S. Sherwood.)

VI.

James Arthur Sherwood.

[Only child of George (Botsford) Sherwood and Betsey Sanford.]

b. May 8, 1867, Easton, Conn.

m. January 6, 1889, Redding Ridge, Conn.

Eva Whitehead.

[Only child of Henry Whitehead and Agnes Banks IX.] (Sanford.)

b. April 3, 1870, Redding Ridge, Conn.

child:

Hazel Elaine Sherwood, b. October 11, 1889, Redding Ridge, Conn.
(Seventh gen., Revd John Beach; eleventh gen., Thomas Sanford.)

(v. Mrs. A. B. Whitehead.)

V.

Charles Sanford.

[Seventh son of James Sanford, Jr., and Eliza French. p. 285.]

b. February 5, 1849, Redding, Conn.

m. February 19, 1879.

HANNAH SHERWOOD.

[Dau. Philo Botsford Sherwood (son of Jno. and Eliza (Botsford) Sherwood), by his third wife, Jerusha Stilson. p. 288.]

b. May 31, 1852.

CHILDREN:

ELSIE SANFORD, b. June 7, 1880, Redding, Conn.
LUCY SANFORD, b. February 19, 1882, Redding, Conn.

(rec'd Mrs. S. S. Duncombe.)

————o————

III.

Hannah Beach.

[Third dau. of Lazarus Beach and Lydia Sanford. p. 246.]

b. April 11, 1767.

d. January 25, 1814. (T. S. Christ Ch. Grave Yard.)

m. January 29, 1786.

PHILO LYON.

[Son of Daniel Lyon of Weston.]

b. October 29, 1764.

d. April 12, 1813. (T. S. Christ Ch., Redding Ridge, Conn.)

CHILDREN:

HENRY LYON, b. November 16, 1786; d. December 30, 1873 (old age), Redding Ridge.

m. ESTHER TAYLOR.

LAZARUS LYON, b. Oct. 16, 1788; d. March 18, 1810, æ. 22 yrs.

(T. S. Ch. Church.)

INFANT, b. January 13, 1792; died same day.

ZIBA LYON, b. January 10, 1793; d. Sept. 4,   , Utica, N. Y.

m. MINERVA NICHOLS (no children).

PHILO LYON, JR., b. August 24, 1794; d. May 7, 1839. p. 290.

ISAAC BEACH LYON, b. Apr. 24, 1796; d. July 4, 1837. p. 291.

INFANT, b. Oct. 10, 1798; d. Nov. 11, 1798.

LYDIA LYON, b. Nov., 1799; d. Feb. 3, 1816.

PHILEMON LYON, b. July 28, 1802; d. Dec 23, 1857, Utica, N. Y.
m. ELIZA ANN LEWIS.
d. July 4, 1895, Utica, N. Y. (no ch.)
(Copied from an old bible belonging to Ziba Lyon, which at his death was sent to my mother, Mary Lyon Morse.—Mrs. H. G. M. Penfield.)

IV.

Philo Lyon, Jr.

[Fourth son of Philo Lyon and Hannah Beach.]

b. August 24, 1794.
d. May 7, 1839.
m. October 29, 1815.

LUCY STARR.

[Dau. of Peter and Mary (Polly Boughton) Starr.]

b. July 18, 1796.
d. May 10, 1882.

CHILDREN :

HENRY LYON, b. Aug. 16, 1816; d. March 9, 1841.
m. May 22, 1837, Lydia Disbrow.
a son, MELANCTHON STARR LYON, b.   , d. 1863.
MARY LYON, b. January 26, 1821. p. 290.

V.

Mary Lyon.   ·

[Only dau. of Philo Lyon, Jr. and Lucy Starr.]

b. January 26, 1821.
d. April 2, 1889.
m. May 19, 1847.

IRA MORSE.

[Son of Ira and Polly (Judson) Morse.]

b. October 19, 1819.

CHILDREN :

HELEN GERTRUDE MORSE, b. October 10, 1848. p. 291.
PERCIVAL GLEASON MORSE, b. November 5, 1850, Danbury, Conn.
m. May 11, 1877, Brooklyn, N. Y.
EMMA JOSEPHINE OLIPHANT.
[Dau. of James and Anna Maria (Hutchinson) Oliphant.]
b. January 28, 1850, N. Y. C.   (v. Mrs. P. G. Morse.)
EZRA STARR MORSE, b. December 6, 1853; d. June 29, 1889. (unm.)
(v. H. G. M. Penfield.)

VI.
Helen Gertrude Morse.

[Only dau. of Ira Morse and Mary Lyon.]

b. October 10, 1848.

m. February 21, 1878, Danbury, Conn.

DAVID GIDDINGS PENFIELD.

[Son of Levi Penfield (b. Sept. 1, 1807 ; d. June 9, 1851); m. Dec. 24, 1835, Eunice Giddings (b. June 3, 1807; d. Nov. 8, 1892.)]

b. August 8, 1842, New Fairfield.

d. May 20, 1897, Danbury, Conn.

CHILDREN :

PERCIVAL STARR PENFIELD, b. November 21, 1878, Danbury, Conn.

ALLAN MORSE PENFIELD, b. February 2, 1884, Danbury, Conn.

(v. H. G. M. Penfield.)

———o———

IV.
Isaac Beach Lyon.

[Fifth son of Philo Lyon and Hannah Beach. p. 289.]

b. April 24, 1796, Redding, Conn.

d. July 4, 1837, Redding, Conn.

m. JULIA HIBBARD.

CHILDREN :

PHILO L. LYON, b. November 31, 1826, Redding, Conn. p. 291.

JULIA LYON, b. June 8, 1833, Redding, Conn. p. 292.

JOHN BEACH LYON, b. November 8, 1836, Redding, Conn. p. 292.

(rec'd Ethalinda E. Lyon.)

V.
Philo L. Lyon.

[Elder son of Isaac Beach Lyon and Julia Hibbard.]

b. November 31, 1826, Redding, Conn.

d. June 27, 1896, Macedon, N. Y.

m. March 17, 1850, Lakeville, Livingston Co., N. Y.

MARIA MILLIMAN.

[Dau. of Abiram and Ethalinda (Scott) Milliman.]

b. December 19, 1827, Ann, Livingston Co., N. Y.

CHILDREN :

AUGUSTA M. LYON, b. Mar. 16, 1851 ; d. Mar. 21, 1890, Macedon, N. Y.

PHILO SCOTT LYON, b. May 22, 1853; d. April 3, 1870, Macedon, N. Y.

PHILEMON LYON, b. Nov. 1, 1857, Macedon, Wayne Co., N. Y. p. 292.

(rec'd Ethalinda E. Lyon.)

VI.

Philemon Lyon.

[Younger son of Philo L. Lyon and Maria Milliman.]

b. November 1, 1857, Macedon, Wayne Co., N. Y.
m. May 1, 1879.

EMMA S. FISHER.

[Dau. of George and Eliza (Perry) Fisher.]

b. January 30, 1857, Troy, N. Y.

CHILDREN:

ETHALINDA E. LYON, b. Feb'y 28, 1880, Macedon, Wayne Co., N. Y.
LIZZIE M. LYON, b. June 28, 1881; d. March 25, 1890, Macedon, N. Y.
GRACE E. LYON, b. April 7, 1883, Macedon, Wayne Co., N. Y.
GEORGIA A. LYON, b. September 3, 1884, Macedon, N. Y.
FLORENCE J. LYON, b. Nov. 16, 1886; d. Nov. 21, 1887, Macedon, N. Y.
RUBY A. LYON, b. October 21, 1893; d. May 3, 1895, Macedon, N. Y.
GENEVIEVE LYON, b. December 14, 1896, Macedon, N. Y.

(rec'd Ethalinda E. Lyon).

V.

Julia Lyon.

[Only dau. of Isaac Beach Lyon and Julia Hibbard. p. 291.]

b. June 8, 1833, Redding, Conn.
d. March 20, 1889, Palmyra, N. Y.
m. May 5, 1853, Macedon, Wayne Co., N. Y.

URIAH MILLIMAN.

[Son of Abiram and Ethalinda (Scott) Milliman.]

CHILD:

ETHALINDA JULIA MILLIMAN, b. May 1, 1854, Macedon, N. Y.
d. Nov. 13, 1873, Palmyra, N. Y.   (rec'd Ethalinda E. Lyon).

V.

John Beach Lyon.

[Younger son of Isaac Beach Lyon and Julia Hibbard.]

b. November 8, 1836, Redding, Conn.
m. January 17, 1871, Rose, Wayne Co., N. Y.

ELLEN MOON.

[Dau. of William Moon of England.]

b. 1848, England.

CHILDREN:

\ LYDIA LYON, b. November 21, 1875, Ontario, N. Y.
/ BESSIE LYON, b. November 21, 1875, Ontario, N. Y. p. 293.
CHARLES A. LYON, b. September 4, 1878, Ontario, N. Y.

VI.
Bessie Lyon.
[Twin dau. of John Beach Lyon and Ellen Moon.]
b. November 21, 1875, Ontario, Wayne Co., N. Y.
m. October 16, 1892, Port Gibson, Wayne Co., N.Y.

WILLIAM WITHERDEN, JR.

(rec'd Ethalinda E. Lyon.)

————o————

III.
Eunice Beach.
[Fourth dau. of Lazarus Beach and Lydia Sanford. p. 246.]
b. November 23, 1769, Redding, Conn.
d. September 19, 1822, New Haven, Ill.

m. JONATHAN HULL.
[Son of SETH HULL and Elizabeth Mallory.]   (Hull.)
b. October 25, 1763.
d. December 1, 1820.

CHILDREN:

LEMUEL BEACH HULL, b. April 10, 1792. p. 293.
SETH HULL, b. July 13, 1796. p. 294.

IV.
Rev'd Lemuel Beach Hull.
[Elder son of Jonathan Hull and Eunice Beach.]
b. April 10, 1792.
d. Oct. 22, 1843, Nashotah Cem'y, Milwaukee, Wis.
m. October 18, 1824.

POLLY WATERBURY.
[Dau. Nathaniel Waterbury and Hannah White.]
b. April 9, 1800, Darien, Conn.
d. Aug. 7, 1881, "laid at rest," Nashotah Cem'y,
Milwaukee.

CHILDREN:

HANNAH WHITE HULL, died young.
ELEANOR HULL, died unmarried.
JOHN BEACH HULL, b. September 17, 1828. p. 294.

(v. Walter Belden Hull.)

V.

John Beach Hull.

[Only son of Rev'd Lemuel Beach Hull and Polly Waterbury.]

b. September 17, 1828.
d. March 17, 1891.
m. September 10, 1856.

ELLEN CLARISSA SABIN.

[Dau. of Eben Hamilton Sabin and Nancy Cramer.]

b. February 19, 1833.

CHILDREN:

CLARA FRANCES HULL, b. November 20, 1858. (unm.)
AMY WHITE HULL, "Entered into Rest" on Saturday, July 30, 1881.
WALTER BELDEN HULL, b. September 11, 1867. (unm.)

(v. W. B. Hull.)

IV.

Seth Hull.

[Younger son of Jonathan Hull and Eunice Beach.]

b. July 13, 1796.
d. April, 1835, Beardstown, Ill.
m. May 22, 1823.

NABBY EVOLETH.

Known to have had one son, HENRY HULL, who m. and had a family.

(unfinished correspondence.)

———o———

III.

Isaac Beach.

[Third son of Lazarus Beach and LYDIA SANFORD V. p. 246.]

b. May 19, 1773, Redding, Conn.
d. July 20, 1822, Alexander, N. Y.

(T. S. Redding Ridge.)

first m. December 7, 1794.

ELIZABETH SILLIMAN, of Easton, Conn.

b. December 11, 1769.
d. February 14, 1796.

second m. September 26, 1797, Redding, Conn.

HANNAH HILL.

[Dau. of Andrew Lane Hill and HANNAH LYON.]   (Hill.)

b. January 7, 1776.
d. May   , 1846.

CHILDREN (of second marriage):

BETSEY BEACH, b. Nov. 12, 1798; d. Sept. 1, 1846, Redding. (unm.)
LYDIA BEACH, b. February 27, 1800, Redding, Conn. p. 295.
CHARLES BEACH, b. November 27, 1801, Redding, Conn. p. 296.
WYLLIS BEACH, b. August 20, 1803; d. Feb'y 3, 1851, Redding. (unm.)
LAZARUS BEACH, b. July 28, 1805, Redding, Conn.
     d. September 20, 1850, Redding, Conn.
     m. May 14, 1829, Redding, Conn.
          BETSEY FOSTER.
         [Dau. of Joel and Esther (Seymour) Foster.]
     b. January 6, 1811, Redding, Conn. (no descendants.)
ISAAC BEACH, JR., b. July 14, 1808, Redding, Conn. p. 296.

(Redding Records.)

IV.

Lydia Beach.

[Younger dau. of Isaac Beach, by his second wife, HANNAH HILL.]

b. February 27, 1800.
d. May 3, 1871.
m. March 28, 1822, Redding, Conn.

JAMES ROGERS HAWLEY.

[Sixth son of Joseph and Chloe (Rogers) Hawley.]   (Hawley Rec'd.)

b. September 18, 1797.
d. August 29, 1876.

CHILDREN:

ISAAC BEACH HAWLEY, b. March 7, 1823.
    d. December 8, 1853.
 • m. February 27, 1848.
         MARIA ANDERSON.
        [Dau. of James and Elizabeth Anderson.]
    b. February 14, 1832.
(After her husband's death, m. Charles Ward.)   (v. Mrs. Chas. Ward.)

JULIA AMELIA HAWLEY, b. December 11, 1824.
m. February 10, 1847.
GEORGE H. CHASE.
b. July 5, 1815.
d. March 24, 1885.   (rec'd Mrs. Chase.)

IV.

Charles Beach.

[Eldest son of Isaac Beach, by his second wife, HANNAH HILL.]
b. November 27, 1801, Redding Ridge, Conn.
d. March 14, 1864, Danbury, Conn.
m. November 20, 1832, Danbury, Conn.

LUCY PECK.

[Dau. of Eliakim and Polly Peck.]
b. August 29, 1804, Danbury, Conn.
d. May 31, 1856, Danbury, Conn.

CHILDREN:

MARY PECK BEACH, b. August 14, 1833, Redding Ridge, Conn.
d. June 10, 1838, Redding Ridge, Conn.
SARAH LOUISA BEACH, b. August 4, 1835, Redding Ridge.
m. June 6, 1872, Danbury, Conn.
EDWARDS ELY BARNUM.
[Son of Ira and Clarissa Barnum.]
b. Feb. 6, 1824, New York City.
d. June 24, 1893, Brooklyn. (no children.)
JULIA HILL BEACH, b. September 24, 1840, Danbury, Conn.
d. February 7, 1842, Danbury, Conn.   (v. S. L. B. Barnum.)

IV.

Isaac Beach, Jr.

[Fourth son of Isaac Beach by his second wife, HANNAH HILL.]
b. July 18, 1808, Redding, Conn.
d. July 10, 1862, Forrestport, N. Y.
m. November 1, 1840, Redding, Conn.

MARY REBECCA WINTON.

[Dau. of James and Parthenia (Seeley) Winton.]
b. April 6, 1821, Bridgeport, Conn.

CHILDREN :

WILLIAM H. BEACH, b. November 23, 1841, Redding, Conn. p. 297.
EMILY PARTHENIA BEACH, b. April 6, 1843, Redding, Conn. p. 297.
CHARLES WINTON BEACH, b. October 20, 1845, Remsen, N. Y.
     m. January 15, 1889, Easton, Conn.

FRANCES AGNES WILSON.
[Dau. of John B. Wilson and Clarina Middlebrook.]
     b. at Easton, Conn. (no children.)   (v. F. A. W. Beach.)
AARON SOMERS BEACH, b. April 30, 1847, Remsen, N. Y. (unm.)
ISAAC H. BEACH, b. October 18, 1851, Remsen, N. Y. p. 299.
MARY L. BEACH, b. March 8, 1856, Remsen, N. Y. p. 299.
*LYDIA JULIA MARA BEACH, b. June 22, 1857, Remsen, N. Y.
     m. MEEKER.   (rec'd Isaac (H.) Beach, 3d.)

V.

William Henry Beach.

[Eldest son of Isaac Beach, Jr. and Mary R. Winton.]
     b. November 23, 1841, Redding, Conn.
     d. Feb'y 15, 1873, Greenbush, Clinton Co., Mich.
     m. October 13, 1869, Victor, Clinton Co., Mich.

MARGARET JANE BALLANTINE.
[Dau. of William Ballantine (b. Oct. 17, 1804, Belfast, Ireland; d. June 6, 1882,
Laingsburgh, Mich.) and Jane Graham (b. Dec. 20, 1806, Armagh.
Ireland; d. July 16, 1888, Laingsburgh.)]
     b. January 15, 1842, White Oak, Mich.

V.

Emily Parthenia Beach.

[Eldest dau. of Isaac Beach, Jr., and Mary Rebecca Winton.]
     b. April 6, 1843, Redding, Conn.
     m. January 6, 1863, Booneville, N. Y.

MARCUS JOLLEY.
[Son of Stephen Jolley and Charity Hicks.]
     b. June 26, 1839, Georgetown, N. Y.

CHILDREN :

FRANK A. JOLLEY, b. March 14, 1864, Granby, N. Y. p. 298.
ARMENIA CHARITY JOLLEY, b. Sept. 13, 1865, Granby, N. Y.
     d. November 3, 1869, Greenbush, Mich.
MINNIE R. JOLLEY, b. Sept. 16, 1869, Greenbush, Mich. p. 298.
EUGENE S. JOLLEY, b. Sept. 27, 1871, Greenbush, Mich. p. 298.
HENRY ISAAC JOLLEY, b. December 2, 1879, Greenbush, Mich.
                             (v. E. P. B. Jolley.)

* Letter returned, not found at address given.

VI.

Frank Alwyn Jolley.

[Eldest son of Marcus Jolley and Emily P. Beach.]

b. March 14, 1864, Granby, Oswego Co., N. Y.

d. March 12, 1896, Chicago, Ill.

m. June 19, 1890, Sedalia, Pettis Co., Mo.

SARAH ELLIVET McCORD.

b. October 11, 1868, Ohio.

CHILD:

FOREST GLENN JOLLEY, b. March 10, 1891, Sedalia, Mo.

VI.

Minnie Rebecca Jolley.

[Second dau. of Marcus Jolley and Emily P. Beach.]

b. Sept. 16, 1869, Greenbush, Clinton Co., Mich.

m. January 12, 1898, Greenbush, Mich.

WALLACE J. ROCKWOOD.

[Son of David Rockwood and Caroline Osborn.]

b. July 27, 1856, Bloomfield, Penna.

VI.

Eugene Steven Jolley.

[Second son of Marcus Jolley and Emily P. Beach.]

b. September 27, 1871, Greenbush, Mich.

m. November 28, 1894, Greenbush, Mich.

ANNIE LOIS FLEAGLE.

[Dau. of Peter and Mary (Cole) Fleagle.]

b. May 24, 1871, Greenbush, Mich.

CHILD:

CLAIRE FLEAGLE JOLLEY, b. June 1, 1897, Greenbush, Mich.

V.

Isaac (Hill) Beach, 3rd.

[Fourth son of Isaac Beach, Jr., and Mary R. Winton.]

b. October 18, 1851, Remsen, Oneida Co., N. Y.
m. February 17, 1887, Mt. Pleasant, Mich.

VIRGINIA (JENNIE) GRIMM.

[Dau. of John Jordan Grimm and Elizabeth Fox. (m. Oct. 29, 1844, Penn'a.)]

b. March 11, 1865, Parkersburg, West Virginia.

CHILDREN:

JESSE JORDAN BEACH, b. January 10, 1888, Van Decar, Mich.
LOREN LLEWELLYN BEACH, b. September 24, 1889, Van Decar, Mich.
ARTHUR ANDREW BEACH, b. November 4, 1891, Van Decar, Mich.
ESTHER MARY ELIZABETH PANSY BEACH, b. May 25, 1894, Van Decar.

(v. Isaac (H.) Beach, 3d.)

V.

Mary Lucy Beach.

[Second dau. of Isaac Beach, Jr. and Mary R. Winton.]

b. March 8, 1856, Remsen, Oneida Co., N. Y.
m. December 24, 1873, Bingham, Clinton Co., Mich.

ARLINGTON CYRUS LEWIS.

[Son of Cyrus Lewis and Clarissa Easton.]

b. Oct. 12, 1847, Middlefield, Geauga Co., Ohio.

CHILDREN:

ARTHUR EUGENE LEWIS, b. August 27, 1875, Lake City, Mich.
GERTRUDE EFFIGENE LEWIS, b. August 28, 1877, Lake City, Mich.
BLAINE IRVING LEWIS, b. April 7, 1880, Lake City, Mich.
EVERARD ARLINGTON LEWIS, b. September 15, 1884, Lake City, Mich.

(v. M. L. B. Lewis.)

SANFORD.

THE ANCESTRY AND DESCENDANTS OF JOHN AND ANNA (WHEELER) SANFORD OF REDDING, CONN.

[MSS. Researches of Henry Sanford, Gloucester, Mass.]

From Mr. Edward Jackson Sanford's Records, Knoxville, Tenn.

SANFORD FAMILY.

Thomas Sanford, born in England early in the seventeenth century, say from 1600 to 1610, was, we have reason to believe, son of Anthony Sanford (and Joane, daughter of John Stratford), who was son of Raulf Sanford of Stowe, Co. Gloucester, England; he married, about the time he left England, Dorothy, daughter of Henry Meadows of Stowe; he came to Boston, Massachusetts, with the John Winthrop colony, 1631-3. We first find him in Dorchester, Mass., where he received land with others in 1634, also 1635; he became a freeman in the Colony, March 9th, 1637. In 1639 he removed with a colony from Dorchester and Watertown to Connecticut and settled in Milford, New Haven County, where his name appears in the earliest records. He was a leader in organizing the town and was intimately associated with Gov. Treat, Lieut.-Gov. Leete, Buckingham, Law and other noted and leading men of the times. Probably Stratford, Conn., was named by him for his maternal grandfather, John Stratford. His grandson Thomas Sanford, son of Ezekiel Sanford, was an early settler there.

I. gen.—Thomas Sanford, born in Stowe, Co. Gloucester, Eng., son of Anthony Sanford, mar'd about 1630, Dorothy, dau. of Henry Meadows of Stowe, Co. Gloucester, Eng., by whom he had two children born before he went to Connecticut, and his wife Dorothy, we think, died in Dorchester. He died in Milford, Conn., October, 1681.

Children of Thomas and Dorothy Sanford:

II. gen.—I. Ezekiel Sanford.

II. Sarah Sanford, who mar'd Richard Shute of East Chester, Conn., August 14th, 1656.

Thomas Sanford, mar'd for his second wife, Sarah; maiden name unknown to writer. She was in Milford, May 14th, 1681.

Children by second wife:

III. Mary Sanford, b. Jan'y 16th, 1641, in Milford, Conn.

*IV. Samuel Sanford, b. Apr. 20th, 1643, in Milford, Conn., mar'd April 16th, 1674, Hannah Bronson, by whom he had six children; he settled in Milford and died there, 1691.

V. Thomas Sanford, Jr., b. Dec., 1644, in Milford, Conn., mar'd Oct. 12th, 1666, Elizabeth Payne, dau. of William Payne of New Haven, Ct., by whom he had nine children; he settled in New Haven, and died there.

†VI. Ephraim Sanford, b. May 17th, 1646, in Milford, Conn.; mar'd Nov. 18th, 1669, Mary, b. 1645, dau. of Thomas Powell of New Haven, Ct., by whom he had seven children; he settled in Milford, a farmer, and died there 1685.

VII. Elizabeth Sanford, b. Aug. 27th, 1648, in Milford, Conn.; mar'd Oct. 21st, 1669, Obadiah Allyne of Middletown, Conn.

WILL OF THOMAS SANFORD OF MILFORD, CONN., DATED
SEPT. 23rd, 1681. ·

I give and bequeath to my eldest son Ezekiel Sanford twenty pounds besides what I have already given him.

I give unto my son Thomas Sanford ten pounds besides what I have already given him.

I give unto my son Ephraim Sanford that piece of Meadow I bought of Adam Blackman, lying on an Island in Stratford, containing seven acres, besides what I have already given him.

I give to my daughter Sarah Shute wife of Richard Shute of East Chester the sum of fifty shillings besides what I have already given her.

I give unto my daughter Elizabeth Allyne wife of Obadiah Allyne of Middletown, the sum of five pounds besides what I have already given her.

My Will is that my Endowment of twenty pounds to my grand daughter Sarah Shute should be fulfilled by my Executor as also all the forementioned Legacies within.

I give unto my grand son Thomas Allyne five pounds to be paid when he attains the age of twenty-one.

* Rev. David A. Sanford, B'p't, Okla.
† Mary Roland (Sanford) Beach, VIII. gen. from Ephraim and Mary Powell.

I give unto my son Samuel Sanford my dwelling House, out housing
with my home lot and all the rest of my land both arrable and meadow
ground with in the bonnds of Milford, that I have not formerly desposed
of with all the appurtenances there unto belonging to him and to his
heirs and assigns forever and I do hereby make my son Samuel Sanford my whole and sole Executor of this my last will and testament
and I do will and desire and appoint Hon. Major Robert Treat, and
Mr. Daniel Buckingham and Samuel Ells to be overseers to this my
will fulfilled and in witness that this is my last will and testament.

I have here unto set my hand and seal this three and twentieth day
of Sept, 1681

Signed sealed and delivered
In presence of
Daniel Buckingham   Thomas Sanford   [seal]
Samuel Ells
Jonathan Law

Sept. 26ᵗʰ, 1681. It is my Will that my son Ezekiel Sanford receive
ten pounds in Addition to that before given.

I further give to Elizabeth Allyne five pounds and to my maid Servant Sarah Whitlock I give fifty shilling

The Estate was appraised by John Beard and Samuel Clark, Oct.
21ˢᵗ 1681. Am't £450. 18ˢ. 3ᵈ Homestead £130 „ Meadow £108

From Records at Milford, Connecticut.

ORDER OF SEARCH FOR COL. WHALLEY AND GOFFE.

May 17ᵗʰ. 1661 for the Marshalls or Deputies at Milford.

You are to make deligent search by the first throughout the
whole town of Milford and the precincts there of taking with
you two or three sufficient persons and—calling in any other
help you shall see need of who are hereby required for your
assistance upon call! and this to be in all dwellings houses,
barns or other buildings whatsoever and all vessels in the
harbor for the finding and aprehending of Colonel Whalley
and Colonel Goffe who stand charged with crimes as by his
Majestie's letter appears: and being found you are to bring
them to the Deputee Governor or some other Magistrate to
be sent over for England according to his Majestie's orders
whereof fail at peril.

Attest   by order of General Court
Jasper Crane   WILLIAM LEETE, Dep. Gov.
Nathan Gilbert
Robert Treat   Iⁿ the Marshalls Absence, I do appoint

and empower Thomas Sanford, Nicholas Camp and James
Tapping to the above named power according to the tenor of
the warrant and to make a return there of under your hand
to me by the first.   ROBERT TREAT, Gov.

We the said persons appointed to serve and search by
virtue of this order warrant do hereby declare and testifie that
to our best light we the 20ᵗʰ May, 1661 made deligent search
according to the tenor of this warrant as Witness our hand.

The Judges remained con-   THOMAS SANFORD
cealed in the Cave at West
Rocks, from May 15ᵗʰ to   NICHOLAS CAMP
June 11ᵗʰ, the record adds.   JAMES TAPPING   } searchers
No doubt Thomas Sanford   his
helped supply them with LAWRENCE WARD ×
food and other comforts.   mark

II. gen.—Ezekiel Sanford, son of Thomas Sanford, married April 25th, 1665, Rebecca Wickla. (In Schenk's Fairfield, Rebecca Whelpley, dau. of John and Rebecca Whelpley
of Fairfield.) He settled in Fairfield, Conn., and died there
1683; was a large land-holder, as the records show, a large
portion he gave to his children, while living, his widow
Rebecca administered upon the estate. She died before it
was settled. In 1697 a final settlement was made by mutual
agreement, as will be seen hereafter.

Children of Ezekiel and Rebecca Sanford:

III. gen.—I. Sarah Sanford, b. Mch. 5th, 1666, in Fairfield,
Conn.; mar'd Cornelius Hull (Jr.)

II. Ezekiel Sanford, Jr., b. M'ch 6th, 1668, in Fairfield,
Conn.

III. Mary Sanford, b. Apr. 3rd, 1670, in Fairfield, Conn.;
mar'd Theophilus Hull.

IV. Rebecca Sanford, b. Dec. 13th, 1672, in Fairfield, Conn.;
mar'd John Seeley.

V. Thomas Sanford, b. May 2d, 1675, in Fairfield, Conn.

VI. Martha Sanford, b. June 29th, 1677,   "   "

VII. Elizabeth Sanford, b. Sept. 6th, 1679,   "   "

Then follows the settlement of his estate—a lengthy and
involved document, wherein by much circumlocution they

arrive at a just and satisfactory distribution to which they agree by signature—the 2nd day of November, 1679.

In presents of   Ezekiel Sanford
ye witnesses   Thomas Sanford
Samuel Squires   Cornelius Hull in behalf
John Bartow   of Sarah his wife.
     Theophilus Hull, in right
     of Mary his wife
Inventory Estate Jany 2nd John Seely in right of
     1685/,   £356   Rebecca his wife
     her
     Martha × Sanford
Widow administered upon   mark
the Estate, rec^d ⅓ the land   her
during her life and £56,   Elizabeth × Sanford
out of the personal Estate.   mark

The subscribers to the above instrument appeared in court this 2^d of November 1697 and acknowledged the same to be their free act and deed.

NATHAN GOLD, *Clerk.*

III. gen.—Ezekiel Sanford, b. M'ch 6th, 1668, in Fairfield, Conn., son of Ezekiel Sanford and Rebecca Wickla, mar'd 1696 Rebeckah Gregory; he died M'ch 1728–9, leaving a large landed estate [see synopsis of will annexed]. She was living in 1764 [see paper annexed].

Children of Ezekiel and Rebecca (Gregory) Sanford.

IV. gen.—I. Joseph Sanford, b. M'ch 27, 1697, in Fairfield, Conn., mar'd Feb. 11th, 1725, Catherine Fairchild, by whom he had nine children, seven sons and two daughters; he settled in Fairfield.

II. Lemuel Sanford, b. Dec. 16th, 1699, in Fairfield, Conn., mar'd May 12th, 1730, Rebecca Squires, b. 1703; he settled in Redding, which at that time was part of Fairfield; he died there Apr. 25th, 1780. They had ten children, three sons and seven daughters. She died M'ch 26th, 1779.

III. Zachariah Sanford, b. Nov. 24th, 1701, in Fairfield, Conn., mar'd Oct. 11th, 1736, Ann Hall, and they had seven children, one son who died quite young and six daughters.

IV. Ezekiel Sanford, b. July 27th, 1704, in Fairfield, Conn.

V. Samuel Sanford, b. Feb. 20th, 1707-8, in Fairfield, Conn., mar'd Jan. 11th, 1733-4, Sarah Meeker, by whom he had twelve children ; settled in Redding, Conn. He died there Nov. 6, 1768; she died Nov. 30, 1803.

VI. Ephraim Sanford, b. Feb. 12th, 1708-9, in Fairfield, Conn.

VII. Rebeckah Sanford, b. Nov. 21, 1710, [m. about 1730 Wm. Hill].

VIII. Abigail Sanford, b. Aug. 29th, 1714 ; mar'd Dec. 4th, 1735, James Bradley.

IX. Elnathan Sanford, b. Sept. 1st, 1717, in Fairfield, Conn.; died probably young ; no mention made of him in his father's will.

Synopsis of Will of Ezekiel Sanford, Jr., made Jan'y 29, 1728-9:

"Touching my worldly estate—after just debts *⁰⁄ₑ*.—to my beloved wife Rebecca one full third personal absolutely and one third real estate for life. * * * daughters Rebecca and Abigail two hundred pounds apiece * * * beloved and eldest son Joseph, heirs *⁰⁄ₑ* one hundred pounds more than an equal part with his brothers * * * Samuel twenty pounds more * * having considered my son Zachariah in ye like amount in my life time * * * beloved sons Joseph, Lemuel, Zachariah, Ezekiel, Samuel and Ephraim * * all the rest of my estate to be equally divided." Then follows some particulars as to lands—"and my pleasure is that my said son Ephraim live with his mother to be helpful to her during his non age." Zachariah and Ezekiel Exectors—John and David Down and Samuel Cooke, Witnesses. The will is Probated M'ch 28, 1728-9.

"Covenant between Joseph Sanford and brothers : To all people to whom these presents shall come greeting,

Know ye that where as Rebeckah Sanford of said Fairfield, Mother, sons ye Subscribers.

viz: Joseph Sanford, Lemuel Sanford, Zachariah Sanford, Ezekiel Sanford and Samuel Sanford all of said Fairfield, is become impotent and poor by age &c and the burthen of her support naturally and by Law devolves upon us and that an equal distribution of expense for her support may be had : we ye said Subscribers do here by covenant and agree each with ye other to yield and pay our Respective and equal part and proportion for her support and do also bind our several and respective heirs to pay ye same and enforce this our agreement, we said Subscribers do bind ourselves and our Heirs Executors and Administrators in ye sum of one pounds Lawful money to be paid by him or his Heirs Executors &c who shall not yield and pay such proportionable part as aforesaid to him or them who shall fulfil said agreement.

In witness whereof ye party have hereunto sett their hands and Seal in Fairfield this seventh day of January 1764/₅

Signed sealed and Delivered	Joseph Sanford	[L. S.]
in presence of	Lemuel Sanford	[L. S.]
John Sherwood	Zachariah Sanford	[L. S.]
John Sherwood Jr.	Ezekiel Sanford	[L. S.]
Silas Griffith	Samuel Sanford	[L. S.]
Elnathan Sanford."		

The Sanford who sent me the above says there is not another copy in the world.

Ephraim Sanford died in 1761.

Redding was a part of Fairfield at the time this was written, and I have been told the *long lots* mentioned in the will extended to Redding 17 miles.

IV. gen.—Ephraim Sanford, b. Feb. 12th, 1708–9, in Fairfield, Conn., son of Ezekiel Sanford Jr., mar'd Oct. 7th, 1730, Elizabeth Mix; he settled in the village of Redding, being the northern portion of Fairfield and was incorporated as town of Redding, 1767; the place where he settled was and is still called Sanfordtown. Was a large land-owner there, as is shown by deeds now in possession of his descendants, some of which date as early as 1733. He was engaged at an early day in the mercantile business, his being the first store in what is now called Redding; his goods were purchased in Boston, Mass.; he was very successful, leaving a large estate for those days. He died Feb. 6th, 1761–2, leaving a widow and eleven children, four sons and seven daughters. By will he left the widow £967 3 shillings; to each of his sons, £760. 2ˢ. 6¼ᵈ; to each of his daughters, £253. 7ˢ. 6¼ᵈ. The division was made May 26th, 1763.

V. gen.   *Children of Ephraim and Elizabeth Sanford.*

I. Elizabeth Sanford, b. July 3d, 1731, in Fairfield, Conn., mar'd Oct. 17th, 1747, Jonas Platt.

II. Rachel Sanford, b. July 23d, 1733, in Fairfield, Conn., mar'd Oct. 31st, 1751, Stephen Mead.

III. Abigail Sanford, b. May 12th, 1735, in Fairfield, Conn., mar'd Oct. 9th, 1755, Daniel Jackson; they were grandparents of Edward Jackson, who married Lydia Ann Sanford.

IV. Hannah Sanford, b. M'ch 3d, 1737, in Fairfield, Conn., mar'd Sept. 19th, 1756, David Lyon.

V. John Sanford, b. April 26th, 1739, in Fairfield, Conn.

VI. Oliver Sanford, b. Sept. 17th, 1741, in Fairfield, Conn., mar'd April, 1767, Rachel Coley, dau. Dea. David Coley of Weston, Ct.

VII. Lois Sanford, b. Sept. 14th, 1743, in Fairfield, Conn., mar'd May 21, 1761, Joseph Lyon.

VIII. Tabitha Sanford, b. Feb. 28, 1746, in Fairfield, Conn., mar'd June 26th, 1766, Thomas Rothwell.

IX. Hulda Sanford, b. Apr. 25th, 1748, in Fairfield, Conn., mar'd Oct. 28th, 1779, Thomas White.

X. Ephraim Sanford, b. May 25th, 1750, in Fairfield, Conn.

XI. Augustus Sanford, b. July 12th, 1753,   "   "

XII. Esther Sanford, b. April 24th, 1755, in   "   " died early, not mentioned in will.

V. gen.—John Sanford, b. Apr. 26th, 1739, in Fairfield, Conn., son of Ephraim and Elizabeth Sanford, mar'd, 1757, Anne, maiden name unknown to writer; settled in the Foundery district of Redding, Conn., where he died (Ap'l 18) 1784. His descendants reside there at the present time.

VI. gen.   *Children of John and Anne Sanford.*   [*See Gen.*]

SANFORD.

Of John we have been able to secure very little to add. The quotation from the State records places him politically, while that from the Probate Court of Danbury gives us, at last, the maiden name of his wife. In the volume of the State records comprising the year 1777, page 163, we read: "An order was given to the committee of prisoners at Mansfield to take a bond of John Sanford [a person confined in Mansfield, an enemy to this country] for 1000 pounds, conditioned that, where-as the said John Sanford is found guilty of being inimical and dangerous to this and the rest of the United States of Am⍤, Ordered, to be removed and sent to the Governor and Committee of Safety to have his place of residence assigned, and hath for some time resided in Mansfield according to said order, and now moving for liberty to return to Reading for the settlement of his Mother's estate, and promising his good behavior,—now if the said John Sanford shall well and truly return to Reading, dwell and abide within and not depart from out of the limits of said Town, and shall do nor say nothing in prejudice of the interests or rights of this or any other of the rest of the United States of Am⍤ or any of the measures pursuing by them for their defense, and shall not hold any correspondence with or give any intelligence to the enemies of said States, and shall repair to any place assigned by the Governor and Committee of Safety of this State upon requisition, then the foregoing bond to be void, else, to remain in full force and virtue, and upon his executing said bond, to give said John Sanford a permit to return to Reading without molestation ⁰/₀ ⁰/₀." Let not your present patriotism condemn that of your forefather who was thus faithful to his oath and King.

In the administration of his own estate, in the Danbury probate records there is this note: "Aug 22, 1791—Whereas by the death of Anne Wheeler formerly the relict and widow of John Sanford, her portion shall be divided equally . . . . " This is most important, and both the Judge of that Court and the town clerk of Redding (Mr. Nickerson) are agreed that the evidence is conclusive. We have tried to find whose daughter she was, and hope to accomplish this additional fact when opportunity is given for a further personal search.

The names of John's children as given in the will are in this order: the five sons, "James, John, Stephen, Eli, Ephraim," and then the daughters, "Elizabeth Hill, wife of Daniel Hill Jun', Huldah Lyon, wife of Lemuel Lyon, Anne Lyon, wife of Abraham Lyon, Lois and Esther." This is probably the correct order, and differs somewhat with that sent by the family. The name of Ann's first husband is by them given as "*Levi*," and her second "Webb Lyon." Now it is evident that the first is a mistake and, we have authority for adding, the second also, for in the Bridgeport probate records there is the will of Levi Lyon, before referred to, by which we learn the name of his wife Lusinda and his sister-in-law Anne, the widow of *Nehemiah* Lyon. Besides these evidences, Webb Lyon, or rather, "Nathaniel Webb Lyon," was the father of Hanford Lyon, and it is known that Anne Lyon left no children. Elizabeth Sanford had married Daniel Hill, Jr.; he died before his father, leaving her with one son John, who is called "grandson" in Captain Daniel's will. Of the sons, James, John, Stephen, Eli and Ephraim, from small beginnings we have harvested large crops, making food for much digestion.

James, the eldest, was called "Squire James," and must have been a man of mark as well of means. As a boy he had run away from home to be a teamster in the army, and though we do not find him enrolled in any particular company, his name is mentioned in 1841 on the pension list, as "of Reading, aged 81." This was the year before his death. It is a pity we have no record of his personal reminiscences, they would have added greatly to these pages; however, his children and his children's children even to the sixth generation still remain in and about Redding, and some of the family reside in the old homestead of the following deed recorded in Vol. 3d of Land Records at Redding:

REDDING. Vol. 3. 1784-1801
" Know all men by these presence that I John Sanford of Redding in Fairfield County and State of Connecticut,
for the Consideration of the natural love & affection that I have for my son James Sanford of the Town and County afore said and as a part of his Portion of my eftate which I intend to beftow upon James Sanford and to his Heirs and Assignees forever, three several pieces of Lands lying in Redding at a place called Rock houfe hill, the firft piece

lying the Eaſt side of the highway—part in Hubbels and part in Sherwoods long lots so called with a dwelling houſe there on, bounded
Northerly upon Andrew Hill's land, Easterly upon Daniel Hill's Land,
Southerly upon Land belonging to the Heirs of Nehemiah Seeley
Deceas[4] & Eaſterly upon highway, and in quantity one acre & 39
Rods of Land.—The other piece lying acroſf the way, from deſcribed
piece in Jacksons long lot so called and in quantity two Acres beginning at a heap of stones at yᵉ South part of the gate where it
now stands, then running West five rods to a heap of Stones, thence
South two rods, thence Weſt sixteen rods to a heap of stones, thence
Southerly fourteen rods & 3 quarters of a rod to a walnut pole stones
to it, then Easterly by twenty one rods to the highway, thence northerly sixteen rods & three quarters by the highway to yᵉ bounds began
at and bounded Northerly, Weſterly and Southerly by my own land
and Easterly by Highway. The other piece lying below the croſs
highway and in quantity twenty Acres be it more or leſs being the
souther most part or piece of Land I have in Redding it lying & being
in Jacksons, Grummond & Sanfords long lots, bounded West upon
Lazarus Beaches land, Southerly upon Jonathan Lyons, Easterly upon
highway and—Northweſterly upon the cross highway—With all the
privileges and....appurtenances there unto belonging unto him the s
James Sanford his Heirs and assigns for his and their own proper
use and Behoof. *And furthermore,* I the said John Sanford—do by
these present bind myself my Heirs forever to warrant and Defend
the above granted and bargained Premises to him the said James
Sanford his Heirs and Assigns, against all claims and Demands what
soever—*in Witness* here of I have here unto set my Hand and Seal
this Day of April in the year of our Lord 1784

                                        JOHN SANFORD.

In Prensence of
Stephen Betts.
Oliver Sanford.

Redding in Fairfield County on yᵉ day and Date above....Person-
ally appeared John Sanford....Signer and Sealer of the above written
instrument, and acknowledged the same to be his free Act and Deed
before me

                        STEPHEN BETTS Jus. of Peace

    The above is a true Record Recorded ye 16ᵗʰ of Auguſt 1781

                        LEM¹ SANFORD Town Clerk."

    John, the second son, enlarged his phylacteries and sent his
immediate descendants far afield. Canada was none too distant for their adventurous spirits, and to-day, in the Canadian
house of Parliament, one of his grandsons occupies a prominent place ; another is at the head of a college in Ontario ;

another was, as we shall see later, most prominent in diplomatic life, and a fourth is president of the Knoxville and Tennessee railroad. That some stayed nearer home and peopled that portion of country will be realized when we come to find a large Duncombe connection. This family came originally from Bucks County. "Charles Duncombe, son of William Duncombe of Barley-end near Joinghoe in ye County of Bucks and Elizabeth Hubbart daughter of Zachariah Hubbart were marryed March 16ᵗʰ 1744/5 by ye Rev. Mr. Henry Caner of Fairfield. Children: Charles, born April 24, 1747 ; William, born April 5th, 1749 ; John, born April 18, 1751 ; Elizabeth, born July 23d, 1753, and Thomas, Sepᵗ 1756." John married Catherine Burr, daughter of John and Emma (Booth) Burr, who was born Nov. 5, 1753. [See Burr Gen., p. 171.]

The name of John Duncombe's wife as sent us may be that of a second wife (Eliza Jones). He was the father of David, who married Ruth Sanford, dau. of John, Jr. The youngest daughter, Lydia Ann, married Edward Jackson of Redding ; he was humbly born, and when this gay young favorite of the neighborhood chose him for her life's partner, her father feared and her friends wondered, but the almost immediate influence upon him was such as to show the benefit of this happy and congenial marriage. As time went on and in larger fields they, too, ventured in northern climes to seek larger harvests, their work prospered and rewards both spiritual and worldly crowned their efforts. In a little book published in Toronto in 1876, containing a memorial to these pioneer Methodists in Canada, we read that in their later years they were devoted to a series of great Christian enterprises,—the Wesleyan Female College at Hamilton ; the Orphan Asylum and Benevolent Society (of which Mrs. Jackson was directress and treasurer) ; the Central Methodist church, of which she laid the corner-stone ; the endowment of Victoria College and the establishment of a theological department therein. After Mr. Jackson's death she continued this last to its accomplishment, and as her biographer, the Rev. Mr. Burwash, concludes: "The character of this noble woman was in many respects the complement of her husband."

Before speaking of Stephen's descendants, a word more should be said of two of these spoken of, the one, member of the Canadian Parliament, and the other in Tennessee.

William Eli Sanford, now resident in Hamilton, Ontario, has been actively engaged in commercial pursuits all his life. In addition to being the head of a large manufacturing concern which employs upwards of two thousand people, he has been intimately associated with various monied and educational institutions of Canada. He was president of the Hamilton Provident Loan, a banking institution of $2,000,000; president of the Hamilton Ladies' College; a member of the Board of Regents of Victoria University, and a member of the Senate of the same. He was made a member of the Canadian Senate (a life appointment of Her Majesty) in the year 1887, since which time he has been engaged in various commissions for the Government, spending some weeks at one time in Washington, during a period of important legislation in which Canada was largely interested. He was engaged in negotiating a Reciprocity Treaty with the Cape Colonies and the Cape of Good Hope with the Hon. Cecil Rhodes, the then Premier of the Cape Colonies. Mr. Sanford married for his first wife Emeline Jackson, the only child and daughter of those first Canadian pioneers of whom we have just read.

Edward Jackson Sanford went to Tennessee before the war, and being a Northern man was banished by the Confederates. He remained away until the return of Gen. Burnside, when he was one of that small number who as volunteers defended Fort Saunders at the siege of Knoxville. In 1864 he established the wholesale drug house of E. J. Sanford & Company, which is now Sanford, Chamberlain & Albert. Of the many public offices which Mr. Sanford has well filled, it would be impossible to speak at length: President of the Mechanics National Bank, vice-president of the East Tennessee National Bank, president of the Board of Education and the Board of Trustees of the Medical College, of the Knoxville Woolen Mills, of the Tennessee and Ohio and Knoxville and Ohio Railroad companies, a trustee of the University, director in many companies; in fact, the Knoxville Journal says, "hardly an enterprise for the employment of capital and labor has been started in Knoxville for the last quarter of a century toward the success of which his counsel, his capital and his energy have not contributed." It is largely owing to his interest in this work and kindness in lending valuable papers that I am able to present so complete an early record of this family.

Stephen, the fifth son by his marriage to Sarah, the daughter of Nehemiah Curtis, united with one of the families in the Beach connection [see Curtis] and their children with one exception married at home—Shelton, Morehouse, and Hurd ; none far off, even to the present day. The next generation, however, filled sail and crossed many boundaries. The most noted of these was Henry Shelton Sanford, only child of Hon. Nehemiah Curtis Sanford, who has held many high offices in diplomatic circles, commencing his career as attaché at St. Petersburg in 1847, under Hon. Ralph I. Ingersoll. "The next year, 1848, he was acting Secretary of Legation under Hon. Andrew J. Donelson at Frankfort. In 1849 appointed by President Taylor Secretary of Legation at Paris under Hon. Wm. C. Rives, and on the departure of the latter in 1853, Chargé d'Affaires for nearly a year, arranging for our first postal convention with France. On his resignation and return to this country in 1854, he took up the celebrated Aves Island case, which, in connection with that of Guano Island, has led to most favorable results and the development of enormous agricultural interests. Mr. Sanford made several visits to Central and South America. In 1859, while engaged on his book on International Maritime Law, he was, at the recommendation of the Panama Railroad Company and the Pacific Mail Steamship Company, sent by the President to New Grenada to negotiate for the extension of the Panama Railroad charter. His house in Washington the winter of the Peace Congress (1860–61) was the centre of decisive discussion. Mr. Lincoln, immediately after his inauguration, appointed him Minister to Belgium, and within three days he was on his way to Paris under confidential instructions. His mission to Belgium was made to cover much diplomatic ground.

Gov' Seward said of him : "Mr. Sanford during the first year of the war was the Minister of the United States in Europe." During the eight and a half years Mr. Sanford remained in Belgium he negotiated and signed the treaties of the Scheldt, of commerce and navigation, of trade-marks, and the consular convention, the first ever made by Belgium ; the extradition treaty he had discussed failed by reason of one point, since yielded by Government. He made numerous reports to the State department, for a time fiscal agent for the Government in Europe, he was entrusted with delicate and confidential business both in and out of Germany (among

others to Caprera to confer with Garibaldi), in all of which
the State Department openly sustained and afterward com-
mended its representative. His private fortune contributed
largely to the needs of his position abroad, and at home he
presented a Krupp gun to his native State, and a battery of
steel guns to the First Minnesota regiment.

After Mr. Sanford's resignation and return, he undertook
large interests in Louisiana and other Southern States,
notably in Florida, where he established Sanfordtown, a
large Swedish colony. In 1884, as plenipotentiary of the
International Congo Association, he secured at Washington the recognition of that flag as of a friendly government. This was signed by Secretary Frelinghuysen and
himself April 18th, 1884, and led to most important results.
In 1884–5 he was plenipotentiary of the United States at
the Berlin Conference, and signed, Feb. 26th, 1885, with his
colleague Minister Kasson, the "Act Générale," securing
freedom of access to our commerce and ships, respect for our
missionaries, free trade, and the abolition of the slave trade
in the Congo region. In 1886, General Sanford organized at
Brussels and despatched to the Congo, under the charge of
Lieut. E. H. Tarent, the "Sanford Exploring Expedition," for
scientific and commercial discovery and information. It will
be recalled that in order to get the steamboats "Florida" and
"New York" around the cataracts, they had to be taken apart
and carried around on the heads of native porters, put together
again and launched at Stanley Pool. Naturally they were the
first commercial steamers floated on the upper Congo.

The Sanford exploration became in 1888, in Brussels, a large
stock company, with seven steamers and ten stations. It was
a great regret to General Sanford that he could not interest
American capital in this venture, for our flag, first taken
there by Stanley and afterwards by him, has now been replaced
by foreign colors—"Florida" and "New York" thus oddly
crowned. The "Congo" continued in his thoughts, and it
was in endeavoring to secure its development along good and
temperate lines that he was struck by an incurable disease.
In February of 1891 he sailed for America to visit and direct
his estate in Florida. In May he went to Virginia, hoping
the waters of the Healing Springs would revive him, and
there he breathed his last, on May 21, 1891. Thus closed the
useful life of one whose record contains more years of diplo-

matic service than any of his countrymen. He was the only American who has passed through all its grades from Attaché to Minister Plenipotentiary (that of Ambassador being since created). He departed leaving to his family a beautiful memory of perfect devotion and tenderness, of faithful appreciation and kindness to his friends, of good deeds to the afflicted and unfortunate, of energetic and loyal service to his country, and an example of unfailing unselfishness, generosity, and of dignified disinterested labor to a new generation." I am sorry not to have space to give this very interesting memoir in full, but sufficient quotations must have established every claim made for this excellent gentleman and diplomat. He married a descendant of one of the early Italian families, del Paggio, afterwards du Puy—Hugenots. On the revocation of the edict of Nantes they fled to America, not, however, before several members of the family had suffered martyrdom.

The first Stephen's son John was a member of the 28th Congress, and of the Electoral College of 1856; his son Stephen was a member of the 41st Congress, and of the Electoral College of 1868; and his son John, of the 51st Congress, and the Electoral College of 1896. These were all of Amsterdam, New York State, where for three generations the name has stood for advancement, probity and honorable discharge of public and private duties.

Of Ephraim, the youngest son of John and Anna, we had nothing to begin on. Coming across the marriage of an "E. Sanford and Sally Platt," in the Platt genealogy, at a date to correspond with requirements, we investigated this and found it to be correct. From this point, by dint of advertising in several papers, we have developed the extensive line of descendants here given. He was also that "Ephraim Sanford" who was killed in a runaway accident on the turnpike road between Torrington and New Haven in 1808, his will being probated that year.

Item from Orcutt's History of Torrington, p. 90: "Mr. Potter sold this property to Ephraim Sanford of Newtown, Ct., who took possession and went on with the store, and also bought the tavern, and about a year after Mr. Sanford was on his way to New Haven with a load of cheese, the horses ran away and he was killed. His executors sold the store to R. Butt and Fred Robbins, 1808."

Previously, he had resided in New York State for a few
years; his youngest child born in Johnstown. Sally Platt
was the daughter of Jarvis and Annie (Nichols) Platt and
sister to Charlotte, who married Lemuel Sanford. After
Ephraim's death, his widow married a Wilcox.

The Platts were originally from Milford, Conn., where
Richard's name appears Nov. 20, 1639, with a family of four,
he having landed in New Haven in 1638. He became deacon
in the first church in Milford in 1669; he died in 1684, his wife
having died eight years before. Their names are inscribed on
the Memorial Stone Bridge over the "Wapawaug." The
descent of Jarvis is from Richard and Mary, Jonas and Sarah
Scudder, Obadiah[1] and Mary Smith, Obadiah[2] and Thankful
Scudder-Jarvis. Thankful Scudder was of Huntington, and
her mother dying when she was quite young, was brought up
by Thomas and Abigail Jarvis, whose name she adopted in preference to her own,—and certainly Polly Jarvis is preferable.
Jarvis Platt was born in 1759, and died in 1841. He married
Annie Nichols in 1779. She was the daughter of Richard
and Abigail (Gold) Nichols, grandson of the first Richard,
son of Sergeant Francis. [See Nicholls.]

Among other interesting intermarriages is one which brings
in the Morgan family. Elizabeth, the eldest daughter of John
and Anna, married for her second husband Hezekiah Morgan,
the son of Zedekiah, son of Peter, son of Isaac, son of John,
son of James, thus back to 1607. Ezra, son of Hezekiah and
Elizabeth (Sanford) Morgan, born in 1801, married Hannah
Nash, and their son, the Hon. Daniel Nash Morgan, was
Treasurer of the United States from June 1, 1893, to July 1,
1897. "He was born in Newtown, Fairfield County, Conn.,
August 18, 1844, and received his education at the Newtown
Academy, Bethel Institute, and in the common schools. His
natural bent was towards mercantile pursuits, and the five years
of his minority were passed in his father's store, and the next
year he had control of the business, and then for three years
he was of the firm of Morgan & Booth. He is a Democrat in
politics and was elected a member of the Common Council of
Bridgeport in 1873–74; Mayor of the city in 1880 and 1884;
on the Board of Education in 1877–78; for thirteen years he
was Parish Clerk of Trinity Church, and afterwards Junior and
Senior Warden; he has for years been President of the Bridge-

port Hospital ; was Vice-President of the Consolidated Rolling Stock Company ; was Sinking Fund Commissioner of the
city ; was President of the City National Bank from 1879 to
1893 ; is President of the Mechanics' and Farmers' Savings
Bank ; was State Senator from the 14th District in 1885 and
1886, having been previously a member of the House, in 1883.
In 1892 he was elected State Senator by 1755 majority, the largest
ever given for Mayor, Representative, or Senator in the history
of the town.   He is a Mason and for two years Master of Cor-
inthian Lodge, No. 104, of Bridgeport, and is now a member
of Hamilton Commandery, No. 5, K. T. ; besides which he
is connected with many other offices of trust and consideration in the city.   In the history of the country there have
been eighteen United States Treasurers ; they have been
selected from Connecticut three times and from Fairfield
County twice ; and after the election of President Cleveland,
the choice fell upon Mr. Morgan, who assumed the duties of
his high office with the best wishes of his hosts of friends
throughout the State, and he has held the position since
that time with credit to himself and advantage to the country.   Mr. Morgan lives in Washington, necessarily, but he
has a summer home in Connecticut, where he spends his
vacations with his family.   His wife was Medora H. Judson
of Huntington, and they have two children, a daughter and
a son.

On assuming the position as U. S. Treasurer, Mr. Morgan
gave his predecessor a receipt for *$740,817,419.78⅔*.   When
he retired, he received one from his successor for *$796,925,-
439.17⅔*."

Mrs. Morgan is herself a descendant of John Beach the
first, through John² and Hannah Staples, Ebenezer and Mehitable Gibson, John and Rebecca, Hezekiah and —— Silliman, Rebecca and Agur Judson, William Agur Judson and
Marietta Beardsley.   Marietta Beardsley was the daughter of
Ebenezer Beardsley and Maria Beach, who was the daughter
of Ebenezer (brother to Hezekiah) and Abbe —— Beach.   The
double connection explains itself.   The marriages and full
family records of the two brothers, Hezekiah and Ebenezer
Beach, can be found in the first volume of Town Records
(Huntington) at Shelton, Conn. (Town Clerk's Office).

Descendants of John Sanford and Anna Wheeler

V.

John Sanford.

[Eldest son of Ephraim Sanford (Ezekiel, Jr.; Ezekiel; Thomas) and Elizabeth Mix.]

b. April 26, 1739, Fairfield, Conn.

d. April 18, 1784, Redding Ridge, T. S.

m. —— 1757.

ANNA WHEELER.

[Settlement of Estate, Will of John Sanford, probated, Danbury, Conn.]

d. 1791.

CHILDREN:

JAMES SANFORD, b. 1758, Redding, Conn. p. 255.
ELIZABETH SANFORD, b. October 13, 1763, Redding, Conn. p. 318.
JOHN SANFORD, JR., b. December 21, 1765, Redding, Conn. p. 326.
STEPHEN SANFORD, b. November 24, 1769, Redding, Conn. p. 343.
HULDAH SANFORD, b. August 29, 1771, Redding, Conn. p. 354.
ELI SANFORD, b.   ; d. in Redding; m. Sarah Lyon, of Quaker Hill.
    son: ASAHEL SANFORD, d. in Michigan.
            m. ABBY WHITLOCK.
        [Dau. of Walter W. and Anna (Gorham) Whitlock.]
                                    (rec'd Miss Sanford.)
EPHRAIM SANFORD, b. 1775, Redding, Conn. p. 357.
ANNE SANFORD, b. August 12, 1781, Redding, Conn. p. 309.
LOIS SANFORD;
EASTER SANFORD.   (names according to Will.)

VI.

Elizabeth Sanford.

[Eldest dau. of John Sanford and Anna Wheeler.]

b. October 13, 1763, Redding, Conn.

d. August 5, 1853, Redding, Conn.

first m. (According to Father's Will, Probate Court, Danbury.)

DANIEL HILL, JR.

[Son of Capt. Daniel Hill, by his second wife, Elizabeth Lane.]

b. April 12, 1761.

("Died before his father, 'Grand-son John'" mentioned in Capt. Dan'l Hill's will.)

second m. HEZEKIAH MORGAN.

[Son of Zedekiah Morgan (b. 1744-5, Norwich, Ct.; m. Jan'y 26, 1769, Ruth Dart of New London, Ct.)]

b. July 24, 1773, Newtown, Conn.
d. March 24, 1857, Newtown, Conn.

CHILDREN (of second marriage):

ZERA MORGAN, b.   1797. p. 319.
FANNY MORGAN, b. February 22, 1799. p. 321.
EZRA MORGAN, b. February 21, 1801, Redding, Conn. p. 323.

VII.

Zera Morgan.

[Elder son of Hezekiah Morgan and Elizabeth (Sanford) Hill.]

b.   , 1797.

m. SALLY A. UNDERHILL.

CHILDREN:

CHARLES MORGAN, b. April 7, 1821, Newtown, Conn. p. 319.
REV'D HENRY MORGAN, b. March 7, 1825, Newtown, Conn.
d. March 22, 1884, Boston, Mass. (unm.)

VIII.

Charles Morgan.

[Elder son of Zera Morgan and Sally A. Underhill.]

b. April 7, 1821, Newtown, Conn.
d. February 5, 1891, Newtown, Conn.
second m. March 9, 1851.

(Newtown Records. Rev'd Wm. M. Carmichael.)

POLLY PECK.

[Dau. of Abel Peck.]

b.   1832, Weston, Conn.
d. January 1, 1892.

CHILDREN (of second marriage):

HENRY P. MORGAN, b. March 28, 1852, Newtown, Conn. p. 320.
ORMEL E. MORGAN, b. February 8, 1855, Newtown, Conn. p. 320.
MERWIN D. MORGAN, b. September 4, 1857, Newtown, Conn.
EDITH L. MORGAN, b. October 18, 1862, Newtown, Conn. p. 320.

IX.

Henry P. Morgan.

[Eldest son of Charles Morgan, by his second wife, Polly Peck.]

b. March 28, 1852, Newtown, Conn.

m. ROMELIA GULIVER.

CHILDREN:

CHARLES MORGAN; HENRY MERWIN MORGAN, m. AMELIA CROOK.

(rec'd Mrs. O. E. Morgan.)

IX.

Ormel Eli Morgan.

[Second son of Charles Morgan, by his second wife, Polly Peck.]

b. February 8, 1855, Newtown, Conn.

m. August 28, 1877, Redding, Conn.

ESTHER POTTER BRISCOE.

[Dau. of Bradley Dimon Briscoe and Mary Catherine Glover.]

b. March 11, 1859, Newtown, Conn.

CHILDREN:

ARTHUR BRISCOE MORGAN, b. March 23, 1879, Newtown, Conn.

GRACE EDITH MORGAN, b. March 26, 1892, East Norwalk, Conn.

CLARA LOVISE MORGAN, b. Sept. 8, 1894; d. Sept. 20, 1894, Newtown.

(v. Mrs. Ormel E. Morgan.)

IX.

Edith Louisa Morgan.

[Only dau. of Charles Morgan, by his second wife, Polly Peck.]

b. October 18, 1862, Newtown, Conn.

m. April 8, 1879.

WILLIAM JAMES COOK.

[Son of William H. and Emeline (Foxworth) Cook.]

b. February 25, 1852.

CHILDREN:

ELSIE MAY COOK, b. July 22, 1880.

FLORA EDITH COOK, b. February 23, 1883.

WILLIAM M. COOK, b. February 2, 1885.

EDWARD R. COOK, b. January 14, 1893.   (v. E. L. M. Cook.)

VII.

Fanny Morgan.

Only dau. of Hezekiah Morgan and Elizabeth (Sanford) Hill. p. 318–19.]

b. February 22, 1799.
d. September 5, 1856, Bridgeport, Conn.
first m. March 18, 1818, Redding, Conn.

JEREMIAH BANKS.

[Son of Hyatt and Sarah Banks.]

b. March 18, 1794.
d. March 2, 1851, (æ. 56 yrs., 11 m., 24 d.), Redding.
second m. September 10, 1854.

STURGES FANTON.

[Son Serg't Abel Fanton and Jerusha Sturges.]

b. December 21, 1791, Weston, Conn.

(Edw. J. Sanford.)

d. 1865, Sag Harbor, Long Island. (Miss Sanford.)

CHILDREN (of first marriage) :

GEORGE W. BANKS, b. February 22, 1819; d. April 29, 1837. (unm.)
CHARLES M. BANKS, b. March 4, 1821, Redding, Conn. p. 321.

(rec'd A. B. Whitehead.)

VIII.

Charles Morgan Banks.

[Younger son of Jeremiah Banks and Fanny Morgan.]

b. March 4, 1821, Redding, Conn.
d. September 22, 1887, Redding, Conn.
m. November 3, 1844, Weston, Conn.

SOPHIA BRADLEY.

[Dau. of Medad and Catherine M. Bradley.]

b. April 27, 1825, Greenfield, Conn.
d. November 17, 1897, Redding Ridge, Conn.

CHILDREN :

AGNES BANKS, b. November 15, 1846, Greenfield, Conn. p. 322.
ELIZABETH S. BANKS, b. November 14, 1847, Redding, Conn. p. 322.
ALMA L. BANKS, b. October 28, 1867, Redding, Conn. p. 323.

(v. A. B. Whitehead.)

IX.

Agnes Banks.

[Eldest dau. of Charles Morgan Banks and Sophia Bradley.]

b. November 15, 1846, Greenfield, Conn.

m. June 30, 1867, Redding, Conn.

HENRY WHITEHEAD.

[Son of Harvey and Laura (Stevens) Whitehead.]

b. January 28, 1842, Redding, Conn.

(v. A. B. Whitehead.)

X.

Eva Whitehead.

[Only child of Henry Whitehead and Agnes Banks.]

✓ b. April 3, 1870, Redding Ridge, Conn.   ⌄

m. January 6, 1889, Redding Ridge, Conn.

JAMES ARTHUR SHERWOOD.

[Only child of George Botsford Sherwood and BETSEY SANFORD. p. 288.]

b. May 8, 1867, Easton, Conn.

CHILD:

✓ HAZEL ELAINE SHERWOOD, b. Oct. 11, 1889, Redding Ridge, Conn.
(11th gen. in descent from Thos. Sanford; 7th gen. from Rev⁴ Jno. Beach.)
(rec'd Mrs. Henry Whitehead.)

IX.

Elizabeth Savery Banks.

[Second dau. of Charles Morgan Banks and Sophia Bradley.]

b. November 14, 1847, Redding, Conn.

m. January 18, 1871, Redding, Conn.

JOHN KENNEDY DUNCAN.

[Son of Jesse and Frances (Lewis) Duncan.]

b. January 31, 1847, Brownville, Penn³.

d. January 31, 1884, Chicago, Ill.

CHILDREN:

KATHERINE DUNCAN, b. January 28, 1872, Chicago, Ill. p. 323.
JESSE HENRY DUNCAN, b. February 2, 1876, Chicago, Ill. (unm.)

(v. E. S. B. Duncan.)

X.

Katherine Duncan.

[Only dau. of John Kennedy Duncan and Elizabeth Savery Banks.]

b. January 28, 1872, Chicago, Ill.
m. October 19, 1893, Chicago, Ill.

HENRY WARD DIETRICH.

[Son of Henry S. and Sarah Jane (Clark) Dietrich.]

b. May 24, 1869, Chicago, Ill.

CHILDREN:

DUNCAN WARD DIETRICH, b. August 30, 1894, Chicago, Ill.
DOROTHY DIETRICH, b. Oct. 29, 1895, Chicago, Ill.   (v. K. D. Dietrich.)

IX.

Alma Louisa Banks.

[Youngest dau. of Charles Morgan Banks and Sophia Bradley.]

b. October 28, 1867, Redding, Conn.
m. November 7, 1888, Stamford, Conn.

FRANCIS COLEY LEE.

[Son of Henry and Julia (Coley) Lee.]

b. January 1, 1865, Redding, Conn.

CHILDREN:

CHARLES HENRY LEE, b. August 15, 1889, Redding, Conn.
JULIAN LEE, b. August 21, 1892, Redding, Conn.
COLEY FANTON LEE, b. January 10, 1897, Redding, Conn.

(rec'd A. B. Whitehead.)

———o———

VII.

Ezra Morgan.

[Younger son of Hezekiah Morgan and Elizabeth (Sanford) Hill. p. 318–19.]

b. February 21, 1801, Redding, Conn.
d. June 9, 1871, Newtown, Conn.
m. June 5, 1838, Westport, Conn.

HANNAH NASH.

[Dau. of Daniel and Rebecca (Camp) Nash.]

b. February 6, 1816, Westport, Conn.
d. April 15, 1883, Newtown, Conn.

CHILDREN :

ELIZABETH S. MORGAN, b. March 31, 1839, Newtown, Conn. p. 324.
MARY CAMP MORGAN, b. July 17, 1842, Newtown, Conn.
    d. August 6, 1890.
DANIEL N. MORGAN, b. August 18, 1844, Newtown, Conn. p. 325.
HARRIET LOUISA MORGAN, b. June 17, 1846, Newtown, Conn.
    d. February 22, 1874.
CORNELIA JANE MORGAN, b. October 4, 1847, Newtown, Conn.
    d. September 30, 1877.
HANNAH SOPHIA MORGAN, b. July 14, 1851, Newtown, Conn.
    d. July 2, 1863.
FREDERICK EZRA MORGAN, b. August 13, 1853, Newtown, Conn.
    d. June 17, 1862.
EDWARD KEMPER MORGAN, b. March 16, 1859, Newtown, Conn. p. 325.
                       (v. Hon. Dan'l N. Morgan.)

VIII.

Elizabeth Sanford Morgan.

[Eldest dau. of Ezra Morgan and Hannah Nash.]

b. March 31, 1839, Newtown, Conn.
m. October 15, 1862.   (Newtown Records.)

RUFUS DAVENPORT CABLE.

[Son of George (Lewis) Cable and Mary Mallory.]

b. December 9, 1831, Westport, Conn.
d. August 19, 1889, Westport, Conn.

CHILDREN :

JOHN HENRY CABLE, b. August 27, 1863, Westport, Conn.
    d. July 19, 1873, Westport, Conn.
MARY ELIZABETH CABLE, b. July 16, 1865, Westport, Conn. p. 324.
GEORGE EZRA CABLE, b. Nov. 7, 1867 ; d. June 13, 1868, Westport, Conn.
SOPHIA MORGAN CABLE, b. June 9, 1870 ; d. Sept. 15, 1871, Westport.
HANNAH LOUISA CABLE, b. January 3, 1873, Westport, Conn.
ANTOINETTE CORNELIA CABLE, b. December 1, 1874, Westport, Conn.
                      (v. E. S. M. Cable.)

IX.

Mary Elizabeth Cable.

[Eldest dau. of Rufus Davenport Cable and Elizabeth Sanford Morgan.]

b. July 16, 1865, Westport, Conn.
m. June 1, 1886, Westport, Conn.

MARCUS BAYARD BUTLER.

[Son of Marcus B. and Emily (Lacy) Butler.]

b. November 26, 1859, Milford, Conn.

CHILDREN:

DOROTHY MORGAN BUTLER, b. February 28, 1888 ;
 d. March 28, 1888, Bridgeport, Conn.
VIRGINIA LACEY BUTLER, b. August 10, 1889, Bridgeport, Conn.
MARCUS BAYARD BUTLER, b. October 7, 1891, Bridgeport, Conn.
(v. M. E. C. Butler.)

VIII.

Hon. Daniel Nash Morgan.

[Eldest son of Ezra Morgan and Hannah Nash.]

b. August 18, 1844, Newtown, Conn.
m. June 10, 1868, Huntington, Conn.

MÉDORA HUGANEN JUDSON.

[Dau. of Hon. William Agur Judson and Marietta Beardsley.] (Orcutts.)

b. August 14,   , Huntington, Conn.

CHILDREN:

MARY HUNTINGTON MORGAN, b. Nov. 29,   , Huntington, Conn.
FLORENCE NEWTON MORGAN, b. Dec. 5, 1876, Huntington, Conn.
 d. April 18, 1878, Huntington, Conn.
WILLIAM JUDSON MORGAN, b. May 17, 1881, Bridgeport, Conn.
(v. Hon. Dan'l N. Morgan.)

VIII.

Edward Kemper Morgan.

[Youngest son of Ezra Morgan and Hannah Nash.]

b. March 16, 1859, Newtown, Conn.
m. September 27, 1883, Huntington, Conn.

CHARLOTTE ADELAIDE JUDSON.

[Dau. of Charles Judson and Eleanor Booth.]

b. December 1, 1861, Huntington, Conn.

CHILDREN:

DANIEL JUDSON MORGAN, b. June 10, 1885, Huntington, Conn.
FREDERICK EDWARD MORGAN, b. February 13, 1890, Bridgeport, Conn.
(v. Edw. K. Morgan.)

VI.

John Sanford, Jr.

[Son of John Sanford and Anna Wheeler. p. 318.]

b. December 21, 1765, Redding, Conn.
d. June 5, 1842, Redding, Conn.
first m. 1788.

LYDIA WHEELER.

[Dau. of John Wheeler of Weston, Conn.]

b. 1771.
d. November 9, 1807, Redding, Conn.

second m. "ELIZABETH PARSONS,"

[Wife of John Sanford, Jr.]

d. November 23, 1848, æ. 75." (T. S. Redding Ridge.)

CHILDREN (of first marriage, none by second):

ELIZABETH SANFORD, b. August 15, 1790, Redding, Conn. p. 326.
RUTH SANFORD, b. April 22, 1792, Redding, Conn. p. 328.
MARGARET SANFORD, b. October 20, 1794, Redding, Conn.
    m. HENRY DEAN. (no descendants.)
SARAH SANFORD, b. January 25, 1797, Redding, Conn. p. 336.
JOHN W. SANFORD, b. May 21, 1799, Redding, Conn. p. 338.
ELI SANFORD, b. August 4, 1801, Redding, Conn. p. 340.
LYDIA A. SANFORD, b. March 17, 1804, Redding, Conn. p. 342.

(rec'd Edw. J. Sanford.)

VII.

Elizabeth Sanford.

[Eldest dau. of John Sanford, Jr., and Lydia Wheeler.]

b. August 15, 1790, Redding, Conn.
d. January 7, 1881.

m. AARON LYON.

[Son of Lemuel Lyon and HULDAH SANFORD. p. 189.]

CHILDREN :

LEMUEL LYON.
MARY ELIZA LYON, b. March 11, 1825. p. 327.
LYDIA LOUISA LYON, b. June 17, 1830.
    d. August 22, 1856, Chatham, Ont., Canada. (unm.)

(v. Rev⁴ Edw. N. English.)

VIII.

Mary Eliza Lyon.

[Elder dau. of AARON LYON and ELIZABETH SANFORD.]

b. March 11, 1825.

d. February 18, 1857, Chatham, Canada.

m. June 20, 1847.

REV'D NOBLE FRANKLIN ENGLISH.

[Son of Noble English and Elizabeth Forsyth.]

b. Sept. 24, 1820, Co. Middlesex, Ont. (Lond.), Can.

d. May 23, 1874, London, Ont., Canada.

CHILDREN :

LEMUEL NELSON ENGLISH, b. Apr. 22, 1848 ; d. May 7, '48, Pictou, Can.

LYDIA EMELINE ENGLISH, b. July 17, 1849, Rockville, Canada. (unm.)

EDWARD N. ENGLISH, b. June 17, 1851, Brockville, Canada. p. 327.

ELIAS FRANKLIN ENGLISH, b. May 3, 1853, Bytown (Ottawa) Canada.
d. Sept. 11, 1854, Brantford, Canada.

GEORGE ALBERT ENGLISH, b. May 18, 1855, Brantford, Canada.
d. December 24, 1861, Goderich, Ont., Canada.

(v. Rev⁴ Edw. N. English.)

IX.

Rev'd Edward Noble English.

[Second son of Rev⁴ Noble Franklin English and Mary E. Lyon.]

b. June 17, 1851, Brockville, Ont., Canada.

m. August 21, 1871, Stapleford, Co. Wilts, Eng.

MARY STOUGHTON MULKINS.

[Dau. of H. Mulkins, the Vicar of Stapleford, and Jane Grey Dennis.]

CHILDREN :

STUART NOBLE ENGLISH, b. June 12, 1878, London, Ont., Canada.

EDWARD LYON ENGLISH, b. June 24, 1879, London, Canada.
d. August 18, 1879, Kirkton, Canada.

THERESA MARY ENGLISH, b. July 16, 1880, Kirkton, Canada.
d. February 27, 1885, London, Tw'p, Ont.

(v. Rev⁴ Edw. Noble English.)

———o———

VII.

Ruth Sanford.

[Second dau. of John Sanford, Jr., and Lydia Wheeler.]

b. April 22, 1792, Redding, Conn.
d. May 11, 1881, Redding Centre, Conn.
m. November 25, 1810, Redding, Conn.

DAVID DUNCOMBE.

[Son of John Duncombe and Eliza Jones. p. 311.]

b. October 21, 1788, Redding, Conn.
d. February 5, 1857, Redding Centre, Conn.

CHILDREN:

HENRY B. DUNCOMBE, b. November 4, 1811, Redding, Conn.
d. December 20, 1836.
m. December 31, 1832.

ANN HULL.

[m. as second husband Walstein Gorham.]

d. æ. 84, 1898, buried Hull Cem⁷ (son by her 1st m. d. æ. 17 yr.)
DAVID S. DUNCOMBE, b. October 1, 1813, Redding, Conn. p. 328.
ASAHEL S. DUNCOMBE, b. September 1, 1815, Redding, Conn. p. 329.
CHARLES DUNCOMBE, b. October 24, 1817, Redding, Conn. p. 331.
HARRIET N. DUNCOMBE, b. April 29, 1820, Redding, Conn. p. 331.
LYDIA A. DUNCOMBE, b. March 4, 1824, Redding, Conn. p. 332.
AARON H. DUNCOMBE, b. May 2, 1826, Redding, Conn. p. 334.
WILLIAM E. DUNCOMBE, b. February 17, 1830, Redding, Conn. p. 334.
(v. Wm. E. Duncombe.)

VIII.

David Sanford Duncombe.

[Second son of David Duncombe and Ruth Sanford.]

b. October 1, 1813, Redding, Conn.
d. March 19, 1883, Redding, Conn.
first m. June 29, 1845, Sherman, Conn. (?)

JANE CHARLOTTE LEACH.

[Dau. of William and Charlotte (Steadwell) Leach of Sherman, Conn.]

b. January 31, 1818, Sherman, Conn.
d. March 9, 1852.   (v. M. P. D. Cook.)
second m. January 17, 1854, New York City.

MARIETTA WRIGHT.

[Dau. of Joel Wright of Pompey, N. Y., and Cynthia Pratt of Pratt's Hollow, N. Y.]

b. October 31, 1830, Pompey, N. Y.

CHILD (of first marriage):
MARY P. DUNCOMBE, b. August 15, 1848, New York City. p. 329.

CHILDREN (of second marriage) :
WILLIAM S. DUNCOMBE, b. Feb. 14, 1856, New York City. p. 329.
NELLIE C. DUNCOMBE, b. September 6, 1863, New York City. (unm.)
(v. W. S. Duncombe.)

ı   IX.

Mary Paulina Duncombe.

[Only child of David Sanford Duncombe, by his first wife, Jane C. Leach.]

b. Aug. 15, 1848, New York City.
m. June 11, 1874, Elizabeth, New Jersey.

WILLIAM CROWELL COOK.

[Son of Elisha Worth Cook, Trenton, N. J., and Lois Crowell, Phila., Penna.]
[Crowell corruption of Cromwell.]

b. March 7, 1836, Philadelphia.

CHILDREN :

HELEN CROWELL COOK, b. February 9, 1877.
SANFORD CROWELL COOK, b. October 26, 1881.   (v. M. P. D. Cook.)

IX.

William Sanford Duncombe.

[Only son of David Sanford Duncombe, by his second wife, Marietta Wright.]

b. February 14, 1856, New York City.
m. October, 25, 1887, San Francisco, Cal.

LILLIE NICHOLS MURDOCK.

[Dau. of Albert Hamilton Murdock and Charlotte Dorothy Hills.]

b. Feb. 27, 1858, Arcata, Humboldt Co., Cal.

CHILD :

DOROTHY DUNCOMBE, b. October 5, 1888, San Francisco, Cal.
(v. Wm. S. Duncombe, Cal.)

———o———

VIII.

Asahel Sanford Duncombe.

[Third son of David Duncombe and Ruth Sanford. p. 328.]

b. September 1, 1815, Redding Centre, Conn.
d. February 28, 1873, Brooklyn, N. Y.

m. December 25, 1837, Redding, Conn.

Betsey Ann Canfield.

[Dau. of Lemon and Betsey (Jenkins) Canfield.]

b. December 2, 1814, Redding, Conn.
d. April 7, 1873, Brooklyn, N. Y.   (v. Mrs. Leich.)

CHILDREN:

William Henry Duncombe, b. July 5, 1839; d. under four years.
Emma Josephine Duncombe, b. August 2, 1841; d. under four years.
Edward Jackson Duncombe, b. December 25, 1843, Redding, Conn.
    m. March 25, 1883.
              Frances Grant. (no children.)
Mary Emma Duncombe, b. January 23, 1846; d. under four years.
Henry C. Duncombe, b. September 21, 1849, Redding, Conn. p. 330.
Franklin Duncombe, b. September 20, 1851; d. under four years.
Isabella R. Duncombe, b. June 2, 1854, Flatbush, N. Y. p. 330.
                        (rec'd Wm. E. Duncombe.)

IX.

Henry Clay Duncombe.

[Third son of Asahel Sanford Duncombe and Betsey A. Canfield.]

b. September 21, 1849, Redding, Conn.
m. July 16, 1872, Brooklyn, N. Y.

Delia Frederica Wedekend.

[Dau. of Frederick and Harriet E. Wedekend.]

b. November 17, 1853, Brooklyn, N. Y.

CHILDREN:

Henry Augustus Duncombe, b. November 24, 1873, Brooklyn, N.Y.
Lillian May Duncombe, b. December 8, 1875, Brooklyn, N. Y.
                        (v. H. C. Duncombe.)

IX.

Isabella Ruth Duncombe.

[Third dau. of Asahel Sanford Duncombe and Betsey A. Canfield.]

b. June 2, 1854, Flatbush, N. Y.
m. January 16, 1884, Brooklyn, N. Y.

Adam Henry Leich.

[Son of Adam and Catharine (Barker) Leich.]

b. May 5, 1854, Brooklyn, N. Y.

CHILDREN :

OLIVER DUNCOMBE LEICH, b. January 19, 1887, Brooklyn, N. Y.
EDNA MONROE LEICH, b. June 4, 1888, Brooklyn, N. Y.
BARKER LEICH, b. Dec. 3, 1890, Brooklyn, N. Y.   (v. I. R. D. Leich.)

————o————

VIII.

Charles Duncombe.

[Fourth son of David Duncombe and Ruth Sanford.]

b. October 24, 1817, Redding, Conn.

m. ELIZA FANTON.

[Only dau. of Curtis Fanton and REBECCA LYON, p. 354.]

CHILDREN.

EDMUND DUNCOMBE, b.   ; m.
LYDIA ANN DUNCOMBE, b.   ; d.   ;
    m. WM. JENNINGS : son FREDERICK JENNINGS.
HARRIET DUNCOMBE, b.   ;
    m. JOHN BOUTON of Norwalk, Conn.
Son : DUNCOMBE BOUTON, m.   .   (rec'd Mrs. Leich.)

————o————

VIII.

Harriet N. Duncombe.

[Elder dau. of David Duncombe and Ruth Sanford. p. 328.]

b. April 29, 1820, Redding Centre, Conn.
d. April 27, 1893, Redding, Conn.
m. May 4, 1840, Redding, Conn.

JOHN LEE HILL.

[Son of John Read Hill and BETSEY SANFORD VII, (Aaron, Hezekiah, Lemuel,
    Ezekiel, Jr., Ezekiel, Thomas.)]   (Hawley Record.)

b. June 15, 1810, Redding, Conn.
d. January 18, 1852, Redding, Conn.

CHILDREN :

WILLIAM H. HILL, b. May 1, 1845, Redding, Conn. p. 332.
JOSEPHINE E. HILL, b. May 22, 1848, Redding, Conn. p. 332.
                        (rec'd Wm. E. Duncombe.)

IX.

William H. Hill.

[Only son of John Lee Hill and Harriet N. Duncombe.]

b. May 1, 1845, Redding, Conn.

first m. October 5, 1869, Redding, Conn.

MARY A. HOTCHKISS.

[Dau. of Frederick A. Hotchkiss and Mary Parsons.]

b. August 7, 1851.

d. October 1, 1886.

second m. October 10, 1888.

LAURETTA C. BALLARD.

b. October 10, 1850.

CHILDREN (of first marriage, none by second) :

JOHN READ HILL, b. December 27, 1870, Redding, Conn. (unm.)

CARRIE L. HILL, b. Nov. 5, 1872 ; d. June 20, 1876.

FREDERICK H. HILL, b. July 18, 1874, Redding, Conn.

ERNEST WILLIAM HILL, b. January 1, 1876, Redding, Conn.

(rec'd Wm. E. Duncombe.)

IX.

Josephine Elizabeth Hill.

[Only dau. of John Lee Hill and Harriet N. Duncombe.]

b. May 22, 1848, Redding, Conn.

m. May 11, 1870, Redding, Conn.

REV'D EDSON WYLLIS BURR.

[Fifth son of Linus Burr and Betsey Kelsey of Killingworth.]

(Burr B'k, p. 280.)

b. March 29, 1841, Middletown, Conn.

CHILDREN :

HARRIET BURR, b. June 14, 1872, Jersey City, N. J.

EUGENE WYLLIS BURR, b. October 14, 1875, Bloomfield, N. J.

(v. J. E. H. Burr.)   (rec'd Wmʳ E. Duncombe.)

———o———

VIII.

Lydia Ann Duncombe.

[Younger dau. of David Duncombe and Ruth Sanford. p. 328.]

b. March 4, 1824, Redding Centre, Conn.

d. March 2, 1884.

m. April 18, 1842, Redding, Conn.

JOHN OSBORN.

[Son of Turney and Sarah (Parsons) Osborn.]

b. December 5, 1813.

d. July 24, 1891.

CHILDREN :

JOHN A. OSBORN, b. June 29, 1847. p. 333.

EUGENE E. OSBORN, b. May 1, 1854, Norwalk, Conn. p. 333.

IDA MEDORA OSBORN, b. November 17, 1855, Norwalk, Conn.

d. February 6, 1857, Norwalk, Conn.   (v. Jno. A. Osborn.)

IX.

John Arthur Osborn.

[Elder son of John Osborn and Lydia A. Duncombe.]

b. June 29, 1847.

m. March 15, 1882, Trenton, N. J.

ELLA FRANCES PERRY.

[Dau. of Truman G. Perry and Harriet F. Scholefield.]

b. December 17, 1847.

CHILDREN :

HELEN PERRY OSBORN, b. April 15, 1883, Norwalk, Conn.

HARRIET LYDIA OSBORN, b. July 21, 1888, Norwalk, Conn.

(v. Jno. A. Osborn.)

IX.

Eugene Ernest Osborn.

[Younger son of John Osborn and Lydia A. Duncombe.]

b. May 1, 1854, Norwalk, Conn.

m. August 27, 1879, Washington, D. C.

ADA MARIENETTE GIBBS.

[Dau. of Thomas F. Gibbs and Sarah M. Andrews.]

b. October 18, 1858, Boston, Mass.

CHILDREN : .

ETHEL OSBORN, b. July 14, 1880, Ishpeming, Michigan.

d. August 6, 1893, Ishpeming, Michigan.

EDITH OSBORN, b. May 8, 1885, Ishpeming, Michigan.

EUGENE OSBORN, b. June 4, 1888, Ishpeming, Michigan.
RUTH OSBORN, b. January 21, 1894, Ishpeming, Michigan.

(v. Eugene Ernest Osborn, Ill.)

————o————

VIII.
Aaron Hawley Duncombe.
[Fifth son of David Duncombe and Ruth Sanford.]
b. May 2, 1826, Redding Centre, Conn.
m. October 9, 1849, Redding, Conn.

MARY GORHAM EDMONDS.
[Dau. of John and Maria (Mallory) Edmonds.]
b. June 28, 1830, Redding, Conn.

(No children.)   (v. A. H. Duncombe, Wisconsin.)

————o————

VIII.
William Edgar Duncombe.
[Sixth son of David Duncombe and Ruth Sanford. p. 328.]
b. February 17, 1830, Redding Centre, Conn.
first m. November 24, 1852, Redding, Conn.

SARAH FAIRCHILD.
[Dau. of Joseph B. Fairchild and Phœbe Shepard.]
b. April 4, 1828, Redding, Conn.
d. May 7, 1857, Redding Centre, Conn.
second m. November 9, 1858, Redding, Conn.

SARAH SANFORD[V].
[Second dau. of JAMES SANFORD, JR., and Eliza French. p. 285.]
b. June 7, 1833, Redding, Conn.

CHILDREN (of first marriage):
DAVID S. DUNCOMBE, b. Dec. 15, 1854, Redding Centre, Conn. p. 335.
GEORGE F. DUNCOMBE, b. April 1, 1857, Redding Centre, Conn. p. 335.

CHILD (of second marriage):
EMMA ELIZA DUNCOMBE, b. June 1, 1864, Redding Centre, Conn. p. 335.

(v. Wm. E. Duncombe.)

IX.
David Sanford Duncombe.
[Elder son of William Edgar Duncombe, by his first wife, Sarah Fairchild.]

b. December 15, 1854, Redding Centre, Conn.
d. September 20, 1892, Knoxville, Tenn.
m. June 17, 1880, Mount Vernon, N. Y.

LYDIA LANE LOCKWOOD.
[Dau. of John Millington Lockwood and Nancy Howe.]

b. October 27, 1856, Pelham, Westchester Co., N. Y.

CHILDREN:

WILLIAM MILLINGTON DUNCOMBE, b. Mar. 24, 1881, Knoxville, Tenn.
FREDERICK HOWE DUNCOMBE, b. Sept. 1, 1883, Mount Vernon, N. Y.
RAYNOR SANFORD DUNCOMBE, b. Oct. 4, 1886, Knoxville, Tenn.
DAVID SANFORD DUNCOMBE, JR., b. Sept. 30, 1891, Knoxville, Tenn.
(v. Mrs. David Sanford Duncombe.)

IX.
George Fairchild Duncombe.
[Younger son of William E. Duncombe, by his first wife, *Sarah Fairchild.]

b. April 1, 1857, Redding Centre, Conn.
m. April 10, 1878, Newtown, Conn.

LUCY BEERS.
[Dau. of David Hard Beers and *Lucy Fairchild.]

b. August 10, 1854, Newtown, Conn.

CHILD:

JULIA BEERS DUNCOMBE, b. March 13, 1881, Newtown, Conn.
(v. Geo. F. Duncombe.)

IX.
Emma Eliza Duncombe.
[Only child of WILLIAM EDGAR DUNCOMBE, by his second wife, SARAH SANFORD. p. 287-324.]

b. June 1, 1864, Redding Centre, Conn.
m. November 11, 1896, Redding, Conn.

GEORGE BENJAMIN BEERS.
[Son of Benjamin and Eliza (Wheeler) Beers.]

b. November 15, 1861, Easton, Conn.

(No children.)   (v. E. E. D. Beers.)

———o———

* First cousins.

VII.

Sarah Sanford.

[Fourth dau. of John Sanford, Jr., and Lydia Wheeler. p. 326.]

b. January 25, 1797, Redding, Conn.
d. August 4, 1846, Bridgeport, Conn.

m. GARRY DAYTON.

[Son of Brewster Dayton, Jr., by his second wife, Betsey Willoughby.]   (Orcutt.)

b. September 10, 1791.
d. before 1842.

" John L. Hill left Guardian of Sally Dayton and Betsey Lyon."   (Will of Jno. S.)

CHILDREN :

BETSEY; CAROLINE; BETSEY; LYDIA ANN; SANFORD; *CHARLES W.

VIII.

*Charles Willoughby Dayton.

[Younger son of Garry Dayton and Sarah Sanford.]

b. August 8, 1835.
d. April 29, 1897, Mount Vernon, N. Y.
m. July 24, 1858, Carmel, N. Y.

ELIZABETH ARCHER.

[Dau. of John and Elizabeth (Barger) Archer.]

CHILDREN :

JOSEPH HENRY DAYTON, b. September 26, 1860, Carmel, N. Y. p. 336.
CHARLES HARRISON DAYTON, b. January 2, 1863, Carmel, N. Y. p. 337.
FANNIE DAYTON, b. May 24, 1869, Brewster, N. Y. p. 337.
DAVID JESSE DAYTON, b. January 25, 1873, Brewster, N. Y. (unm.)
JENNIE GERTRUDE DAYTON, b. July 29, 1875, Brewster, N. Y. p. 338.
LYDIA LOUISE DAYTON, ⎱ died in infancy.
CARRIE DAYTON.   ⎰   (v. Jos. H. Dayton.)

IX.

Joseph Henry Dayton.

[Eldest son of Charles Willoughby Dayton and Elizabeth Archer.]

b. September 26, 1860, Carmel, N. Y.

* Will of Sally Dayton, dated "July 23, 1846 . . mentions daughters Betsey and Lydia Ann, son Charles W."   (John L. Hill of Redding, Ex. B'p't Probate Rec'd.)

m. October 3, 1880, Shrub Oak, N. Y.

ABBIE J. LENT.

[Dau. of Robinson and Robenia (Denike) Lent.]

b.   Putnam Valley, N. Y.

CHILDREN :

ERNEST ROBINSON DAYTON, b. August 11, 1881, Putnam Valley, N. Y.
ERA MAY DAYTON, b. January 29, 1884, Putnam Valley, N. Y.

(v. Jos. H. Dayton.)

IX.

Charles Harrison Dayton.

[Second son of Charles Willoughby Dayton and Elizabeth Archer.]

b. January 2, 1863, Carmel, N. Y.
d. May 5, 1897, Mount Vernon, N. Y.
m. January 25, 1890, Patterson, Putnam Co., N. Y.

ELLA CLARKSON.

[Dau. of Charles Clarkson and Rebecca Russell.]

b. August 29, 1867, Patterson, N. Y.

CHILDREN :

EDITH MAY DAYTON, b. July 14, 1893, Mount Vernon, N. Y.
BENJAMIN WILLOUGHBY DAYTON, b. July 26, 1895, Mt. Vernon, N. Y.

(v. Mrs. Chas. H. Dayton.)

IX.

Fannie Dayton.

[Eldest dau. of Charles Willoughby Day and Elizabeth Archer.]

b. May 24, 1869, Brewster, N. Y.
m. January 8, 1889, Patterson, N. Y.

FREEMAN SPRAGUE.

[Son of Ferris J. Sprague and Sarah M. Smalley.]

b. November 14, 1867, Kent, Putnam Co., N. Y.

CHILDREN :

HOMER SPRAGUE, b. November 20, 1889, Kent, Putnam Co., N. Y.
CHARLES W. SPRAGUE, b. Dec. 21, 1891 ; d. Apr. 29, 1892, Kent, N. Y.
HOWARD SPRAGUE, b. September 19, 1893, Kent, N. Y.
FREEMAN SPRAGUE, JR., b. February 4, 1896, Kent, N. Y.

(v. F. D. Sprague.)

22

IX.

Jennie Gertrude Dayton.

[Youngest dau. of Charles Willoughby Dayton and Elizabeth Archer. p. 336.]

b. July 29, 1875, Brewster, N. Y., U. S. A.

m. September 2, 1896, Mt. Vernon, N. Y., U. S. A.

RODERICK MACKENZIE.

[Son of William Roderick MacKenzie and Elizabeth Pearson.]

b. February 17, 1868, Dingwall, Co. Ross, Scotland.

CHILD :

CHARLES RODERICK MACKENZIE. b. March 10, 1897, Dingwall, Scotland.
(v. J. G. D. MacKenzie, Scotland.)

────o────

VII.

John Wheeler Sanford.

[Elder son of John Sanford, Jr., and Lydia Wheeler. p. 326.]

b. May 21, 1799, Redding, Conn.

d. November 24, 1890, Redding Ridge, Conn.

m. March 5, 1822.

ALTHA FANTON.

[Dau. of Capt. Abel Fanton and Jerusha Sturges.]

b. April 11, 1800, Weston, Conn.

d. February 23, 1890, Redding Ridge.

CHILDREN :

MARY ANN SANFORD, b. March 23, 1823, Redding Ridge. (unm.)
GEORGE WHEELER SANFORD, b. October 3, 1824, Redding Ridge.
  d. December 6, 1842, Redding Ridge.
HARRIET STEVENS SANFORD, b. September 11, 1826, Redding Ridge.
  d. February 4, 1853, Redding Ridge.
FLORA MARIA SANFORD, b. November 3, 1828, Redding Ridge.
  d. April 30, 1894, Redding Ridge.
EDWARD J. SANFORD, b. Nov. 23, 1831, Redding Ridge. p. 338.
GEORGIANA SANFORD, b. November 19, 1843, Redding Ridge. p. 340.
(v. Miss M. A. Sanford.)

VIII.

Edward Jackson Sanford.

[Younger son of John Wheeler Sanford and Altha Fanton.]

b. November 23, 1831, Redding Ridge, Conn.

m. August 21, 1860, Knoxville, Tenn.

EMMA CHAVANNES.

[Dau. of Rev⁴ Adrian Chavannes and Anna Francillion of Lausanne, Switzerland.]

b. March 20, 1841, Vevey, Switzerland.
d. October 1, 1895, Battle Creek, Michigan.

CHILDREN:

EDWARD T. SANFORD, b. July 23, 1865, Knoxville, Tenn. p. 339.
EMMA SANFORD, b. February 18, 1869, Knoxville, Tenn. p. 339.
ALFRED FANTON SANFORD, b. February 21, 1875, Knoxville, Tenn.
MARY SANFORD, b. October 27, 1877, Knoxville, Tenn.
HUGH WHEELER SANFORD, b. April 22, 1880, Knoxville, Tenn.
LOUISE SANFORD, b. April 29, 1882, Knoxville, Tenn.

(v. Edw. J. Sanford.)

IX.

Edward Terry Sanford.

[Eldest son of Edward Jackson Sanford and Emma Chavannes.]

b. July 23, 1865, Knoxville, Tennessee.
m. January 6, 1891, Knoxville, Tenn.

LUTIE MALLORY WOODRUFF.

[Dau. of William Wallace Woodruff and Ella Connelly.]

b. September 26, 1866, Knoxville, Tenn.

CHILDREN:

DOROTHY SANFORD, b. December 5, 1891, Knoxville, Tenn.
ANNA MAGEE SANFORD, b. December 19, 1892, Knoxville, Tenn.

(v. Edw. J. Sanford.)

IX.

Emma Sanford.

[Eldest dau. of Edward Jackson Sanford and Emma Chavannes.]

b. February 18, 1869, Knoxville, Tenn.
m. February 25, 1892, Knoxville, Tenn.

EDWARD JACKSON SANFORD IX.

[Elder son of HON. WILLIAM ELI SANFORD, M.P., by his second wife, Sophia Vaux. p. 341-2.]

b. June 24, 1867, St. Paul, Minn.
d. March 13, 1897, Hamilton, Ont., Canada.

CHILD:

CONSTANCE PHYLLIS SANFORD, b. January 3, 1893, Hamilton, Canada.

(v. Edw. J. Sanford, Tenn.)

VIII.

Georgiana Sanford.

[Fourth dau. of John Wheeler Sanford and Altha Fanton. p. 338.]

b. November 19, 1843, Redding Ridge, Conn.

m. July 11, 1876, Redding Ridge, Conn.

REV'D CHARLES WALLACE KELLEY.

[Son of William Robinson Kelley (b. Exeter, N. H.) and Nancy Hancock (descendant of John Hancock.]   (v. G. S. Kelley.)

b. February 6, 1832, Boston, Mass.

———o———

VII.

Eli Sanford.

[Younger son of John Sanford, Jr., and Lydia Wheeler. p. 326.]

b. August 4, 1801, Redding, Conn.

d. August 31, 1839, New York City.

m. February 26, 1826, New York City.

EMELINE ARGALL.

b. July 12, 1808.

d. June 26, 1836.   (v. Wm. S. Alley.)

CHILDREN :

ELIZA SANFORD, b. February 7, 1828, New York City, N. Y. p. 340.

LYDIA ANN SANFORD, b. March 29, 1829, New York City.

d. February 28, 1852, Redding, Conn.

m. ANDREW MEEKER.

[Son of Arza and Adelia (Gorham) Meeker.]

(one child, died.)   (rec'd Miss M. A. Sanford.)

HANNAH J. SANFORD, b. December 2, 1831, New York City.

d. May 5, 1849, New York City.

WILLIAM E. SANFORD, b. August 21, 1834, New York City. p. 341.

(v. Wm. S. Alley.)

VIII.

Eliza Sanford.

[Eldest dau. of Eli Sanford and Emeline Argall.]

b. February 7, 1828, New York City.

d. August 11, 1886, Clifton Springs, N. Y.

first m. July 8, 1846, New York City. (?)

Elijah Phillips Farmer.
[Son of Aaron Dwight Farmer and Lucretia Phillips.]

b. July 5, 1812, Bolton, Mass.
d. May 12, 1857, Ellington, Conn.

(rec'd Cornelius Farmer).

second m. July 23, 1861, Buffalo, N. Y.

Doctor James T. Alley.
[Son of Moses and Dorcas (Doland) Alley.]

b. March 20, 1831, LaGrange, Duchess Co., N. Y.
d. September 17, 1878, St. Paul, Minn.

(rec'd Miss J. D. Alley).

child (of first marriage)
Hannah Eliza Farmer, b. August 8, 1849, New York City.
d. September 17, 1852, Ellington, Conn.

IX.

William Sanford Alley.
[Only child of Doctor James T. Alley and Eliza (Sanford) Farmer.]

b. April 19, 1863, Rome, Italy.
m. February 6, 1889, Syracuse, N. Y.

Julia Eliza Chamberlain.
[Dau. of Webster R. Chamberlain and Julia Avery.]

b. March 29, 1863, Syracuse, N. Y.

(v. Wm. S. Alley, Canada).

VIII.

Hon. William Eli Sanford, M.P.
[Only son of Eli Sanford and Emeline Argall.]

b. August 21, 1834, New York City.
first m. April 25, 1856. (?)

Emeline Sanford [VIII] Jackson.
[Dau. of Edward Jackson and Lydia Ann Sanford [VII]. p. 342.]

b. August 21 (?), 1838, Hamilton, Canada.
d. 1858, Hamilton, Canada.

second m. Ottawa, Canada.

SOPHIA VAUX.

[Dau. of Thomas Vaux, Wisbeach, Cambridgeshire, Eng., and Margaret Marshall, Toronto, Canada.]

b. Montreal, Canada.

CHILDREN (of second marriage) :

EDWARD J. SANFORD, b. June 24, 1867, St. Paul, Minn. p. 339.
HENRY VAUX SANFORD, b. 1871, Hamilton, Canada.
d. 1872, Hamilton, Canada.
EDNA SANFORD, b.   Hamilton, Canada.
MURIEL SANFORD, b.   Hamilton, Canada.
(rec'd Hon. Wm. E. Sanford.)

————o————

VII.

Lydia Ann Sanford.

[Youngest dau. of John Sanford, Jr., and Lydia Wheeler. p. 326.]

b. March 17, 1804, Redding, Conn.
d. May 5, 1875, Hamilton, Ontario, Canada.
m. August 14, 1826, Redding, Conn. (Town Records.)

EDWARD JACKSON.

[Grandson of Daniel Jackson and ABIGAIL SANFORD V. (Ephraim, Ezekiel, Jr., Ezekiel, Thomas.)]

b. April 20, 1799, Redding, Conn.
d. July 14, 1872, Hamilton, Ont., Canada.

CHILDREN :

Two children, died young.
EMELINE SANFORD JACKSON, b. 1838, Hamilton, Canada. p. 341.

————o————

VI.

Stephen Sanford.

[Son of John Sanford and Anna Wheeler.]

b. November 24, 1769, Redding, Conn.
d. October 20, 1848, Roxbury, Conn.

m. SARAH CURTIS.

[Dau. of Nehemiah Curtis and Martha Clarke.]   (See Curtis.)

b. September 5, 1771, Zoar, Conn.
d. May 8, 1856, Roxbury, Conn.

CHILDREN:

NEHEMIAH C. SANFORD, b. October 29, 1792, Roxbury, Conn. p. 343.
CHARLOTTE SANFORD, b. December 15, 1797, Newtown, Conn.
        d. January 19, 1813, Roxbury, Conn.
PHŒBE SANFORD, b. January 20, 1800, Newtown, Conn. p. 344.
JOHN SANFORD, b. June 3, 1803, Roxbury, Conn. p. 346.
CHARLES SANFORD, b. July 20, 1805, Roxbury, Conn. p. 347.
STEPHEN SANFORD, JR., b. February 12, 1808, Roxbury, Conn. p. 348.
NELSON SANFORD, b. May 15, 1810, Roxbury, Conn. p. 353.
                                (rec'd Charles Sanford, Roxbury.)

VII.

Hon. Nehemiah Curtis Sanford, LL.D.

[Eldest son of Stephen Sanford and Sarah Curtis.]

b. October 29, 1792, Roxbury, Conn.
d. June 23, 1841, Derby, Conn.
m. September 2, 1822, Huntington, Conn.

NANCY BATEMAN SHELTON.

[Dau. of Joseph and Charity (Lewis) Shelton.]   (Tuttle B'k.)

b. January 30, 1800, Lary Hill, Huntington, Conn.
d. December 21, 1880, Derby, Conn.

VIII.

Hon. Henry Shelton Sanford.

[Only child of Nehemiah Curtis Sanford and Nancy B. Shelton.]

b. June 15, 1823, Woodbury, Conn.
d. May 21, 1891, Healing Springs, Virginia.

m. September 21, 1864, Paris, France.

GERTRUDE ELLEN DU PUY.

[Dau. of John du Puy and Mary Richard Haskins.]

b. June 27, 1841, "du Puy Place," Banks-of-the-Schuylkill, Philadelphia, Penna.

CHILDREN:

HENRY SHELTON SANFORD, b. July 17, 1865, U. S. Legation, Brussels, Belgium. d. October 1, 1891, New York City.

GERTRUDE ELLEN DUPUY SANFORD, b. November 16, 1869, Brussels, Belgium. d. April 28, 1893, New York City.

FRIDA DOLORÈS SANFORD, b. Feb'y 28, 1871, Brussels, Belgium.

ETHEL SANFORD, b. September 2, 1873, Brussels, Belgium. p. 344.

HELEN CAROLA NANCY SANFORD, b. Apr. 10, 1876, Brussels, Belgium.

LEOPOLD CURTIS SANFORD, b. July 27, 1880, Brussels, Belgium. d. Dec. 1, 1885, Château de Gingelona, Belgium.

EDWYN EMELINE WILLIMINE GLADYS MCKINNON SANFORD, b. November 27, 1882, Brussels, Belgium.

(v. Ethel Sanford–Sanford.)

IX.

Ethel Sanford.

[Third dau. of Hon. Henry Shelton Sanford and Gertrude E. du Puy.]

b. September 2, 1873, Brussels, Belgium.

m. February 17, 1892, Sanford, Florida.

HON. JOHN SANFORD.

[Eldest son of HON. STEPHEN SANFORD VIII and Sarah J. Cochran. p. 347.]

b. January 18, 1851, Amsterdam, N. Y.

(v. Ethel Sanford–Sanford.)

————o————

VII.

Phœbe Sanford.

[Younger dau. of Stephen Sanford and Sarah Curtis. p. 343.]

b. January 20, 1800, Newtown, Conn.

d. January 30, 1879, Washington, Conn.

m. May 18, 1823, Roxbury, Conn.

* DIMON MOREHOUSE.
[Son of Benjamin and Jane (Hill) Morehouse.]

b. April 22, 1790, Washington, Conn.
d. March 28, 1846, Washington, Conn.

CHILDREN:

STEPHEN S. MOREHOUSE, b. January 25, 1825, Washington, Conn. p. 345.
HENRY H. MOREHOUSE, b. June 7, 1829, Washington, Conn. p. 345.

(v. S. S. Morehouse.)

VIII.

Stephen Sanford Morehouse.
[Elder son of Dimon Morehouse and Phœbe Sanford.]

b. January 25, 1825, Washington, Conn.
m. March 27, 1850, Roxbury, Conn.

MARIA BARBARA PATTERSON.
[Dau. of Samuel Patterson and Susan Hartwell.]

b. June 18, 1828, Roxbury, Conn.
d. May 7, 1882, Washington, Conn.

CHILD:

AMY AUGUSTE MOREHOUSE, b. October 22, 1853, Washington, Conn.
d. August 31, 1873, Washington Conn.   (v. S. S. Morehouse.)

VIII.

Hon. Henry Hobart Morehouse.
[Younger son of Dimon Morehouse and Phœbe Sanford.]

b. June 7, 1829, Washington, Conn.
m. May 20, 1851, Washington, Conn.

PAULONA MARGARET TITUS.
[Dau. of Styles Titus and Loretta Arnold.]

b. August 7, 1831, Washington, Conn.
d. April 27, 1894, Washington, Conn.

---

* In the " Gershom Morehouse " Book a previous marriage is mentioned, thus : " Married February 3, 1817 Huldah Titus," in this case Phoebe Sanford was probably his second wife.

CHILDREN:

FRANCESE ELLEN MOREHOUSE, b. March 10, 1852, Washington, Conn.
d. November 13, 1869, Washington, Conn.
HENRY S. MOREHOUSE, b. Nov. 14, 1856, Washington, Conn. p. 346.
(v. H. H. Morehouse.)

IX.

Henry Sanford Morehouse.

[Only son of Henry Hobart Morehouse and Paulona M. Titus.]

b. November 14, 1856, Washington, Conn.
d. November 5, 1882, Washington, Conn.
m. November 27, 1879, Bristol, Conn.

CARRIE MARIA WARNER.

[Dau. of Cyrus Alonzo Warner and Angeline Elizabeth Sullivan.]

b. December 29, 1855, Bristol, Conn.

CHILD:

HENRY WARNER MOREHOUSE, b. Sept. 29, 1881, Washington, Conn.
(v. Mrs. Henry S. Morehouse.)

———o———

VII.

Hon. John Sanford.

[Second son of Stephen Sanford and Sarah Curtis. p. 343.]

b. June 3, 1803, Roxbury, Conn.
d. October 4, 1857, Amsterdam, N. Y.
m. August 3, 1822, Amsterdam, N. Y.

MARY SLACK.

[Dau. of John and Rachel (Winchel) Slack.]

b. March 2, 1803, Amsterdam, N. Y.
d. November 11, 1888, Amsterdam, N. Y.

CHILDREN:

SARAH CAROLINE SANFORD, b. March 27, 1824, Amsterdam, N. Y.
d. March 27, 1871, Amsterdam, N. Y.
m. November 19, 1845.
JOHN STEWART.
STEPHEN SANFORD, b. May 26, 1826, Mayfield, N. Y. p. 347.
NELSON SANFORD, b. June 1, 1828, Mayfield, N. Y.
Aug. 15, 1848 (accidently killed on cars bet. Amsterdam and Albany.)

DAVID SANFORD, b. May 4, 1830, Glen, Montgomery Co., N. Y.
    d. August 11, 1885.
    m. November 3, 1851.
                CARRIE E. PEARL.
ALEDAH SANFORD, b. March 8, 1833, Glen, N. Y.
    m. December 29, 1856, Amsterdam, N. Y.
                JAMES E. WARRING.
HARRIETTE SANFORD, b. 1836, Amsterdam, N. Y.
    m. July 15, 1856, Amsterdam, N. Y.
              HENRY SACIA. (rec'd Ethel Sanford-Sanford.)

VIII.

Hon. Stephen Sanford.

[Eldest son of John Sanford and Mary Slack.]

    b. May 26, 1826, Mayfield, Montgomery Co., N. Y.
    m. December 12, 1849, Amsterdam, N. Y.

SARAH JANE COCHRAN.

[Dau. of Alexander Gifford Cochran and Sarah Dempster Phillips.]

CHILDREN :

JOHN SANFORD, b. January 18, 1851, Amsterdam, N. Y. p. 344.
WILLIAM C. SANFORD, b. July 14, 1854, Amsterdam, N. Y.
    d. March 17, 1896.
HENRY CURTIS SANFORD, b. July 30, 1859, Amsterdam, N. Y.
    d. April 19, 1874.
CHARLES FRANCIS SANFORD, b. Sept. 21, 1864, Amsterdam, N. Y.
    d. July 10, 1882.
STEPHEN SANFORD, JR., b. October 9, 1868, Amsterdam, N. Y.
    d. February 20, 1870.   (rec'd Ethel Sanford–Sanford.)

————o————

VII.

Charles Sanford.

[Third son of Stephen Sanford and Sarah Curtis, p. 343.]

    b. July 20, 1805, Roxbury, Conn.
  *d. August 10, 1848, Newburgh, N. Y.

first m. EMELINE OLIVER, Newburgh, N. Y.

  *d. May 29, 1836, Newburgh, N. Y.

second m. CHARLOTTE SAUCHY, Newburgh, Conn.

  *d. March 27, 1864, Newburgh, N. Y.

CHILD (of first marriage):

LEMUEL CURTIS SANFORD, b. August 1830, Newburgh, N. Y.
d. 1848, Roxbury, Conn.

CHILD (of second marriage):

CHARLES CURTIS SANFORD, d. *Apr. 4, 1859, æ. 18 or 19 yrs., Newburgh.

———o———

VII.

Stephen Sanford, Jr.

[Fourth son of Stephen Sanford and Sarah Curtis. p. 343.]

b. February 12, 1808, Roxbury, Conn.
d. December 4, 1888, Roxbury, Conn.
m. November 5, 1828, Roxbury, Conn.

EUNICE MARINDA HURD.

[Dau. of Wait Hurd and Hepsey Thomas.]

b. February 11, 1810, Roxbury, Conn.
d. October 12, 1887, Roxbury, Conn.

CHILDREN:

NATHAN W. SANFORD, b. December 27, 1829, Roxbury, Conn. p. 348.
SARAH J. SANFORD, b. March 7, 1832, Roxbury, Conn. p. 349.
WATSON C. SANFORD, b. August 24, 1834, Roxbury, Conn. p. 350.
CHARLOTTE H. SANFORD, b. March 10, 1837, Roxbury, Conn. p. 350.
CHARLES SANFORD, b. March 10, 1841, Roxbury, Conn. p. 351.
JOSEPHINE M. SANFORD, b. March 4, 1846, Roxbury, Conn. p. 352.
ELIZABETH SANFORD, b. October 20, 1848, Roxbury, Conn. p. 352.
(rec'd Mrs. Charles Sanford.)

VIII.

Nathan Wait Sanford.

[Eldest son of Stephen Sanford, Jr., and Eunice Marinda Hurd.]

b. December 27, 1829, Roxbury, Conn.
d. October 24, 1856, Roxbury, Conn.
first m. August 19, 1851, Roxbury, Conn.

JULIA FRANCES BURRITT.

[Dau. of Daniel Fairchild Burritt and Betsey Morris.]

b. July 21, 1832, Roxbury, Conn.
d. August 17, 1853, Woodbury, Conn.

* " Dates from off their gravestones at Newburgh, N. Y."—S. S. Morehouse.

second m. February 26, 1855.

AMELIA ELIZABETH ROBERTS.
[Dau. of John and Elizabeth (Dawson) Roberts.]
b. June 4, 1836, Woodbury, Conn.

IX.

Herland Burritt Sanford.
[Only child of Nathan W. Sanford by his first wife, Julia F. Burritt.]
b. April 21, 1852, Roxbury, Conn.
m. November 24, 1897, New Britain, Conn.

MARY BOEHM.

(rec'd Mrs. Lemmon—Mrs. Vorce.]

VIII.

Sarah Jane Sanford.
[Eldest dau. of Stephen Sanford, Jr., and Eunice Marinda Hurd. p. 348.]
b. March 7, 1832, Roxbury, Conn.
d. May 9, 1894.
m. April 23, 1857, Roxbury, Conn.

SAMUEL SANFORD UTTER.
[Son of Samuel Utter, Troy, N. Y., and Mahala Cecilia Sanford, Roxbury.]
b. June 4, 1829.
d. May 19, 1896, Brooklyn, N. Y.

IX.

John Leiddle Utter.
[Only child of Samuel Sanford Utter and Sarah Jane Sanford.]
b. June 21, 1852, Roxbury, Conn.
m. March 4, 1885, New York City.

SOPHIA AUGUSTA CLAFFY.

CHILD:
SARAH S. SANFORD UTTER, b. July 11, 1886, Brooklyn, N. Y.
(rec'd Mrs. Chas. S.—Mrs. Vorce.)

VIII.

Watson Curtis Sanford.

[Second son of Stephen Sanford, Jr. and Eunice Marinda Hurd.]

b. August 24, 1834, Roxbury, Conn.
d. March 2, 1878, Roxbury, Conn.
m. March 9, 1858, Woodbury, Conn.

JENNIE SUMMERS.

[Dau. of David Summers and Sarah Maria Upson.]

b. September 1, 1837, Woodbury, Conn.

CHILDREN :

LILLIAN A. SANFORD, b. August 8, 1860, Woodbury, Conn. p. 350.
STEPHEN SANFORD, b. January 22, 1865, Roxbury, Conn.
d. March 18, 1887, Russell, Kansas.

IX.

Lillian Amelia Sanford.

[Only dau. of Watson Curtis Sanford and Jennie Summers.]

b. August 8, 1860, Woodbury, Conn.
m. November 30, 1880, Kent, Conn.

JULIUS HENRY ALLEN.

[Son of Stephen and Sophia (Fairchild) Allen.]

b. March 21, 1854, Newtown, Conn.

CHILDREN :

HOWARD SANFORD ALLEN, b. May 18, 1882, Woodbury, Conn.
ARTHUR STEPHEN ALLEN, b. February 9, 1884, Woodbury, Conn.
(v. L. A. S. Allen.)

VIII.

Charlotte Hepsey Sanford.

[Second dau. of Stephen Sanford, Jr. and Eunice Marinda Hurd.]

b. March 10, 1837, Roxbury, Conn.
first m. December 29, 1858, Roxbury, Conn.

ANDREWS WELLER.

[Son of Elisha Andrews Weller and Maria Peck.]

b. May 10, 1837, Roxbury, Conn.
d. July 18, 1860, Roxbury, Conn.

second m. January 17, 1871, Roxbury, Conn.

DANIEL SHELDON LEMMON.

[Son of Jedidiah and Dolly (Sanford) Lemmon.]

b. March 29, 1817.

d. May 30, 1886, Woodbury, Conn.

(No children.) (v. Mrs. Lemmon.)

VIII.

Charles Sanford.

[Third son of Stephen Sanford, Jr., and Eunice Miranda Hurd.]

b. March 10, 1841, Roxbury, Conn.

first m. June 2, 1863, Roxbury, Conn.

SARAH AMELIA BRADLEY.

[Dau. of Eli Nichols Bradley and Elizabeth Rising.]

b. October   , 1842, Roxbury, Conn.

d. August 17, 1877, Roxbury, Conn.

second m. January 27, 1880, Bridgewater, Conn.

JULIA ALMIRA TREAT.

[Dau. of Harmon Treat and Mary Emeline Wooster.]

b. October 10, 1854, Bridgewater, Conn.

CHILDREN (of first marriage, none by second):

EDELBERT L. SANFORD, b. May 22, 1864, Roxbury, Conn. p. 351.

ANDREWS W. SANFORD, b. Feb. 23, 1866, Roxbury, Conn. p. 352.

(v. Mrs. Chas. Sanford.)

IX.

Edelbert Lincoln Sanford.

[Elder son of Charles Sanford, by his first wife, Sarah A. Bradley.]

b. May 22, 1864, Roxbury, Conn.

m. July 14, 1887, Bridgeport, Conn.

LETTIE MARY BUTLER.

[Dau. of Charles and Fannie (Hart) Butler.]

b. October 9, 1865, New Britain, Conn.

CHILDREN:

CHARLES WISE SANFORD, b. August 21, 1889, Derby, Conn.
    d. May 7, 1891, Derby, Conn.
JAMES NELSON SANFORD, b. May 9, 1891, Derby, Conn.
MILDRED ANITA SANFORD, b. Apr. 27, 1893; d. Apr. 28, 1893, B'p't.
CHARLOTTE AMELIA SANFORD, b. October 24, 1895, Derby, Conn.
ANNA VORCE SANFORD, b. August 12, 1897, Roxbury, Conn.

(v. Mrs. Chas. Sanford.)

IX.

Andrews Weller Sanford.

[Younger son of Charles Sanford, by his first wife, Sarah A. Bradley.]

b. February 23, 1866, Roxbury, Conn.
m.   1884.

ELIZABETH BOOTH.

[Dau. of Silas and Caroline (Baldwin) Booth.]

CHILDREN:

ARTHUR EDELBERT SANFORD, b. January 20, 1885.
Twins.   Died.   (rec'd Mrs. Chas. S.—Mrs. Vorce.)

VIII.

Josephine Marinda Sanford.

[Third dau. of Stephen Sanford, Jr., and Eunice Marinda Hurd. p. 348.]

b. March 4, 1846, Roxbury, Conn.
m. October 5, 1870, Roxbury, Conn.

REV'D JUHA HOWE VORCE.

[Son of Lewis B. Vorce and Althea Nims.]

b. March 19, 1843, Crown Point, N. Y.
d. February 20, 1896, Hartford, Conn.

(v. J. M. S. Vorce.)

VIII.

Elizabeth Sanford.

[Fourth dau. of Stephen Sanford, Jr., Eunice Marinda Hurd.]

b. October 20, 1848, Roxbury, Conn.
d. October 12, 1878, Woodbury, Conn.

m. May 8, 1872, Roxbury, Conn.

*EDWARD JOHN CURTISS.

[Son of Daniel Curtiss and Julia Frances Strong.]

b. January 24, 1845, Woodbury, Conn.

CHILD:

SARA MARINDA CURTISS, b. March 12, 1874, Woodbury, Conn.

(v. Edw. Jno. Curtiss.)

———o———

VII.

Nelson Sanford.

[Fifth son of Stephen Sanford and Sarah Curtis. p. 343.]

b. May 15, 1810, Roxbury, Conn.

d. September 5, 1846, New Milford, Conn.

m. September 20, 1833.

MARY JANE MOREHOUSE.

[Dau. of †Col. Hawley Morehouse and Betsey Maria Hartwell.]

b. December 3, 1811, Washington, Conn.

d. May 26, 1889, Brookfield, Conn.

VIII.

John Hawley Sanford.

[Only child of Nelson Sanford and Mary Jane Morehouse.]

b. September 23, 1840, New Milford, Conn.

d. July 9, 1864, Amsterdam, N. Y.

m. MARGARET NEWCOMB of Poughkeepsie, N. Y.

CHILD:

WILLIAM SANFORD, b. ——, 1864, Amsterdam, N. Y.

(rec'd Mr. S. S. Morehouse.)

---

*Remarried, June 7, 1882, Woodbury, Conn., Ella L. Ahaurs (dau. of Truman and Elizabeth (Lambert) Ahaurs, b. June 27, 1855, Washington, D. C.; d. April 25, 1884, Woodbury, Conn.; one child, Eula Lambert Curtiss, b. April 15, 1884.

† Probably elder brother of Dimon Morehouse—see "Gershom Morehouse" Book.

VI.

Huldah Sanford.

[Dau. of John Sanford and Anna Wheeler. p. 318.]

b. August 29, 1771, Redding, Conn.
m. October 25, 1787, Redding, Conn.

LEMUEL LYON.

[Son of Eli Lyon and Betty Hill.]   (see Hill).

CHILDREN :

AARON LYON, b.   , Redding. p. 326.
ELI LYON, b. Jany 16, 1790.   (Redding Record.)
SIMEON LYON, b. June 13, 1792; March 15, 1795.   (Redding Record.)
SUSE LYON, b. Jany 10, 1795.   (Redding Record.)
        m. WILLIAM PLATT, of Newtown.
REBECCA LYON, b. Jany 11, 1799, Redding Record, p. 354-31.
ALANSON LYON.

VII.

Rebecca Lyon.

[Youngest dau. of Lemuel Lyon and Huldah Sanford.]

b. January 11, 1799.   (Redding Record, Conn.)
d. January 23, 1877.   (Danbury Record, Conn.)

m. CURTIS FANTON.

[Son of Rowland Fanton and Polly Burr.]

b.   , 1797, Redding, Conn.
d. August 16, 1871.   (Danbury Record, Conn.)

CHILDREN :

HENRY B. FANTON, b. April 8, 1822, Redding, Conn. p. 354.
ELIZA FANTON, b.   p. 331.
RUFUS SANFORD FANTON, b. 1827, Redding; d. 1860, Danbury. (unm.)
                    (rec'd Henry B. Fanton, Jr.)

VIII.

Henry Burr Fanton.

[Elder son of Curtis Fanton and Rebecca Lyon.]

b. April 8, 1822, Redding, Conn.
d. May 29, 1897, Rutherford, N. J.

m. September 26, 1843, Redding, Conn.

ELIZA ANN CHAPMAN.

[Dau. of Daniel and Eliza (Andrews) Chapman.]

b. March 14, 1825, Redding, Conn.

CHILDREN:

EMMA E. FANTON, b. October 5, 1848, Redding, Conn. p. 355.
ANN AUGUSTA FANTON, b. August 22, 1850, Redding, Conn.
m. December 29, 1890, Brooklyn, N. Y.
LOUIS HENRY MYERS.
[Son of Louis Henry Myers and Bertha Obershelf.]
No children.
HENRY B. FANTON, JR., b. July 18, 1852, Redding Conn. p. 356.

IX.

Emma Eliza Fanton.

[Elder dau. of Henry Burr Fanton and Eliza Ann Chapman.]

b. October 5, 1848, Redding, Conn.
d. April 13, 1882, Brooklyn, N. Y.
m. October 17, 1866, Danbury, Conn.

HANFORD BENNETT FAIRCHILD.

[Son of Edward Platt Fairchild (b. June 26, 1818, Newtown, Conn.) and Mary Williams (b. September 22, 1823, Danbury).]

b. August 19, 1843, Brookfield, Conn.

CHILDREN:

TWO CHILDREN died young.
HANFORD B. FAIRCHILD, JR., b. October 22, 1872, New York City. p. 355.
(v. H. B. Fairchild.)

X.

Hanford Bennett Fairchild, Jr.

[Son of Hanford Bennett Fairchild, by his first wife, Emma E. Fanton.]

b. October 22, 1872, New York City.
m. October 26, 1891, Brooklyn, N. Y.

ALLIE EMMA HATHORN.

[Dau. of George C. Hathorn and Emma L. Rollins.]

b. August 10, 1873, Brooklyn, N. Y.

CHILDREN:

EMMA ALMIRA FAIRCHILD, b. Brooklyn, N. Y.
HANFORD BENNETT FAIRCHILD, 3rd, b. Brooklyn, N. Y.

(rec'd H. B. Fairchild, Jr.)

IX.

Henry Burr Fanton, Jr.

[Only son of Henry Burr Fanton and Eliza Ann Chapman.]

b. July 18, 1852, Redding, Conn.

m. February 21, 1877, New York City.

EMMA GLADYS WOODRUFF.

[Dau. of Hiram Stewart Woodruff and Asenath Hall.]

b. June 30, 1854, Auburn, N. Y.

CHILD:

VÉRA PALISSE FANTON, b. August 26, 1878, Oakland, Cal.

(v. Henry B. Fanton, Jr.)

VI.

Ephraim Sanford.

[Son of John Sanford and Anna Wheeler. p. 318.]

b. about 1775.
d. 1808.
m. —— 1796.

SALLY PLATT.

[Dau. of Jarvis Platt and Anna Nichols.]   (See Nichols.)

CHILDREN:

EPHRAIM M. SANFORD, b. January 15, 1797, Litchfield, Conn. p. 357.
ANNA SANFORD, b. May 8, 1799. p. 362.
JARVIS P. SANFORD, b. June 15, 1801. p. 362.
ALOSIA SANFORD, b. July 1, 1803, Johnstown, N. Y. p. 363.
(rec'd Geo. P. Sanford.)

VII.

Ephraim Mix Sanford.

[Elder son of Ephraim Sanford and Sally Platt.]

b. January 15, 1797, Litchfield, Conn.
d. May 1, 1871, Easton, Conn.
m. January 15, 1822.   (Easton Record.   v. Miss Mallette.)

REBECCA LACY.

[Dau. of Stephen Lacy and Sally Somers.]

b. June 3, 1805, Easton, Conn.
d. March 23, 1890, Easton, Conn.

CHILDREN:

EPHRAIM L. SANFORD, b. July 11, 1824, Newtown, Conn. p. 358.
SARAH A. SANFORD, b. September 7, 1826, Easton, Conn. p. 359.
ALOSIA E. SANFORD, b. July 13, 1830, Easton, Conn. p. 359.
PAULINE R. SANFORD, b. November 5, 1833. p. 360.
FANNIE E. SANFORD, b. March 7, 1836, Easton, Conn. p. 361.
GEORGE P. SANFORD, b. June 27, 1838, Easton, Conn. p. 362.
MARY J. SANFORD, b. July 16, 1844, Easton, Conn.
     m. January 12, 1874, Easton, Conn.
     LEVI H. EDWARDS, son of Albert Edwards.
(v. Geo. P. Sanford.)

VIII.

Ephraim Lacy Sanford.

[Elder son of Ephraim Mix Sanford and Rebecca Lacy.]

b. July 11, 1824, Newtown, Conn.
d. March 26, 1895, Easton, Conn.
first m. September 22, 1851.

ANN REBECCA MALLETTE.

[Dau. of Jesse Mallette and Jennette Sherman, of Tashua, Conn.]

b. November 11, 1829, Tashua, Conn.
d. March 8, 1861, æ. 31 yrs. 3 mo. 18 da.

(Tashua Cemy.)

second m. October 26, 1863.

SARAH A. WYATT.

b. September 9, 1833.

CHILDREN (of first marriage, none by second):

SARAH J. SANFORD, b. September 2, 1853, Trumbull, Conn. p. 358.
YULU E. SANFORD, b. December 30, 1855, Trumbull, Conn. p. 358.

(v. S. J. S. Tyler.)

IX.

Sarah Jennette Sanford.

[Elder dau. of Ephraim Lacy Sanford, by his first wife, Ann Rebecca Mallette.]

b. September 2, 1853, Trumbull, Conn.
m. March 11, 1874, Easton, Conn.

JAMES SMITH TYLER.

[Son of John and Mary (Loden) Tyler.]

b. December 24, 1850, New York City.

CHILDREN:

JOHN LACY TYLER, b. July 17, 1875, Trumbull, Conn. (unm.)
YULU MAY TYLER, b. May 22, 1880, Easton, Conn.
MARY TYLER, b. April 22, 1896, Easton, Conn.   (v. S. J. S. Tyler.)

(rec'd Geo. R. Sanford.)

IX.

Yulu Eberdine Sanford.

[Younger dau. of Ephraim Lacy Sanford, by his first wife, Ann R. Mallette.]

b. December 30, 1855, Trumbull, Conn.
d. March 16, 1894.

m. July 25, 1885.

CHARLES FRENCH OSBORNE.

[Son of Charles Osborne and Catherine Ann French.]

b. April 16, 1859.

CHILDREN:

CHARLES HERBERT OSBORNE, b. November 9, 1886, Trumbull, Conn.
GEORGE WALTER OSBORNE, b. February 16, 1888, Trumbull, Conn.
GRACE ANN OSBORNE, b. June 4, 1891, Trumbull, Conn.

(rec'd Geo. P. Sanford. S. J. S. Tyler.)

———o———

VIII.

Sarah Anna Sanford.

[Eldest dau. of Ephraim Mix Sanford and Rebecca Lacy. p. 357.]

b. September 7, 1826, Easton, Conn.
m. October 15, 1854, Newtown, Conn.

HORACE GILBERT.

[Son of Ezra Gilbert (b. Aug. 28, 1792) and Sarah Kimberly Smith (b. July 27, 1788, New Haven).]

b. June 8, 1812, Newtown, Conn.

CHILDREN:

FLORINE GILBERT, b. April 13, 1856, Newtown, Conn. (unm.)
IDA MAY GILBERT, b. November 16, 1858, Newtown, Conn. (unm.)
FANNIE ADELA GILBERT, b. March 13, 1861, Newtown, Conn. (unm.)

(v. S. A. S. Gilbert.)

———o———

VIII.

Alosia Ellen Sanford.

[Second dau. of Ephraim Mix Sanford and Rebecca Lacy.]

b. July 13, 1830, Easton, Conn.
d. March 4, 1878, Danbury, Conn.
m. October 30, 1853, Newtown, Conn.

CHARLES ROBERTSON.

[Son of Levy and Polly (Patchen) Robertson.]

b. September 23, 1832, Weston, Conn.

CHILDREN:

CHARLES S. ROBERTSON, b. October 16, 1854, Easton, Conn. p. 360.
GEORGE H. ROBERTSON, b. August 8, 1864, Danbury, Conn. p. 360.

(v. Chas. S. Robertson.)

IX.

Charles Sanford Robertson.

[Elder son of Charles Robertson, by his first wife, Alosia E. Sanford.]

b. October 16, 1854, Easton, Conn.
m. September 21, 1887, Danbury, Conn.

AUGUSTA ELIZABETH EDWARDS.

[Dau. of Albert S. Edwards and Emily Wilson.]

b. Nov. 16, 1859, Danbury, Conn.

CHILDREN:

CHARLES A. ROBERTSON, b. September 7, 1888, Danbury, Conn.
HAROLD E. ROBERTSON, b. March 7, 1897, Danbury, Conn.

(v. Chas. S. Robertson.)

IX.

George H. Robertson.

[Younger son of Charles Robertson, by his first wife, Alosia E. Sanford.]

b. August 8, 1864, Danbury, Conn.
m. December 24, 1888, Danbury, Conn.

HARRIET KEYS.

[Dau. of Christopher Columbus Keys and Harriet Spencer.]

b. March 7, 1867, Mattewan, N. Y.

CHILD:

MINA A. ROBERTSON, b. December 26, 1889, Danbury, Conn.

(rec'd Chas. Sanford Robertson.)

———o———

VIII.

Paulina R. Sanford.

[Third dau. of Ephraim Mix Sanford and Rebecca Lacy. p. 357.]

b. November 5, 1833.
d. May 10, 1887, Trumbull, Conn.
m. February 10, 1865.

WILLIAM A. BURR.

[Son of William Burr.]

IX.

George Ernest Burr.

[Only child of William A. Burr and Paulina R. Sanford.]

b. July 28, 1866.

m. January 19, 1888.

WINIFRED HINKEY.

CHILD:

WILLIAM E. BURR, b. May 31, 1889.   (rec'd Geo. P. Sanford.)

---o---

VIII.

Fanny Elizabeth Sanford.

[Fourth dau. of Ephraim Mix Sanford and Rebecca Lacy.]

b. March 7, 1836, Easton, Conn.

m. June 2, 1860, Long Hill, Trumbull, Conn.

GEORGE ABLE MALLETTE.

[Son of Jesse Mallette and Jennette Sherman. p. 358.]

b. March 20, 1834, Tashua, Trumbull, Conn.

d. April 22, 1891, Bridgeport, Conn.

CHILDREN:

IRVING S. MALLETTE, b. April 2, 1862, Easton, Conn. p. 361.

GEORGIE MAY MALLETTE, b. May 13, 1874, Bridgeport, Conn. (unm.)

FANNY EDITH MALLETTE, b. Oct. 21, 1876; d. Dec. 27, 1876.

(v. G. M. Mallette.)

IX.

Irving Sanford Mallette.

[Only son of George Able Mallette and Fannie E. Sanford.]

b. April 2, 1862, Easton, Conn.

m. June 2, 1886, West Stratford, Conn.

OTALGE ELIZABETH FRICKE.

[Dau. of Gottfried George Fricke and Henriette Dorothy Kutcher.]

b. August 4, 1862, Hartford, Conn.

CHILDREN:

GEORGE ALFRED MALLETTE, b. May 5, 1889, Bridgeport, Conn.

ETHEL HENRIETTA MALLETTE, b. May 21, 1894, Bridgeport, Conn.

(v. Irving S. Mallette.)

---o---

VIII.

George Platt Sanford.

[Younger son of Ephraim Mix Sanford and Rebecca Lacy.]

b.   June 27, 1838, Easton, Conn.

m.   January 16, 1884, Rochester, N. Y.

SARAH M. (BENNETT) FAIRMAN-DAY.

[Dau. of John Cotton Smith Bennett and Sarah M. Curtis.]

b.   February 20, 1845, Trumbull, Conn.

(No children.)   (v. Geo. P. Sanford.)

———o———

VII.

Anna Sanford.

[Elder dau. of Ephraim Sanford and Sally Platt. p. 357.]

b.   May 8, 1799.

d.   August 12, 1889, Urbana, Ohio.

first m. June 14, 1818.

SHERMAN BARBER.

second m. AUGUSTUS ADAMS.

CHILDREN (of first marriage):

SANFORD BARBER; SHERMAN BARBER; ORVILLE H. BARBER.

———o———

VII.

Jarvis Platt Sanford.

[Younger son of Ephraim Sanford and Sally Platt.]

b.   July 15, 1801.

d.   March 8, 1847.

first m. ——

second m. CLARISSA BURT.

CHILD (of first marriage):

SHERMAN SANFORD.

CHILDREN (of second marriage):

CLARISSA J. SANFORD, b. June 1, 1836. p. 363.

ANNA E. SANFORD, b. May 10, 1838. p. 363.

PHILO N. SANFORD, b. July 6, 1840. p. 363.

MARY SANFORD, b. Feby 16, 1843; d. August 5, 1847.

(rec'd Geo. P. Sanford.)

VIII.
Clarissa J. Sanford.
[Eldest dau. of Jarvis P. Sanford, by his second wife, Clarissa Burt.]

b. June 1, 1836.
d. August, 1887.
m. —— COLGROVE.

CHILD:

PHILO S. COLGROVE, b.   (rec'd Geo. P. S.)

VIII.
Anna E. Sanford.
[Second dau. of Jarvis P. Sanford, by his second wife, Clarissa Burt.]

b. May 10, 1838.
d. March 1, 1873.

m. —— WILCOX.

CHILD:

CLARA A. WILCOX, b.   (rec'd Geo. P. S.)

VIII.
Philo N. Sanford.
[Only son of Jarvis P. Sanford, by his second wife, Clarissa Burt.]

b. July 6, 1840.
m.   , 1861.

SOPHIA C. KETCHUM.

CHILDREN:

NELBERT SANFORD, b. March 31, 1866; d. Dec. 12, 1891.
MERTON J. SANFORD, b. March 23, 1869.
JENNIE SANFORD, b. October 17, 1871.
NORA SANFORD, b. December 2, 1873.   (rec'd Geo. P. Sanford.)

————o————

VII.
Alosia Sanford.
[Younger dau. of Ephraim Sanford and Sally Platt. p. 357.]

b. July 1, 1803, Johnstown, N. Y.
d. January 20, 1889, Goshen, Conn.

first m. December 23, 1821, Goshen, Conn.

(2nd wife of) LUMAN OVIATT.

b. September 6, 1777.

d. December 7, 1838.

second m. December 19, 1873.

HOSEA CRANDALL.

CHILDREN (of first marriage):

SARAH L. OVIATT, b. November 28, 1822, Goshen, Conn. p. 364.

LYMAN B. OVIATT, b. September 27, 1826, Goshen, Conn.
      d. January 12, 1850.

SAMUEL P. OVIATT, b. July 14, 1831, Goshen, Conn. p. 365.

VIII.

Sarah L. Oviatt.

[Only dau. of Luman Oviatt by his second wife, Alosia Sanford.]

b. November 28, 1822, Goshen, Conn.

d. August 9, 1849, Goshen, Conn.

m. September 25, 1839, Goshen, Conn.

JAMES WADHAMS.

[Son of Norman Wadhams and Patty North.]

b. February 4, 1815, Goshen, Conn.

d. September, 1883.

CHILDREN :

URI M. WADHAMS, b. July 26, 1840, Goshen, Conn.
      Killed September 25, 1863, Virginia.
            (2nd Conn. Heavy Artillery.)

FREDERICK L. WADHAMS, b. December 4, 1842. p. 364.

ABNER H. WADHAMS, b. May 29, 1844. p. 365.

JAMES SANFORD WADHAMS, b. October 10, 1848; d. September, 1870.
                        (rec'd Fred'k L. Wadhams.)

IX.

Frederick L. Wadhams.

[Second son of James Wadhams and Sarah L. Oviatt.]

b. December 4, 1842.

m. June 19, 1870.

SARAH MARIA GOODWIN.

[Dau. of George and Sally (Weekes) Goodwin.]

b. November 10, 1852, New Hartford, Conn.

CHILDREN:

FREDERICK URI WADHAMS, b. December 6, 1871. (unm.)
SANFORD H. WADHAMS, b. March 21, 1874. (unm.)
HERBERT GOLD WADHAMS, b. April 30, 1877.
CLARENCE G. WADHAMS, b. June 13, 1886. (rec'd Fred'k L. Wadhams.)

IX.

Abner H. Wadhams.

[Third son of James Wadhams and Sarah L. Oviatt.]

b. May 29, 1844.
m. May 13, 1873.

HATTIE P. THOMSON.

CHILDREN:

SARAH L. WADHAMS, b. October 16, 1876.
DARIUS T. WADHAMS, b. May 26, 1878.
JENNIE LOUISA WADHAMS, b. April 14, 1887.

(rec'd Fred'k. L. Wadhams.)

VIII.

Samuel P. Oviatt.

[Younger son of Luman Oviatt by his second wife, Alosia Sanford.]

b. July 14, 1831.
d. June 5, 1895.
m. October 13, 1858.

MARY JANE CRANDALL.

CHILD:

SAMUEL OVIATT, b. July 9, 1879.   (rec'd Fred'k. L. Wadhams.)

INDEX

IN LINE OF JOHN, Jr.

IN LINE OF LAZARUS

25

MARRIED BEACH, BOTH LINES

SANFORD

SANFORD MARRIAGES

ERRATA.

Page 22, for "Lemenuel" read Lemuel Camp
Page 161, for "And" read "An" ever so short a voyage. . .
Page 232, for "Cyrenus" read Cyreneus Hurd.
Page 272, for Margaret Spanctou read Spancton.
Page 297, Aaron Summers Beach.
Page 297, Lydia Julia Maria Beach.

ADDENDA.

Page 162, Hezekiah Thompson always called in old records "Judge," but never held such office.

Page 247, Samuel Beach Ladd died in London, England, May 30, 1898.

Page 276, Emma Estella Shepard died Dec. 17, 1892. Horace Butler Hunter, son of William B. and Mary M. (Butler) Hunter, born Dec. 29, 1852, Madison, Conn. William Shepard Hunter born Aug. 31, 1889.

Page 281, William Chapman, son of Pelatiah (and Mary White), son of Obadiah, son of John. Amy Lovell, daughter of John, born March 28, 1760.

Page 282, Amos *Chapman* Sanford married —— Foster.

Page 282, David *Porter* Sanford married Adela Newton, son Amos C. in New York City; daughter Lillie married —— Williams, Palmyra.

Page 285, Senah Sanford, died July 7, 1898.

Page 297, Lydia Julia Maria Beach married Nov. 11, 1885 at St. John's, Mich., James Neelands of Owen Sound, Canada, born June 9, 1857 and died at Caulkinsville, Isabella Co., Mich., Dec. 11, 1892. Their children were Andrew Winton, Aug., 1886, Isaac Beach, Feb., 1887, Robert Henry, Aug., 1889, Deborah Mary, Jan., 1891 and Ellen Jane, May, 1893. Mrs. Neelands married June 14, 1895, Edward A. Meaker of New York State; present address, Weidman, Isabella Co., Michigan.

www.ingramcontent.com/pod-product-compliance
Lightning Source LLC
Chambersburg PA
CBHW021343110726
47900CB00005B/1590